THE STONE OF VITALITY

THE STONE CYCLE BOOK 5

THE STONE CYCLE SERIES

The Stone of Knowing (The Stone Cycle Book 1)
The Cost of Knowing (The Stone Cycle Book 2)
The Stone of Authority (The Stone Cycle Book 3)
The Struggle for Authority (The Stone Cycle Book 4)
The Stone of Vitality (The Stone Cycle Book 5)
...with more to come

Companion Novelettes
The Seer: A Prequel to The Stone of Knowing (The Stone Cycle)
The Rending: A Prequel to The Cost of Knowing (The Stone Cycle)

THE STONE OF VITALITY

THE STONE CYCLE BOOK 5

ALLAN N. PACKER

LUMINANT PUBLICATIONS

*To Adeline, Cressida, Sebastian, Reuben, Annabeth, and Genevieve.
In expectation that as you grow and develop your imaginations will thrive.
In confidence that you will think, dream, and act in a way that leaves the
world better than you found it.*

Castel
Castel Citadel
Deadman's Pass
Steffan's Citadel
Arven
Maranelle
Duchy
of
Erestor
N
W
E
S
Arvenon
& surrounding Kingdoms

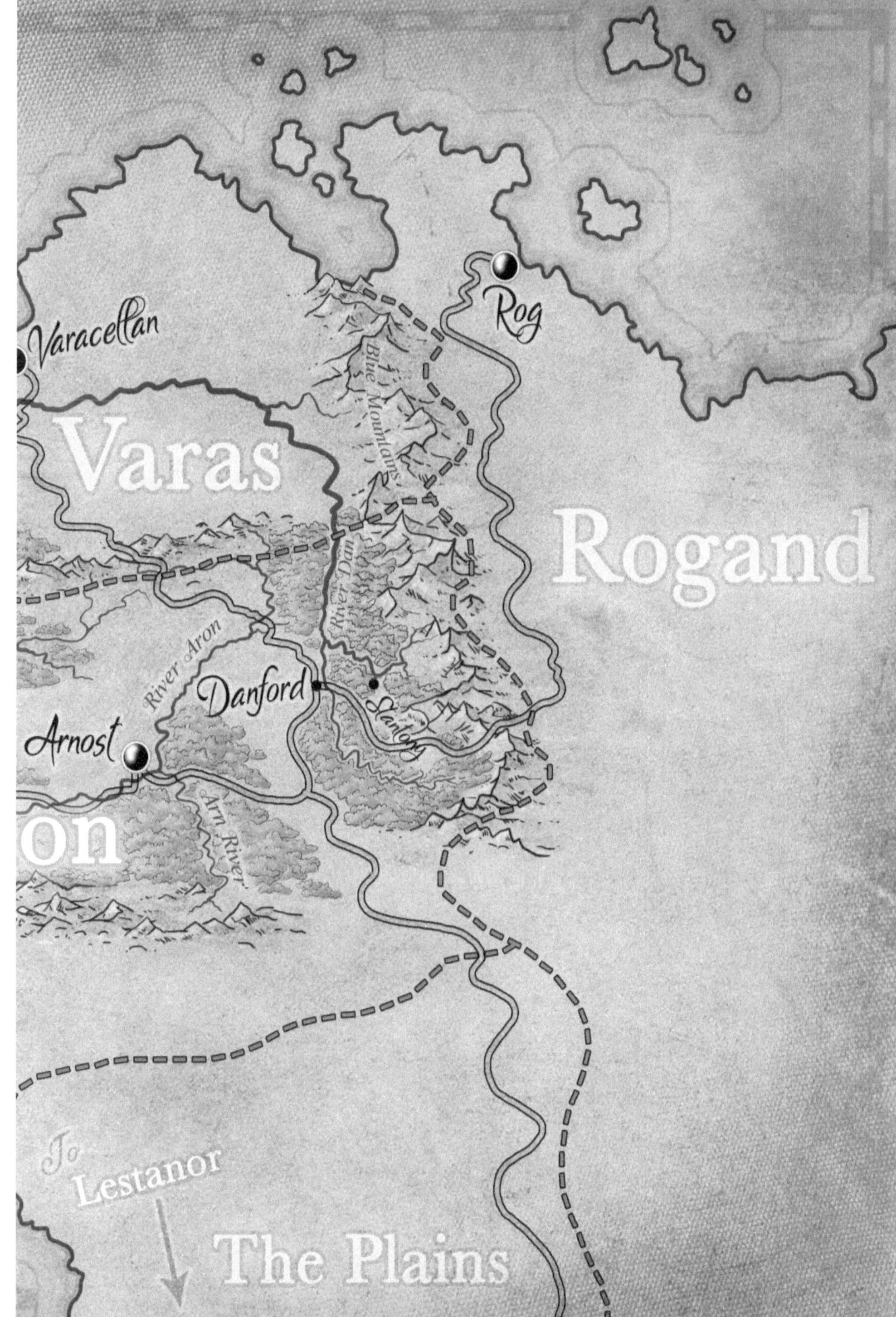

Varacellan
Rog
Varas
Blue Mountains
Rogand
River Dam
River Aron
Danford
Arnost
Stanton
on
Arn River
To
Lestanor
The Plains

VOLUME 1—THE INEVITABILITY OF PERIL

1

———

A gray morning dragged painfully into a pallid afternoon, and still she didn't come. Kamash sat on the rocky promontory in growing misery, gazing out to sea. It had been more than two weeks since last he saw her.

As the sun began to set, he faced the unpalatable truth—she was gone. Her quiet intelligence would brighten his eyes no more. Her carefree exuberance had lifted his spirits for the last time. It was over.

The old man clambered slowly to his feet. As always he had brought a gift, and without a second thought he tossed it carelessly into the ocean. Then he turned his back on the endless slap-slap of the waves and trudged reluctantly across the small sandy beach, heading for his shelter.

Some of the people he'd once called friends might say he had sunk low indeed to be mourning such a loss. He didn't care. Decades had slipped by since he'd worked up the courage to sail away from his old life. He had relinquished his former friends without remorse, and they had undoubtedly forgotten him as quickly as he'd forgotten them. He had watched with no regret as the mainland dwindled in the wake of his boat. Civilization and its complexities held no appeal for him, any more than the restless human hordes that sustained it.

Choosing instead to embrace the remote exile of his island retreat, he had quickly been captivated by the wonders of a timeless world unspoiled by the vanity and folly of men.

The months turned slowly to years, and even as he celebrated his escape from the grasping avarice of his kind, he discovered that loneliness had begun to gnaw at him. Contented as he was in his own company, it was disconcerting to discover that he nevertheless needed a companion.

One morning he had noticed an injured sea lion pup, stranded in the shallows of the little beach where he liked to swim each day. Having become adept at catching fish, he offered his latest takings to the pup. Frightened and resistant at first, the young sea lion eventually accepted the gift, perhaps sensing that the alternative was starvation. Kamash's compassion was rewarded with gratitude, and in time an unlikely affection developed between the lanky land dweller and the glistening creature of the sea.

He had named her Sparkle, as much for her lightness of being as for the sunlight that bounced so readily from her body. They became firm friends throughout the seasons of her life. He swam with her when the waves and the weather permitted it, and watched her antics from the shore whenever the sea refused to respect his puny strength. She came and went as nature demanded. Sometimes she was gone for days, and on a number of memorable occasions she'd returned bringing a new pup for his inspection.

He had made a raft, and she glided effortlessly beside him as he sailed beyond the fringes of his tiny circle of land, out into the deep ocean. Once, falling unexpectedly into the water, he watched in helpless dismay as the wind quickly carried the raft beyond his reach. Sparkle had accompanied him on his long swim back to shore, nudging him encouragingly whenever he flagged and refusing to let him give in to exhaustion and despair. Somehow he made it back. Even now he marveled at his own endurance.

Kamash had always known it could not last. He made no attempt to count the advancing years, but two decades might have slipped away before he first began to notice that she was failing. One telltale sign was the increasing enthusiasm with which she accepted the fish he offered each morning.

The end when it came still haunted his nightmares. A huge shark appeared from the deep as she lay basking in the shallows, snatching her away in little more than a heartbeat.

In her youth she would have danced aside to evade the predator. That day she had barely moved. Kamash watched in unbelief as the boiling water subsided, leaving no more than a red stain to mark the passing of his only friend.

He had surged into the water in mindless defiance of the departed monster, shouting at the top of his lungs as he called down curses upon the creature and its offspring forever. When his anger eventually faded he returned to the shore, falling to his knees and crying like a baby.

Years passed before he found a way to impress another of her kind. Once more he had embraced life with energy, choosing to ignore the inconvenient reality that in time this season too must come to an end.

The absence that day of his latest companion was no surprise—having enjoyed her companionship for many years, he had long been aware that her lifespan was almost at an end.

The inevitable termination had left him bereft and alone again. What would he do now? Did he have the heart and the resolve to start over a third time?

He was no closer to an answer when night fell and he headed for his bed. Forsaken, friendless, and utterly miserable, he lay down and attempted to sleep.

KAMASH FIRST SPOTTED the sail on his daily ascent to the highest point of the island. He had occasionally observed ships in the distance before, although none bothered to approach the unpretentious pimple of land that he called home. Seeing no reason to expect a different outcome this time, he took little notice of the intruder.

He was no longer a young man, but he found the climb invigorating as always. Reaching the top, he scanned the horizon. The rocky outcrop that crowned the summit offered an uninterrupted view in every direction and provided a perfect vantage point for assessing the weather. A cloudless sky with excellent visibility awaited him; he could just make out the low smudge to the southeast that represented his nearest island neighbor.

Otherwise there was nothing visible but sea beyond the rocky cliffs that surrounded the island. Nothing apart from the sail drawing noticeably closer.

It was hard to imagine anyone wanting to explore his domain. He had deliberately settled in a location both isolated and relatively unappealing. The larger island to the southeast was well watered and boasted several beaches where a boat could safely land. And as far as he knew it had never been occupied. Kamash therefore watched on with surprise and growing unease as the ship continued to head in his direction.

The only seaward access to the island was a small beach, its white sand clearly visible below him. He maintained a simple shelter among the trees, but his main dwelling was further inland beside the only reliable spring that watered the island. Neither structure was visible from the beach, and in the current balmy weather he had no reason to maintain a fire that might draw attention with its smoke. A search party would soon discover evidence of his presence of course, but he could not imagine any possible reason why anyone would want to land a search party.

The ship drew closer, and he squatted down so his silhouette would not be visible to any sailor keeping a lookout. He was no master mariner, but he could tell there was something unfamiliar about the design of the three-masted ship. It must surely be foreign. The sailors launched a rowboat, and he watched as it found its way to his beach. Two people were put ashore—at this distance they appeared to be a slight youth and a burly man—before the boat resumed its circumnavigation of the island.

It appeared unlikely that the two trespassers would be leaving anytime soon, so avoiding them would not be an option. After so long away from his own kind, Kamash wasn't sure what to think about interacting with people again. But loneliness had nagged at him since the disappearance of his latest companion, and he could not entirely ignore the lure of human contact. Curiosity eventually got the better of him, and he made his way down to the beach.

A young woman in strange garb sat on the sand beside a thickset man who appeared to be a guard. The old man watched them curiously from behind a tree for some time before deciding to take his chances.

As soon as he stepped into the open, the young woman leaped to her feet and called out in a language he didn't recognize. Her guard drew a knife and hovered protectively in front of her.

"Greetings," said Kamash, stretching out both hands palms upward to show he was no threat. "Do you speak Rogandan?"

"Who are you?" the young woman demanded imperiously, answering in the same language. She clearly understood Rogandan, although she spoke it strangely.

"My name is Kamash," he replied. "Who are you?"

Her head went up instantly. "I am Princess Neira of the Empire of Ahr," she replied, staring down at him over her nose. "I am the treasured daughter of the emperor—may his name ever be exalted!—and the only sister of the emperor-to-be." Almost as an afterthought she flicked a finger in the direction of her protector. "This is Uman," she sniffed.

"I bid you welcome," he said with a tentative smile.

She glared at him disdainfully. "You are a commoner, little better than a dog," she told him. "Why do you not abase yourself before me?"

He raised an eyebrow. "You are not in your empire now, Princess Neira. You are in my domain." His lip curled up in a wry smile as he glanced around at the sand and the trees. "On my little island I like to think of myself as emperor."

"It isn't much of an empire," she snorted.

"It's modest," he admitted, "but it's where you've landed. I'm sure the Empire of Ahr is mighty indeed, but it must be a long way from here." He gave her a wink. "To be honest, I know almost nothing about it."

She glowered at him. "When my sailors return you will answer for your insolence!" she snapped.

He studied her for a moment. "Why have they left you here?" he asked.

"I demanded to be put ashore," Neira replied haughtily. "How can any normal person be expected to tolerate constant rocking and shaking for weeks on end? Much less the daughter of the emperor!"

"When are they coming back for you?" he asked.

"As soon as they've rowed around the whole island. I instructed them to search for a more appealing beach." She waved an arm about her disparagingly. "Even a refuse heap like this ought to have *something* pleasant to offer."

Kamash ignored the insult to his tiny empire. "Who is in charge of your ship?" he asked. "What brought you here?"

She rounded on him. "Be very careful," she warned. "I advise you not to pry into affairs beyond your station."

With no answers forthcoming from the young woman, Kamash redirected his attention to Uman. "Do you know what your captain is up to?" he asked.

Uman's face was unreadable. Perhaps he didn't understand Rogandan. Perhaps he was giving nothing away. Either way, he offered no response.

Kamash turned back to the girl with a sigh. "I'm sorry to have to tell you this, Princess, but it looks as if your sailors have abandoned you and left you to your fate."

She didn't seem at all concerned. "Nonsense!" she replied dismissively.

He shrugged. "They did indeed row around the island. Then they returned to the ship and were taken on board. I watched them sail away."

It was obvious that the girl did not believe him. But the guard had understood what Kamash was saying, and he appeared shaken by the news.

"Follow me for a couple of minutes, and you'll be able to draw your own conclusions," Kamash told them, pointing away from the beach.

The princess glared at him with narrowed eyes. The guard joined him without hesitation.

Ignoring the path he had worn to the summit, the old man turned instead to a nearby hill and began to climb. He emerged at the top with Uman close behind him. Neira appeared a moment later, the sour look on her face making it abundantly clear what she thought of him and his assertions.

The ship was already far enough away that the sails could barely be seen above the horizon. Had they waited much longer, the vessel's current location would have been visible only from the summit.

The immediate reaction of the princess was one of fury. She shrieked and ranted in words that Kamash could not understand. Uman did not respond, although Kamash thought he saw compassion in his eyes. When her anger failed, she threw herself to the ground and dissolved into tears.

Many years had passed since Kamash's last contact with a young woman, and he looked on helplessly. Eventually, with nothing better to suggest, he turned to the guard. "I can offer you food and fresh water," he said.

Uman nodded once, before reaching down and lifting Neira into his arms. They set off, carefully descending the path to the beach.

They had not gone far before Neira began protesting noisily in her own language. Uman put her down, and she made her way independently back to the white sand.

As soon as they reached the beach, Kamash invited them to sit.

"Please, make yourselves comfortable," he said. "I will prepare some food."

The old man had departed from the mainland with a generous quantity of seeds, and after cultivating several small strips of land he had been able to establish a reliable supply of vegetables, more than enough to feed one person. He now prepared a platter of fresh produce, carving off slices of fresh fish to go with it.

By the time he returned, Neira appeared to have mastered herself, although her eyes wore a haunted look, and she seemed distracted and ill at ease.

Both of his guests came to life when the food arrived. They accepted the vegetables readily. Uman looked at the fish uncertainly before placing a piece in his mouth and chewing slowly. Deciding he liked it, he helped himself to more.

The princess had an entirely different reaction. "What is this?" she demanded, screwing up her face in disgust.

"It's fish," he said simply, "freshly caught today."

"It isn't cooked!" she protested.

"My people regard it as a delicacy served this way," he told her in surprise.

"Your people are barbarians!" she spat.

Horrified at her slur, Uman bowed a mute apology.

Kamash shrugged. "I am happy to cook some fish if you prefer it," he said mildly. "I will build a fire."

She glared at him without otherwise responding.

As he got up, Uman turned to the girl, waving his hands animatedly. The princess reacted sharply in her own language. Kamash left them to battle it out.

After completing his preparations, the old man cooked the fish absently, his mind rehearsing the unexpected events of the day. *People* had arrived. Words had been spoken to him, and he had replied. He must have said more that day than in the previous few years combined.

The new arrivals had done a lot more than just shatter the stillness. Intrigue clung to them as a web binds itself to a fly. He heaved a deep sigh. He was already missing the simple solitude he had enjoyed for so long. He wondered if he would ever get it back.

After staring bemusedly into the fire for a while, he hefted his shoulders in a shrug of resignation. He would choose to embrace his new reality. What else could he do anyway?

The first priority was to make sense of what had just happened. The princess had insisted on feeling solid earth beneath her feet again. It had been a straightforward request, but a cynical game was being played out in response. Whoever commanded the foreign ship had grasped the opportunity to dump her. She hadn't been killed outright, but she had been deposited in a place where she was unlikely to survive for long, even with the help of her protector.

The girl might be self-important and demanding, but that could hardly be a reason for abandoning her, especially if she really was a princess.

It seemed ironic that in spite of his self-appointed exile to a place of no interest to anyone, Kamash had apparently found himself caught up in a political power play of some significance. Neira was not in the emperor's direct line of succession, but she was close enough to have become a target.

When Kamash returned with the cooked fish, he saw that the food he'd served previously was gone. All of the raw fish had been eaten, presumably by Uman. Seeing Neira eyeing the latest offerings hungrily, he presented her with the cooked fish immediately.

Before she ate, she mumbled an apology. "I'm sorry." Getting out the words was an obvious struggle. He had the impression she wasn't accustomed to apologizing to anyone.

Uman glared at her pointedly, and she tried again. "I'm sorry I didn't thank you for the food." After a nudge from the guard's elbow, she grudgingly added, "And I'm sorry for calling you a barbarian."

"I've been called worse," he told her with a smile. "I accept your apology." Then he pointed to the fish. "Enough talk—the food is getting cold!"

She needed no further urging, devouring it all without ceremony.

While she was eating Kamash took the opportunity to study the guard. It seemed unlikely that Uman was related to the princess in any way, yet he behaved like a parent disciplining a loved and pampered child. He was not frightened to demand appropriate conduct from her. He had engineered her apology and prodded her until satisfied by her contrition.

The question of his identity was by no means the only mystery surrounding the guard. Uman had not uttered a word, and Kamash could only guess at the reason.

After the food had all been eaten, the old man waded into the sea and swam lazily for a while in the shallow waters adjacent to the beach. The guard soon followed him in. The princess contented herself with watching the two men from the shore.

Leaving the water first, Kamash took the opportunity to satisfy his curiosity. "Why does Uman never speak?" he asked the girl.

"He has no need to speak," she sniffed. "It is enough for him to faithfully serve his princess."

Not satisfied with her answer, the old man tried again. "Is he capable of speech?"

The princess frowned in annoyance at his persistence. Then she shook her head. "He has been mute for as long as I can remember," she told him.

Kamash watched thoughtfully as Uman floated on his back, his eyes closed. If the big guard was enjoying himself, his face showed no sign of it. He was a difficult man to read.

The sun was low in the sky when the three of them gathered around the embers of his fire. The old man prepared and served a little more food, then led them to the spring. After they had slaked their thirst in its crystal clear water, he invited them to follow him to his main shelter inland.

His hut had been sturdily constructed, designed to withstand the worst of the storms that battered the island in the rainy season. It was too small for three people, but after offering his own tiny bedroom to the princess he somehow managed to find space for himself and the guard on the floor of the little living area.

Normally he had no difficulty falling asleep, but that night he tossed and turned restlessly, unsettled by the quiet sobbing of the abandoned princess. He didn't doubt that Uman was equally troubled by Neira's misery, but the guard respected her privacy, making no attempt to console her.

Much of the night had worn away before Kamash finally succumbed to weariness and slept.

2

———————

The raft skipped across the surface of the water, its sail flapping in the stiff breeze. Kamash pulled hard on the makeshift mainsheet to flatten the sail. In response, the raft began to punch through the low waves, picking up speed.

"Now!" he called.

Uman put the tiller over, and the bow began to come around as the raft swung slowly across the wind. The breeze filled the sail from the opposite side, thrusting it across the boat.

"Watch out for the boom!" Kamash shouted to Neira, anxiously eyeing the swinging spar.

She dodged gracefully, clinging to the mast and laughing as spray splashed across her face. The burly guard grinned up at them both as the raft settled into its new tack.

Neira was unusually animated when they sat around the fire that evening. As always, Uman said nothing, but the light in his eye spoke almost as expressively as her words.

Kamash watched them both with considerable satisfaction. Out on the water battling with the elements had been the first time he'd witnessed either of his new friends abandoning themselves to pure delight. The hours he'd invested preparing the raft had not been wasted.

For the first few days the princess had spent the greater part of the daylight hours at the summit of the island, watching in vain for a sail to appear on the horizon. Eventually she'd been forced to accept that the ship was not coming back for her.

Her prospects must have seemed bleak indeed. Nothing had equipped her for the life she now faced. Having clearly been cosseted and indulged from her earliest years, she had acquired none of the skills needed in a primitive environment with no luxuries and few amenities.

The old man might have expected her to wallow in despondency. She had surprised him by undergoing a rapid transformation, taking only a few days to become proficient in catching, cleaning, and filleting fish. Neira even routinely dirtied her hands tending gardens and preparing and cooking food.

After a while Kamash complimented her on her helpfulness. "Your resilience impresses me," he told her. "I've never heard of a princess stooping to menial tasks."

"A princess exists to be served," she snapped. "Don't dare to imagine I'm becoming a servant."

When he didn't respond, she added fiercely, "It wasn't my choice to take up residence on this refuse heap." She swept her arm about contemptuously. "But I'm not going to mope. I'll do whatever I need to do to become stronger."

So she was dreaming of revenge. And she had realized she needed to do much better than survive if she ever hoped to achieve it.

Whatever Kamash thought of her motivation, her new competencies bore eloquent testimony to her ability to adapt.

However skilled the princess might become, an uncertain future lay ahead for her, and for them all. Kamash felt sure that Neira, at least, had little real awareness of the trouble she was in. Enlightening her wasn't something he was looking forward to, but the urgency had been growing with every passing day. That night, as they relaxed before the fire with an evening meal settling comfortably in their bellies, he decided he could wait no longer.

"We can't stay here," he told them bluntly.

They looked at him, surprise on their faces.

Neira wasn't speechless for long. "If you thought I was enjoying myself today," she said, "let me make it absolutely clear I have no desire to stay here a minute longer than I have to." When he held his peace, she asked impatiently, "What is your concern? Are we going to run out of food?"

He slowly shook his head. "It's much worse than that. I will speak frankly. Sooner or later the people responsible for leaving you here are going to return. They will be expecting to find you dead from starvation, exposure to the elements, or a combination of both. Their reason for coming back will be to satisfy themselves that your lives have indeed ended that way. They will search the island for your bodies, and they won't be happy if they find you alive. It won't go well for me either when they learn I was responsible for your survival."

Uman stared back at him, his face expressionless apart from a narrowing of his eyes. Kamash had the impression that none of this came as a complete surprise to him. Neira looked stunned.

"Unfortunately, we have no time to waste," he continued. "After they abandoned you here, it probably took them a day or two to sail to Rog, and it will take them about the same to return. I have no idea how much time they will need to finish their business in Rog, but I expect they'll only stay away long enough to be certain you have starved. We might already be out of time. If not, we will be very soon."

When the princess found her voice again, it wasn't to argue with him. She seemed remarkably willing to accept his conclusions.

"We can use the raft, can't we?" she asked. "We could just relocate to another island."

He shook his head again. "It wouldn't help. As soon as they discovered signs of permanent habitation here—and it wouldn't be possible to erase those signs entirely—they'd immediately search all of the nearby islands. It would only be a matter of time before they found us. Moving would create other problems, too. The islands near here are uninhabited, so we would be entirely on our own. We might run out of food in the months it would take to establish productive cultivated strips."

A frown creased the face of the princess as she grappled with his words.

Kamash transferred his gaze to the fire, staring absently into the dancing flames. He hadn't bothered to spell it out, but he was impacted no less than they were by the turn of events. His way of life had effectively ended the moment the sailors dumped the princess on his island.

The island had nurtured and sustained him from the day he first arrived as a refugee. It had provided him with a home as the years slipped away. But it would quickly forget him. Everything he had labored so long to build would slowly be swallowed up by the vegetation. Only his fading memories would remain.

The princess broke into his thoughts. "What can we do?" she asked, a hint of panic in her voice.

He returned a wan smile. "Our circumstances might be grim, but the situation isn't entirely hopeless. I foresaw this outcome when you first arrived, and I haven't been idle. Teaching you the rudiments of sailing was not just for your entertainment—it was an important step in my preparations. I've also been gathering supplies." He took a deep breath. "We will sail to the mainland. And we're not going to delay any longer. We leave at dawn."

Their shocked faces stared back at him.

"But how can we possibly reach the mainland?" asked Neira. "Surely it wouldn't be safe to cross the open sea in a raft. It was bad enough in a ship!"

"We won't use a raft," Kamash told her. "We don't need to. I have a boat."

THE OLD MAN sat grimly at the tiller, defying the turbulence of the sea. The wind had picked up steadily over the past few hours, and the waves tossed the little boat about unmercifully, apparently determined to unseat him. The clouds to the west were looking especially ominous, and he was unable to restrain himself from making constant furtive glances in that direction.

He had schooled his face into an unexpressive mask, unwilling to acknowledge how much the conditions were beginning to alarm him. His passengers probably wouldn't have noticed his demeanor anyway. Heads down, both of them clung wretchedly to the sides of the tiny craft. They had long since emptied their stomachs into the roiling waters.

The outlook had turned bad almost from the moment they were ready to set out from the island. For two days the weather had toyed with Kamash, presenting lowering skies that threatened storms to come. Yet the storms never eventuated. They could have left while conditions were merely difficult; instead the old man was forced to endure the frustration of wasted opportunity.

The prospect of enemies returning to trap them loomed larger with every passing day. Kamash was sure the sailors would reappear at any moment. It would be too late to leave when that happened.

In the end, caught between the certainty of the human threat and the uncertainty of the elements, he decided to hope for the best and launch the boat. He set a course for the northwestern tip of the Rogandan coastline, to the west of Rog.

He had become well acquainted with raging seas, and no less with the cold ferocity of the predators that lurked in their depths. He would be leaving all that behind him, returning to a world of ruthless tyrants and scrabbling commoners. Mercurial weather and ravenous sea creatures seemed tame compared to the perils that awaited him.

He acknowledged that the turbulent seas were at least having one positive effect—the prospect of reaching Rogand was becoming more attractive by the minute.

After promising himself he would never go back, he was now doing exactly that. He couldn't entirely comprehend his own reasons.

Risking himself to help people he barely knew presented no real mystery—he could never have retained his honor if he'd simply left his visitors to their fate. The greater puzzle was that having decided to return, he found himself readily able to do so, and only because he had long prepared against such a day.

When he originally decided to settle on the island, he no longer needed his boat. He could easily have released it to drift away with the currents, or left it to slowly fall apart on the sand. Why then, had he painstakingly sheltered it from the elements, setting aside time and effort over the years to maintain it? He told himself he was simply being prudent, retaining a way of escape in case of emergency, but his own reasoning had never satisfied him. He could only conclude that some part of him had always known that one day he would return, in spite of the risk.

That day had finally come, his hand forced by an unlikely pair of castaways. He had little idea what he would find when they reached Rogand. Embracing the easiest and perhaps also the most cowardly course, he simply decided not to think about it.

KAMASH SOMEHOW MANAGED to reef the sail as the gale began to build in strength, rigging a small storm jib instead. Then he turned the boat and allowed it to run before the storm, stern toward the waves.

It hadn't taken long for the wind to shred his jib. He'd asked far too much of his aging sails—new material would have been severely tested in these conditions.

He turned to the others and shouted, "If you have gods, now's the time to pray to them!" He had no idea if they heard him over the howling of the wind.

He threw out a sea anchor and secured the tiller. There was little else he could do now. They were at the mercy of the wind and waves.

When the sun set they were still afloat, huddling fearfully together as the sea tossed the little craft up and down. Kamash had passed far beyond the point of exhaustion, completely spent from the effort of peering ahead in the dark. He decided to rest his eyes, just for a couple of minutes...

SOMETHING DISTURBED KAMASH, dragging him out of a strange dream. Baffled and disoriented, he opened his eyes and glanced around. He was lying on the bottom of the boat with daylight shining about him. Astonishingly, the tiny craft was still afloat, rising and falling with the swell. Neira and Uman lay prostrate nearby, either asleep or unconscious. The storm seemed to have passed, and the wind had eased to little more than a stiff breeze.

A voice was calling insistently, although Kamash could make no sense of the words. Had it been the voice that awakened him?

He tried to sit up, the effort leaving him weak and faint headed. Squinting around he spotted a vessel nearby. It appeared to be a fishing boat. When the voice called again, he raised his arms in a gesture of helplessness.

For all he knew, the sailors were Varasan, or perhaps Castelan. Both kingdoms spoke the same language, but he didn't understand a word of it.

The fishing boat drew closer, and a net was thrown down to him. The men seemed friendly enough. He grabbed the net and allowed his little boat to be drawn alongside the larger vessel. A couple of the fishermen clambered down and waved him to the net, inviting him to board their boat. Then they tended to the girl and her guard. He watched them stupidly for a moment before crawling to the net and stiffly beginning to climb. Hands reached down for him, pulling him onto the deck.

They lifted Neira aboard next. Uman presented more of a challenge—it took three of them to retrieve the big man.

A fisherman offered Kamash a blanket, and he wrapped it gratefully around his shoulders. He sat on the deck as the net was retrieved. His little boat began to drift away, disappearing behind a wave only to reappear as it crested the next, all the while dwindling in size. Before long it was lost to sight entirely.

His boat might not have delivered them to Rogand, but it had at least preserved their lives. Now it was gone. The final vestige of his decades in exile had been removed. Tears threatened to well up in his eyes before he steeled himself. Now was not the time to become sentimental.

Redirecting his attention to his companions, Kamash found Uman beginning to stir. Walking cautiously across the pitching deck he approached the guard, quietly explaining to him what had happened. Neira woke as he was finishing, and the two of them hurried to her side.

"Where am I?" she asked groggily.

"We've been rescued by fishermen," he replied. "I don't speak their language—they're not from Rogand. But they have treated us kindly."

Seeing that all three of them were awake, one of their rescuers came to join them. He was the captain if his demeanor offered any clue. As soon as he spoke it was apparent that Neira understood no more than Kamash of his language.

"Rogand?" he asked, directing a finger at Kamash.

The old man nodded.

The captain rattled off a number of other words, pointing into the distance as he spoke. The only word recognizable to Kamash was 'Varacellan.'

"I think they're Varasan," the old man told his companions. "And I think they're taking us to Varacellan, their capital."

"Will there be anyone there who speaks Rogandan?" asked the princess.

"Most certainly," he replied. "Varacellan is a major trading hub, and people gather there from many places. There will be traders and diplomats from Rogand. Provided Rogand and Varas aren't at war, that is," he added. He had no idea what might have happened in the world in the decades since he left Rogand.

Neira's eyes went wide. "Why would they be at war?" she asked.

Before he could reply, a sailor arrived with food and some kind of hot drink. Kamash accepted it gratefully, nodding his thanks to the man before he left.

As soon as they were alone again, Neira faced Kamash. "I know a little of Rogand," she said. "I had a slave who taught me the language. She told me stories, too. Uman was never far away, so he heard the lessons and the stories." She stole a glance at her guard. "Most of them, anyway," she added mysteriously. "That's why he understands Rogandan." Her head went up. "He doesn't understand it as well as I do of course."

"So you were on the ship because of your Rogandan language skills?" Kamash ventured.

"Certainly not!" she snorted. "My slave taught me in secret. My father would never have let me go if he thought I would be able to communicate with the Rogandans independently." Her lip twisted up in a crooked grin. "As it was, he granted permission reluctantly. I nagged him incessantly, and even my brother decided to support me. But he only agreed because of who was in charge of the expedition." The smile faded from her face. "I expected it would be such a wonderful adventure."

Kamash gazed at her sympathetically. He wondered what the purpose of the voyage might have been. There was a great deal he didn't understand about the princess and the people who had sailed with her before abandoning her.

She recovered quickly. "Tell me about the kingdoms in this region," she demanded.

"Rogand is on the eastern side of the continent, with Lestanor below it to the south," he told her. "A mountain range that runs north-south forms the western boundary of Rogand. On the other side of the mountain range is Varas in the north, and Arvenon in the south. Castel lies to the west of Varas, and it also borders Arvenon in the south."

"What languages do these kingdoms speak?" she asked.

"We Rogandans have our own tongue, as you know," he replied. "The Arvenians, Varasans, and Castelans all speak the same language. It's generally known as Arvenian. People from Lestanor have their own tongue. And there is a Plains region to the south of Arvenon. Nomad tribes live there. They speak many different dialects."

"Which kingdom is the biggest?" asked Neira.

"Rogand is the largest, and has the most people. Arvenon is next, then Lestanor. Varas and Castel are smaller."

"And why did you think there might be a war?" she asked.

He shrugged. "Only because Rogand has fought Arvenon more than once in the past. But I know of no reason why they should be fighting now."

"You seem to know a lot about all this. Why did you leave Rogand, and how long have you been away?" she asked curiously.

"I've been away a long time. Many years," he said evasively.

To his relief, she did not pursue it further. She clearly had secrets of her own. Perhaps that was why she chose not to dig too deeply.

BEFORE THE SUN set the harbor of Varacellan hove slowly into view. It was completely dark by the time they finally docked.

The captain had already shown them great consideration, and when he realized they had no money to pay for lodgings, he thoughtfully arranged for a port official to conduct them to the Rogandan embassy. The port official knew enough Rogandan to explain the captain's intentions to the old man and his friends.

Kamash was grateful beyond words. Meeting with the ambassador was precisely what he had been hoping for. Being unable to thank the captain in his own tongue, all of them, even Neira, bowed low in gratitude before waving a farewell.

As they approached the ambassador's building, Kamash tried to calm his racing heart, reminding himself he was well acquainted with dealing with royal officials. Of necessity his skills had remained dormant, but he felt sure that conventions would not have changed significantly, even over the course of his long life. Leaning closer to Neira, he whispered, "Would you allow me to do the talking, at least for now?"

She looked down her nose at him for a moment, then to his surprise she responded with a nod.

When they arrived, they were ushered inside after a short delay and greeted by a Rogandan official. "What brings you to the ambassador?" the official asked. "I heard you were rescued from a tiny boat far out at sea."

"We were," Kamash acknowledged. "We were fortunate indeed to be found by Varasan fishermen. My name is Kamash," he continued with a bow, "and this is Neira and Uman. Uman does not speak."

The official surveyed them with raised eyebrows, but didn't comment. They must surely provide a curious spectacle. The great age of Kamash would itself be an object of curiosity, and the foreign features of the others could hardly have been more apparent.

"I am sure the ambassador has more important priorities than providing comfort to shipwrecked mariners," Kamash continued. "But I am confident he will want to hear what we have to tell him."

"I don't doubt you have a story worth listening to," the official told them, "but it will need to wait until the morning. The ambassador is not available at present. In the meantime, I will arrange for food to be sent to you. After you have taken refreshments, you will be shown to our guest quarters."

The official was as good as his word. A light meal soon appeared, then they were led to a cluster of small rooms equipped with beds and other amenities. After being invited to make themselves comfortable, they were told that someone would come for them in the morning.

Entering the room assigned to him, Kamash threw himself down onto the low bed and fell immediately into a deep sleep.

3

———

The afternoon had almost worn away before the ambassador called for Kamash and his companions. An aide ushered them into a small reception room where the ambassador sat at a large mahogany desk, his attention fixed on a parchment spread out before him.

"The castaways, Lord Daris," the aide announced before excusing himself with a bow.

The ambassador glanced up from the parchment. He appeared anxious and distracted.

"I heard of your ordeal," he said. "A terrible business." He waved a hand vaguely. "I will arrange for you to be transported to Rog at the earliest opportunity." His eyes drifted down to the parchment again.

If Kamash was reading Lord Daris correctly, this promised to be a short interview.

"We apologize for disturbing you, My Lord. I am Rogandan and my name is Kamash," he said. "My companions understand our language, although they are not from Rogand or from any of the kingdoms in this region."

The ambassador's head jerked up. He directed a sharp glance toward the girl. "Who are your companions?" he asked.

Kamash opened his mouth to respond, but Neira got in first. She had either forgotten her agreement to let Kamash do the talking, or she'd chosen to ignore it.

"This is Uman," she said, indicating the guard. "He cannot speak. My name is Neira. We have journeyed here from the Empire of Ahr."

Neira's answer was direct, but it was more restrained than the old man might have expected. Discovering he had been holding his breath, he released it slowly, allowing the air to escape between his teeth.

Lord Daris had gone pale. He turned to Neira. "Could it be possible?" he murmured. "Are you...?"

She shot a glance at Kamash.

Apparently she hadn't entirely forgotten her promise. But the ambassador needed to know the truth, and it was her story. He nodded once.

She raised her head proudly. "I am Princess Neira, beloved daughter of our most august emperor—may his name be exalted!"

"This is...most unexpected," the ambassador stammered. He shook his head, attempting to recover himself. Pushing back his chair, he clambered to his feet and offered her a formal bow. "I am greatly honored to host you, Your Highness," he said. "I beg your forgiveness if our welcome has been somewhat lacking."

"You are pardoned," she replied condescendingly, looking down at him over her nose. "I have endured much worse in recent times," she added with a dark glance in the direction of Kamash.

The ambassador pulled a cord beside his desk, and a servant hurried in. "Bring refreshments at once for our honored guests!" he ordered.

The servant bowed and scurried away. It was apparent that they now had the ambassador's full attention.

"How did you come to be adrift on the open seas?" Lord Daris asked them.

Neira glanced at Kamash, clearly inviting him to respond on behalf of them all.

"It is a matter of some delicacy, My Lord," he said. "But the simple answer is that a few weeks ago, the princess and her guard found themselves stranded as a result of misadventure on the island where I have been living. I offered to sail them to Rog. Unfortunately for us all, my small vessel was disabled in a major storm. We somehow remained afloat until Varasan fishermen found us and brought us here."

The ambassador eyed him shrewdly. "It is obvious to me that there is a great deal more to your tale than you have revealed. Much as I respect your discretion, it is crucial that I, and other interested parties, learn the full details of everything that has happened. Once the right people are in the room, would you be willing to speak openly?"

Kamash stared back at him determinedly. "On one condition," he said.

"What is it?" asked Lord Daris.

"Both you and the king of Varas must guarantee the safety of Princess Neira and her guard."

The ambassador appeared relieved. "I can readily agree to that, and I have no doubt that King Delmar will do the same."

At that moment servants arrived bearing food and drink. After ordering that his guests be served, the ambassador directed one of his servants to find new clothing for them.

He turned to Kamash. "I am going to leave you for a while, to gather a few key people who will want to hear your news. You have my word that you will receive the guarantee you requested before anything needs to be said. I will, of course, send a full report to King Krasmir, and I have no doubt that he will underwrite my guarantee."

"Who is King Krasmir?" asked Kamash curiously.

Lord Daris gazed at him in surprise. "The king of Rogand, of course."

The old man's eyebrows went up. "I expected Agon—the son of King Ugar—would be king now."

The ambassador stared at him strangely. "How long have you been away from Rogand?"

To Kamash's relief, an aide scurried up to Lord Daris with a message, saving the old man the necessity of a reply. Upon reading the message, the ambassador regretfully informed them that he was urgently needed elsewhere. After promising he would return soon, he excused himself and hurried away with the aide.

THE SUN HAD BARELY SET when Kamash and his companions, newly clad in fine clothing, were taken to the Rogandan ambassador. On the way, Kamash sidled alongside the princess.

"Do you wish to speak for yourself?" he asked her.

"Certainly not!" she retorted. "It would not be dignified for me to talk about my abasement on your primitive island. And although I entrusted my life to your puny little boat—very unwisely as it turned out—I have no desire to glorify either the vessel or the experience by talking about it. I will withhold comment until matters of substance are raised."

The old man nodded, unable to keep a smile from his lips. Whether born and bred in empires or in kingdoms, royals were the same everywhere.

They were ushered into a lavishly appointed reception room where food and drink were being served in bountiful supply. A buzz of voices greeted them as they arrived, but all conversation ceased the moment they entered the room, and every eye turned in their direction.

The ambassador stood waiting for them along with five other people. All of them studied Kamash and his friends with considerable interest.

"Welcome!" said Lord Daris, his lips parting with the practiced smile of a diplomat. He addressed the others already in the room. "May I introduce to you Princess Neira of the Empire of Ahr, her guard, Uman, and Kamash, one of my own countrymen who has been accompanying them."

Then he turned to the new arrivals. "Allow me to introduce my other guests. We are privileged to have with us King Delmar of Varas, along with one of his senior nobles, Lord Karevis."

The Varasan king aimed a nod in their direction. Lord Karevis bowed.

"I am also pleased to introduce to you King Rupert of Castel and Lord Mardone, one of his nobles. We are fortunate that they happened to be visiting Varacellan and were able to join us."

King Rupert and Lord Mardone added their greetings.

"We are also grateful that Count Ranauld has made himself available to join us. The count is a nobleman in the court of King Steffan of Arvenon and a close confidante of the king. His presence in Varacellan is also timely."

The count bowed a welcome.

Kamash eyed them curiously. He was impressed. Four of the five kingdoms in the region were now represented. And Lord Daris had introduced the foreigners almost as if they were on friendly terms with Rogand, maybe even allies. A great deal must have changed since he was last abroad in the world.

Two kings had made themselves available at very short notice, along with highly ranked nobles representing two more. Kamash was left wondering what might have prompted such a response. He didn't doubt that princesses rarely visited Varacellan from far off empires, especially as castaways. But surely curiosity alone could not account for a gathering such as this.

His experience told him that these people had more than a casual interest in the princess. He felt sure they knew something of her already and had information Kamash wasn't aware of.

"Please," said the Rogandan ambassador, "tell us from the beginning how you came to be here. Leave nothing out. I will translate for the benefit of those who speak only Arvenian."

Kamash exchanged a glance with the princess. She nodded briefly.

Pausing for a moment to calm his racing pulse, he began. "I have been living for some years on a tiny island far from the mainland."

He waited for Lord Daris to translate before continuing.

"Several weeks ago, I watched as a boat was rowed to the little beach of my island. Two people—the princess and her guard as I later discovered—were put ashore. I watched as the sailors rowed around the island before returning to their ship and sailing away."

Muttering broke out at his words. The ambassador and his guests appeared troubled.

Kamash continued. "I made myself known to the princess and her guard and was able to satisfy their immediate need for food and shelter. After they had endured a few weeks of their unexpected isolation, I offered to sail them to Rog. My intent was to commit them into the care of the king. Soon after we left, a severe storm blew up. It prevented us from completing our journey. We might well have perished at sea had it not been for the intervention of Varasan fishermen who were kind enough to bring us here."

Heads nodded once his words were translated.

"What prompted you to risk the elements?" asked Lord Daris, frowning. "Why not simply wait for the princess's people to return for her?"

Before responding, Kamash stole a glance at the princess. She returned a tight nod, and the old man faced the ambassador once more.

"I acted out of concern for the well-being of the princess," Kamash replied. "When she first arrived she told me that she had been weary from a long sea voyage and asked to spend a short time on solid ground. The sailors were delivering her to the island in response to that request. They promised to return for her after circumnavigating the island in search for a more attractive place to land. For reasons known best to themselves, they chose not to do that."

Kamash furrowed his brows. "There can be little doubt that the sailors believed the island to be uninhabited." He paused before adding, "And also incapable of sustaining life for any length of time, given the lack of shelter and readily available food supplies."

Further muttering broke out as soon as his words were translated.

"I had food enough for the three of us," Kamash continued. "But I formed the opinion that the sailors would return at some point, expecting to find the bodies of the princess and her guard. I could only guess at their reaction on finding them alive and well. But I deemed it unsafe for any of us to remain on the island to find out."

"Who was in charge of the Ahran vessel, and what was the purpose of the voyage?" the ambassador asked.

A stubborn look came to the princess's face. "You surely cannot expect that I would disclose matters of state to foreigners," she said haughtily.

The ambassador and his guests exchanged glances.

King Delmar spoke, addressing himself to the princess.

"His Majesty King Delmar asks if you know why the sailors left you on the island," the ambassador translated.

Her reply was brief and terse. "I do not. But my father will have the heads of those responsible when he finds out."

An animated conversation broke out in Arvenian, and the ambassador turned aside for a time to participate in it.

Kamash waited patiently. Thus far he had been the only one providing information, and he would have greatly appreciated any member of his audience returning the favor. But his experience of kings and noblemen left him with low expectations.

Nor was he disappointed. The interaction that followed went on for long enough that Kamash began to wonder if the kings and their retainers had forgotten entirely that the princess and her little party were still present in the room. After a while he decided to ignore them, choosing instead to eat heartily from the tantalizing array of food and wine laid out in the reception room.

Eventually the talking came to an end.

"The hour is late," Lord Daris told Kamash and his companions. He waved at the tables still laden with food. "Please, take your fill. King Delmar is kindly arranging for you to be shown to more appropriate accommodations at the palace. We will remain here in Varacellan while a suitable vessel is being prepared. It might take a day or two, but as soon as one is available we will take ship to Rog. I will accompany you."

The ambassador addressed the princess. "I presume you would wish your guard to remain at your side, Your Highness?" he asked.

"Most certainly," she replied.

Lord Daris turned to Kamash. "All of us thank you for your efforts on behalf of the princess. You will be free to go your own way in the morning."

"He will be coming with us," the princess interjected bluntly. "I will not go to Rog or anywhere else without him."

Lord Daris raised his eyebrows, but he didn't argue. "Are you willing?" he asked the old man.

Kamash nodded slowly. He was no less surprised than the ambassador by the princess's demand, but he didn't show it. "I find myself with no pressing engagements," he said with a wry smile. "So I am willing."

"Very well," said Lord Daris. "I will see to the arrangements."

A detachment of honor guards duly arrived to escort them to their new accommodations. The palace was close enough for them to walk, and as they passed through the broad streets Kamash gazed curiously at the happy crowds that thronged them. Well before they arrived at their destination he had decided he liked Varacellan very much.

The room allocated to Kamash in the palace was noticeably different from the one he had occupied the previous night, and bore no comparison at all with his primitive dwelling on the island. The feather and down pillow beneath his head was luxurious. Nevertheless, soft though it might be, it was quickly forgotten once sleep reached out for him.

THE CITY of Varacellan glittered in the early morning light, beautiful and peaceful. Splendid as it was, King Rupert of Castel would have exchanged it in a heartbeat for the less sophisticated grandeur of his own capital city. There was no place like home when you'd slept badly and woken to a fresh day of troubles.

He had plenty on his mind. Needing to clear his head, he left the palace buildings and wandered aimlessly into the large garden within the outer walls of the castle.

Life had changed dramatically for Rupert in the years since he was crowned king. At first, deceived entirely by the former Lord Eisgold, an impressionable King Rupert had made a series of monumentally bad decisions that brought his kingdom to the brink of disaster. His blindness had also very nearly cost him his own life.

Thanks entirely to the bold initiatives of a determined band of loyalists, Lord Eisgold's duplicity had been exposed in time to save Rupert and free his kingdom. Greatly humbled by the impact of his mistakes, the unseasoned young king had chosen to embrace responsibility for his actions and learn from the experience.

Eight years had now passed since the deaths of the traitorous Lord Eisgold and Eisgold's sponsor King Agon of Rogand. During that period he had worked hard at growing into the shoes vacated by King Istel, his beloved father, struck down before his time. The nobles who rescued Rupert had unstintingly provided help and guidance, proving their value and their loyalty many times over.

Everything had been proceeding as well as Rupert could have hoped. As he slowly began to mature, he dared to imagine that better times lay ahead for him and his kingdom. As little as a month ago his world had seemed predictable and his kingdom secure. He felt sure that the troubles of the past lay behind him.

Then a ship sailed into the harbor at Rog, bearing the Grand Vizier of the Empire of Ahr. Disaster now threatened to engulf Rogand—and Arvenon, Varas, and Castel along with it. Any notion that Rupert's world was stable had been stripped away in a moment.

Dangerous as the situation was, Rupert and his fellow monarchs at least thought they understood what was happening. The arrival of Princess Neira demonstrated that none of them understood anything.

Rupert groaned aloud and shook his head. At the sound, a face he recognized appeared from behind a flowering bush.

The narrowed eyes of Princess Neira peered up at him. "King Rupert, isn't it?" she sniffed. "I don't remember the name of your kingdom."

He groaned again, inwardly this time. Why did he have to bump into the princess, of all people? And she'd spoken to him in Rogandan. He'd been working hard to master the language, but he suspected that her fluency exceeded his own.

"My kingdom is called Castel, Princess Neira," he replied.

"I see," she said, somehow managing to convey that neither he nor his little kingdom registered at all in her reckoning.

"What brings you into the garden this morning?" he asked, unable to overcome his awkwardness enough to conjure up a more sharp-witted question.

Her eyebrows drew together. "Don't women in your kingdom enjoy gardens?" she asked, a sarcastic tinge to her tone.

He winced inwardly. "Yes, they do," he acknowledged. Then, speaking mostly to himself, he added, "The real surprise is that I'm here."

"Well?" she demanded. "Why are you here?"

Was it necessary for her to be so blatant about her rudeness? Perhaps she had been hoping for solitude, but so had he.

"You're not the only one with more questions than answers," he retorted with a frown. "Nor are you the only one who'd rather be speaking your own language, and preferably to someone vaguely interested in hearing what you had to say."

She looked at him wide-eyed for a moment, then she burst out laughing.

He flushed, taken aback by her response and annoyed with himself for being so forthright.

"I'm not laughing at you," she said, struggling to suppress another chuckle. "I'm appreciating the absurdity of this situation."

Her response didn't help, and it must have shown on his face, because she added, "On Ahr-Chitani I was never allowed to spend time alone with a male. Much less one with the impertinence to treat me as an equal. My chaperones would be horrified." A new bout of giggling overtook her.

He stared back at her, unsure how to respond.

She looked at him boldly. "I must say there are aspects to the situation I'm finding very interesting." Then her brows knit together delicately. "Would you like to kiss me?"

He frowned, beginning to feel even more uncomfortable.

"Apparently not," she said, sounding a bit peeved. Then she shrugged. "I've always been told that I'm much too brazen for my own good." The trace of a grin appeared on her lips. "But this is the first time I've stooped to inviting a man to kiss me."

He couldn't prevent his eyes flicking to her lips. He felt himself blushing.

She frowned again. "Back home no one would dare of course. You're probably the first person who could actually do it without losing your head." She grinned at him.

Abruptly she glanced over his shoulder. "There's Uman! I need to leave."

And with a swish of her skirts she was gone.

Rupert shook his head. He couldn't begin to figure her out. The fate of kingdoms hung in the balance, with her positioned at the center of the maelstrom. And here she was trying to orchestrate her first kiss. What on earth was she playing at?

The stakes had never been higher for him and for his kingdom. Yet a single trivial issue occupied far too much of his attention as the morning slipped away. "Would you like to kiss me?" she had asked. The question was absurd. And his inability to banish it entirely from his mind annoyed him intensely.

4

The first glimmers of daylight slowly lightened the sky, revealing a broad beach lapped by the gentle swell of a tranquil ocean. Nestled behind the sand dunes lay a fishing village, a haven to the small boats spreading out at that moment across the bay, their sails billowing in a freshening breeze.

Suddenly a monstrous reptilian form burst from the ocean, shattering the stillness. The creature threw back its head and bellowed, the unearthly roar drowning out the cries of the fishermen. Then it bent low, opening its gigantic maw wide to enclose a fishing boat. As the mouth snapped shut, a long tail whipped out to lash another vessel, splintering timbers as though they were twigs.

Boats dodged back and forth across the bay as fishermen tried frantically to evade the monster. Their efforts were in vain. One by one the boats succumbed to its fury until nothing but wreckage remained to rise and fall with the swell.

Surging from the ocean, the beast fell upon the village, thrashing about in a frenzy until the settlement had been utterly destroyed. Then, raising its head and roaring once more, it headed inland.

. . .

BROTHER ANDER WOKE WITH A START, struggling to separate imagination from reality. Lurching unsteadily from his bed in a tower room of the royal castle at Arnost, he shuffled to the window, sweating profusely in the cool air. He stared wide-eyed up into the brilliant display of stars, unnerved by the vividness of the dream.

As he watched, a shooting star flashed across the heavens, rapidly followed by several more. Fully alert now, the monk's brows drew together as he labored to make sense of the demonstration.

Had the dream been a premonition? Had he witnessed signs in the heavens to confirm it?

Only one conclusion made sense to him—trouble was coming. His gut tightened as he pondered the implications.

What should he do?

Once a soldier and a leader in battle, the big monk knew that the mightiest of armies were powerless to defeat some enemies. The greatest warrior could not strike down a pestilence that might be conquered by the frailest of healers. He had come to recognize that true strength was often disregarded, dismissed as weakness by those unable or unwilling to penetrate its disguise.

What should he do?

Lighting a candle, he glanced down at the scroll that lay beside it. His eye fell upon the words he had been studying before he surrendered to sleep, 'Devote yourselves to prayer, being watchful and thankful.'

A wry smile crossed his lips as he considered the seeming feebleness of prayer.

His question had been answered. Heaving a deep sigh, he gazed once more out into the night sky. Then kneeling on the rough stone floor, he directed his forebodings heavenward.

QUEEN ESSANDA HAD FINALLY FOUND time to focus on her youngest child, Princess Charlotte, to the great delight of the three-year-old. Sweet and demure, Charlotte was also unusually astute for her age.

She unfailingly showered her father with affection, but showed a clear preference for the company of her mother. Everyone said she was a miniature of the queen.

"Mother! Mother!"

Queen Essanda sighed as her sons appeared at the door. Unusually spirited, they somehow managed to commandeer a disproportionate share of her available time. Her eldest, the eight-year-old Crown Prince Aiden, hobbled into the room with an arm over the shoulder of his younger brother, Prince Leonid, recently turned six.

Little Charlotte jumped up in alarm and ran to them. "Are you hurt, Aidie? What happened?"

"I was riding, and I fell off," Aiden replied through gritted teeth. "I hurt my ankle."

"Come over here," commanded the queen. "Ava!" she called. "Could you please fetch Brother Ander? Quickly!"

"At once, Your Majesty," her maid replied, dropping her needlework and scampering for the door.

Essanda settled her injured son on a sofa and tried to make him comfortable. He appeared overwrought. After a moment's reflection, she decided she'd have been more concerned if he was pale and subdued. Children certainly had a taste for the dramatic.

The monk arrived before many minutes had passed. He walked into the room, taking in the scene at a glance. Approaching the prince, he quickly examined his ankle, moving it back and forth gently. He smiled at the queen. "It appears to be a sprain," he assured her. "Nothing seems to be broken."

He turned to the prince. "What's the problem, young Aiden?" he asked. "Have you been up to mischief again?"

"I was riding, and I fell off," Aiden repeated, not making eye contact with the monk.

"That's curious," said Brother Ander. "I wouldn't have expected that pony of yours—Prince, isn't it?—to do anything too adventurous. He seems barely able to raise a trot."

Aiden colored slightly.

The monk grinned at him. "Perhaps you fell off a horse?"

The prince didn't reply, but the look on his face was revealing.

"You didn't tell me you were riding a horse!" his mother exclaimed. "You know you're not supposed to be doing that!"

"I didn't lie!" he insisted. "You never asked me what I was riding!"

She raised an eyebrow at him.

Aiden threw up his hands. "How will I ever become a warrior if I never get to ride real horses?"

"You're much too young to be thinking about becoming a warrior," Essanda told him sternly.

"But you were only a girl when you went to battle!" Aiden protested.

"That was different," Essanda replied, "and I certainly was a lot older than eight." She frowned at him. "How did you find out about that anyway?"

Brother Ander cleared his throat guiltily. "I suspect I might have been to blame for that, Your Majesty," he admitted.

"It isn't his fault," retorted Aiden, his lips forming a pout. "Everyone in the kingdom knows about it! Everyone except us, that is."

Essanda turned to the monk with a sigh, determined to change the subject. "What does he need to do about the ankle?" she asked.

"It needs rest," Brother Ander replied. "It would help if he stays off it for a while."

"If I promise to keep away from the horses, can I ride my pony?" Aiden asked hopefully.

"Most certainly not!" his mother replied. "You heard what Brother Ander said. You need to rest your ankle."

Aiden glowered at the monk.

"You appear to be cross with me," Brother Ander observed. "Why don't you punch me? If you dare, that is," he challenged, standing before the prince with hands on his hips.

Aiden hopped up immediately. Leaning against a sofa for support, he began flailing about with both fists, grunting aloud as he strained to hit his target.

Brother Ander grinned back at him, stretching out a hand lazily and placing it on the prince's forehead. His reach was so much longer than the boy's that Aiden was unable to land a single punch.

"Argh! It isn't fair!"

Still grinning, the monk removed his hand and let the young prince pound him for a few moments. "Enough!" he cried with a laugh. "I'll need a doctor myself in a minute."

Aiden stopped punching and sat down again with a grunt of satisfaction.

The monk ruffled his hair. "Promise me you'll take better care of yourself, young prince!" he said.

Aiden grinned up at him. Then he stood once more and hobbled to the door, calling for his brother to lend him a shoulder again.

Turning to Ava, the queen jerked her head after him. The maid nodded an acknowledgment, following them out the door to keep an eye on them.

Essanda smiled indulgently after their disappearing forms. Then she turned her full attention to Brother Ander and studied him for a while. "You seem more thoughtful than usual," she said.

"You're uncommonly observant, Your Majesty," he replied. "I thought I was behaving normally."

"You were," she said. "But I've known you a long time. You have something on your mind."

"I do," he acknowledged. "I had a dream last night, a disturbing dream. And it was followed by shooting stars in the heavens."

She raised her eyebrows. "Can you tell me about it?"

He nodded. Surprisingly, he was still able to remember it clearly. He described it without further comment.

She stood silently for a while. Finally, she asked, "Did you say the sun rose over the sea?"

"Yes," he replied.

"So the setting was not Arvenon. The sun sets over our coastline —it doesn't rise over the sea."

He looked at her in surprise. "You're right! I never thought of that."

"Rogand, perhaps?" she asked.

He nodded. "Perhaps. If the dream represents anywhere known to us, it would have to be Rogand."

"So something is threatening Rogand. Do you think it's a natural disaster? A plague, or a flood?"

He shook his head slowly. "My heart says otherwise." He gazed down at her. "You understand better than most the damage caused by human greed and lust for power, Your Majesty. You and King Steffan have suffered from it yourselves."

"What can the king and I do to prepare?" she asked.

He shrugged. "I have no advice to offer, Your Majesty. I can only say I'm confident you'll find a way through, as you have in the past."

She gazed up at him silently for a moment. Then she said, "Thank you, Brother Ander. I truly don't know how we would manage without you."

He stared back at her in surprise. "I contribute so little. I do know I'm supposed to pray, and I've been doing that. For you and the king especially, because the burden of leadership weighs heaviest during difficult times. But beyond that..."

She smiled. "You do much more than you realize."

He thanked her with a bow and left.

Princess Charlotte was overdue to reclaim her mother's attention. Essanda reached out and drew her in for a hug, and the three-year-old settled in with a sigh of satisfaction.

Nevertheless, the queen was unable to entirely banish the previous conversation from her mind. Brother Ander feared that trouble was coming. She could wish it otherwise, but wishing achieved very little. Perhaps the monk was right, and they would somehow find a way through when the need arose.

She very much hoped so.

AFTER CONCLUDING A SCHEDULED meeting with the Castelan ambassador, Queen Essanda left the reception room to discover her husband waiting for her.

"Essanda, I need to speak with you. Urgently." The king looked worried.

She followed him into a private meeting room and closed the door behind them. "What's the problem, Steffan?" she asked.

"I've just received a dispatch," he told her grimly. "There's trouble."

She grimaced. "The dispatch is from Rog. And whatever the trouble is, it came from the sea."

His brows puckered in astonishment. "How did you know?"

"A lucky guess," she replied. "I can explain later. What's the trouble? Relations with Rogand have never been better since King Krasmir ascended the throne."

"Krasmir isn't the problem," he exclaimed. "It's much worse than that. A ship arrived from the Empire of Ahr, bearing the Grand Vizier."

"The Empire of Ahr? I've barely heard of it. It's on another continent isn't it?"

"Yes," he replied. "Going there requires a long and dangerous sea voyage. Only the boldest traders are willing to risk the journey."

"What's the problem?" she asked.

"The Grand Vizier says he was heading for Rogand on a goodwill visit. He claims they were attacked at sea as they approached Rog. The emperor's daughter was traveling with them, and she was abducted from their ship, supposedly by men from a customs ship bearing the Rogandan flag."

Essanda frowned in disbelief. "It's hard to imagine King Krasmir sanctioning such an action. What does he have to say about this?"

"He strenuously denies that any of his people were involved," Steffan told her. "He thinks it might have been pirates. It's very surprising, though, to say the least."

His brows furrowed. "The Grand Vizier says this act has brought intolerable dishonor to the empire, and the emperor will have no choice but to send soldiers to find his daughter. They will conduct a search throughout Rogand, Castel, Varas, and Arvenon! They will poke their noses into every corner of the four kingdoms looking for the princess, and they will do it with or without our cooperation."

"What? That would amount to an act of war!"

"Exactly. The Grand Vizier has promised to return with an army big enough to crush any kingdom unwilling to cooperate with them."

Essanda was horrified. "Have Varas and Castel been informed? Are Delmar and Rupert aware of this?" she asked. "And what is Krasmir planning to do?"

"I don't know what Krasmir intends to do. But he's sent urgent messages to Varacellan and Castel Citadel as well as to us." He shrugged helplessly. "That's all I know."

Essanda shook her head slowly. "What can we do?"

"I've sent for Will," Steffan told her. "We'll need him and his insights. I've also sent a messenger to Lord Burtelen, and asked him to ride to Arnost with Will."

She nodded. "It's a pity the duke isn't still with us. I always valued his wisdom."

"Yes, I'm sure it won't be the last time we'll find ourselves missing my uncle," Steffan replied. "Even if he hadn't passed away last year, though, it wouldn't have been reasonable to expect him to travel from Maranelle to Arnost."

"Are you hoping to send Will to Rog?" Essanda asked.

"The thought had crossed my mind," he acknowledged.

"He won't want to go unless Amyra is with him," she said. "I hear the two of them are inseparable. And he'll want Thomas with him too."

The king looked surprised. "Why would Will want Thomas to go with him?"

Essanda quirked her eyebrows at him. "Are you serious? Whenever anything significant is going on, he always involves Thomas."

"Well I was expecting him to take Rufe. But you're undoubtedly right. For that matter he'll probably want Jonas and Haldek and Breysen..."

"It's all very well to make light of it," she chided. "I have a feeling we'll soon be wishing there were plenty more like them."

"You're probably right," he told her seriously. "You usually are. Now tell me how you guessed the news from Krasmir."

She gazed up at him. "Earlier today Brother Ander told me about a dream he had recently," she said. "He dreamed that a monster attacked the coast. The sun was rising over the sea, so it must have been an eastern coastline. I guessed it was Rog. He got up from the dream in time to see a shower of shooting stars. After receiving a dream that was followed by a sign in the heavens, he became convinced that trouble was coming."

"How does any of that help us?" asked Steffan.

She shrugged. "I don't know. But he told me he's praying for us."

The king raised his hands in a mute appeal. "We're going to need all the help we can get," he said grimly.

5

———————

"There's been another dispatch from Rog, Essanda."

The queen looked at Steffan hopefully. "Good news?"

He shook his head. "Nothing useful to report, I'm sorry to say."

"Is the Grand Vizier still in Rog?"

"He was still at Rog when the messenger left," Steffan replied. "The man is apparently unyielding. The Rogandans have been meeting with him every day, but the meetings have led nowhere. The Ahrans don't seem in any hurry to leave, which seems odd. There's no real reason for them to stay—other than to assess Rogandan military strength," he added darkly.

"Still, while the Grand Vizier remains in Rog the Rogandans can at least keep trying," Essanda said hopefully.

Steffan nodded. "Maybe they'll somehow find a way to get through to him. Once he leaves, it's likely that we'll see him next at the head of an invasion army."

"Any word from Castel or Varas?" she asked.

"Yes, I've heard from our ambassador to Varas. King Rupert recently arrived in Varacellan on a diplomatic visit, so he'll be able to consult directly with King Delmar. As it happens Count Ranauld is there too. He will represent our interests."

Essanda sighed. "Will and Lord Burtelen should be arriving before long. Maybe they will have suggestions."

"AIDEN! You'll never guess who I just saw riding in!"

The crown prince of Arvenon looked at his younger brother blankly. "Who?"

"It was Will!"

Aiden's eyes lit up. "I'll beat you to the courtyard, Leo!"

Both boys leaped to their feet and raced for the stairs.

The princes flew out of the royal castle at Arnost to find Will separating from the large party that had accompanied him. Having just dismounted, he was handing the reins to a stable hand.

When he saw the boys coming, he faced them with both hands on his hips. "Who might these urchins be?" he asked with a mock frown. "Young vagabonds, I don't doubt—dashing around, disturbing the peace."

He knelt with a grin, opening his arms wide to receive them. Both boys barreled into him at the same time. Knocked off balance, he tumbled backward helplessly, grasping the boys tightly to his chest. The combatants rolled about in the dirt, the boys wriggling and squirming energetically as they tried to free themselves. Loud hollering interspersed with gales of laughter issued from all three of the wrestlers.

The queen appeared on the scene, accompanied by her daughter. "Who's creating all this racket?" she demanded, peering down at the pandemonium before her. "Are those my sons attacking Lord Torbury?"

Princess Charlotte watched on wide-eyed, a giggle on her little lips.

Will staggered to his feet with both boys still hanging off him.

"I'm exhausted, Your Majesty!" he wheezed. "I've fought bandits who were less ferocious than this welcoming party."

She frowned down at her sons, an eyebrow raised admonishingly. "Let the poor man go!" she commanded.

Loud protests sounded from the boys, but they released Will as instructed.

After tousling their hair, he brushed at his clothes in an attempt to dust himself off. Then he knelt before Princess Charlotte. "Can you spare a hug for an old campaigner?" he asked.

"You're very dirty," she told him seriously. "But I think I might have one hug for you."

He reached out for her, and she leaped into his arms, squealing with delight as he swept her off her feet.

"It's an energetic end to a long journey, Will," the queen told him with a laugh. "But you're very welcome, as you can see."

King Steffan appeared. "I thought the castle was under attack!" he exclaimed. "Now I see that it's only Lord Torbury arriving."

Will bowed with a smile, Charlotte still in his arms, and the king grinned back at him.

"Your arrival is perfectly timed, My Lord," the king told him. "Please join me and Essanda." He turned to a servant. "I believe I saw Lord Burtelen riding in. Could you please ask him to join us?"

As the king led them away, Prince Aiden called to Will, "Come find us when your meeting finishes. Promise?"

"I promise!" Will called back with a laugh.

AFTER ORDERING refreshments for the weary travelers, Steffan led them to a small meeting room. They made themselves comfortable while waiting for Lord Burtelen to join them. He arrived as the food and drinks were being served.

"Thank you both for coming so promptly," the king told the new arrivals. "It's been two weeks since a disturbing dispatch arrived from Rog, and I've just received a new dispatch, this time from Varacellan. Before I share its contents, let me brief you on the situation to date."

He quickly outlined all he knew about the Ahran situation. Then he retrieved a parchment.

"This dispatch just arrived from Varas," the king told them. "The news is so bizarre it's difficult to know what to make of it. The missing princess has turned up. In Varacellan."

"Surely that's good news!" exclaimed the queen.

He shook his head grimly. "I'm afraid not. It seems she wasn't kidnapped at all. Her own people dumped her with her bodyguard on a tiny remote island and left them there to die."

The news was greeted with stunned silence.

Lord Burtelen was the first to speak. "How did she get to Varacellan?" he asked.

"Fortunately for us, the Ahrans decided to abandon them on the one remote island that was inhabited. An old hermit was living there, and he took them in and fed them. He also had a boat, and they all set out for Rogand in it. They were caught in a storm and would have died if they hadn't been rescued by some Varasan fishermen who took them to Varacellan."

"Is Delmar planning to return the princess to the Ahrans?" asked Will.

"You won't be surprised to hear there are a range of views on the wisdom of handing her over," the king replied. "There'd be no way to guarantee her safety. But they are planning to send her to Rog."

"At the very least the Grand Vizier needs to know that his lie has been exposed," said Lord Burtelen.

"It might not be possible to confront him with the truth," said the king. "He may have already left Rog by the time the news reaches King Krasmir."

"It seems that the Ahrans want a pretext for war," said Will. He shook his head grimly. "If you can't find a reason, create one. Fabricate an incident, then blame the victim. The only thing that remains is to invade."

"I fear you're right, Will," said Lord Burtelen. "Producing the princess might not stop the Ahrans. If they're determined enough, they'll find another excuse to invade."

Will nodded. "The question is why they've done this. What are their motives?"

The king spread his hands helplessly. "That's what we need to find out."

"Perhaps the princess has answers," said Will. "Do we have anyone who speaks the Ahran language?"

"I've learned that the princess speaks Rogandan, and apparently speaks it well," the king told him.

Will raised his eyebrows.

Everything went quiet until Will asked the king directly, "I'm the only person among your nobles who speaks Rogandan, Your Majesty. Were you planning to send me to Rog?"

"It did occur to me, Will," the king acknowledged.

"You've finally had a chance to settle down, Will," the queen observed. "How would you feel about leaving your family?"

"I won't deny that having a wife and children has changed my outlook on life," Will acknowledged. "But I haven't forgotten that my position of privilege comes with responsibilities—to you and to the kingdom. I'll go if you want me to."

"What will Amyra think about that?" asked Essanda.

"I'd like to discuss it with her," Will replied. "It's possible she'll want to go herself. She speaks Rogandan at least as well as I do."

"And your children?" persisted the queen.

"I'm not sure. With your permission, Your Majesties, I'll return home to properly plan for the journey. Would the delay cause a problem?"

"I trust not," the king replied. "Given you'll be starting from Erestor, it might be quickest to sail to Rog from Maranelle. That should allow you to save quite a bit of time."

Will grimaced. "I can't pretend to have positive memories of my last voyage."

"It did take you a while to find your sea legs," the king acknowledged with a chuckle. "If you're going by ship, perhaps you should take Breysen with you. He's living on your holdings now, isn't he?"

"Yes, he is. It's a good thought. I'll send a message to Newhaven to see if Thomas can come too. He traveled to Rogand with me last time."

Essanda and Steffan exchanged a glance.

"What about Elena and the children?" asked the queen.

"Thomas and Elena will need to decide that for themselves," Will replied.

He turned to the king. "I will follow through on your suggestion, Your Majesty. Traveling to Rog by sea should save a considerable amount of time."

"You'll go as my personal representative, Will," Steffan replied. "I'll prepare some letters of introduction to confirm your role. You can take them with you when you leave for home."

"Thank you, Your Majesty," Will replied with a bow.

"How many people will you take?" Steffan asked.

"Just a small party," said Will. "A large force won't be appropriate for a diplomatic mission. It could send the wrong message."

Steffan nodded his agreement. "You'll be able to consult with Ranauld when you arrive. He's currently in Varacellan, and he's planning to travel with King Delmar and King Rupert when they take the princess to Rog."

"I will look forward to meeting with him," Will said with evident satisfaction.

The king eyed Will thoughtfully. "I'm sure I don't need to remind you that you'll be going as Lord Torbury. I'll avoid any mention in your credentials about your role as commander of the Arvenian army. The less said about that the better, I imagine. It's now been several years since the war ended, and another king is on the throne. But we need to avoid any unnecessary tension with the Rogandans."

Will nodded. "Of course, Your Majesty. I have no more desire than you to resolve this or any other issue by fighting."

<hr>

A NEW MORNING HAD DAWNED, and the road beckoned. After carrying out a final check of his horse's girth straps, Will swung into the saddle. With his credentials from the king stowed safely in a saddle-bag, nothing remained to delay his departure.

A myriad of thoughts flooded through Will's mind as he watched his riding companions mount up. He was looking forward eagerly to seeing his wife and children again. He wouldn't be with them for long, though, and he was already suffering pangs of regret.

The truth was that wandering the world held little appeal for him now. Given the climactic events that had taken place in Rogand, those who knew Will best might have expected life to seem monotonous for him once he returned from there. Nevertheless, he'd readily found new outlets for his restless energies. Returning to his devastated holdings in Erestor with a bride, he set about the process of rebuilding, ably assisted by his new steward, Jonas. Other friends had worked tirelessly alongside him too. Rufe had taken responsibility for animal husbandry as well as security on the holdings, and Breysen, reunited at last with his family, was thriving as the community blacksmith.

Will had put down deep roots into Erestor. Having learned the hard way the value of relationship and credibility with the local nobility, he now took an active interest in the affairs of Erestor's Council of Lords. Many of the nobles had reacted coolly to him at first, but after patience and perseverance he could now count a good few of them as friends. Showing generosity at strategic moments hadn't hurt either.

The Duke of Erestor had eased him into the role, continuing to provide support until his recent death. The whole country mourned the passing of the duke, and Will missed his skillful supervision and wise counsel as much as anyone. Nevertheless, he was gratified when leadership of the council passed to Lord Burtelen, a good friend and staunch ally of Will's.

Regular visits to the capital to consult with the king and queen were still required. Once they were added to the tally, Will had more than enough to occupy his attention.

His musing was interrupted by a familiar voice. "Will, can I please have a word?"

Will turned to the newcomer with a welcoming smile. "It's good to see you, Brother Ander. Unfortunately I'm about to leave—I'm sorry I haven't spent time with you. It's been a very short visit this time."

"I understand," the monk replied. He lowered his voice. "Are you going to Rogand? Because if you are I'd like to go with you."

Unsure of how much he was at liberty to say, Will had no ready reply to offer.

Apparently understanding the reason for his silence, Brother Ander added, "I know there's trouble, but I don't know the details. Would you be willing to wait long enough for me to ask the king and queen for permission to join you?"

"Of course," Will replied without hesitation. He dismounted from his horse. "I'll let my companions know about the delay."

Less than an hour passed before Brother Ander returned. If the big man was still eager to join Will, there was little outward sign of it. At that moment he looked more sober than enthusiastic.

"The king and queen have released me and given me permission to join you," said the monk.

"Reluctantly, if I know anything about the queen," said Will with a smile. "All of them will miss you."

A horse was found for Brother Ander, and he rode out beside Will.

"The king gave me a confidential briefing," said the monk. "The situation doesn't sound encouraging."

Will shook his head. "No. Not encouraging at all."

After they had ridden on in silence for a while, Will addressed the monk again. "The queen told me about your dream. Is that why you want to join us?"

The monk shook his head. "The dream was terrifying. It didn't leave me enthusiastic about heading into the eye of the storm. The reason has more to do with my desire to visit Rogand. Brother Vangellis went there, and he learned the language. I suppose I see myself as following in his footsteps." He stole a glance at Will. "I've been learning Rogandan myself."

Will's eyebrows went up. "You'll be doubly useful then. Would you like to practice while we're riding?"

Brother Ander agreed readily.

"I'm sure you'll be happy to see some of your old friends when we reach my holdings," said Will, switching to Rogandan.

"Most definitely. I will look forward to it," the monk replied in the same language. "It's been far too long."

Will's eyebrows went up even further. "Very impressive! You clearly have a gift for languages."

Brother Ander smiled, but didn't comment.

"I'll be interested to show you the progress we've made," said Will. "And there might be some other surprises too. Involving Rufe."

The monk's eyes went wide. "A lady?" he asked incredulously.

Will nodded. "I suspect he might have met his match at last," he confided with a wink.

6

Kamash leaned over the rail, watching the water as it slid past the hull of the ship and wrestling with his thoughts.

Thus far this voyage was diverging in every imaginable way from the final ill-fated voyage of his own boat. On this ship he had been assigned a comfortable berth and given access to a seemingly endless selection of delicious food. Everything reeked of luxury and quality. None of that was surprising, of course, given the status of the passengers.

Up to that point the voyage had proven uneventful, and he'd been informed that they were already more than halfway to Rog. He was still struggling with his apprehensions about returning to the capital he had fled so many years earlier.

He was no longer ignorant about the recent history of Rogand. A little careful research and a few discreet inquiries had yielded a deluge of information. Agon had indeed ascended the throne after the death of his father, King Ugar. During his eventful reign he had managed to make enemies throughout the region, invading Arvenon and briefly annexing Varas. Frequent mention was made of his army commander, Lord Drettroth, and the name was never mentioned without a snarl.

King Agon might have alienated his neighbors, but rumor had it that he had been equally unpopular within his own kingdom. His careless disregard for the common people had resulted in widespread poverty and oppression. In the end the king had apparently been assassinated on the orders of Drettroth, his own commander, with the killer not surfacing until years after Drettroth was dead and buried.

Lord Drettroth was a person known to Kamash, although it was certainly not the same man. The nobleman he knew was fabulously wealthy, but also fat, lazy, and the most subservient of King Ugar's boot lickers. Kamash could not imagine him invading anything more threatening than a banquet hall. The man who commanded Agon's armies and ultimately brought down the king must have been the successor to the man known to Kamash, most probably his son.

There was also much talk about the Arvenian army commander, a man called Will Prentis. He seemed to have featured prominently in defeating the Rogandan invasion, and rumor said he was also present when Agon was killed.

None of this history had been provided by Rogandans. They seemed unwilling to dwell even for a moment on their former king or anything associated with him. Without exception the old man's sources were Varasan, Castelan, or Arvenian.

The current monarch of Rogand was another matter entirely. Everyone—Rogandans and foreigners alike—wanted to talk about King Krasmir. The new king had captured the popular imagination. He seemed to be a strong ruler who was tolerated by his nobles and loved by the commoners of Rogand. And he had ushered in a new era of cooperation with the neighboring kingdoms.

A single crucial question remained: what did all of this mean for Kamash? Frustratingly, he knew of only one way to find an answer— he would have to wait and see.

The arrival of Princess Neira pushed such thoughts from his mind.

She came and leaned on the rail beside him, gazing off toward the horizon. Peering at her out of the corner of his eye, Kamash wondered what she must be thinking and feeling, so far from home and targeted by enemies from her own empire. He had no desire to ask. She would speak if she had a mind to.

"You handle yourself well in front of royalty," she eventually offered.

His eyebrows rose involuntarily. She wasn't given to handing out compliments, so her praise took him by surprise.

"I wonder where you learned to do that?" she continued, narrowing her eyes to stare at him.

Kamash's heart skipped a beat. Was he so transparent? His mind in a whirl, he could think of no suitable response.

She didn't leave him suffering for long; her next comment snapped him out of his agitation entirely.

"I have decided to appoint you as my spokesperson," she announced matter-of-factly.

He turned to her with a frown. "Whatever do you mean? I can't speak on your behalf!"

"Why not?" she demanded.

"I'm not even from your empire."

Her nose went up. "What difference does that make when my own countrymen have betrayed me?"

Kamash shook his head slowly. "I can't do it, Princess. I'm willing to help you as I've done already, but I can't be your official representative."

Her mouth turned down at the corners and tears began to fill her eyes. "Here I am, far from any real civilization—alone and friendless —cut off from everything and everyone. You're the only person I've met who has shown any kind of concern for me. Now you want to abandon me too. And to the mercy of barbarians!"

She stood there sniffing pathetically, dabbing at her eyes.

Kamash could not bear it. "Please don't cry," he told her. "I'll be your spokesperson if it means that much to you."

The tears vanished in a heartbeat. "Good," she said with evident satisfaction. "You needn't worry—I'll instruct you about what you should and shouldn't say on my behalf."

Another figure emerged onto the deck. It was the young Castelan king.

"Ah, there's that other supposed royal—King Rupert, as he styles himself," she said brightly. "Goodbye, loyal spokesperson. We'll talk more later."

And with that she was gone, heading in the direction of the new arrival.

Kamash watched her retreating form in astonishment. What had just happened? Had he been played?

He sighed in resignation, shaking his head. Whether or not she'd taken advantage of him, he was a man of his word and he'd committed himself now.

Neira's arrival had upended his life. And she'd just made it more complicated than ever.

THE YOUNG KING Rupert groaned when he noticed Princess Neira approaching. Their last interaction had left him extremely uncomfortable. She was disconcerting and unpredictable, and he had no idea how to deal with her.

"*King* Rupert!" she said. The emphasis on his title seemed a trifle pointed, and the smile on her face was as oily as it was friendly. It could easily have been interpreted as mocking.

"Princess," he said tersely, with a crisp nod of his head.

She stared out over the water, the picture of innocence. "Have you been enjoying the voyage?" she asked sweetly.

He grunted noncommittally. "For the most part. And you?"

"More and more," she confirmed with a broad grin.

He remained silent, unwilling to risk even an innocuous comment.

Abruptly she turned to face him. "I suppose I should warn you," she said. She spoke casually, but her voice had taken on an ominous tone.

Rupert looked at her blankly. He couldn't even begin to imagine what might come out of her mouth next.

"My father is not likely to receive it warmly when he learns of your intentions toward me."

His brows drew together, even as his heart began to thump in his chest. "What intentions?" he asked, his voice sounding shrill even to his own ears.

"We talked about you kissing me. In the garden."

"There wasn't any conversation," he protested. "You asked me to do it! That was it!"

"Can you honestly pretend you haven't been thinking about kissing me since?" She paused, studying him intently with narrowed eyes. Then a gloating smile appeared on her lips. "There's no point in denying it! It's written all over your face."

What could he possibly say? He'd certainly thought about kissing her—he'd even obsessed about it briefly—but he'd emerged with no desire whatsoever to do it. And he certainly didn't have intentions toward her. The princess wasn't at all the kind of person he was drawn to. She was far too mercurial.

He opened his mouth to speak, but the right words didn't come readily. She seemed so volatile. How would she react if he set her down? He snapped his mouth shut again, struggling to decide what to say.

"Look, *King* Rupert. I need to be honest with you," she told him condescendingly. "You'd be quite unsuitable as my consort. It simply wouldn't work. I can't settle for a man just because he has some kind of a title. I need someone with presence, a person who can't be trifled with." She released an exaggerated sigh. "I'm sure this must hurt. But I'm being kind to you, even if it doesn't feel like it."

Patting him on the shoulder, she turned on her heel and flounced off across the deck.

Rupert blinked his eyes, trying to make sense of what had just happened. Assuming he was willing to overlook the excruciating awkwardness of the whole incident, it was actually good news, wasn't it? He couldn't imagine her wanting to trouble him any further. As for her humiliating assessment of his manhood and her bizarre conclusions about what he wanted from her, he would simply need to ignore them.

As he stood staring down at the waves, a figure appeared beside him at the rail. It was the old man.

"King Rupert?" asked the newcomer.

"Yes," Rupert acknowledged.

"Do you speak Rogandan?"

"I do," he confirmed, nodding cautiously, "although not particularly well."

"I am Kamash. I witnessed your interaction with the princess from afar."

Rupert felt himself blushing.

"I don't know what Her Highness said to you, but I hope you will extend understanding if that should be needed. The princess has not been called upon to represent her empire before, and I'm sure you can appreciate how much there is to learn when taking on such a role." He paused, apparently choosing his words carefully. "It must be especially difficult for one who has been offered very little freedom in the past."

A guffaw burst out of Rupert before he could stop it. He looked at the old man in amusement. "You're worried about her creating an international incident, aren't you?"

The old man hesitated for a moment, then he responded with a tight nod.

"You have abundant reason to worry!" Rupert told him with another burst of laughter.

He grinned at Kamash. With no more than a few carefully chosen words, the old man had somehow managed to restore both his good humor and his sense of perspective.

He clapped Kamash on the back. "Please don't alarm yourself. I'm willing to overlook her insults and her baseless insinuations," he said, still smiling. "You can tell her I said that, too."

The young man gazed out over the sea. "The salt air is doing me good," he said. "I'm hungry. I think I'll head below decks."

Clapping Kamash on the back once more, he headed for the hatch.

LEFT ALONE to his thoughts again, Kamash grimaced as he ran a hand across his face. Things had been complicated enough already. How had he gotten into this mess?

Even if it turned out to be a disaster for him, good might still come from it. The princess might have manipulated him into a role on her behalf, but in doing so she'd shown surprising good sense. Kamash's interaction with the young Castelan king made it obvious that she needed help—help that her new spokesperson was well placed to offer. A single important question remained to be answered: would she pay any attention to his advice?

In his short time on the island with Neira, he had learned that beneath her haughty and impulsive exterior lay a good heart. She'd simply never been taken in hand. Could he succeed with her when the best teachers in her empire had clearly failed?

She had at least found herself in a unique learning environment. She had sailed into the unknown with men who were honor-bound to care for her and protect her, men who had sworn allegiance to her father the emperor. They had abandoned her to her fate. Would that crush her spirit, or would she grow from it? Humility was a necessary stepping stone on the path to true wisdom; if she chose to embrace it there was a glimmer of hope.

His stomach abruptly growled loudly. Apparently his body had no respect for his need to withdraw and contemplate. King Rupert's comment about being hungry must have triggered the reaction.

Putting his uncertainties to one side, he set off after the young king.

7

———

The robed and hooded priest of the dark gods stood silently, eyeing the worshipers as they approached. Stationed as he was at the busiest of the shrines under his supervision, he had little opportunity for quiet reflection.

Such holy places played an important role in the worship of the dark gods of Rogand. Common people never entered the Temple of the Dark Gods at Rog, and not even the noble born had access, except by particular invitation. All of the people instead attended one or other of the shrines dotted throughout the cities and in the countryside.

The priest assigned to each shrine came at scheduled intervals to enact rituals, to lead worshipers in chants like the Call to Fear, and to receive pledges and gifts in support of the priesthood.

The people made their petitions to the dark gods directly; the presence of a priest guaranteed that the petition would be heard by the dark gods, if not granted.

Key rites of passage took place at shrines, with priests consecrating every birth, marriage, and death. Major civic appointments and significant commercial agreements also traditionally incorporated a brief ceremony at a shrine in the presence of a priest.

This particular shrine was located in a regional town, a place of no apparent significance. Appearances could be deceptive though. A priest who kept his ears open could learn a lot, even in a backwater like this. Whatever he learned would be passed on to a senior priest who passed through the region regularly. Any information of value soon made it back to the temple at Rog.

Fewer people were attending the shrines in recent years. The prosperity and comfort associated with the reign of King Krasmir undoubtedly had a lot to do with that. People were more attentive to the dark gods when they were fearful.

Returning his focus to the worshipers, he saw that next in line was a woman he recognized—the wife of an influential nobleman. Since the time a few months previously when her only daughter had almost succumbed to a crippling illness, the noblewoman had become a frequent visitor to the shrine. The priest knew a little of her circumstances and her story—given the prominence of her husband, he made it his business to do so.

Momentous events were afoot in the kingdom, and the nobleman in question had been summoned to Rog to participate in confidential meetings convened by the king. Perhaps she knew something about the topics to be discussed, perhaps not.

Dropping the traditional gift into the locked box, the noblewoman stepped forward and bowed respectfully. Then she opened her mouth and began to make her petition to the gods.

Blotting out all other distractions, the priest leaned in, straining his ears to catch every word.

Wisps of smoke rose lazily in the air, mingling with the incense that drifted up from the bowls scattered liberally throughout the chamber. This room was not the most heavily frequented in the Temple of the Dark Gods at Rog, and it was not the place from which Goultzar directed his vast network of subordinates, but he liked to spend a portion of each day there worshiping with the acolytes.

Glancing around in the hazy air, he paused to savor the atmosphere of the place. Unexpectedly recalling his reaction on first entering this temple, he shook his head in bafflement, unable to make sense of his initial revulsion.

A sharp twinge in his lower back intruded painfully on his thoughts, prompting him to push himself up from the rough stone floor to stretch uncomfortably. As Archprimus, second only to the High Priest himself, Goultzar's exalted station granted him a range of privileges. But it did not free him from the ravages of advancing age. He was no more exempt from mortality than any other priest.

An image of his leader came unbidden to his mind, and he reluctantly corrected himself: *most* priests could certainly not claim to be exempt from mortality. He still hadn't made up his mind about His Eminence. The celebrated longevity of the High Priest became ever more remarkable as the years advanced.

At risk of being caught in the grip of a thought process that was neither new nor welcome, he dismissed his musings with a frown, directing his attention instead to the observance going on around him.

Goultzar knew where he needed to focus his energy. His primary role was to direct the activities of the priests, not just here in the temple at Rog, but throughout Rogand. He had been appointed to this role—many years previously—largely in recognition of his outstanding abilities as an organizer and administrator. His overarching purpose, though, was to ensure that devotion to the dark gods never flagged. For him the significance of this purpose had grown as the years passed. It now went far beyond a mere calling; it had become the consuming passion of his life. His burning desire to express his own devotion was a key reason he participated in the daily ritual before him now.

He had only just seated himself again when a junior priest arrived, bending low to reach his ear. "His Eminence awaits you," he whispered respectfully.

The Archprimus clambered to his feet once more and made his

way to the small room where the High Priest spent each day. He knocked at the door before pushing inside.

The High Priest, seated as usual in his carved wooden chair, observed his progress with apparent disinterest, offering no greeting and failing to acknowledge Goultzar's bow of obeisance. The visitor, more than familiar with the ways of his master, was not surprised.

Goultzar sat in silence on the low stool that faced the High Priest, granting His Eminence the courtesy of speaking first.

A long silence ensued as the aged Superior observed his underling. "You are troubled," he finally offered.

Goultzar tried to mask his surprise. He shouldn't have been caught off guard by the perceptiveness of the old priest. It was true. Goultzar's thoughts had been increasingly darkened by a new concern.

"As always, nothing escapes you, Your Eminence," he said dipping his head low. He paused to collect his thoughts. "Of late it has seemed to me that zeal for the worship of the dark gods is flagging in the kingdom."

He paused to allow the High Priest to respond. No reply was forthcoming. He permitted a soft sigh to escape his lips.

"The people revere their monarch, as is appropriate." He hesitated for a moment, undecided about the wisdom of being entirely frank. "They seem almost delirious in their acclaim for King Krasmir and his reforms."

Once more he paused to allow a reply.

Knowing that the High Priest's patience far exceeded his own, Goultzar gave up waiting. "King Krasmir observes the traditions, and he does not neglect the required festivals and rituals," he said frankly. "But he shows little enthusiasm for it." Deciding at last to throw caution to the winds, he added, "Does our king respect the dark gods? Does he fear them as his predecessor did?"

The High Priest stared back at him.

Had Goultzar spoken out of turn? The priesthood had always been fiercely independent of the crown, but the Archprimus was well aware that there were limits. He clamped his mouth shut. This time he would wait for the Superior to speak, however long it took.

His mind continued to churn as he waited. Much more could have been said. Goultzar's role as Archprimus allowed him to observe the kings closely. Agon had gone out of his way to avoid the priests, and there was little doubt that the king had privately feared the dark gods. Such deference from the earthly ruler was both desirable and appropriate.

Agon's successor was different. The dark gods and their ways had no hold over Krasmir. Goultzar was certain of it, and it disturbed him deeply. The people always followed the lead of their king.

All this time His Eminence remained silent, studying the priest before him. Uncomfortable at first, Goultzar slowly began to feel affronted. Shocked by his own reaction, he turned his attention to the floor in front of him, determined not to think about anything more significant than the flagstones at his feet.

After what felt like an age, the High Priest finally spoke. "Kings are mortal."

Goultzar looked up sharply with eyes narrowed. What had prompted such a comment? Had his ancient master somehow guessed at Goultzar's questions around the High Priest's own mortality?

Both men sat in silence. Goultzar remained still for long enough that his lower back pain returned, and he began to experience pins and needles in his feet. He was soon struggling to prevent physical discomfort from dominating his consciousness.

Finally his master released him. "A man waits at the temple gate. He has requested an audience with me. You will see him."

Goultzar stood up. After sitting for so long he felt light headed, and he paused while attempting to recover himself. How could his master bear to remain motionless for so long in that chair?

At last able to trust himself to move, Goultzar bowed deeply and left the room.

Once clear of the building, he headed for the temple gates. As he walked he allowed himself to revisit his meeting with the High

Priest. His Eminence had revealed no more about his inner thoughts than he ever did. That came as no surprise. If the Archprimus was honest, he knew that he had a reputation of his own for being cryptic.

The important question was whether the Superior took his concerns seriously. The High Priest had reason to be concerned if the dark gods failed to receive the respect due to them.

The High Priest was a man who said little and moved even less. At first glance he could easily be taken to be a characterless figurehead well into his dotage. But anyone foolish enough to underestimate him soon learned that he was not a person to be trifled with. When he saw fit, the Superior acted, and acted decisively.

Arriving at the gates, the Archprimus found four hooded priests standing quietly before a man clad in strange garments. Like Goultzar, the visitor wore a hood that hid his face almost completely.

Stepping around the priests, he faced the man, studying him quietly without offering a word.

"Are you the High Priest?" the newcomer demanded impatiently.

Goultzar could not place the man's accent. He allowed the minutes to stretch out before answering. "I am not."

"I will speak to no one but the High Priest."

The Archprimus stretched a hand toward the open gates behind the newcomer. "You are free to leave."

"So who are you, then?" growled the man.

"I am the Archprimus," Goultzar replied after a dignified pause.

The visitor considered that for a moment. "The second in charge," he muttered. Then, in a louder voice, "I will speak with you. But not with these present." He swept an arm disdainfully across the little cluster of priests.

None of them moved.

The newcomer slowly pulled back his hood to reveal a hard face bearing a prominent scar below one eye. "Perhaps you are frightened, old man," he sneered, leaning forward provocatively.

Goultzar leaned forward himself until his face was inches from the stranger's. "I do not fear you," he replied with casual contempt, reaching up to pull back his own hood. He exposed enough to reveal skin etched deeply with scars and daubed with fresh blue paint.

The visitor drew back in shock at the sight. Hastily recovering, he steadied himself, schooling his features into an impassive mask.

Covering his face once more, the Archprimus nodded to his fellow priests. They slipped quietly away, leaving him alone with the visitor. "Well?" he asked.

"Does your religion provide a way to achieve immortality?"

Goultzar started momentarily. Then, narrowing his eyes, he intoned, "The gods offer life, and the gods snatch it back."

"But is there a way to bargain for extended life?"

The Archprimus frowned. "How would such a bargain be made?"

"With blood, of course," replied the stranger. "One life extended, in exchange for other lives ended before their time."

"Who has spoken to you of such an arrangement?" demanded Goultzar coldly.

"I'm not here to answer your questions," the stranger growled. "You're wasting my time. I want to speak with the High Priest."

"He is not available," the priest said flatly. Then he turned on his heel, leaving the stranger at the gate.

Goultzar had conveyed cold indifference to his visitor. Inwardly, he was struggling to contain his shock. What did the High Priest know of these matters? The stranger's questions had poked and prodded uncomfortably at his own uncertainties around the longevity of the High Priest.

Profoundly unsettled by the interview, Goultzar decided to return to the Superior immediately. Uninvited and not expected, he nevertheless pushed past the startled young priest on duty outside the High Priest's room.

The bright eyes of the old man followed him as he entered the room. If the High Priest was at all surprised by the intrusion, he gave no sign of it.

Goultzar bowed tightly before planting himself once more on the stool opposite his master. He did not wait for permission to speak. "The visitor at the temple gates came to inquire about a bargain with the dark gods. A bargain intended to deliver unending life. He wished to discuss these matters with you, and with you alone." Try as he might, he could not entirely eliminate a tone of accusation from his voice.

The High Priest responded with his habitual tranquility. "Nehrvina the Awful grants life. She reclaims it when she chooses," he said with apparent indifference.

The Archprimus frowned. He was not in the mood for riddles. "Do you know of any such bargain?" he asked bluntly.

The eyes of the Superior bored into him. No response was offered.

Goultzar sat motionless on his stool staring at the older man. He had no idea what else to do.

Finally the old man intoned, "The ways of Nehrvina are inscrutable." Then the High Priest closed his eyes, signifying that the conversation was at an end.

Confused and defeated, the Archprimus got to his feet and departed from his master's presence.

THE ARCHPRIMUS'S visitor made his way to a rough inn in the dockside district of Rog. He occasionally glanced back over his shoulder, but it didn't appear that he was being followed.

Reaching his destination, he pushed through the door and threaded his way between the revelers to a table on the far side of the public room. A stool was pushed out from beneath the table, and he sank onto it gratefully. He found a pitcher of ale waiting for him.

The face of the man opposite was hidden behind a cowl. "Did you learn anything useful, Kaifet?" The question was spoken softly.

The new arrival shook his head. "I wasn't allowed to speak with the High Priest. The fool who met with me knows nothing."

The first man grunted. "It's time to try a more direct approach."

"Easier said than done," Kaifet warned.

"You know what to do," growled his companion. "Get onto it, and don't waste any more time."

Kaifet paused for long enough to drain his ale. Then he got up and headed for the door.

No sooner had Kaifet left the inn than a rough-set man at an adjacent table pushed himself to his feet and disappeared out of the door after him. When Kaifet's cowled companion decided to leave, he was tailed as well.

None of the other patrons in the inn noticed anything unusual. For them it was just another rowdy night in a seedy establishment serving cheap ale. All they cared about was getting drunk as quickly as possible.

One week had passed since Kaifet visited the Archprimus. It had been an unusually busy time, but the preparation was finally complete. Kaifet was ready.

A group of men stood silently beside him as he peered through the darkness toward the Temple of the Dark Gods at Rog. On that night the moon was entirely hidden behind clouds. It suited Kaifet perfectly. The element of surprise would be crucial.

"You all know what to do," he growled. "Once we're inside the temple, kill anyone who gets in your way. Not the High Priest—we need him alive."

"How many guards can we expect?" one of the men asked.

"No one has ever seen guards in or around the temple. And none of our informants are aware of priests being armed. The priests are deranged though—don't eyeball them too closely. Stay focused on what we're here to do. We go in, we grab the High Priest, and we get out. Do you understand?"

His words were met with a chorus of grunts.

He drew his sword and raised it aloft.

Twenty swords cleared their scabbards, and Kaifet crept forward, followed closely by his handpicked band.

No one was anywhere in sight when they reached the gates of the temple. Hurrying through the entrance, they headed for the main temple building where the High Priest reportedly spent his entire life.

The High Priest was a fool. He should have met with Kaifet when he had the chance, instead of hiding behind a subordinate. Secreting himself in the temple wouldn't save him.

As he approached the temple, Kaifet had the uneasy feeling that he was being watched. He brushed it off. He'd felt that way for days, without ever finding the slightest evidence to support the notion. It had to be nothing more than nerves.

Stealing around to the rear of the building, he found a door left ajar. Could it really be this straightforward? Pushing inside, he waited until all of his men had filed in after him.

It was pitch dark inside the doorway. Moving quietly forward he came to another door, also lying open. Through the door lay a chamber. Even in the dark he could tell it was large. It appeared to be empty.

Prowling across it he came to yet another large room, dimly illuminated by a small cluster of candles suspended from the ceiling. No priests were anywhere to be seen.

Three other doorways led out of the chamber—the temple building was beginning to feel like a maze. Where were the priests? And where was the High Priest hiding? His men would have no choice but to search every corner until they found him.

Choosing a door at random, he headed toward it. His men bunched tightly together behind him, their figures casting huge shadows on the walls in the candlelight. Hardened soldier as he was, he couldn't pretend it wasn't unnerving.

Seen from outside, the temple was eerie enough in the daytime. Inside it in the dark was infinitely worse. And something he didn't recognize hung in the air—a cloying odor, perhaps incense mingled with the smell of blood. He grimaced with distaste.

Reaching the door, he opened it and peered inside. Another dark space awaited. Thrusting aside his misgivings, he went through.

The smell in the air was much stronger now. It was becoming difficult to breathe. Beginning to feel disoriented, he brushed uneasily at the beads of sweat on his brow and pushed on, more lightheaded with every step.

A thud sounded behind him. Peering sluggishly back over his shoulder, he saw one of his men sprawled on the ground. Another slumped to the floor even as he watched. He blinked stupidly, dimly aware of a mounting sense of panic but unable to think straight.

Why was he here? Was there something he needed to achieve?

Such questions were beyond his grasp. Abruptly losing control of his limbs, he collapsed, his head hitting the ground hard.

FOUR AT A TIME, a steady stream of hooded priests filed from the temple. Each group hefted an unmoving form.

The procession disappeared into the night, the darkness masking the departure of the intruders as effectively as it had masked their arrival. Nothing was heard of them again.

8

Kamash stood at the rail as the ship bearing the princess and the foreign royalty glided into Rog's bustling harbor. The ship had traveled in convoy with four accompanying ships that bristled with armed soldiers, and these escorts now drew back to allow the royal vessel to dock.

Having recently visited the harbor at Varacellan, Kamash eyed the vista before him with heightened interest. The contrast could scarcely have been more marked. If the harbor of the Varasan capital exuded orderliness, the Rogandan equivalent could only be described as chaotic. The appearance of the two cities from the sea only added to the contrast. Varacellan was fair and grand with tall and stately towers. What little could be seen of Rog from the harbor was unremarkable and grimy.

The princess was probably turning away from the sight in disgust. Not so Kamash. He had gone into exile by his own choice, but the tug on his spirit could not be denied. Swallowing hard against a lump in his throat, the old man brushed a tear from his eye. He was coming home.

A great deal had changed since he last glimpsed the harbor from the seaward side. The volume of shipping had increased enormously.

A host of local vessels of every shape and size lay at anchor beside tall ships displaying the colors of other kingdoms. The proportion of ships bearing three masts had grown, and his memory told him that almost all of the vessels before him were in better repair than they used to be. Rogand had apparently prospered, and its neighbors with it.

A figure appeared beside him at the rail. It was the princess. Uman hovered nearby while maintaining a respectful distance, apparently willing to permit his mistress a private conversation with her spokesperson.

A steady breeze swept the long hair from Neira's face as she gazed toward the docks that were growing steadily closer. She shifted restlessly, unable to stand still for more than a moment. A wave of sympathy washed over Kamash. Everything familiar to the princess had been swept away, and he had little doubt that anxiety was threatening to overwhelm her.

He was not unduly alarmed. Neira was not the same girl who had stepped onto the sandy beach of his island. A new sadness cloaked her now, but she had grown stronger too. He was confident that she would win through. And she was not alone. She had Kamash to support her, as well as Uman.

"Do you feel ready to face the barbarians?" he asked, a wry smile on his lips.

She glowered at him, refusing to rise to the bait.

"They will ask questions that deserve answers," he warned her. "If you want me to help you, I need to know a lot more than you've told me so far."

Her nose went up. "Don't expect me to gossip sensitive information," she said stiffly. "You needn't think I'm stupid just because I'm young."

"I don't see you as stupid," he replied patiently. "But both of us need to understand what's going on here, and they can help."

"How could they possibly help?" she asked dismissively.

"They know a great deal more than they're telling us," he replied.

She raised her eyes heavenward, apparently unconvinced.

The old man persisted. "After we arrived in Varacellan, do you remember the reaction of the Rogandan ambassador when I told him you and Uman were not from any of the kingdoms in the region?"

She frowned. "He seemed surprised."

"He was a lot more than surprised," Kamash assured her. "He was stunned. When he realized who you were, he immediately assembled an astonishing collection of royalty. He did it in no more than a few hours."

She snorted. "There's nothing surprising about that. I'm an important person."

He shook his head impatiently. "Those royals weren't there out of politeness."

"Why were they there then?"

"That's the point! We don't know. They told us nothing. They just asked questions."

She scowled, no doubt belatedly recognizing how one sided the exchange had been. "What makes you think they can help us?"

"They could tell us what they know. That might help us understand what's going on. But we need to give them a reason to be frank with us. If we refuse to speak openly, we shouldn't expect them to do it."

The ship's sails had been reefed and its forward movement had almost ceased. Lines were thrown down to row boats, and they began towing the ship toward a dock.

The princess appeared absorbed in the scene before her. She hadn't responded to his comment. Kamash decided it was time to become bolder.

"Who was in charge of your expedition?" he asked.

Neira looked at him sharply.

"I need to know if I'm going to be able to help you," he insisted.

She glared at him for a moment, then she sighed. "The Grand Vizier of the Empire of Ahr was in charge of the mission."

"So he's the one who ordered that you be left behind?"

"Never! He would never dream of doing any such thing."

"Because he likes you?"

"Pah! He has no great love for me. But he is the most loyal and most reliable of all my father's subjects. My father would never have allowed me to come if anyone else was in command."

"Who would have ordered such an action then?"

She scowled off into the distance. "I want to know that as much as you do. I can only think it was the ship's captain. I do not know him well, and I cannot guess why he would do such a thing."

"What of the Grand Vizier? Why didn't he prevent it?"

"I have been wondering about that," she said with a frown. "I fear for his safety! The captain must surely have restrained him—or worse."

"And what was the purpose of your expedition?" asked Kamash.

She glared at him. "Enough questions!"

He shrugged. It was a start. It was nowhere near enough though.

He locked eyes with her. "If you want me to help you, then you need to trust me," he told her pointedly.

THE RECEPTION that awaited the travelers was impressive by any standard. Bright banners of every imaginable color whipped in the breeze, soldiers clad in ceremonial finery lined the streets, and the royal party waited in the shelter of an arresting canvas pavilion of great size.

The king sat on an ornate throne surrounded by a small crowd of nobles. Kamash knew that King Krasmir had a wife and children, although they were nowhere in sight. The throne must have been heavy, and the old man could not help wondering how such an object had been transported to the dockside reception area.

Pushing such irrelevancies from his mind, he focused his full attention on the task at hand. Taking Princess Neira's arm, he steered her forward, noting with satisfaction that the other royal visitors stood aside to allow her through. Uman followed in their wake.

The king stood up from his throne to greet her. "You must be Princess Neira of the Empire of Ahr," he said smoothly, dipping his head respectfully. "I bid you welcome to Rogand. I trust that your voyage from Varacellan was both comfortable and uneventful."

The princess performed an unfamiliar curtsy in return. "I thank you, King Krasmir," she returned. "Our journey was brief, but pleasant. I am honored to visit your kingdom and gratified to be received so graciously."

Kamash quietly released a breath, allowing the tension to ease from his body. He had set out to prepare the princess of course, but she had proven to be an indifferent student. She must have paid some attention though, because she had remembered the king's name and observed enough royal protocol to avoid any suggestion of a veiled insult.

King Krasmir then turned his attention to his other guests, greeting King Delmar and King Rupert warmly, and welcoming others among the noble guests by name.

As the introductions proceeded, the old man allowed himself to study the Rogandan king. The monarch was a big man with bushy eyebrows and a generous beard. Loose talk had likened the king to a bear, and the comparison might have been credible had Krasmir dressed himself differently. The king's demeanor was another matter. He appeared refined and intelligent, and in no way beast-like.

There was nothing weak about the king though. Kamash sensed a toughness beneath the monarch's polished manners. Rogand had apparently done well to find itself ruled by its current sovereign.

Whatever else could be said, this king bore little resemblance to Ugar, a ruler with whom Kamash had been only too familiar.

Royal receptions were exhausting work, and Kamash had become both hungry and thirsty. While keeping a close eye on the princess, he took the opportunity to sample the generous selection of refreshments on hand.

Momentarily distracted, upon looking up he was startled to find himself staring into the face of King Krasmir.

"You are the Rogandan known as Kamash?" It was a statement more than a question.

"I am, Your Majesty," he replied, bowing deeply.

"I understand we have you to thank for the survival of the princess."

"Along with a liberal dose of good fortune," he said, managing a weak smile.

"Indeed," the king agreed. He studied Kamash closely. "I believe the princess has asked you to remain at her side."

"That is true," the old man confirmed. "She has requested me to act as her spokesperson."

"Perhaps a surprising title to confer upon a hermit," the king observed casually.

The old man bowed, but offered no other response.

"But I am told there is much more to you than meets the eye," the king concluded.

Kamash fought down the wave of panic that threatened to rise up and overwhelm him. His heart pounded painfully in his chest, and he could only hope that his agitation was not visible to the king.

The king watched him closely for a few moments before observing, "I am pleased that one of my own subjects stands beside the princess, rather than a person driven by more obscure agendas."

The old man took a deep breath, working hard to steady himself. "I will strive to further the well-being of the princess," he managed, "but my efforts will never be to the detriment of Rogand."

"I am gratified to hear it," the king replied smoothly. He studied the old man for a moment longer before adding with a shallow nod, "Please accept my personal welcome. I am sure we will see more of each other."

Kamash bowed deeply, holding the pose for longer than protocol demanded. When he rose he found that the monarch had gone.

King Krasmir was clearly a shrewd operator. He had taken the trouble to find out about Kamash, and he had skillfully reminded the old man where his loyalty lay.

Surely the king knew nothing of substance about Kamash though. How could he?

The old man stood without moving for a very long time until his heart had settled into a more normal rhythm. His interaction with the king had come as a salutary reminder. He would need to exercise unusual caution in the days to come.

SEVERAL ROBED PRIESTS were included in the delegation that greeted the foreign royalty. King Krasmir had arranged for them to be kept largely out of sight, perhaps mindful of the way their appearance affected unpracticed observers.

None of them said a word, not even to each other. They looked, they listened, and when it was over they quietly melted away.

One of them made his way immediately to the Archprimus, who led him to a private location.

"What did you learn?" Goultzar asked.

"The main arrival was a young princess. From the Empire of Ahr," the priest replied.

"The one all the fuss is about?"

The priest nodded. "I assume so."

"Who were the others?"

"The king of Varas. His name is Delmar. And the king of Castel—Rupert. There were other nobles with them, including from Arvenon."

"And what was King Krasmir's reaction?"

"He greeted them cordially. Warmly, even."

The Archprimus scowled. "Our own king, consorting with unbelievers." He spat in disgust. "Who else was with the princess?"

"A big guard. And an old man. He appeared to be Rogandan."

"Who is he?"

"I heard the king talking to him. His name is Kamash. He's the one who rescued the princess, and he's her spokesperson. He told the king he won't do anything to harm Rogand. The king seemed surprised that she picked him. Supposedly he's been a hermit."

"This hermit story sounds fanciful to me. I don't believe a word of it!" exclaimed the Archprimus. "Find out more about this Kamash.

And keep a close watch on the princess. I'll make sure the other foreigners are watched."

The priest nodded.

Goultzar frowned at him. "Was anyone aware that you were listening?"

The priest shook his head emphatically. "I know how to keep my eyes down and my ears open," he asserted.

The Archprimus placed a hand on his heart, clenching his fist before flinging open all his fingers except the little one. The priest repeated the gesture before turning and slipping away.

MUCH LATER ANOTHER of the priests present at the royal reception paid a lengthy visit to the High Priest to deliver his report. No one apart from the Superior knew of the visit, and what was said between the two men was privy to them alone.

The visit remained secret thanks to a hidden doorway in the small room set aside for the exclusive use of the High Priest. The priest used it to enter and leave the room, and during his visit he ensured that both other entrances to the room were locked from the inside.

Only a very small and select group of priests knew of the High Priest's secret doorway. The Archprimus was not one of them.

9

Amyra aimed a welcoming smile at Dahra, who had emerged looking bleary-eyed. "Good morning, Mother. Did you sleep well?" Without conscious thought she had asked her question in the language of the Aen-ur.

"Very well, thank you. For some reason I seem to need more sleep these days than I ever used to," replied Dahra in the same language. "Perhaps it's the climate," she added with a wink.

Her mother wasn't as young as she once was, and Amyra didn't begrudge her an extra hour or two of sleep. She was grateful beyond words that Dahra had chosen to leave Aen-irac and make her home on the Torbury holdings in Erestor.

Having a grandmother on hand to help with young children was invaluable, of course, especially when Will was away in Maranelle attending meetings of Erestor's Council of Lords, or in Arnost consulting with the king. But beyond that, Dahra was the last remaining link with Amyra's old life. Aen-irac seemed far away, and her life among the Aen-ur was only a memory now. Amyra had embraced a new identity, setting down roots among a different people.

"Are you happy, Amyra?" her mother asked, fixing her with a knowing look.

"You know that I am," she replied. "I get tired, of course, but I'm happy tired. I love being a mother." No further words on that topic were necessary—her own mother understood as no one else could.

"I'm quite fond of Will too," she added with a grin.

Dahra laughed at the understatement. "I always knew that the man who captured your heart would need to be special," she said. "Taming you was never going to be a job for the faint-hearted. Will seems to have risen to the challenge."

"I hope I haven't become too tame!" she protested.

"You needn't be too concerned," laughed her mother. "You've tamed the famed commander at least as much as he's tamed you."

"I'm not so sure," grumbled Amyra. "He spends a lot of time away from home."

"He only leaves because he needs to," her mother assured her. "His heart is here—with you and the children on his holding. I see it in his eyes."

Their conversation was interrupted by an insistent voice outside. "What are you about, young Jem! There'll be nothing left of the mistress's garden if you don't take those goats in hand!"

Raising an eyebrow, Amyra headed for the door. "I'll see what's going on," she called back over her shoulder with a parting wave to her mother.

She emerged in time to see a young man chasing away a flock of goats. His face was red—with exertion, embarrassment, or perhaps both.

The garden had been saved by an attractive young woman in her mid-twenties who stood glaring at the unfortunate Jem with hands on her hips. She might be slender of frame, but Amyra knew her as a force to be reckoned with.

"I appear to be in your debt, Peggy!" said Amyra with a smile.

Peggy shook her head, frowning. "Jem was swooning over a couple of girls that wandered by, instead of paying attention to his work. I hope the goats didn't do too much damage."

Amyra chuckled. "My garden is a little overgrown—I can afford to lose a plant or two, I'm sure."

Peggy gave a little bow. "I'm sorry if I'm disturbing you, My Lady," she said self-consciously. "The truth is I was hoping for your advice."

Amyra returned a smile. Looking into Peggy's plaintive eyes, it wasn't hard to guess what was on her mind. "Walk with me," she replied.

Wandering anywhere near the manor house was always distracting—there was so much going on. Constant effort was expended maintaining strips of plowed land, animal pastures and shelters, barns and dwellings, and a range of farm implements. Turning her back on the activity, Amyra led Peggy around the side of the manor house to a grassy sward beside a row of fruit trees. They lowered themselves onto a strategically placed wooden bench.

"How can I help, Peggy?" Amyra asked with a gentle smile.

"I don't understand it," the young woman replied miserably. "I thought we were getting along so well. But he doesn't seem interested in anything more than friendship."

There was no need for her to name the person behind her distress. Amyra knew she had set her sights on the formidable guardsman known as Rufe Sarjant.

As single-minded as she was kindhearted, Peggy had managed to capture a healthy share of the big soldier's attention. Nevertheless, her dream of joining him at the altar was proving unexpectedly elusive. Amyra felt sure that Rufe was drawn to Peggy too, but he seemed almost entirely lacking in confidence when it came to matters of the heart.

"You haven't done anything wrong, Peggy," Amyra assured her. "You just need to give him time."

"But how long is it going to take, My Lady?" she wailed. "I'll be in my dotage soon!"

"Peggy!" chided Amyra, barely restraining her mirth at the young woman's dire pronouncement. It was true that marrying young was the usual expectation, and it was also likely that some of the young men found Peggy intimidating. But the same might have been said of

Amyra before she met Will. Sometimes you just needed to hold out for the right person. And then you had to wait until they were ready.

"Perhaps you need to try a different approach. Storming a fortress isn't the only way to capture it," she said seriously.

"Are you suggesting I should starve him into submission?" Peggy asked gloomily. "Maybe it's a good idea. I know he doesn't like my cooking."

"Whatever do you mean?" asked Amyra.

"I overheard him telling Jonas that my rock buns are well named."

"Oh Peggy!" cried Amyra, bursting into laughter in spite of herself. "If I made rock buns they wouldn't just be hard, they'd be inedible! Yet Lord Torbury seems to like me anyway. I don't think you should read too much into Rufe's comment."

Peggy didn't reply—she seemed lost in thought.

Amyra was sure Peggy truly cared about Rufe. He was a man of contradictions—both fierce and gentle at the same time—and she wondered how successful his admirer had been at understanding him in all his guises.

"What do you know about Rufe's history?" asked Amyra.

"He's been a soldier most of his life. Just like his father and his father's father before him."

"Do you understand what that was like for him?" Amyra persisted.

Peggy looked puzzled. "I'm sure it must have been frightening at times. But it's behind him now."

Could Peggy be ignorant of the specifics of Rufe's story? Even before Torbury Scarp he had become renowned as an army commander under Will Prentis. Fewer people, perhaps, were aware that he had achieved almost legendary status as a berserker in his early years on the battlefield. Amyra knew through Will that the giant guardsman had never been proud of this reputation.

Unfailingly gentle to all who knew him in normal life, Rufe had long since learned to master his impulses on the battlefield as well. But he had never entirely shaken off the shame of his early unbridled destructive impulses.

If Peggy was not yet aware of Rufe's discomfort with his past, it wasn't Amyra's place to reveal it to her.

Perhaps a different tack was needed. "Rufe is big and imposing and incredibly effective at what he does," Amyra said. "But he's also very good at dismissing himself. Sometimes I think he believes that the credit for any success he's achieved belongs entirely to Lord Torbury."

"That's nonsense!" exclaimed Penny. Remembering suddenly who she was talking to, she hastily added, "No disrespect intended, My Lady!"

Amyra smiled. "There's no need to apologize, Peggy. I'm simply suggesting that a more delicate approach might be fruitful. Don't expect him to always understand you. He's spent most of his adult life interacting with men."

The young woman was frowning thoughtfully.

Amyra rose to her feet. "Give him room to take the initiative, too. It might even be worth playing a little hard to get," she suggested with a grin.

"Thank you for your kindness, My Lady," the young woman replied, getting up and bowing gratefully.

"Off with you then, Peggy," Amyra replied. "I hope you know you'll be going with my best wishes!"

Returning to the manor house, Amyra found a grizzled man waiting for her.

"A good day to y', M' Lady," he said respectfully, taking off his cap. "I am Hernholt, steward to Lord Beldisel."

"I remember you, Hernholt, and I bid you welcome," she replied. Lord Beldisel's lands bordered the Torbury estate to the south, and Amyra had met the steward once or twice when visiting their neighbor. "What brings you here today?"

"M' Lord has heard that y' might be looking to buy some cattle. 'E has some very fine specimens, and 'e is willing to sell some of 'em, y' see. Two score, if that many take y'r fancy."

"I can ask Jonas to visit you to take a look at them," she replied. "What's your master's asking price?"

An hour passed before the haggling was over. Jonas appeared not long after Hernholt had left.

"As you know, Will wants to buy a few more cattle. I've just had Hernholt here. Apparently Lord Beldisel is looking to sell some of his herd."

Jonas furrowed his brows. "There'll be a reason he wants to get rid of them," he growled. "They're probably inflicted with rinderpest."

"You're far too suspicious, Jonas!" she laughed. "Lord Beldisel might be canny, but he would never knowingly defraud us."

Her assertion was met with a noncommittal grunt. "I'll find time to inspect them tomorrow," Jonas promised. "I'll go with an open mind, but I'll also take a couple of the older retainers. Between them they know just about everything there is to be known about cattle."

THE DAY CONTINUED AS it had begun, keeping Amyra busy with a seemingly endless succession of duties almost until the time for the evening meal. Returning to the manor house, she allowed her mother to guide her to a comfortable chair. She sank into it with a weary sigh.

Before she could say a word, her daughter, Millie, burst into the room. "Mother! One of the men asked me to say that Jonas needs you!" Without waiting for a response, the girl dashed back out of the door.

Heaving a sigh, Amyra raised her hands helplessly. Pushing herself out of the chair, she set off after the disappearing form of the seven-year-old.

Her mother's voice chased her out of the manor house. "I'll keep an eye on Ethen!"

Amyra called for a horse. After mounting it, she leaned down and lifted Millie, placing the child in front of her.

"Where's Jonas?" Amyra asked, speaking in Rogandan.

"Mother!" complained Millie in Arvenian.

"You need to practice your language skills," Amyra insisted, this time using the language of Lestanor.

"Even Father doesn't speak much Lestanorian," Millie grumbled, reluctantly accepting the switch.

"No, and he regrets it!" her mother replied firmly. "Now, where is Jonas?"

"He's supposed to be at the ford," Millie replied.

Clicking her tongue, Amyra guided the horse forward. She arrived at the ford to find Jonas standing among a crowd of people beside the river. A large cart lay in the river just beyond the ford. Somehow the cart horses had been released. It must have been an extremely challenging operation, given that the cart was completely submerged.

"What happened?" called Amyra, helping Millie down from the horse.

"The cart was driven too close to the edge of the ford," Jonas replied. He shot a disgruntled look in the direction of a man who seemed unusually downcast. "It slid part of the way into the river, then the force of the water carried it the rest of the way."

Drawing him aside to continue the conversation in private, she asked, "What's in the cart?"

"A full load of produce on its way to the market," he replied. "Potatoes, carrots, turnips, cured meat, to name a few of the contents. It's not just the value of the load that upsets me," he said, "it's the time spent planting, cultivating, harvesting, and preparing it all. It's a frustrating waste. And then there's the loss of the cart."

"If the contents could be removed from the cart, would any of it be salvageable?"

"At this early stage, most of it. But there's no way to safely retrieve it."

Amyra fell silent. She glanced at the cart, then began staring intently upstream.

"Look!" a voice cried suddenly. "The water has stopped flowing!"

"There must be a blockage upriver," someone else called.

The river slowed to a trickle, gradually exposing the cart.

"Can you unload it?" Amyra asked tensely.

Jonas didn't bother to reply. He was already shouting orders. A line quickly formed, and bulging sacks and heavy barrels were passed from one person to another until they could be dumped on the river bank.

"I'll try to see what's happening," Amyra called, remounting her horse and heading for a hill that overlooked the river.

The moment she reached the top she leaped from the horse's back. She had been holding back the water with nothing but her willpower, empowered by the Stone of Authority.

Her first act with the stone, years earlier in Aen-irac, had been to hold back a river, releasing the pent up waters to end a battle before it started. Now, with water beginning to spill freely over the banks of the river, she diverted attention to fallen branches lying nearby. She watched as one branch after another tumbled into the river, massing until they formed an effective barrier at a point where the river narrowed.

Less effort was now required to hold back the water, and she stole a glance toward the ford. The wagon was almost empty, and Jonas had harnessed the horses to it. The horses struggled forward, dragging their lighter load out of the river and clear of the ford.

A huge volume of water had been steadily building up behind her makeshift dam, and the strain was mounting to the point where she almost couldn't bear it.

"Get out of there!" she yelled frantically. "The blockage looks like it's about to be swept away!"

Amyra watched in growing tension as people scrambled clear of the river.

Seeing that all of them had made it to safety, she released her control over the water. The dam burst with a roar, and water spewed downward, sweeping branches and other debris before it. For a brief moment the ford disappeared from view as the river overflowed its banks. Flood waters reached out to lap at the pile of salvaged produce before subsiding.

A few short minutes later, everything had returned to normal.

Amyra rode down to Jonas. "Did you retrieve all of the contents?" she asked.

"Thankfully yes. Given time it will dry out. I'm hopeful that most of it will survive a brief soaking. And the wagon is safe too," he replied. He shook his head in wonder. "That was astonishing. No one can avoid disaster entirely, but it's uncanny how often we manage to do it. I'd say that Lord Torbury is just plain lucky."

"It's her ladyship that's brought the luck," asserted one old woman, nodding her wrinkled brow wisely toward Amyra. "I've always said so."

Feeling extremely uncomfortable, Amyra turned away.

She noticed Millie looking back and forth between the river, the cart, and her mother, a puzzled frown on her face. Amyra's heart sank. Her daughter had already witnessed far too many things she should never have seen. One day she might begin to put it all together.

Will would be horrified at the risk she had taken. He would tell her it was madness to use the stone in the presence of all these witnesses, and he was probably right. A brief glimpse of the wagon driver offered a different perspective though. The man looked as if he had just been rescued from a deep, dark pit, and the look on his face went a long way to convincing her that she'd done the right thing.

Perching Millie before her once more, Amyra rode back to the manor house.

Millie was rarely lost for words, but on that occasion they rode in silence. Too weary even to think straight, Amyra felt only relief.

———

Almost a week had passed since the incident with the wagon at the ford. For a time people could talk of nothing else, but thankfully as the days passed life settled into a more normal rhythm.

Conversation turned instead to a new topic: the smoke in the sky to the west. At first it was a subject of idle chatter, but curiosity turned to alarm as the wind shifted and the smoke increased. Dense forest bordered the Torbury holdings to the west. Timber was widely used on the farm in the construction of buildings and for a range of other purposes. All of it came from the forest.

Soon the sky to the west darkened ominously, the air becoming foul with the smell of smoke. That night people went to bed fearful of what might await them in the morning.

Biding her time until all the members of her family were settled and asleep, Amyra stole from the manor house and crept quietly in the direction of the fire. The sky glowed red now, and the whinnying of horses could be heard from the stables. The air stung her face and lungs.

Coming to a halt just clear of the manor buildings, Amyra faced west and thrust out her arms. Almost at once she felt the change as the breeze stiffened and the wind changed direction. She was forcing the fire back onto itself.

Weariness soon forced her to lower her arms, but the gesture had never been necessary. She remained in place, directing the elements until the glow in the west had diminished and the air had cleared. Unutterably weary, she turned and trudged back to the manor house.

IN THE MORNING Amyra emerged much later than usual. Dahra was there to greet her, handing her a small bowl filled with fresh milk. After draining it gratefully, Amyra sat down, still yawning sleepily.

Dahra said nothing, calmly watching her daughter.

Before long Amyra found her mother's scrutiny unnerving. "What?" she demanded, sounding more testy than she had intended.

"The smoke has cleared," said Dahra. "People are saying that the fire has burned itself out."

"That's good to know," Amyra replied with another yawn.

Her mother continued to gaze at her. This time Amyra ignored her.

Dahra eventually broke the silence. "It's going to get you into trouble," she said quietly. When there was no reply, she added, "I should know."

"You had Drettroth chasing you," said Amyra. "This is different."

Dahra shook her head. "By the time I realized I was being chased it was already too late. If you keep using it trouble will find you."

"You're worried for no reason, Mother," Amyra said coolly.

Dahra shrugged. "Don't say I didn't warn you," she replied.

10

———

The sun had barely passed its zenith when Will's party reached his holdings in Erestor. Spotting Amyra outside the manor house, he jumped down from his horse and embraced her enthusiastically. Then he held her at arm's length, admiring her as she grinned back at him.

Their reunion was abruptly shattered by a shout, quickly followed by the arrival of a pair of human hurricanes. Will's seven-year-old daughter, Millie, and her younger brother, Ethen, aged five, burst from the house and leaped on their father.

A smiling Amyra observed the chaotic reunion for a while before turning her attention to Will's companions. "Thank you for bringing him back safely!" she called.

Noticing the monk, she added, "Brother Ander! It's so good to see you again."

Dismounting, the monk greeted her warmly. Having officiated at the wedding of Will and Amyra in Arnost, Brother Ander later made the effort to visit them at their home in Erestor. At their insistence, he had returned to stay with them several times in the intervening years.

Hearing Brother Ander's name, and having satisfied their immediate need to jump on their father, the children turned their attention to the monk. They were soon swarming noisily over him as well, ignoring his laughing protests at their continued assaults.

Amyra was eventually forced to intervene. "Children! That's enough! Leave Brother Ander in peace for a while."

Denied their latest source of entertainment, the children surrounded their father once more, an eager light in their eyes.

"Did you bring me a bigger bow, Father?" asked Ethen. "You promised!"

"What about the pony I asked for?" demanded Millie.

"I've only been home for five minutes," protested Will with a laugh. "Can't you enjoy my company for a while before asking for handouts?"

"A pony isn't a handout. It's an animal," Millie protested. "I was supposed to get it for my birthday!"

"And you *did* promise," insisted Ethen.

Will exchanged a glance with Amyra before rolling his eyes and shaking his head. "Oh, very well," he said. "Presents first."

Both children erupted in squeals of delight.

Will disappeared behind the horses of the party that had ridden in with him. He hadn't yet dismissed his companions, but they didn't seem in any great hurry to leave. They were clearly enjoying the spectacle too much.

When the children's noise showed no sign of abating, Amyra finally intervened. "I'd suggest you both calm down," she said firmly. "Unless you want your father to wait until tomorrow for presents."

The volume decreased at once, although the children continued to bounce up and down irrepressibly.

Will reappeared, leading a bay pony he'd collected by prior agreement from a neighboring holding. Millie ran to it excitedly and hugged its neck. The animal whickered softly, but didn't seem too upset by the attention.

Ethen observed the excitement restlessly, trying desperately to be patient.

Eventually Will seemed to notice him. "Ethen!" he said with a grin. "I almost forgot about you. Now what did I do with that bow?"

By that time Ethen was barely able to contain himself.

"Don't tease the poor boy!" chided Amyra.

"Is this what you're looking for, Will?" asked Brother Ander, holding out a bow.

"Ah, of course! Thank you, Brother Ander."

Will took the bow and handed it to his son, who held it out excitedly, his eyes shining. "It's perfect! Much bigger than my old one! Will you help me with it, Father?" he asked.

"You'd be better off asking Brother Ander for lessons," Will replied.

"Brother Ander? But he's a *monk*!" said Ethen, prompting a burst of laughter from a number of the onlookers.

"He's also a better archer than I'll ever be," Will assured his son.

Ethen looked at the big monk in surprise. "Will you teach me, Brother Ander?" he asked.

"My fighting days are long behind me," the big man replied. "But perhaps I could offer you a tip or two."

"Thanks!" enthused the boy, leaning into the bow and straining to bend it.

"Run along, children," commanded their mother. "It's my turn to have your father's attention for a while."

She turned to the other riders. "Thank you again," she said with a smile. "Please feel free to go. I'm sure you must be eager to return to your own families."

As the riders dispersed, Dahra appeared from inside the house, calling a greeting to Will and Brother Ander.

"Brother Ander will be staying with us in the manor house, Mother," Amyra told her. "Could you please make sure he's comfortable? We'll join you as soon as we've caught each other up on the news."

She took Will's arm, and they strolled off together, wandering aimlessly across the fields.

"Any dramas during my absence?" he asked.

"One of the bulls got loose," she replied. "It would have gored a child if one of the sheep dogs hadn't chased it off. And a farm laborer nearly had his house burned down. Sparks from the cooking fire set some clothing alight. Fortunately no children had been left unattended in the house at the time, because the fire was almost out of control before anyone noticed it. Some of the women were able to douse the flames with water. That sums up everything worth mentioning—at least from today," she concluded.

He grimaced, shaking his head. "I notice you made no mention of the long list of demands that were undoubtedly placed on you," he said.

"It's certainly been busy," she acknowledged breezily. She seemed eager to change the subject. "What of your time in Arnost though?"

"The news is bad, I'm sorry to say. Very bad indeed," he told her grimly. He sighed. "I've become comfortable with peace and quiet, and it's a shock to find it threatened again."

She peered up at him with a frown of concern. "Surely there isn't trouble with Rogand again?"

"There is, but not the kind of trouble anyone could possibly anticipate. It's a very long story, but I'll try to give you the abbreviated version."

Her frown turned to alarm as he outlined the facts as he knew them.

"What are the king and queen planning to do about it?" she asked.

"They want me to go to Rog," he told her.

"They want *you* to go? Surely not!" she cried. "What can they expect you to do about a situation like this?"

"I can represent the interests of Arvenon."

"Why doesn't King Steffan go? You've said that King Delmar and King Rupert are in Rog."

"Neither of the other kings have families to consider. King Steffan does."

"So do you!" she exclaimed.

Will sighed. "Let's defer this conversation for a while. I've sent a messenger to Newhaven asking Thomas to join us here. Let's discuss it when he arrives."

"I hope you're not planning to ask Thomas to go to Rog with you!"

she protested. "You can't expect him to abandon Elena and the children!"

Will ran a hand through his hair. "This isn't exactly the homecoming I was hoping for," he said.

She glared at him for a moment, then she threw up her hands. "I'm sorry, Will. I know this isn't your fault. The trouble is you're so...so responsible!"

"How can I avoid being responsible?" he asked. He waved an arm around him. "I can't take any of this for granted. I only have the holding because the king gave it to me, along with my title."

"You more than earned it!" she exclaimed. "And it wasn't exactly a gift, considering the expectations that came with it," she grumbled.

He shook his head. "Those expectations didn't come with the holding. I was carrying them long before the king made me a nobleman."

She went silent.

"You felt responsible for the Aen-ur when you were with them," he pointed out.

"I haven't forgotten," she said. "I was furious with you for knowingly putting them at risk. I thought their world would end if I didn't protect them from you."

His mouth twisted into a grimace.

"But I was wrong," she concluded. "I admit it. The Aen-ur not only survived—they finished up in a stronger position than before."

"Your concerns were not unreasonable though," he acknowledged. "It could have ended very differently."

Her brows drew together. "In any event, I left the Aen-ur behind, along with my responsibilities, and I followed you here. I've adopted a people group that isn't my own. For the second time."

A stern look had come over her face. "It's different this time though. We have a family. You think you have a heavy burden of responsibility to the king, and I understand that. You believe there's more at stake than just our family, and I understand that too. The problem is that someone has to be responsible for our family. Someone still has to bear the day-to-day burdens of caring for the children. And not just for them—for all the people here on the holding who depend on us. Whenever you're off doing your duty to the king, that responsibility falls to me."

She looked him squarely in the eye. "Now you're supposed to go to Rogand to save the world again. What if you don't return this time? One day, Will, it will get to be more than I can bear."

And with that she wheeled and left him, striding back to the manor house.

Will shook his head in misery. He understood her dilemma completely. He was not unaware of his own responsibility to his family, or to the people around him.

His farmers and workers and their families—everyone who depended on his holdings for their livelihoods—had suffered great loss because of him already. He had long since dealt with the mercenaries who had struck down his steward, Timms, and dragged away his retainers after destroying every building on the property apart from the manor house. Since that time he had done everything in his power to rebuild what had been destroyed and to ensure that the people would be well protected into the future.

But he had a special responsibility to his own family. How could he put their needs first and still fulfill his responsibilities to the king and to the kingdom? He shook his head again. He simply couldn't see how it was possible.

And the stakes had never been higher. If the king was right, not only Rogand, but Arvenon and every kingdom in the region now faced a threat of unprecedented magnitude.

That threat was the reason why Will had called for Thomas. Arvenon had been spared from disaster more than once thanks to Thomas and the remarkable talisman he bore. The Stone of Knowing might be hidden from the world, known only to a select few, but it had the potential to change the course of history.

Will stared after the retreating form of his wife. Their conversation had danced over a much bigger issue. Extraordinary as the Stone of Knowing might be, it was not the only such talisman. The Stone of Authority, once abused fearfully by the late King Agon of Rogand, now rested in Amyra's trustworthy hands. Its capabilities far exceeded anything Will had imagined possible. Amyra had used it to save the Aen-ur from certain destruction.

An uncomfortable dilemma now lay before them both. There seemed little doubt that with the Stone of Authority in her hand, Amyra was better equipped than Will to face down this latest threat. She knew it as well as he did.

It came as no surprise that Amyra was frustrated with Will and his troublesome sense of responsibility. His challenges precisely mirrored the tension she herself was facing.

WILL HAD to wait several days before Thomas appeared. When his friend arrived at the manor house, Will wasn't surprised to find Elena and their children with him. Even Haldek had made the journey, eager to see Will and Amyra once more.

Erestor might have appeared to be as peaceful and safe as it had ever been, but Anneka nonetheless insisted on sending an escort with them. In the end the party had included Rellan and Hender along with a couple of other capable young bowmen who professed a desire to see more of the world.

Millie and Ethen were enraptured when they spotted Thomas and Elena's three children, Tamara, Andy, and Delia. The two families made the effort to connect at least annually, taking it in turns to host at either Newhaven or Will's estate, so the children knew each other well. They had their share of arguments and fights, but for the most part they got along very harmoniously. The five of them soon disappeared, leaving the adults free to talk.

After gathering Thomas, Elena, and Amyra, Will invited Brother Ander, Haldek, and Rellan to join them. Of those living on his own estate, he sent for Rufe and Jonas. Then, remembering the king's suggestion, he called for Breysen as well.

As soon as everyone was assembled, he thanked them for attending and came immediately to the point. "I've returned from the capital with news," he said. "Unfortunately it isn't good news. What I am about to tell you needs to stay confidential. The last thing we want is people panicking for no good reason. But Anneka will need to know, so you're welcome to share it with her when you return, Rellan."

Thomas had gone a little pale. "I wondered why you invited me to join you after visiting Arnost," he said.

Will made no attempt to ease Thomas's mind. "Brother Ander is already aware of the situation, and I've briefed Amyra," he told them. "For the sake of the rest of you, I'll start from the beginning."

With that he launched into a detailed description of the entire sequence of events concerning Princess Neira and the Empire of Ahr. A few questions were asked as he spoke, but for the most part his audience sat listening with grim faces.

"I will be going to Rog as soon as is practicable at the request of the king," he said in conclusion, "and Brother Ander has kindly offered to accompany me. He's also surprised me by demonstrating that he's fluent in Rogandan." He grinned at the monk, who contented himself with a dip of his head in response.

"I will also accompany you, My Lord, if you'll allow me to," said Breysen.

"What about your family?" asked Will.

"Providing for my family is my main responsibility, of course," Breysen replied. "But the debt I owe you outweighs everything else. I haven't forgotten that."

Will couldn't resist shooting a glance in the direction of Amyra. Her face was unreadable.

"There is no real reason for concern though," Breysen continued. "I know from bitter experience how uncertain life can be, so for the last few years I have been laying coin aside whenever I can. My family will manage, even if something happens to me. I am pleased to say they are well connected to the community here, too."

"I accept your offer gladly, Breysen," Will told him. "Especially since the king suggested that I travel to Rog by sea to save time."

His remark was met with considerable surprise, and it took a while before the room became quiet once more.

"I traveled to Rogand with you last time, Will," said Haldek, "and I will come this time too, if you will have me. I have no desire to live in Rogand again. But lately I have been feeling that I would like to see it one last time, especially now that Agon is no longer king."

"Thank you, Haldek," Will replied. "I would be very glad to have you with us."

"I will come too," said Rufe, " although I can't speak a word of Rogandan."

"I imagine your Peggy might have something to say about that," said Will with a grin.

Rufe shook his head, a puzzled look on his face. "For some reason she hasn't been around as much lately," he muttered.

"It's about time you did some of the chasing," Jonas told him with a grin. Then he turned to Will. "You can count me in as well," he said.

"I will accept your offer, Rufe," Will replied. "I would be glad to have you too, Jonas, but I need you here. If you wanted to go off wandering again, you should never have let me see how effective you are as a steward," he added dryly. "The truth is that I'm totally dependent on you to keep the estate functioning. Everyone else depends on you as much as I do."

"It's true!" confirmed Amyra.

"As you wish, My Lord," said Jonas with a tight bow. He looked a little disappointed, but Will knew him well enough to see he wasn't too unhappy about being left in charge.

Rellan hadn't spoken yet, but Will got in first. "Don't even think about offering to come, Rellan. Both of us know what Anneka would have to say about it. We'll try to manage without you."

"I'm not sure how much I could add anyway," Rellan replied with a shrug. "But you know Anneka well enough to realize you've just made a new best friend."

Will chuckled as he pictured Anneka's reaction to hearing that Rellan wasn't going.

Important decisions still needed to be made. "I'm planning to leave for Maranelle soon after dawn the day after tomorrow," he told them. "If you're coming with me, you have tomorrow to complete your preparations. In the meantime, Amyra and I would like to talk with Thomas and Elena, so I'm happy to release the rest of you for the moment."

Peggy tracked Rufe down as he was leaving the conference, her slight figure providing a stark contrast to the huge frame of the soldier. The two of them stood a short distance away, but Will was still able to make out their conversation.

"What plans are you hatching?" she asked him suspiciously.

"I'm going to need to go away for a while," he told her. "With Will. I mean Lord Torbury." He sounded uncharacteristically strained.

"And when were you going to tell your friends?" she demanded.

"The decision has only just been made," he assured her.

"I can well understand his lordship turning to you for help and protection," she told him. "He should expect nothing less from you." Then her voice caught in her throat. "And who will provide help and protection to you?"

"I'll be fine," he assured her. "I've been in much worse situations."

"You be careful, Rufe Sarjant! You'd better come back here in one piece!"

They moved away, and Will shook his head with a grin.

The others had left by now, and Will turned his attention to Thomas and Elena and Amyra, carefully studying them to assess their mood.

"I know I'll need to join you," said Thomas, "although I won't pretend I'm excited about it."

"If you're going, then so am I," Elena said doggedly.

"Why?" asked Thomas. "I can't imagine you have even the slightest interest in going to Rogand."

"I know it was difficult for you when you went there last time, Thomas," she replied. "But it was a torment for me. I didn't know what was happening. I wasn't sure if I'd ever see you again. From now on we stay together."

"But what about the children?" he asked.

"I'm sure my father and your parents would agree to look after them," she replied. "But if both of us are going, they're coming with us."

"I'm sorry to have to ask this of you," said Will. "But all of us understand why you're needed. And I won't deny it will be good to have the two of you with us. You seem to work effectively when you share the stone."

All eyes turned to Amyra.

"I'll be going, of course," she said stonily. "It isn't as if I have a choice."

"And the children?" asked Elena.

"They'll have to come too. Our situation's no different."

"The children will be excited to be traveling together," said Thomas, working hard at being cheerful.

Amyra grunted. She was refusing to make eye contact with Will, and he had no desire to push her. The single biggest reason she needed to go to Rog had nothing to do with him. It had everything to do with the Stone of Authority.

11

───────

Breysen rode into Maranelle with the rest of Will's party, weary after many hours in the saddle. Lord Burtelen had kindly agreed to accommodate them until they set sail for Rog, and Breysen was looking forward to hot food and a solid night's sleep in a bed again. All of them were tired, especially the five children, but thankfully the journey from Will's holdings had passed without incident.

With their immediate destination almost in sight, Breysen reminded himself they were not on the estate now, and he was a retainer to Lord Torbury, not to Will Prentis. The challenge was that Breysen, like everyone who had fought at Torbury Scarp, thought of their commander as Will. It didn't help that some commoners had never changed their ways after Will became Lord Torbury. Some of the commander's close associates—people like Rufe, Thomas, Elena, Rellan, and Brother Ander—had known him before his elevation to the peerage, and Will clearly saw little reason for them to use his title. Even Jonas sometimes called him Will in private. And Breysen was in daily contact with Rufe and Jonas.

He sighed. He could think whatever he liked, but in public he needed to carefully watch what he said.

Lord Burtelen came to greet the small party not long after they arrived.

"Welcome! It's good to see you all," the nobleman said with a beaming smile.

"Thank you, My Lord," Will replied, returning a smile of his own.

"Have you managed to secure a ship for us?" Will asked.

"The matter is not resolved," Lord Burtelen replied with an angry frown. "We've had major problems at the docks of late—every initiative I take seems to be blocked. I gave this particular task to someone I trusted, and I was astonished to learn earlier today that nothing whatever has been done about it. I've told him to find a ship, and to do it today."

The news didn't shake Will's composure. "Let me know if I can help in any way."

Lord Burtelen waved his arms. "It won't be necessary. If it isn't resolved by tonight, I'll deal with it myself in the morning. I'll go in hard if I need to."

"The docks seem to operate by a different set of rules," Will replied. "But I'm sure you'll exercise whatever discretion is necessary," he added mildly.

"Discretion has its limits," growled Lord Burtelen. "These people behave as if they owe allegiance to no one but themselves. They've apparently forgotten who rules Arvenon, and it's about time I jogged their memory." He sighed, his shoulders slumping. "Times like these remind me how much I miss the duke. He knew how to handle the wharf rats, and they seemed to respect him."

Breysen was very surprised by the exchange. Lord Burtelen had a reputation for being even tempered as well as effective. He must be very frustrated indeed to be speaking as he was.

A squeal sounded from one of the children. Apparently noticing them for the first time, Lord Burtelen raised his own eyebrows in surprise. "Are you planning to take children with you to Rog?"

"Yes, we are," Will replied evenly. "Thomas and I will be accompanied by our wives, so our children are coming too."

The ghost of a smile lingered on Will's lips, but it seemed a little forced.

Still talking, the two noblemen wandered away, and Breysen heard no more of the conversation.

The brief interaction about the children set Breysen thinking. Will had said that the children were only there because their mothers were going to Rog. For the first time it occurred to him to wonder if Amyra and Elena wanted to go.

He thought back over the journey from the estate. Amyra had seemed unusually terse. Was it because she had come unwillingly? The blacksmith had been as surprised as Lord Burtelen when he first learned that Elena and Amyra were both taking their children. He had assumed it was because the families were eager to visit Rog, but the more he thought about it, the more unlikely that seemed.

Will and Amyra had always presented a united front to the world, but they must surely navigate tensions in their marriage as every couple did. It was easy to think of Will as floating serenely above the trivial thoughts and passions of the rest of humanity, but he was still human. In any event, whatever frustrations Will and Amyra might be harboring, he had never seen it affect the way they behaved toward their children or their retainers, and he respected them enormously for that.

A burly figure appeared at Breysen's side, and he turned toward the newcomer to find a vaguely familiar face. Abruptly it all came flooding back. The late duke had employed this man as his representative in the alien world of the docks. He looked older, and more hard bitten than ever. Most notably his left ear was now missing, leaving him with a lopsided appearance.

"Jaxin, isn't it?" Breysen asked.

The newcomer grunted an acknowledgment. "I don't remember your name."

"I'm Breysen," he returned.

"Lord Burtelen needs a ship for Lord Torbury. You can come with me."

The invitation was curt, but Breysen decided to ignore the tone.

For all he knew, taking him along might have been intended as a compliment. Weary and hungry after the long ride, he guessed that a visit to the docks would be anything but relaxing. He decided to ignore that too.

He nodded. "Let me speak to Lord Torbury first."

Having secured the nobleman's permission, he hurried off in Jaxin's wake.

The docks had once been a home of sorts to Breysen, but the sights and smells that assaulted him as he entered beside Jaxin felt foreign and unfamiliar. Was he still the same person who spent so much of his life as a sailor?

The two men made their way to the tavern they had visited years earlier in search of a suitable ship. Many eyes followed their progress. Curiously, Breysen was largely ignored, all attention being focused instead on Jaxin. The smoldering anger in the watchful eyes suggested that something had happened, because on Breysen's previous visit Jaxin had seemed entirely at ease in the docks.

Jaxin pushed past the two men guarding the tavern door. They glowered at him but said nothing. Breysen was ignored when he followed Jaxin in.

Seeing who had arrived, the bartender's eyes narrowed. He bent his head and concentrated on wiping down the bar.

Two things abruptly became clear to Breysen. First, he was surprised to discover that he did feel at home here. The men at the docks had apparently decided that he belonged, and that undoubtedly helped. Second, he was there because Jaxin was no longer sure of his own welcome. Breysen's thoughts churned as he tried to make sense of this information.

After a brief scan of the men in the tavern, Jaxin approached a grizzled sailor sitting alone at a table. Following him, Breysen recognized the man at once. It was Captain Yordin of the Nomad Lady.

Jaxin took a stool opposite the captain.

"There's a job for you, Captain Yordin. If you're interested."

The captain grunted.

Whether or not Captain Yordin had heard anything about Jaxin, he could surely read the mood of the men around him. He offered no greeting, but he didn't send Jaxin away either.

Breysen wasn't surprised. Most captains were always willing to weigh up the risks if the profit was good.

Jaxin continued in a low voice. "Lord Burtelen wants to arrange passage to Rog for a large party."

Captain Yordin's eyebrows twitched briefly, then he bent his head and concentrated on refilling his pipe.

"A trip to Rog costs extra," he mumbled.

"Why?" demanded Jaxin. "We're not at war with Rogand."

The captain grunted again. "Uncertain times," he said darkly, his eyes flicking around the room.

Jaxin shrugged. "Consider yourself hired," he told the captain, pushing himself to his feet.

"One condition," the sailor replied, holding up a hand in caution.

Jaxin paused without responding.

"If I don't get confirmation by nightfall, the deal's off."

Jaxin nodded once, then turned to leave.

Breysen followed the other man to the door of the tavern, wondering why the captain had insisted on confirmation. The answer became obvious the moment they left the tavern.

A mob was waiting for them outside. Most of the men openly carried clubs and knives, and their faces suggested they meant business.

A glance at Jaxin showed him standing stiffly alert, his face pale.

"You don't belong here," spat a voice. "Neither of you."

The mob began to push forward. Both men retreated until the wall of the tavern was at their backs. Jaxin apparently had nothing to say and no plan to save them.

"Do you want to bring Lord Burtelen's soldiers down on you?" Breysen asked them.

"You're wasting your time appealing to Burtelen," another voice growled. "He doesn't rule here."

Breysen's eyes narrowed as his memory stirred. Perhaps there was something they could do. The idea was desperate, but what other options did he have? He leaned closer to Jaxin. "Is any of this your fault?" he hissed.

"No!" Jaxin snarled back.

"Then why do they hate you so much?" Breysen persisted.

The other man scowled. "I've done nothing to deserve this."

Breysen decided to take the risk. Straightening, he faced the mob. "I appeal to the Peerless Mariner," he said, trying to keep his voice from sounding shrill.

The men confronting him looked confused for a moment. Then someone retorted, "You have no right. You don't qualify."

"We qualify," Breysen asserted, nodding his head firmly to reinforce it. "We were not challenged by the Shoal Watchers when we entered the docks. That means they acknowledged our right to be here."

The mob paused. Almost within striking distance, they had suddenly become uncertain.

"I appeal to the Peerless Mariner," Breysen repeated, more confidently this time.

For a few tense moments silence reigned. Then a voice snarled, "Suit yourself. It'll be your funeral."

Things moved quickly after that. The two men were surrounded and blindfolded before being led away roughly. Breysen had no idea where they were being taken, but he knew that if the Peerless Mariner didn't see fit to release them, they would never be seen again.

When the blindfold was eventually removed, Breysen found himself in a small dark room without windows. The last of their captors left, bolting the door behind them.

"I hope you know what you're doing with this 'appeal' to the Peerless Mariner," Jaxin said brusquely.

"I hope so too," Breysen replied stiffly. "But if it'd been left to you, our throats would be cut by now. What possessed you to come here? Were you out of your mind? It's obvious you no longer have the freedom of the docks. And why did you bring me?"

"I've done nothing to deserve this," Jaxin repeated stubbornly.

"You'll have your chance to be heard," Breysen told him, "and it better be good. Until we get to that point, leave the talking to me!"

They had been sitting in the darkness for about an hour when a small hatch opened in one of the walls. "Your appeal will be heard," a voice told them lazily. "The Peerless Mariner is busy now. You'll need to wait."

"How long?" asked Breysen.

"It's difficult to say," came the response. "Two or three days if you're lucky."

"We can wait," Breysen said calmly. "But I'm not sure about you. We didn't leave Lord Burtelen in a patient mood. If we're not back by nightfall, you can expect to see the docks swarming with his soldiers by the morning."

A snort sounded through the hole in the wall. "Lord Burtelen is no soldier. He doesn't frighten us."

"You won't be facing Lord Burtelen," Breysen replied. "The soldiers will be led by Lord Torbury."

"Never heard of him," scoffed the voice.

"He's better known as Will Prentis," said Breysen mildly.

The voice went suddenly quiet. After a pause, it resumed. "What does Will Prentis have to do with this?"

"He's the one who needs a ship. He's carrying out a mission for the king—a mission of pressing urgency. He won't take it kindly if you hinder him."

"How would you know what his intentions are?"

"I traveled with him from his holdings. We arrived earlier today."

After a further pause, the hatch in the wall snapped shut.

Before another hour had passed, the door opened to reveal an old crone. She stood in the doorway holding a candle.

"Come with me, good sirs," she croaked.

She led them to a room dominated by a long table. One wall held a number of windows, all shuttered and dark. However the table was brightly lit with many clusters of candles. She pointed them to two chairs on one side of the table, and they sat with their backs to the windows.

The door opened and seven men filed into the room. One sat at each end of the table, while the other five took seats opposite Breysen and Jaxin.

Could one of these men be the Peerless Mariner? Breysen had heard that no one had ever seen the Peerless Mariner's face, so it seemed unlikely. Was the Peerless Mariner even a person? Perhaps the title represented a group of individuals.

"Who are you?" asked the man at one end of the table.

Breysen stood and bowed. "My name is Breysen. I am a second generation sailor and onetime soldier, now in the employ of Lord Torbury, who is also known as Will Prentis."

He sat down again.

The man at the opposite end of the table responded. "Breysen—sailor, sailor's son, and retainer to the commander—is recognized."

All eyes turned to Jaxin.

He also rose, bowing grimly. "My name is Jaxin. For many years I was a retainer to the duke, and I frequented the docks on his behalf. Since his passing I have been working for Lord Burtelen." After speaking he sat down.

A long pause ensued. Eventually a third man intoned, "For the sake of the duke, whose memory we honor, Jaxin—retainer to the duke and to Lord Burtelen—is recognized."

As he finished speaking, the door opened again. Several men entered the room bearing platters of food. The platters were set on the table, with the old crone overseeing the operation.

"Eat, good masters!" she wheezed, pouring ale from a large jug into the mugs set before each person at the table.

"You have appealed to the Peerless Mariner," a different man acknowledged, addressing Breysen. "In doing so you invoked an ancient rite, one that is rarely used. Stranger though you might be, you are nevertheless qualified to make petition, as you claimed. You may state your case."

Breysen stood and bowed once more. "I made the appeal on behalf of my companion. He believes he has been wronged."

At least one of the men opposite stiffened momentarily at this statement before recovering himself.

"Will you allow him to speak?" Breysen asked.

The men around the table exchanged glances.

"Your request is unusual," another man replied. "But he may speak."

Jaxin got to his feet.

"On a recent visit to the docks I was attacked without cause," he said, "and later ejected by force. Since that time I have been unjustly mistreated and intimidated whenever my business led me anywhere near the docks. This harassment has constrained Lord Burtelen on multiple occasions. He is now frustrated to the point where armed conflict is an increasingly likely outcome. If that happens, it will serve no one well. I would argue that it has the potential to diminish the respect enjoyed by those in leadership at the docks."

"You need not concern yourself with the reputation of the Peerless Mariner," another man said tartly. "Concentrate on the matter at hand. You have made a serious accusation about your treatment at the docks. We are not familiar with this supposed incident."

"You ought to be," Jaxin replied. "The person responsible for it is sitting directly opposite me."

Breysen saw that he had fixed his attention on the man who reacted earlier.

His target scowled before blurting out, "This fool attacked my brother and offered no payment."

Jaxin glared at him. "Your brother attacked me with a club when he saw that I was alone. He told me I had no right to be on the docks. As far as I could tell his only motive was to demonstrate how tough he was. I was armed only with a knife, and his arm was injured when I defended myself. Anyone who cares to examine him will see that he received nothing worse than a superficial cut. It would be completely healed by now."

"You lie!" spat the other man. He turned to his fellows. "Evin witnessed what happened. He will confirm it."

"If you're referring to a large barrel-chested man with a bushy black beard," retorted Jaxin, "he not only witnessed it, he pinned me down while you cut off my ear! He mentioned the word 'payment' more than once as you were applying the knife. The 'payment' extracted was unreasonable, especially when compared with the hurt it was supposedly compensating for."

Dark looks had appeared on the faces of a number of the men around the table. "Other witnesses?" one asked curtly.

When Jaxin's attacker offered no response, Jaxin replied, "A scrawny man—old, with little hair, and carrying a limp—also witnessed these events. And to my eye he looked less than comfortable about the so-called justice summarily handed out to me."

Jaxin sat down.

It was apparent to Breysen that the second witness was known to others around the table. Two of the men immediately got up and left the room.

Jaxin's attacker began to sweat visibly. He had reason to. If the other witness corroborated Jaxin's account, the consequences for this man would be dire.

Breysen understood the rules as well as any sailor. No one had the right to mete out justice on the docks without the express permission of the Peerless Mariner. And if Jaxin was telling the truth, the retaliation was not just unauthorized, but excessive. Permanently disfiguring a senior retainer of the most senior civil authority figure was inflammatory, and risked an escalation that could significantly damage all parties.

While they waited, most of the men around the table turned their attention to the food. Breysen joined them without hesitation. Hungry as he was, he allowed himself the luxury of eating it slowly and properly enjoying it. Jaxin ate nothing, and neither did the man he had accused.

More than an hour elapsed before the two men returned. The others left the room, taking Jaxin's attacker with them. Even the old crone disappeared. Only Breysen and Jaxin remained at the table. Breysen helped himself to another mug of ale. Jaxin continued to sit there, a grim look on his face.

They did not have to wait long. All of the men apart from Jaxin's opponent filed back into the room and sat down again. The old crone reappeared and began pouring ale.

One of the men stood to address Jaxin. "The Peerless Mariner wishes to convey sincere regret at the inconvenience you have experienced. No one can give you back your ear, but this token should offer at least some compensation." He handed Jaxin a large bronze coin with a hole punched through the middle of it. "This coin marks you as a protected guest of the Peerless Mariner. It will grant you unfettered access to the docks, day and night, in Maranelle and in other ports. Wear it around your neck, and make sure it is visible on you at all times. None will dare to challenge you."

The speaker bowed. "The Peerless Mariner also extends cordial respects to Lord Burtelen, and expresses a desire to work together harmoniously now and into the future."

Breysen stood up and bowed respectfully. "Please convey our respects and grateful thanks to the Peerless Mariner."

Jaxin also stood. "I also extend my thanks—to the Peerless Mariner and to all of you—for giving me a fair hearing." He concluded his words with a bow.

Blindfolds were once again applied, and the two men were led from the building. When the blindfolds were removed they found themselves outside the tavern.

Jaxin headed into the tavern, and the guards held the door open for him. Breysen followed him inside. The bartender greeted them with a wink. No one else paid them the least attention. Spotting Captain Yordin still inside, Jaxin directed a nod to the sailor. Captain Yordin dipped his head in return.

They left the docks as the sun was setting.

"Now that we have a ship, we'd better hurry back to Lord Burtelen before there's trouble," Jaxin said.

He glanced at Breysen when Lord Burtelen's mansion came into sight. "What do you think will happen to the other man?" he asked.

"I don't know for certain. But it won't go well for him."

Jaxin stopped walking and turned to Breysen. "How did you know you could appeal to the Peerless Mariner?"

Breysen shrugged. "I'd heard stories from my father, and also from an old sailor who now lives on Lord Torbury's estate. Between them they've told me some curious tales." He paused. "I couldn't be certain if the old codes still hold, but it seemed likely. Nothing changes quickly on the docks."

"You have my undying gratitude," Jaxin told him soberly. "I am forever in your debt."

"Think nothing of it," Breysen replied, waving a hand.

They resumed walking. "I'm curious about the Peerless Mariner," Breysen said. "Which of them do you think it was?"

Jaxin frowned. "I have no idea," he replied. "Who do you think?"

Breysen shrugged. "I suppose we'll never know. But my money's on the old crone," he said with a wink.

12

———————

Will clung grimly to the rail as another wave sent spray splashing across the deck. A sailor might not describe this as a storm, but the weather was beyond anything Will could cope with. None of his other family members were doing any better either.

The ship rolled drunkenly, and he leaned over the side once more, his stomach heaving painfully. It didn't matter that he had long since emptied his gut into the roiling waters—his belly refused to quit.

Breysen appeared beside him. "Not comfortable below decks, My Lord?" he asked.

"I don't think I'll ever get used to this," Will lamented. "You sailors seem to enjoy it. What's wrong with you?"

A snort of laughter escaped Breysen. "I'm sorry, My Lord, I'm not meaning to make fun of your discomfort," he said repentantly. "The truth is that I do enjoy it." The sailor-turned-blacksmith gazed at the dark clouds on the horizon. "I'm not sure I like the looks of that storm front though."

Will groaned. "Is it going to reach us?"

"We're about to round Baron Island. We'll soon be sailing east. That storm front will probably catch up with us around sunset."

"Unless I'm imagining it, the waves have been growing bigger," Will said. "Is that the storm?"

Breysen shook his head. "Last time on the Nomad Lady we sailed through Savage Strait. The captain decided against it this time. There are shoals scattered throughout the strait, which makes it too risky when the weather is rough. The alternative is to sail around Baron Island, which takes us into open sea. That's why the waves are bigger."

The look on Will's face must have revealed what he was thinking, because Breysen hastily added, "Don't worry—Captain Yordin knows his business, and this ship is well able to handle a storm on the open ocean."

Breysen's assurances offered slim comfort to Will, especially when the first in a series of huge waves came crashing over the ship.

"I'm going to check on the family," he told Breysen. After waiting for the next wave to pass, he headed for the hatch.

Both Millie and Ethen were lying in their hammocks, pale and miserable. If they noticed the arrival of their father, they gave no indication of it.

Amyra was not doing any better. "When is this storm going to stop?" she asked.

"Apparently it isn't a storm. Not yet, anyway."

She grimaced. "You mean it's going to get worse?"

He nodded. "There's a storm front coming. Breysen said it will reach us by nightfall."

She stared at him, appalled. "Why did I agree to come on this trip? And why did you let me bring our children?"

"I told you what the last sea voyage was like," he reminded her.

"I had no idea it would be this bad!" she retorted.

Will realized that further conversation was unlikely to achieve a useful outcome.

"Perhaps you should do something about the weather," he suggested. "I know you've been practicing with the stone."

"Don't start on that," she growled. "I've never attempted anything like this! And I've only ever used it in private." She glared at him. "Even if I knew what to do—which I don't!—there'd be no way to keep it quiet. Exposing the stone is the last thing we need."

She was right of course. He resolved to say nothing further about it.

Elena's face swayed into view. Her little family had taken hammocks nearby. When they first boarded the ship the five children had been inseparable. Everything had changed with the weather.

"Is there anything I can do to help?" she asked.

Amyra gazed up at her for a moment. "Not at the moment, Elena. The children are trying to rest, and I think we'll manage. Thank you for asking though."

Elena nodded, gazing at them sympathetically.

"How are your family coping?" Will asked.

"Tammi's first voyage was very challenging, but she seems to be handling it much better this time. The younger two are finding it more difficult, Andy especially. Delia's managed to get to sleep somehow."

The ship rolled drunkenly, and Elena was barely able to keep her feet.

"I'll leave you in peace," she said. "Call on me if I can help." Then with a smile and a farewell wave, she was gone.

The weather worsened as the hours dragged by. By the time the last light was fading from the sky, the ship was being tossed about unmercifully on towering waves.

Amyra and the children seemed close to breaking point. Will couldn't bear it any longer. After asking Elena to keep an eye on the children, he led Amyra onto the deck, gripping her arm while hanging on grimly to the nearest support. Spray showered them both as they gaped open-mouthed at the tempest.

"You need to do something!" he shouted, trying to make himself heard over the howling of the wind.

"I don't know what to do!" she yelled back feebly.

Breysen appeared once more. "What are you doing above deck?" he shouted. "It's much too dangerous up here!"

He helped them to the hatch and followed them inside. Even with the hatch closed, the howling of the wind was oppressive.

"You need to stay below," Breysen insisted. "This storm is beyond anything I could have imagined. And we haven't seen the worst of it yet."

"What needs to happen with the weather?" Will asked.

Breysen frowned at him, uncomprehending.

Will tried again. "What does the wind need to do?"

Breysen clearly didn't understand, but he apparently decided to humor his lordship.

"We need a change in wind direction. The wind is blowing from the northwest." He pointed. "It needs to blow from the southwest, more from the land." He swung his arm around to demonstrate. "And if the wind eases, the swell will settle as well."

"Go find Brother Ander and tell him," Will urged. "We need him to enlist the aid of the Almighty."

A light came into Breysen's eyes. He nodded once before heading into the bowels of the ship.

As soon as Breysen was out of sight, Will asked Amyra, "Do you know what you need to do now?"

She stared back at him with bulging eyes. After their brief time above decks, her hair was soaked and matted from the spray, and she looked completely wild.

"I can try," she managed, moving unsteadily toward the hatch.

"Where are you going?" asked Will in alarm. "Can't you do it from here?"

She shook her head wearily. "I need to be able to see if what I'm doing is working."

Reluctantly Will opened the hatch and helped Amyra outside once more. After closing the hatch, he struggled to the rail with her, barely avoiding being swept away by a huge wave that washed over the ship. Will could only hope that the captain and the sailors would be too busy to notice them.

Clinging to the rail, Amyra faced the waves, gritting her teeth in concentration. More than once she almost lost her grip as the ship rolled and pitched in the mountainous swell.

Each time Will saved her. Bending one arm around the rail, he hooked his other arm around her slender waist. Then he focused the whole of his energy on maintaining his grip.

At first Will could detect no change in the conditions. Pushed back and forth with the ship, he continued to cling on with all of his might.

The minutes passed agonizingly slowly. But a time came when gradually, impossibly, the sails began to flap as the wind changed direction. The howling of the gale appeared to diminish, and the waves no longer seemed quite so terrifying. Will watched on with awe and relief as a steady wind filled the sails and the ship settled into a new rhythm, rising and falling on a moderate swell.

A ragged cheer went up from the sailors. Will joined them, although he achieved little better than a hoarse croak.

He turned to Amyra. She appeared pale and stricken, close to collapse. With one arm still locked around her waist, he succeeded in catching her as she slumped to the deck. Hefting her into his arms, he staggered to the hatch.

Amyra slept through the night and well into the next morning. Elena and Thomas took charge of the children, allowing Will to maintain an anxious vigil by her side.

When her eyes finally fluttered open, a surge of relief flooded over him.

"You were incredible!" he breathed. "You saved us all."

She gazed back at him with weary eyes. "The children?" she finally whispered.

"They're fine," he assured her. "Below deck, playing with Thomas and Elena's children."

He brought her water and supported her head while she drank. Then he gently laid her head back onto the hammock.

Her eyes soon closed again, and he left her to sleep.

WILL STOOD ON DECK, accompanied by Thomas, Brother Ander, and a jubilant Breysen. Amyra was still resting below.

"You deserve the credit as well as Brother Ander, My Lord!" said Breysen excitedly. "It never occurred to me to ask him to help. But the wind changed and the storm subsided soon after he started praying!"

Will smiled, but said nothing. He had no desire to dent the blacksmith's enthusiasm, and he was determined not to expose Amyra's stone.

Curiously, Brother Ander seemed unmoved by the acclaim. Was it modesty? Did he question his role in the change of weather? Or was it something else?

"It was a huge relief when the storm died down," said Thomas. "I was beginning to feel anxious about my family's safety."

Will nodded. "The main thing is that the worst is behind us. And according to the captain, the ship hasn't sustained any major damage, and we're making good progress."

After a while Brother Ander and Breysen drifted off.

Thomas glanced at Will with eyebrows raised questioningly. "Was it Amyra?" he asked.

Will nodded. "I feel a bit awkward about redirecting the credit to Brother Ander."

"He doesn't seem at all affected by it," Thomas replied.

"He doesn't," agreed Will. "Is that because he doesn't believe he was responsible? Or is calming a storm of no consequence to him?"

Thomas shook his head. "I can't imagine Brother Ander sees it as unimportant," he said. "But he would see God as having done it, not him."

They stood in silence for a time.

"Where did these stones come from?" Will eventually asked.

"I have no idea," Thomas replied. "A monk who was a friend of Brother Vangellis told me he thought the Stone of Knowing might be a sky rock. And you've seen the scroll. It also suggested the stones came from the sky."

"What's their purpose?" asked Will.

Thomas raised his hands helplessly. "I don't know. But Brother Vangellis once told me he saw the Stone of Knowing as a gift."

"From God?" asked Will.

Thomas shrugged. "I suppose so."

"Wherever they came from, they're powerful," Will concluded. "Frighteningly so."

Thomas offered no response.

THE WHARVES of Rog lay before them, crowded with shipping. Delighted to have made it through an entire day without throwing up, Will stood on deck as the Nomad Lady eased her way into the harbor.

In the hours that lay behind them he had pondered Amyra's achievement with the Stone of Authority. Before long they might be facing an invasion fleet. If she could calm a storm, could she contrive to whip one up to prevent the fleet from landing?

He pictured her lying prone on her hammock, utterly spent. Her will was indomitable, but how could her body sustain another such attempt, much less an effort on an even bigger scale? He shook his head. They needed to find another way to resolve the issues.

He thrust such thoughts from his mind, aware that a pressing matter of a different kind demanded his attention. His previous visit to Rogand had been covert; this time he would be appearing openly. He had no doubt that many would see him as the architect of the catastrophic destruction visited on the armies of Rogand during Drettroth's invasion. He wasn't concerned for himself, but his family was another issue entirely. Would they be safe in Rog?

Under normal circumstances he would never have considered bringing any of them on this venture. But the Stone of Authority was too important to leave behind in Erestor, especially at such a time.

And Amyra's participation had inevitably led to the children coming as well.

He had discussed this with Amyra even before they left their holdings, and they had developed a strategy to minimize the risk as much as possible. They needed to talk with the children before they arrived, so it was no surprise when Amyra appeared on deck bringing both Millie and Ethen. Spotting him, they joined him at the rail.

"I don't want any of you to be seen with me until we're safe in the castle, or wherever King Krasmir plans to accommodate us," he told them seriously.

"Why not?" asked Ethen, puzzled.

"It might be risky for you to be associated with me," he replied. "I don't expect to be popular in some quarters here. I was the commander of the army that defeated Rogand a few years ago."

"Does Tammi have to stay away from her dad?" Millie demanded.

Will shook his head. "Thomas is fortunate to not be well known here. So there's no reason for him to stay away from his family."

"That's not fair!" cried Millie.

"Life isn't always fair, I'm afraid," Will told them.

"We can spend time with your father when we're in our own private rooms, " Amyra told the children. "We'll be playing a game while we're in Rogand too. We're going to see who's the best at listening in Rogandan while speaking in Arvenian."

"But I've been looking forward to practicing my Rogandan!" said Millie disconsolately.

"You'll have plenty of opportunities," Will assured her. "When we're together we'll speak only in Rogandan. And you'll get to do plenty of listening at other times."

"It's just a precaution," Amyra said. "People tend to speak more freely when they think you don't understand. So if any of the people we meet have plans that affect us, they might let it slip."

"Do you understand what you need to do?" Will asked the children.

They both nodded.

"You'll be well protected," he assured them. "Rufe will always be with you, and other guards too."

Noticing Rufe emerging from the hatch, Will waved him over. "I'm going to leave you now," he told his children, kissing them both on the head. Then he embraced his wife. She hugged him back, although her response felt more distant than warm.

He chose not to comment. It might have taken him a while, but he was gradually learning that timing was as important in relationships as it was in battle.

A MESSAGE HAD BEEN SENT to the palace when the ship docked, and Will remained on board, not wanting to leave the docks until his party had been formally received by the Rogandan officials.

Several hours passed before a delegation arrived from the palace. Having disembarked, Will was surprised to discover that the delegation was led by King Krasmir himself.

Horses had been provided, along with carriages for the women with children. Once they had all set out for the palace, King Krasmir pulled his horse alongside Will's.

"So you are Lord Torbury. Hosting the commander of the Arvenian army in my capital must surely rank as one of the more unexpected developments of my reign," the king told him dryly.

Will dipped his head. "I hope that my visit to Rog might prove beneficial to both kingdoms."

Krasmir contented himself with a nod. "Your countryman, Count Ranauld, has assured me that you are here only to work for the good of us all."

"That is indeed my sole purpose in coming to Rog," Will confirmed.

"For as long as that remains true, you are welcome."

"Thank you, Your Majesty."

People waved enthusiastically when they saw their king riding through the streets. He waved back serenely.

After a few minutes he turned to Will again. "I must say I never imagined myself escorting the scourge of Rogand's armies through the streets of Rog. Do you know that people here refer to you as the Lash of the Devil?"

Will kept his face impassive. "I prefer to see myself as the defender of Arvenon, Your Majesty. Your kingdom may itself face an unprovoked invasion soon, and I would expect the Rogandan people to defend themselves vigorously if that were to happen."

The king returned a wry smile. "A subtle but effective riposte. I can see that your diplomatic skills are the equal of your skills in battle." He shrugged. "Diplomacy is merely a different kind of warfare, I suppose."

Seeming to come to a decision, the king took a deep breath and released it slowly. "For my own part, I was never in favor of Drettroth's adventure, and his motives remain cloudy to me. Agon's support for the invasion was no surprise—my predecessor was committed to self-aggrandizement at any cost. You will not find me motivated by the same appetites."

Will bowed low. "I appreciate your candor, Your Majesty."

"While I am speaking candidly, it is only fair to let you know that not everyone here is equally enthusiastic about your visit, Lord Torbury. However, while I have heard many differing reports about you, all parties agree that your capabilities are unmatched. I hope they are right, because I expect we will need all the help we can get in the days to come."

Will did not respond.

"My welcome must seem ambivalent at best," the king concluded. "Nevertheless, I want you to know that I am willing to extend to you the full benefit of any doubt. Your visit enjoys my support—please do not harbor doubts about that. I look forward to working with you."

"I am grateful for your gracious response, Your Majesty," Will replied. "There is one matter that I would like to raise with you, with your permission."

King Krasmir nodded an affirmative.

"My party includes children from two families, one of which is my own. I did not expect an enthusiastic reception, so I have asked my wife and children to remain apart from me in public to minimize any risk to them. You might reasonably wonder why I brought them here at all. The reasons are personal and difficult to explain, but the intent is in no way sinister."

He faced the king squarely. "My wife and children are not responsible for any of my past actions. We have people to guard them of course, but would you be willing to extend some of your own protection over them as well?" He made no attempt to hide a tone of pleading in his voice.

King Krasmir did not hesitate. "I will see to it that your family is well protected, Lord Torbury—you have my word on that. It may be necessary at times for them to curtail their movements, but we will keep them safe. I will personally assign men I know to be trustworthy."

13

———

Will and Amyra sat with Count Ranauld in his apartment at the royal castle at Rog.

"It's a great relief to have you both here," Ranauld told them. "The situation is extremely delicate, and properly representing the interests of Arvenon has felt like a heavy burden. I'm beyond delighted to know that the responsibility no longer rests solely on my shoulders."

"I'm sure you've done an excellent job," Will said reassuringly. "What have you learned so far in the meetings with the princess?"

"There haven't been any meetings yet," Ranauld told him. "There is a reason," he added, apparently in response to the surprise on Will's face. "The king wanted to find out if the Ahrans had returned to the island where they abandoned the princess. The hermit, Kamash, agreed to lead a party there. Apparently he was also hoping to retrieve some personal effects he'd left there. They only returned yesterday—just a few hours before you arrived."

"What did they discover?" asked Will.

"When they reached the island they found that others had been there before them. Presumably the Ahrans returned there as expected. The ground around Kamash's dwelling had been trampled by many feet, and the dwelling itself had been ransacked."

Will pondered this information. "So the Ahrans are now aware that they dumped the princess on an inhabited island. I'm sure they would have conducted a thorough search. And since there were no bodies to be found, they also know she didn't die there as they intended."

Ranauld nodded. "The question is what conclusion they might have drawn from it," he said.

"It would have been obvious to them that someone—presumably a castaway—had been living on the island," said Will. "My guess is that they decided the princess and her guard must have put to sea with the castaway, most likely by raft."

"Only a fool would attempt those seas by raft," said Ranauld.

"Very true," agreed Will. "The Ahrans would almost certainly have concluded that the princess perished at sea."

Both men fell to musing.

Will eventually broke the silence. "What has the princess been doing in the meantime?" he asked.

"She's been seeing the sights of Rog, such as they are." Ranauld made a face. "Under heavy guard of course."

"Can you please use your channels to arrange me an audience with King Krasmir?" asked Will.

"Certainly," Ranauld replied. "I'll request a meeting as soon as the king can make himself available."

WILL and Ranauld were ushered into an audience chamber in the palace. The room boasted a small throne at one end, brightly illuminated by many windows. The king had ignored the throne, sitting instead at the head of an ornate table around which a number of chairs had been placed.

"Please take a seat," King Krasmir told them as they entered the room.

They bowed. "Thank you for seeing us so promptly," Will said, handing a letter to the king. "King Steffan asked me to present my credentials at the earliest opportunity."

The letter from King Steffan had been written in Arvenian, but Steffan's agents had confidently asserted that King Krasmir could both speak and read the language.

The king's eyebrows lifted as he read it. "Your king has given you sweeping powers on his behalf, Lord Torbury. He has even authorized you to commit Arvenon to a mutual-defense treaty if you see fit. He clearly places a very high level of trust in you!"

Will bowed. "King Steffan does not want another war," he said. "But if it is clear that Rogand is being attacked without cause by the Empire of Ahr, Arvenon will stand with Rogand."

"I greatly appreciate King Steffan's support," King Krasmir told him. "And I appreciate your willingness to act on his behalf to establish a strong defense against an attack." His face turned grim. "I regret to say that it may well come to that."

"Standing with Rogand is also a prudent step for Arvenon," said Will. "If Rogand falls, Arvenon and the other neighboring kingdoms are likely to be targeted next."

The king nodded.

"There is another matter I wished to explore, Your Majesty," Will said.

"I am listening," the king replied.

"Count Ranauld has briefed me on recent events," Will said. "I understand that the Ahrans sailed away from Rog before the princess arrived, and that they returned to the island where they left her. Since they did not find her there, they would have been forced to guess about what happened. I personally think it likely they concluded she left the island with the hermit, most probably by raft. That being the case, they would not have expected her to survive."

"That is entirely possible," acknowledged the king.

"Nevertheless, even if the news has not yet reached the Grand Vizier, at least some of the Ahrans would since have become aware that the princess is with us here in Rog," Will continued.

King Krasmir frowned. "How can you be certain about that?" he asked.

"I can't be certain, Your Majesty. But it seems reasonable to suppose they have agents in Rog, and the princess has been openly traveling throughout the city."

The king's eyes narrowed. "Are you suggesting I should have hidden her away?" he asked.

"Not at all, Your Majesty," Will replied calmly. "I doubt that the truth about her whereabouts could have been concealed. It was probably already too late for secrecy when the Varasan fishermen found her drifting at sea and brought her into Varacellan harbor. And any serious attempt at concealment would have required her to be deprived of her liberty. From the little I've heard, she is not well equipped to thrive in such an environment."

The king did not seem entirely satisfied. "What point are you wanting to make then?"

"Your predecessor, King Agon, was able to do a great deal of damage with little more than three highly connected malcontents and a relatively modest sum of money."

"You're concerned about traitors?"

"I'm concerned about being blindsided, Your Majesty. The blows struck by the traitors were effective because we were unprepared. By the time we became aware of their intentions, it was too late to prevent their actions and impossible to undo what they'd already done."

"What are you proposing?" King Krasmir asked.

"While we are not entirely unprepared this time, we remain ignorant about the real agenda of the Ahrans. That makes us vulnerable. I would like to offer two proposals. The first is that we invest whatever resources are needed to track down the Ahran agents."

The king looked unimpressed. "Finding and eliminating their agents won't solve anything. Others will be put in place, and the replacements will be more cautious next time."

"The goal would not be to eliminate the agents, Your Majesty. I am proposing that we monitor them covertly. We need to know what they are planning."

The king considered this.

"What is your second proposal?"

"That we take strong steps to ensure that the Ahrans do not become aware of our own plans."

The king's brows drew together. "Do you doubt my commitment to security? I can assure you that our meetings will be heavily guarded. Intruders will not be allowed anywhere near the site."

Will kept his face impassive. "It is difficult to thwart a person who is sufficiently determined, especially with a lot of people actively discussing the issues and servants coming and going constantly on a range of errands. I would like to propose that the venue be changed —without notice and at the last minute—and that only those directly participating be admitted to the meeting room. No servants and no soldiers should be allowed inside. Refreshments could be served in a different location. And before we begin, participants could be admitted only if you are certain they can be relied upon. I'm sure your agents will have no difficulty identifying nobles with loose tongues. Attendees should be required to never discuss sensitive matters unless they are certain beyond doubt that no others are within earshot."

The king listened patiently until Will finished. "Suppose we implement your plan," he said, "and succeed in tightening security to the point where no word of our plans leaks out. Wouldn't the Ahran agents be forced to resort to strong measures to get information?"

"Yes, Your Majesty. I find that possibility disturbing, as I am sure you do. However we need not provoke them to acts of desperation. Some of our number can hold confidential conversations at other locations, conversations capable of being overheard by a person bold enough to risk detection. We will fill their ears with plausible-sounding plans that have no basis in reality. And the strategy should give us further opportunity to identify the Ahran agents."

"You have a shrewd mind, Lord Torbury."

THE CONFERENCE BEGAN AS SOON as the three kings and the most senior of their nobles had gathered. Will noted with satisfaction that the meeting location had been changed without notice. Indeed he was gratified to discover that so far King Krasmir had implemented every one of his suggestions.

Will had managed to include Amyra in the invitation, although they were trying not to be too obvious about their connection. He had also hoped to include Thomas along with his stone, but King Krasmir made it clear that only nobility would be allowed to participate. Since Will was unable to dream up a good enough reason to request an exception, Thomas had gone to a secure location with Elena, Haldek, Rufe, Breysen, Brother Ander, and the five children.

During King Krasmir's brief introductions to those attending the conference, Will had noted that foreigners were outnumbered at least four to one. A number among the Rogandan nobility were women, and Will found himself thinking of Lady Ona. He grimaced involuntarily.

"I expect that every one of us will make extraordinary efforts to follow through on the security measures I have outlined," King Krasmir was concluding.

The king directed an almost imperceptible nod in Will's direction, but stopped short of openly crediting him for the tightened security. Will was grateful. He enjoyed good relations with all members of the Varasan and Castelan delegations, and he felt confident they would view sympathetically any initiatives he might propose. King Krasmir's delegation was another matter. The king had introduced him as Lord Torbury, not Will Prentis, but if the sour glances directed toward him were any indication, the Rogandan nobles had no doubt about who he was. He had no desire to draw more attention to himself than was necessary.

"We are fortunate to have in our midst a man who possesses an inquiring mind," said King Krasmir. "He has used it to amass a formidable store of knowledge. I am pleased to introduce Lord Boedwyk to this gathering."

A tall thin man with bushy eyebrows got up and moved to the front of the room. He bowed as he faced the king.

"Please favor us with a summary of what is known of the Empire of Ahr," King Krasmir requested.

The king seated himself, and Lord Boedwyk turned to his audience. He began speaking rapidly in Rogandan, apparently oblivious to the fact that his words needed to be translated. Will spared a thought for the carefully selected translator sitting among the Arvenian speakers. The man already looked harried.

Was the nobleman set on delivering a none-too-subtle snub to the foreign guests? After studying him closely, Will decided that the reality was more straightforward—Lord Boedwyk's engagement with his subject was so intense it excluded every other consideration.

"Few Rogandans—and perhaps none of us present in this room—have visited the Empire of Ahr," the nobleman was saying. "To begin with, the lengthy sea voyage introduces a number of interesting challenges. I make no mention of the undoubtedly fanciful tales of sea monsters." He blinked rapidly several times and directed his attention up into the ceiling. "The Ahrans are reputedly an insular society, not naturally welcoming of outsiders. Very like some of us perhaps," he added. His mouth opened wide in a chortle, although he managed to hastily smother the sound.

Recovering himself, he continued. "The Ahrans are not unwilling to trade, but their tastes apparently differ considerably from ours. Ships have arrived in Ahr after a punishing voyage only to discover that their carefully chosen cargo was largely regarded as worthless by their potential customers. After dumping their goods at a loss, they have been left with little choice other than to reload their ship with wares that would be barely marketable in Rogand."

"Perhaps these Ahrans are simply canny traders," a nobleman suggested. "By pretending disinterest, they get the goods for next to nothing. Then in return they hand over junk, and even manage to get some coin for it."

Lord Boedwyk shook his head vigorously. "I think not, I think not," he insisted, shaking his head and blinking once more. "Cheating your suppliers has never been a workable recipe for building trade. No, no, I think it has to do with differences in taste." He frowned for a moment before smiling awkwardly and adding, "But I thank you for your contribution, My Lord. Thank you." He aimed a quick bow in the direction of the other speaker.

"I have learned about some very fascinating customs," he continued. "Ahran mating rituals are of particular interest, especially where kissing is involved." His mouth opened wide in a grin. "I could convey some captivating tales," he suggested with a throaty chuckle.

At that moment Will caught a glimpse of King Rupert. The young king seemed to be fidgeting restlessly. Will wondered what could possibly account for his reaction.

Lord Boedwyk's voice had trailed off, his eyes drifting once more to the ceiling. Will noticed others among the Rogandan nobility rolling their eyes.

"The politics and geography of the empire, Lord Boedwyk?" prompted King Krasmir patiently.

"Ah yes, of course, Your Majesty," Lord Boedwyk replied, clearing his throat with a self-conscious cough. "Please excuse my diversion. The emperor of Ahr has two children: the crown prince being the oldest, and the Princess Neira—currently our guest here in Rog— being the youngest. Neither the emperor nor the crown prince are ever referred to by name, only by their title. The chief minister of the empire is Grand Vizier Rheibas, the very man who favored us recently with a visit to Rog."

Grunts and muttering broke out at this last remark. Lord Boedwyk ignored it and pressed on.

"The climate of the empire is warmer than in Rogand," he continued, "and the population is large—much larger than Rogand by all accounts. The landmass is also large. The empire is made up of a single small continent and a large archipelago of islands, several of the islands being of considerable size."

"Does the emperor live on the continent?" another voice asked.

"An excellent question. An excellent question," the nobleman replied soberly. "The emperor does not live on the continent. His capital of Kat Ahket is located on Ahr-chitani, the largest of the islands. The main administrative center is located there as well."

"Does this emperor have a sizable army?" someone asked.

"On that topic, the reports vary widely," Lord Boedwyk said, placing his hands together in a precise movement and examining them carefully.

Will found himself warming to the Rogandan researcher. The nobleman might have unusual mannerisms, but he was clearly knowledgeable. And he seemed entirely artless, betraying no interest at all in self promotion.

"But whatever the final count might be, I think I can safely say that the number of soldiers answering to the emperor far exceeds the armies of all our kingdoms combined."

"Why does he need such a large army?" asked a nobleman.

"It seems that the emperor is frequently forced to put down rebellions against his authority. I imagine he needs a large army for that reason."

"What about his navy?" asked King Krasmir.

"All reports agree that he lays claim to a large navy," the speaker replied. "I heard of one exercise where the entire navy was gathered into the huge bay at Ahr-chitani, the large island. The ships filled the bay to overflowing." He spread his hands wide.

Another noble spoke up. "Are these ships capable of carrying soldiers?"

"They are," Lord Boedwyk replied with a vigorous nod. "Since rebellions have frequently been island-based, the sailors are very practiced at transporting soldiers and landing them from the ships."

This news was greeted with loud muttering throughout the room.

King Krasmir looked grim. "Do we have any idea why they have turned their attention toward us? What is their motivation?"

The speaker steepled his fingers.

"I cannot name their specific motivation," he said thoughtfully. "I have heard, though, that wars generally stem from one of four causes." He gazed up once more into the ceiling, and his voice took on an instructional tone. "The first and most common reason is a desire for aggrandizement on the part of the ruler. The second reason is greed —a ruler's desire to enjoy the spoils of war while expanding the borders of his own kingdom or empire."

Lord Boedwyk had become more animated as he warmed to his subject. Will listened with growing astonishment.

"The third reason is in response to internal dissension," the nobleman continued. "The ruler turns attention away from local problems by uniting the populace against a foreign enemy. The fourth is a desire for revenge or an urge to right a perceived wrong. Which of these reasons might account for the emperor's actions I cannot say, although the fourth reason is unlikely to apply in this case."

Will barely suppressed a wince. Surely only a fool or an innocent could make such statements before an audience that included three reigning kings. He shot a glance around the room. Other nobles appeared equally uncomfortable. Many were desperately trying to decide where to look.

Curiously, none of the kings seemed offended. They must have decided that these comments did not apply to them. They had probably also judged that their instructor was harmless and that challenging his assertions might only add weight to what he had said.

"Thank you, Lord Boedwyk. Your insights have been...more than usually illuminating," King Krasmir said dryly.

The eccentric nobleman got the hint. Bowing low, he returned to his seat.

"We will take a short break," King Krasmir announced. "Servants are waiting down the hall to guide you to refreshments."

The meeting broke up immediately. Most of the nobles couldn't leave the room quickly enough.

When the conference reconvened it seemed to Will that a somber mood had overtaken the participants. Many of them were talking among themselves in low voices, and King Krasmir had to speak sharply to call them to order.

King Krasmir began. "I spent time during the break with King Delmar of Varas and King Rupert of Castel," he said. "Two key questions need to be addressed as a matter of urgency. What can we do to prepare effectively for a possible Ahran invasion? What can we do diplomatically to head off any such invasion?"

Will decided it was time to actively engage. "May I ask a question, Your Majesty?" he asked.

Many of the Rogandan nobility stared at him open mouthed. He wasn't surprised—the reason wasn't difficult to guess. The infamous commander of the Arvenian armies had dared to show his face in Rog, and, instead of seizing him, their own king had allowed him to join their conference.

That was bad enough. But who could have expected to hear him speaking Rogandan as if it were his mother tongue?

"You have the floor, Lord Torbury," King Krasmir replied evenly, opening his palm in invitation.

Will stood and turned toward Lord Boedwyk. "I thank you for your informative presentation about the Empire of Ahr, My Lord. I found it very instructive, as I'm sure we all did. Were you able to discover any information about the construction of the ships in the emperor's navy? Are the vessels equipped for long voyages across open seas, or are they designed primarily for use among the islands of the archipelago?"

Lord Boedwyk rose to his feet and bowed briefly to Will. "A worthy question, Lord Torbury. And nicely expressed. Very nicely expressed indeed! Who would ever have imagined?" He shook his head. His eyes began to drift to the ceiling once more before he caught himself. "Your question is consequential, My Lord, although I am sorry to say I cannot answer it." He sat down abruptly.

Will bowed in response. "An open ocean voyage with a large fleet carries significant risk. However sizable the emperor's army might be, he will not be able to deploy it without appropriately equipped vessels and experienced captains."

"Can you look into it?" King Krasmir asked, directing his question to Lord Boedwyk.

"I will do what I can, Your Majesty," the nobleman replied.

Many of the Rogandan nobles were now speaking in low voices, shooting frequent glances at Will. From the look on their faces, his fluency in their language had not endeared him to them. They appeared more suspicious of him than ever.

He shrugged it off. He was well accustomed to being an outsider.

His question had clearly captured the attention of some though. King Delmar, sitting not far from Will, leaned over to him. "That was a key question, Lord Torbury," he whispered.

The question demanded an answer. It was hard for Will to imagine that the emperor's main fleet had been constructed for the purpose of invading a distant continent. But if the emperor was planning a foreign adventure, it was also possible that a new fleet was being built, consisting of vessels fit for the purpose.

"I am going to invite Princess Neira to join us," said King Krasmir. "She might be able to offer us some useful insights."

He nodded to Lord Boedwyk, and the nobleman rose to his feet and left the room, presumably to usher in the princess.

Will waited impatiently for her arrival. There were far too many unknowns for his liking, and the princess might hold the key to plugging at least some of the gaps. He was eager to meet her, and even more eager for an opportunity to interview her.

14

"Another ship is approaching, Captain."

Captain Gharpin nodded before turning toward the direction the sailor was pointing. A quick scan of the horizon soon revealed the ship. It gradually grew in size as it drew closer. Based on its course, it could well have been sailing from Ahrchitani. Before long it was apparent that the ship was Ahran.

The Grand Vizier appeared at the captain's side. "I understand an Ahran vessel is approaching, Captain."

"Yes, Your Eminence," Gharpin replied with a bow. As always, the chief minister didn't miss much. The captain kept his face expressionless, careful not to reveal the distaste he felt in the presence of the empire's most senior official.

"Send a signal to the ship," commanded the Grand Vizier. "I wish to enlist the aid of their captain."

Gharpin bowed again, torn between curiosity about the Grand Vizier's intentions and satisfaction at the prospect of getting the man off his ship, even temporarily.

The chief minister then disappeared below decks. He was gone for a considerable time, only reemerging as a longboat from the other ship was finally drawing alongside. Six men accompanied him, every one of them laden down with goods of various kinds. It appeared that the Grand Vizier had retrieved all of his possessions. That could only mean one thing—he intended to transfer to the other vessel. The captain was hard pressed to prevent his elation from becoming obvious.

The Grand Vizier drew Gharpin aside. "You have a new mission, Captain," he announced loftily.

Unable to guess what might be coming next, the captain stared back expressionlessly.

"You will return to the island where you left the princess. You will find she has been returned to it. You will retrieve her and make your way to the capital."

The captain bowed, although inwardly he was scoffing. He didn't trust the Grand Vizier for a moment. Nevertheless, if there was even a chance that the princess could be rescued, the mission was worth the delay in returning to Ahr-chitani.

"I must return to Kat Ahket to consult with the emperor," the Grand Vizier concluded.

The chief minister did not wait for a response from the captain. Heading for the side of the ship, he proceeded to oversee the laborious operation of lowering three of his men and all of his possessions to the boat below. The wind had been picking up steadily over the last few hours and the heavy swell made the transfer extremely challenging.

Very little could be heard above the howling of the wind and the creaking of the ship's timbers. Nevertheless the Grand Vizier persisted in shouting instructions. As the longboat tossed and turned on the waves, a number of his belongings fell out of it, quickly sinking out of sight. He turned pale with anger.

Eventually the boat, overloaded and low in the water, was rowed back to the other ship. The chief minister watched from Captain Gharpin's ship, grinding his teeth as more of his possessions were surrendered to the ocean while they were being hauled aboard.

Having offloaded its cargo, the longboat returned for the exasperated Grand Vizier and his remaining three men. The worsening conditions considerably complicated the process of transferring them to the other ship. Nevertheless they were eventually taken on board, the boat was pulled from the water, and the ship turned and set sail for the capital at Kat Ahket.

Gharpin was relieved to have finally seen the last of the scheming official. Turning to his helmsman, he ordered, "Set a course for the island where we left the princess."

The helmsman's face showed his surprise, but he made no comment.

Gharpin watched with considerable satisfaction as the boat bearing the Grand Vizier slowly diminished in size. With the chief minister finally gone, the captain took the opportunity to carefully review in his mind all that had happened since he first left Ahrchitani.

Having both the Grand Vizier and the princess on board as passengers had made the voyage challenging from the very beginning. Gharpin had no great love for the princess. She was conceited and almost unendurable. Nevertheless, she was the emperor's daughter, and the captain had openly questioned the Grand Vizier's order to leave her and her guard alone on the island. He well understood that it was folly to make an enemy of a senior official, especially one as powerful as the Grand Vizier. But, as a loyal subject of the emperor, how could he say and do nothing when her life seemed so obviously at risk?

The chief minister had informed him coldly that he had no business interfering in matters he didn't understand. Gharpin had no choice but to set sail for Rog.

When they reached the Rogandan capital, the captain caught wind that bizarre stories were being told to their hosts. Supposedly Rogandan sailors—or pirates—had kidnapped the princess. He was beginning to get a glimpse of how far the chief minister was willing to go.

After they sailed away from Rog, the Grand Vizier had commanded the captain to return to the island. Gharpin had been under no illusions when they arrived there—he fully expected to find that the princess and her guard had perished. Instead, an exhaustive search of the island revealed no trace of Princess Neira.

The Grand Vizier had casually told the captain that the princess had been collected from the island as planned. He claimed she was supposed to be returned there in time to join the return voyage to the capital of Kat Ahket. Since the timing had apparently gone astray, a ship would be sent to collect her later.

The chief minister had then retired to his cabin.

Unconvinced, the captain had quietly ordered his men to search the nearby islands. The search revealed nothing. The princess and her guard had simply vanished.

Gharpin was convinced that the Grand Vizier was spinning a series of bald-faced lies. But apart from the order to abandon the princess on the island, he had no proof of the man's duplicity.

The captain's men had found obvious signs of long-term habitation on the island. Only one explanation made any sense to Gharpin: whoever had been living there had left the island with the princess and her guard. Whether they had set out for the mainland or for another island, it seemed likely they had succumbed to the elements before reaching land at all. Without access to a suitable vessel, their chances of survival would have been very poor indeed.

Gharpin did have one immediate source of satisfaction. For the first time since departing from their home, the only people aboard his ship were his own crew. That was cause for celebration.

Six men had transferred to the other ship with the Grand Vizier. They had been handpicked, every one of them completely loyal to the chief minister. They had been as aloof and arrogant as their master. If Gharpin had dared, he would have left all of them on the island along with the Grand Vizier, instead of the princess.

Convinced that the chief minister and his lackeys had a hidden agenda, Gharpin had assigned five of his own sailors to watch them. Not one of these men was still alive. One had somehow fallen overboard during a storm, two others had succumbed to sickness—most likely poison—and the other two had mysteriously vanished at different times during the voyage. The captain suspected the last two were thrown overboard after their throats had been cut.

The loss of his men was intolerable, and Gharpin was determined to ensure they had not died for nothing. He would make sure that a full report of the princess's movements reached the emperor. The chief minister would arrive in Kat Ahket first, so he would gain first access to the emperor's ear. But the captain would not be deterred. He would make it his mission to see that the Grand Vizier's actions were exposed in full.

THE CONDITIONS WORSENED as they sailed on. Gharpin soon had no opportunity for musing.

"Captain!"

Hearing the urgent cry, Gharpin labored to the helm.

"She's sluggish!" the helmsman shouted over the wind, "Not responding properly to the tiller!"

A gigantic wave assaulted them, and the captain looked on in alarm as the ship rolled drunkenly in response. Worse, she appeared to be listing to the port side.

It made no sense. Recently built, the ship was one of the finest vessels in the emperor's deep sea fleet.

Gesturing frantically to a sailor to join him, the captain struggled to the hatch and made his way below deck. To his horror he found the lower hold awash, sea water surging about freely as the ship rolled back and forth. Numbed by the scale of the disaster, he explored as far as he dared.

The ship had been holed at the waterline in multiple locations, and water had been pouring in ever faster as the storm continued to build.

Fear was unmistakable in the eyes of the sailor beside him. Gharpin made no attempt to reassure his companion. Repairs were not an option—it was far too late for that. The only certainty was that the ship was going to sink. It was merely a matter of time.

This calamity was no accident; the damage could only have been caused by sabotage. The Grand Vizier's men must have carried out the destruction as they were preparing to leave. They had not been halfhearted. Thanks to the noise of the growing storm, there would have been no need to be furtive about their efforts.

Pushing down his fury, the captain forced his way back onto the deck, his companion behind him.

"We have to launch the boats!" Gharpin yelled to the sailor.

Wide-eyed, the man nodded once before hurrying away.

Squinting against the spray, Gharpin peered across the deck with a heavy heart. The ship carried three longboats. Between them they had nowhere near the capacity needed to accommodate the entire crew. His first instinct was to yield up his own place for the sake of one of his men. But there was no way to evade his responsibility. He needed to get word to the emperor.

Sailors were laboring to launch the boats—no simple task in the conditions. Transferring any of the crew would be an extremely hazardous operation. The sea would toss the boats about relentlessly once they were in the water.

The moment the boats had been released, Gharpin shouted the words most dreaded by every captain: "Abandon ship!"

One by one his crew obeyed, with Gharpin watching on anxiously. Satisfied that he was the last, he waited until the ship lurched in the right direction and jumped over the side.

Hitting the water hard and sinking quickly, he struggled resolutely upward to the light, resisting the remorseless tug into the icy depths below.

He broke the surface gasping for air. Bobbing about in the raging sea, his face covered with spray, he spun around trying to catch sight of a longboat. Carried up on a wave, he spotted a boat nearby and struck out for it at once. Several sailors had already climbed aboard, and they pulled him over the side.

Working frenetically, they rescued as many men as they could. Occasional glimpses of the other two boats confirmed the terrible truth—too few of Gharpin's men had made it to the precarious safety offered by the longboats.

It wasn't until an exhausted Gharpin settled back to rest that he noticed something was wrong. Spray might be splashing over them constantly, but there was far too much water sitting in the boat. A frantic search for leaks soon led him to the holes in the bottom of the boat. Someone had staved in the timbers.

He immediately ordered the men to begin bailing. Even before they started he knew it wouldn't be enough.

Salt water ran freely down his cheeks. It might have been spray, and it might have been tears. Either way, he knew they were finished.

Releasing a despairing sigh, Gharpin closed his eyes in resignation. He had been a fool. He had dared to challenge the highest official in the empire. It was always going to end badly.

THE SLEEK VESSEL beneath Bisri Ahuzza's feet slid gracefully through the swell, speeding him away from the capital of Kat Ahket. Salt water sprayed freely over the aristocrat, but it did not drive him from the rail of the ship. As special envoy to the emperor, he frequently found himself at sea, and he never tired of it.

The captain approached. "A ship has been sighted, Bisri. It appears to be Ahran."

"Send them a signal," the bisri told him. "We need to know if they have information about the Grand Vizier's whereabouts."

Only minutes passed before Ahuzza became aware that the man he sought was aboard the other ship. It took considerably longer for the Ahran aristocrat to transfer to that ship by longboat.

Climbing aboard the Grand Vizier's ship, Ahuzza was quickly ushered into the presence of the Grand Vizier of the empire.

"Bisri Ahuzza," said the chief minister, nodding a greeting.

The bisri bowed low. "Matters of a sensitive nature have arisen, Your Eminence—matters that require your urgent attention. The emperor has placed a fast warship at your disposal." He gestured in the direction of the vessel that had borne him from Kat Ahket.

The chief minister dismissed his attendants immediately. "What is the nature of this business, Bisri?" he asked curtly.

Ahuzza lowered his voice. "A rebellion has been brewing on Ahr-kasahn, Your Eminence. Reports indicate that it is about to boil over."

The Grand Vizier studied him for a moment. "What are the wishes of the emperor?" he asked.

"That you take charge of the situation and resolve the matter," the bisri replied simply.

The chief minister remained silent, his face expressionless. Then he nodded, turning away to call for the captain of his vessel.

The captain hurried to his side.

"I must leave you, Captain," said the chief minister. "My servants will remain. They can oversee the transfer of my personal effects to my palace when you arrive in Kat Ahket."

The captain bowed, and the Grand Vizier faced Bisri Ahuzza once more. "Lead the way," he said, indicating the waiting longboat.

Bisri Ahuzza stood silently in the private reception room of the governor's mansion on Ahr-kasahn. The Grand Vizier sat in state immediately to his left, waiting patiently for the arrival of a delegation. The governor of Ahr-kasahn was nowhere in sight. He had been excluded from the meeting.

Several men and women were ushered into the reception room. A tall man in late middle age strode in at their head. His face revealed tension, but he was otherwise calm. Three men and three women trailed in after him. Two of the women looked angry. All of the others looked terrified.

The Grand Vizier eyed them darkly. "I have been called away from urgent business," he told them brusquely. "Why am I here?"

The tall man bowed. "My name is Hirath, Your Eminence. Thank you for agreeing to meet with us. We are loyal subjects of the emperor, and it was never our desire to cause a disturbance. But the situation here on Ahr-kasahn has become intolerable."

When the Grand Vizier did not respond, Hirath continued.

"On Ahr-kasahn, justice is extended only to those who can afford massive bribes. Taxes have become so crushing that many have been forced into poverty. And new taxes are levied regularly—taxes that do not apply on other islands."

"Why haven't you taken these concerns to the governor?" demanded the Grand Vizier.

"Anyone who dares to raise such matters with the governor is thrown into prison, Your Eminence," Hirath replied. "The situation has become so bad that a large crowd recently gathered in the main public square to air their grievances. The governor's response was to send in soldiers."

"People were slaughtered!" one of the women moaned. "My husband and son among them!" She began to weep.

"I have been informed by the governor that the crowd was armed and aggressive," the Grand Vizier returned. "He assures me that the soldiers were merely defending themselves."

"That is not true, Your Eminence," Hirath said firmly. "Fighting did not break out until later, and only as a direct response to the massacre in the square."

"Who led the armed resistance?" demanded the Grand Vizier.

"I did, Your Eminence," Hirath acknowledged.

The chief minister studied him for a moment, then he rose to his feet. "A thorough and impartial investigation will be carried out," he announced. "Any officials who have been corrupt or negligent will pay a heavy price."

Hirath bowed. "And the governor?" he asked boldly.

"Every senior official will be investigated," declared the Grand Vizier. "That includes the governor."

Hirath bowed once more. "We thank you, Your Eminence. Your reputation gives us hope that justice will finally be done."

"Hirath will remain here," said the Grand Vizier. "The rest of you are dismissed. I can promise that your concerns will be taken seriously. But let me warn you that any new attempt to take up arms will be met with a ruthless and overwhelming response."

Hirath's companions bowed low before scurrying away.

The chief minister turned to Hirath. "You have the makings of an effective leader," he observed. "Draw closer."

Hirath bowed before stepping forward.

"You say you are aware of my reputation."

"I am," Hirath acknowledged.

"Then you know that I cannot allow you to live," the chief minister informed him quietly. "Not after you have led an armed rebellion."

Hirath had gone pale, but he did not respond.

"The only possible alternative would be to offer you a job," mused the Grand Vizier. He studied the other closely. "Something tells me a role of that nature would not suit you."

The silence from Hirath seemed to offer confirmation.

"It is as I expected," said the chief minister with a shrug.

He got to his feet. "Execute this man at dawn," he ordered.

As he prepared to leave the room, the Grand Vizier leaned in to speak quietly to the condemned man. Bisri Ahuzza was close enough to hear the comment.

"If it's any comfort to you," murmured the chief minister, "I think it likely that the governor will be executed at your side."

The Grand Vizier left the room without a backward glance.

Bisri Ahuzza hurried out behind him.

15

Bisri Ahuzza stood at the prow of the emperor's ship and watched as a tiny smudge appeared on the horizon.

A distinctive cone gradually took shape above the landmass: the crater-capped mountain that towered over the extensive island of Ahr-chitani. Fantastic tales were still told of the last time the mountain had erupted, but that was ancient history. No wisps of smoke hung over the mountain today, nor on any other day in living memory.

Beside the bisri stood the Grand Vizier of the glorious Empire of Ahr. The formidable dignitary had once been a low-ranking aristocrat known simply as Bisri Rheibas—a man with few prospects and nothing obvious to commend him. How he had ascended to the lofty rank of Grand Vizier was hotly debated.

Some pointed to his obvious abilities. On Ahr-kasahn, Bisri Ahuzza had witnessed firsthand the most recent example of the chief minister's renowned prowess. A single meeting, a swift investigation, and two summary executions had ended a rebellion that threatened to plunge one of the most populous islands in the archipelago into chaos. The Grand Vizier had almost made it look effortless.

Behind closed doors, the chief minister's opponents murmured that Bisri Rheibas could most accurately be characterized as a vicious schemer, and that his rise to prominence owed more to his effectiveness at disposing of rivals than to any honest skills. No one had ever offered proof in support of these slurs, and the Grand Vizier's supporters dismissed all such talk as malicious slander. His detractors whispered that no one with proof had ever stayed alive long enough to present it.

Bisri Ahuzza had no reason to believe the critics. Nevertheless he frequently reminded himself not to cross a man who could order executions without first obtaining the emperor's approval.

In any event, it was widely acknowledged that the emperor trusted his chief minister implicitly. That said a great deal, because Ahuzza knew that the emperor was no idiot, and he had access to more information than anyone. If Bisri Rheibas was truly devious and self-serving, he was unusually adept at keeping it hidden.

No one disputed that Rheibas was useful to the emperor. What Ahuzza had just witnessed on Ahr-kasahn amply reinforced his effectiveness.

Seeing that they were nearing their destination, Ahuzza redirected his attention to the scene before him.

As the ship approached the generous bay that led to the capital of Kat Ahket, it glided among a multitude of vessels of every size. Ships bearing two or three masts dominated the harbor, their flags and pennants snapping in the breeze, fishing boats weaved their way between the larger ships, and smaller craft ferried passengers and cargo across the bay.

Palm trees stood tall among the sturdy buildings of white stone that stretched out beyond the water's edge in every direction. Even from this distance, the towering walls of the imperial palace gleamed brightly in the afternoon sunshine.

Ahuzza stole a glance at the figure beside him. What was passing through the Grand Vizier's mind as he approached Kat Ahket? The powerful official had just returned from Rog. Bisri Ahuzza had never visited the place himself, but he had heard reports about it. The docks of Rog, with their untidy wharves and mismatched architecture, provided a squalid gateway to the Rogandan capital.

The scene here must surely offer a complete contrast. Before him lay the glorious city of Kat Ahket, the heart of the empire. It was also the main power base of Rheibas, reputed to be the most powerful Grand Vizier the empire had known.

Word of the Grand Vizier's arrival must have spread quickly, because by the time they were ready to disembark, a crowd had gathered. Most of them were just curious bystanders, but one of them carried a message bearing an imperial seal. The chief minister scanned the message briefly before securing it within his cloak.

A carriage was waiting for them, and they climbed aboard immediately. The chief minister ordered the curtains closed as the carriage rumbled through the streets of Kat Ahket. Some would assert that Rheibas disdained the dregs of the empire and studiously avoided all contact with them. It seemed equally likely to Ahuzza that he was simply weary and craved a brief moment of solitude.

Either way, Ahuzza enjoyed the view and was sorry to be shut off from the world.

Presumably the dispatch waiting for the chief minister at the docks had been a summons to the crown prince, because the carriage delivered them to the door of a gleaming residence outside the palace walls favored by the emperor's son.

It was rumored that the prince liked to conduct his business away from prying eyes at the palace. Ahuzza thought it implausible. Only a fool would imagine he could avoid the notice of the emperor. A smattering of the emperor's spies were surely numbered among the crown prince's most trusted aides.

It was, however, tempting to wonder what the emperor would think about his Grand Vizier visiting the prince before calling at the palace.

The Grand Vizier was ushered directly into a reception room. Ahuzza hung back, but the chief minister waved him forward. Perhaps it was in the interests of the Grand Vizier to have a witness to the conversation.

The crown prince was already on hand to receive his visitor.

Ignoring Ahuzza, he waved the chief minister to a seat. "Rheibas," he said. "I see you received my summons."

"Your Highness," replied the chief minister, bowing before settling himself.

The crown prince had a name of course—Ahreitas—but protocol demanded that he could only be directly addressed by his title. The emperor's son and heir apparently regarded such conventions as beneath him—he had not bothered to use the Grand Vizier's title.

Perhaps he was determined to ensure the chief minister never forgot his humble beginnings. Ahuzza had heard rumors that on one occasion when the prince was younger he had told the Grand Vizier, "I have divine blood coursing through my veins, Rheibas. What do you have in your veins? Pig's blood? Or something worse? Urine, perhaps?"

If the story was true, the crown prince must have since learned to moderate his impulses. His manner on this occasion was not openly contemptuous, but his words had nevertheless failed to show appropriate respect for the Grand Vizier. Ahuzza could only wonder what Rheibas might think about that.

The crown prince seemed to notice his father's envoy at last. He eyed Ahuzza coolly for a moment before apparently deciding that a witness held some value to him as well.

He redirected his attention to the chief minister. "I hear you have been attending to business on Ahr-kasahn. Did you follow through on my request while you were in Rog?" the crown prince asked Rheibas.

Request? Ahuzza barely refrained from snorting. The crown prince had never been given to making requests.

The chief minister dipped his head. "I did, Your Highness. One of my people has prepared a detailed assessment of the Rogandan army, as well as estimates of the armies of other kingdoms in the region. The Rogandans have a large force. The Arvenian army is smaller, although more effective by all accounts. The Varasan and Castelan armies are smaller again, but not to be entirely discounted."

"How do they compare with our armies?"

"Our armies are much larger. And more practiced at fighting, thanks to the continuing unrest on some of our islands."

The crown prince scowled.

It appeared that the Grand Vizier was delivering an indirect reminder to the arrogant young prince that his position was not entirely secure. The unrest on Ahr-kasahn, clearly known to the prince, also provided a timely reminder that the chief minister was the empire's primary safeguard against rebellion.

The Grand Vizier did not dwell on these topics. "Transporting our armies to Rogand would present the greatest challenge," he continued.

"Could their navies prevent it?"

Rheibas shrugged. "Even combined, they would not compare with our own fleet, Your Highness. Nevertheless, nothing can be taken for granted where tide and weather are concerned."

Ahreitas grunted. "These kingdoms would be weaker if driven apart," he said. "That outcome should be easy to achieve given their history."

Before the prince could speak again, the chief minister changed the subject. "Important as these issues might be, Your Highness," he said, "I am sorry to report that I bear news of much greater import."

"Has my sister gotten herself into trouble on her little adventure?" the prince asked dryly.

Rheibas bowed his head. "The news does indeed concern your sister, Your Highness. On the way to Rog our ship was intercepted by Rogandan sailors—or pirates if the Rogandan king is to be believed—and the princess was kidnapped. There was nothing our men could do to prevent it."

The crown prince snorted. "I'm not asking for whatever story you've concocted for my father," he scoffed. "I want the truth!"

The chief minister's brows bristled indignantly. "How could you imagine I would deceive you about such an important matter?" he asked stiffly.

The prince continued to glower at the official, but he subsided. "So what have you done about it?" he demanded.

"There was little we could do, either at the time or later," the Grand Vizier replied.

"How could you have allowed such a situation to arise in the first place?" demanded the prince.

"Perhaps Your Highness has forgotten who supported the princess when she pleaded with your father for permission to go," Rheibas observed coolly.

The prince glared back at him but didn't reply.

After a loaded silence, the chief minister added, "I am hopeful that our representatives in Rog will soon receive a ransom demand."

The crown prince eyed him darkly for a long moment. "Go to the palace at once!" he commanded irritably. "My father will be impatient for your report."

His Imperial Majesty the Emperor Hourahn II of Ahr sat in state in the splendor of his royal palace, surrounded by guards clad in imperial finery and waited on by an army of servants. He watched without expression as his Grand Vizier approached the throne and bowed low in homage. Bisri Ahuzza followed close behind.

Turning to his servants, the emperor flicked a finger. "Leave us," he commanded. He glanced at Ahuzza. "My envoy will remain."

All of the servants scurried away, accompanied by most of the guards. A dozen guards remained, positioned watchfully just out of earshot.

"I have been made aware of your intervention on Ahr-kasahn, Chief Minister Rheibas. Once more you have demonstrated your value to me and to the empire."

The Grand Vizier bowed humbly.

"I am, however, much more interested in the outcome of your mission to Rog," he continued, a troubled look on his face. "I am not referring to trading rights. I have heard that my daughter did not return with you. Where is she?"

A grave expression covered the face of Rheibas. "I bring terrible news, Your Imperial Majesty. The princess has been kidnapped. Our vessel was boarded before we reached Rog, by men from a ship bearing the Rogandan flag. The foreigners claimed their role was to intercept smugglers. After removing anything of value, they took the princess by force. They came with such overwhelming numbers that our sailors were unable to prevent them."

The emperor rose from his throne, pacing restlessly around it. "You did not sail alone!" he exclaimed. "Why did the other ships in your squadron not support you?"

"Our ships became separated in a storm," Rheibas told him. "We were boarded at a time when we were entirely without support."

"Have you confronted the Rogandan king?"

"I have, Your Majesty. He denies all responsibility. He asserted that the princess must have been taken by pirates."

"What has been done to recover her?"

"I made it clear to the Rogandans that they risked the fierce wrath of the emperor of Ahr if they failed to secure her. I propose that we return immediately with a fleet of our deep sea ships."

The emperor waved a hand dismissively. "You know as well as I do that any such operation would take many weeks to prepare."

"Then I implore you to send me back with as many ships as can be made available at short notice."

"For what purpose?" demanded the emperor.

"To continue to apply pressure on the Rogandans and their allies, Your Majesty. If there is a delay in our response, or if someone junior is sent to act on your behalf, it might send the wrong message."

"You will return at once," the emperor told him. "Find yourself a vessel. A small squadron of three ships will accompany you to provide protection. This will not be a show of force. Our initial negotiating position will emphasize our desire to resolve the matter peacefully. To demonstrate our intent, you will lead the negotiations, and another will command the squadron."

He glanced at Ahuzza. "The other commander can be Bisri Ahuzza."

He returned his attention to the Grand Vizier. "I have no need to explain to you the importance I place on securing my daughter's safe return, Chief Minister Rheibas. I am placing great faith in you. You have repeatedly demonstrated your formidable skills as a negotiator. When you arrive in Rog, you will inform the Rogandans that I am granting them one month to retrieve the princess. In the meantime, you do not have my permission to declare war or to make threats on my behalf. I will not enter into hostilities against a distant kingdom without clear evidence of their complicity. I expect a comprehensive report from you before the month comes to an end. Do you understand?"

Rheibas nodded, bowing deeply. "Yes, Your Imperial Majesty."

"I wish to speak with the captain of the vessel that took you to Rog," the emperor informed him. "Have him sent to me at once."

A grim look came to the face of Rheibas. "I regret to say that Captain Gharpin is not in Kat Ahket," he replied. "Knowing him to be effective and reliable, I transferred to another ship and sent him back to Rog to continue the search for the princess. I hope I did not err, Your Majesty," he concluded.

The emperor paused before responding with a tight nod to indicate his acceptance of his chief minister's action.

"You are dismissed," the emperor told them. "I will look forward to a rapid and successful outcome from your efforts."

Ahuzza left with the chief minister after both of them had bowed respectfully.

The emperor had not given the chief minister an entirely free hand—he clearly intended Ahuzza to remain independent. But the chief minister would undoubtedly find a way to achieve his purposes. He always did.

16

Kamash and the princess had been summoned to another section of King Krasmir's palace for a meeting. After being offered food and drink, they were requested to wait until someone came for them.

They had been waiting for a couple of hours when a tall and somewhat awkward looking man approached them. To Kamash's eye he had the refined air of a country nobleman, although a pair of sharp eyes peered out from beneath his rampant eyebrows.

"My name is Lord Boedwyk." The man grinned broadly as he said it, as though he had just made a joke.

Ignoring his unusual manner, Kamash returned a bow.

"Please come with me," the nobleman continued, setting off without waiting to see if anyone was following him.

Kamash accompanied him into a large meeting room with at least thirty people in it. Princess Neira walked stiffly at his side, her nose in the air.

Every eye turned in their direction.

King Krasmir stood to greet them. "I welcome Princess Neira and her spokesperson, Kamash, to this gathering." He addressed the princess directly. "We are looking forward to discussing recent events with you and exploring possible ways to proceed."

The king briefly introduced the others in the room. Kamash had always had an ability to remember names, and he made special note of the most important of the attendees.

A quick glance at Neira told Kamash that she was leaving it to him to respond. He bowed low. "On behalf of Princess Neira of the Empire of Ahr, I thank you for your welcome, King Krasmir, and for your hospitality at Rog." He bowed to the rest of the room. "King Delmar, King Rupert, other honored guests."

It was immediately obvious to Kamash that this meeting was already in progress. The subtle signs told him that the others present in the room had been there for some time. King Krasmir and his guests had probably already drawn conclusions based on the information available to them. It remained to see if they were willing to talk openly about that information and the positions they had reached.

"We are eager to understand the purpose of your visit to Rogand, Princess Neira," King Krasmir began.

Kamash decided to be direct. "Before the princess addresses such questions, she has a question of her own. Having endured a great deal in recent weeks, she would be grateful to hear news of the ship that carried her to this part of the world."

The Rogandan monarch briefly exchanged glances with his Varasan and Castelan counterparts before responding. "The ship visited Rog," King Krasmir confirmed.

"And did they mention the princess?" Kamash asked.

"They told us that their ship had been attacked at sea and the princess abducted. They said that this act of piracy brought shame upon the empire. They promised to return with an army to search Rogand and all the nearby kingdoms for the princess, with or without our support."

"Who told you these lies?" demanded the princess, outrage in her voice.

"The Grand Vizier," King Krasmir replied.

The face of the princess went bright red with anger, then slowly paled with shock. She muttered under her breath in her own language.

"What are you saying?" whispered Kamash.

If she heard his question she gave no sign of it. Her face had set hard like granite.

A wave of frustration washed over the old man. How could he help her if she closed herself off to him?

"The Grand Vizier has invented an excuse to invade. Is he likely to follow through with it?" asked King Krasmir.

The princess offered no response.

The king tried again. "Do you understand the purpose of this deception by the Grand Vizier?"

Still she remained silent.

A Rogandan nobleman broke the silence. "The invasion threat is empty," he said dismissively. "Rogand is too far away. The Empire of Ahr has no ships suitable for transporting soldiers over open seas."

King Krasmir glared at the speaker.

The princess erupted.

"I have been to Varacellan as well as to Rog," she spat. "The fishing villages of Ahr-chitani outshine your pitiful little harbors. You are so proud of your ships—all of them pale beside the glory of the emperor's navy. You try to tell yourself that the emperor has no ships capable of carrying soldiers across open seas. You are an ignorant fool! The Grand Vizier has spent the past few years building just such a fleet at Kat Ahket."

The wide-eyed looks on the faces of many of the attendees told Kamash that the princess had just provided a crucial piece of missing information.

Glancing back at the princess, Kamash saw her face flush with anger as she realized that she had been goaded into saying much more than she intended. She clamped her mouth tightly shut.

The old man sighed. Each party had revealed a single piece of valuable information, but no one appeared willing to say more. He had hoped for a meeting of minds, yet the conference already seemed bogged down.

An Arvenian noblewoman, introduced by King Krasmir as Lady Torbury, addressed herself to Kamash. "Does the princess wish to return to her own country? Or would she prefer to remain in Rogand under King Krasmir's protection?"

It was an important question, and one for which he had no answer. He turned to Neira. She stared back at him with tears in her eyes. "There is no one I can trust," she whispered. "No one but you, old man."

For a moment his heart melted. Then he reminded himself that the princess was capable of shameless manipulation if she thought it suited her purposes.

He tried to make sense of it all. Kamash had no doubt that the Grand Vizier's betrayal had shaken the princess to the core. In spite of her bluster in defense of the honor of the empire, she must surely be aware that she had become little more than a puppet in a bold power play. Her exalted status as daughter of the emperor had not protected her. Whatever games she might be playing at that moment with Kamash, the simple truth was that Neira was a vulnerable young woman adrift in a dangerous world.

"What *do* you want, Princess?" he whispered back.

Apparently coming to a decision, she swallowed once then turned to King Krasmir.

"It seems I must continue to intrude upon your hospitality, Your Majesty, at least for the moment," she managed.

The king's face was impassive. "If your people return, Your Highness, do you wish to be reunited with them?"

She paused for a long moment. Then she shook her head. Her face appeared stricken, and her lower lip trembled. Kamash was certain she was not faking her reaction this time.

King Krasmir nodded to Lord Boedwyk, and the nobleman led Kamash and the princess from the room.

THE PRINCESS HAD BARELY LEFT before animated conversation broke out across the chamber. Everyone seemed to be talking at once.

Will ignored it, his mind working on the problem before them. If the princess had spoken the truth, the empire had the means to invade Rogand. The reason for doing so remained obscure, although Lord Boedwyk had accurately outlined a number of possibilities. Was it the will of the emperor, or did it have more to do with intrigues fomented by the Grand Vizier? Was the crown prince in any way involved? The princess had suggested that the Grand Vizier had been building a fleet. Why?

Will wondered how the Ahran motivation could be exposed without traveling to Kat Ahket. And even if they did that, understanding the reasons might not make any difference. If the motivation was greed, what could they do about it?

Perhaps all that mattered was to vigorously prepare their defenses.

"We will meet again tomorrow," King Krasmir told the gathering. "In the meantime, do not speak of these matters to anyone. We cannot afford to allow our security to be compromised. You may consider yourselves dismissed."

As the attendees rose and left the building, Will's mind returned to the princess. She undoubtedly could have said much more than she did.

He needed to find a way to get her in front of Thomas.

King Krasmir was one of the last to leave the meeting chamber, and Will waited outside for him to emerge.

The king soon appeared, accompanied by several of his nobles.

"Your Majesty," said Will with a bow. "Could I have a word?"

King Krasmir hesitated for a moment, then he nodded. "Of course, Lord Torbury." He turned to his nobles. "Would you excuse me?"

The men bowed and moved out of earshot, leaving the king with Will.

"Some of my nobles find it difficult to adjust to change," the king began. "Please pay no mind to their aloofness."

Will waved a hand unconcernedly. "I understand their hesitancy, Your Majesty," he said. "But that was not what I wanted to speak to you about. I have a request. Would it be possible for me to interview the princess? There are some questions I would like to put to her."

The king looked uncertain. After a significant pause he nodded reluctantly. "I suppose I could arrange for that." He lowered his voice a little. "I need to avoid a situation where every noble thinks they should be afforded the same opportunity," he said frankly. "But I would like to briefly meet with the princess myself, and I suppose I could include you in that meeting. I will need to ask you to be very discreet."

It was immediately obvious to Will that asking permission for Thomas to join the conversation would be inappropriate.

Will was grateful to the king for his consideration. Presented with a difficult choice, the king had been willing to place the request of his foreign guest above the need to indulge his nobles. However Will had no pressing reason to meet with the princess if Thomas was to be excluded.

"I have no desire to place you in a delicate position, Your Majesty," said Will with a bow. "Please ignore my request. My questions can wait until the princess next meets with the nobles."

King Krasmir considered him for a moment before nodding his acceptance and rejoining his nobles. It was apparent that the king was relieved.

Concocting a reason to include Thomas in a meeting with the princess was clearly not going to be easy. Nevertheless, a glimpse was all Thomas needed. Some kind of opportunity would surely arise before long.

THE NEXT MORNING Thomas was approached by Will. A serious look covered the commander's scarred face.

"Amyra and I will probably be spending most of the day in meetings with the nobles, Thomas," said Will. "Again." His expression suggested that he expected the benefit to be questionable.

"I've had no success at all arranging for you to meet with the princess," Will continued, his brows furrowed. "The princess is not always included in the meetings though. See if you can wander around where the meetings are held. The guards will prevent you from getting too close, but you might still manage to catch a glimpse of her at some point."

The prospect of poking around where he knew he wasn't wanted held no appeal to Thomas, but he agreed to do it. He couldn't see that he had any choice.

There was unlikely to be any real risk to him, of course, provided he kept a close eye on the people around him. If one of the guards decided he was a threat, he would become aware of it immediately—the stone would leave him in no doubt about their thoughts and intentions.

Leaving it until the meeting was well underway, Thomas set off for the meeting site. He arrived in the general area to find a large contingent of guards controlling access to the meeting rooms.

He was by no means the only curious bystander. Located as they were inside the palace grounds, for the most part people with time on their hands were probably spouses and dependents of the nobles attending the meeting. Perhaps that explained why the soldiers were making no attempt to disperse onlookers as long as they stayed well out of the way.

While waiting for something to happen, Thomas positioned himself far enough from others to avoid unwanted attention, but near enough to overhear their conversation. Having worked at his Rogandan for a number of years with the support of Haldek, he had sufficient mastery of the language to understand what was being said around him.

"This foreign princess wanders about as if she owns the place," grumbled one woman.

"And I know for a fact that she's being helped by an old man who's Rogandan!" added another. "He's supposedly her spokesper-son. What's a Rogandan doing helping a foreigner?"

"The king should have him arrested!" protested the first woman.

Abruptly all conversation ceased, a buzz going up as a few people emerged from the meeting rooms.

"It's the princess! a voice exclaimed. "And her Rogandan lackey!"

Thomas stood on tiptoes and peered forward to catch a glimpse.

In little more than a moment the figures had disappeared from sight, and the conversation around Thomas moved on to other topics.

He remained unmoving, his mouth hanging open stupidly. It had taken only a brief glimpse to leave him stunned speechless.

17

———

"I'm bored!" exclaimed Ethen, pushing himself away from the window. He gazed at Andy and Delia. "Let's go!" he said.

Brother Ander, the only other occupant of the room, couldn't resist a grin. If he knew anything about Ethen, he wouldn't be satisfied until he'd gotten into some kind of trouble.

At five years of age, Ethen might have been two years younger than Andy, but he was a natural leader like his father, Lord Torbury. Delia, also aged five, followed Ethen around like his shadow.

When Ethen wandered out of the room, soon trailed by both Delia and Andy, Brother Ander decided he'd better go with them. Someone needed to keep an eye on them.

Most of the Arvenian adults as well as the five children had been accommodated in an isolated wing of the royal palace at Rog. Will and Amyra were attending the conference with Count Ranauld, and Thomas and Elena had agreed to take responsibility for Millie and Ethen as well as their own three children, Tamara, Andy, and Delia. Thomas was temporarily absent on an errand for Will, but Elena had as much help as she needed from the other adults.

The building provided some space for the children to run around, but all of them were used to spending time outdoors riding horses and throwing themselves energetically into a range of other physical activities. Confining five children in a lifeless building in a foreign city for an entire day was beginning to wear down the patience of everyone.

Most of the adults had sequestered themselves in a large room that boasted several comfortable armchairs. More than once a couple of children had run into the room squealing loudly; on the most recent occasion they had been promptly sent out and told to play elsewhere.

Ethen wandered into the room currently occupied by his older sister, Millie, and Tamara, the oldest of Thomas and Elena's children. Brother Ander trailed in behind them.

At seven, Millie was three years younger than Tamara, but they seemed to enjoy each other's company. Each of them was the oldest child in their respective families, and the monk guessed that they were enjoying the break from their energetic younger siblings.

"Are you two *still* prattling away in Rogandan?" demanded Andy.

No reply was forthcoming.

"I know why you want to learn!" he told Tamara. "Mother and Father talk in Rogandan when they don't want us to understand what they're saying. You just want to listen in on their secrets!"

"And you just want to get me into trouble!" Tammi retorted. "Tattletale!"

Brother Ander stepped in before it came to blows. "Come along, Andy. You, too, Ethen," he said with a smile. "Let's leave the girls in peace. I'm sure we can find something more interesting to do."

As they were leaving, Andy mumbled "Tattletale yourself!" in the direction of Tammi.

She responded by poking out her tongue.

"Let's explore the upper story of the building," suggested the monk.

He led them onto a staircase that wound its way upward until it emptied into a narrow passage covered with worn out carpet. Choosing a direction at random, he headed down the passageway, the three children tagging along behind enthusiastically.

Coming to a closed door halfway along the passage, he tried the handle. The room was unlocked, and the three of them filed in.

The room was empty apart from two old couches positioned opposite each other. The children launched themselves energetically onto the couches, raising clouds of dust. Brother Ander headed for the passageway in search of clear air.

Ethen's voice pulled him up short. "What's *he* doing down there?"

The monk and both of the other children joined Ethen at the window, peering down to the ground below. Brother Ander realized that they were positioned almost directly above the large room where the other adults were sitting. A man, clad entirely in black, stood outside the building leaning on the wall beside one of the windows. He was clearly trying to listen in on their conversation. Royal guards had been positioned at the entrance to the building, and some were stationed at various points around the building as well. None appeared to be located anywhere nearby.

"Let's find out what he's up to!" cried Ethen, running from the room.

"Wait!" called the monk. He was too late. All three children were racing down the staircase before he could stop them.

Brother Ander reached the bottom of the staircase in time to see the last of the children disappearing outside. "Stop!" he called uselessly.

A couple of doors led outside the building. They were all locked, preventing access from outside. But the key was still sitting in the lock of at least one of the doors, and it was that door that the children had used.

Hurrying outside, he saw the children disappear around a corner of the building. A cry of alarm caused him to quicken his pace. He rounded the corner to see Ethen writhing in the grip of the man clad in black. When the huge monk swung into view, the dark figure hefted Ethen into his arms and bolted for a hedge that stood adjacent to the building.

"Go back inside and get your parents," yelled the monk to the other children.

They stood there wide-eyed, rooted to the ground. They needed to move, but he didn't have time to wait for them to do it. Sprinting for the hedge, he set off after the man who had dared to abduct the son of Lord Torbury.

Reaching the hedge, Brother Ander plunged in and forced his way through. He emerged to find two black clad men before him. He could see no sign of Ethen, until alerted by a faint cry, he caught a glimpse of him being hurried away in the grip of another man, presumably the one who had taken him.

The men waiting by the hedge both pulled knives and lunged for the monk. He swayed easily aside, avoiding their thrusts without difficulty.

Years had passed since the monk had last resorted to violence. Renouncing it was no longer a decision he questioned, nor did he doubt his ability to avoid it. Nevertheless, he had no intention of standing by while the boy was abducted. When one of the men thrust his knife again, Brother Ander grabbed his hand and squeezed, at the same time swinging his attacker around to face his companion. The second man, failing to adjust his strike quickly enough, plunged his knife deep into the side of the first attacker, who cried out in pain. The monk thrust the limp form of the injured man onto the other attacker, bringing them both to the ground with the injured man on top. The second man struggled to free himself, pinned down by the dead weight of his friend.

Ignoring the men he had forced to the ground, Brother Ander raced after the one escaping with Ethen.

The man disappeared into a stand of pines, and the monk heard the nickering of horses as he approached the trees. Catching a glimpse of his quarry ahead, he put on an extra spurt.

He emerged into a small clearing to see the man mounting a horse, still grasping hold of the struggling child. As he closed on them, a heavy blow struck him on the back of his head. He crumpled to the ground, everything around him going dark.

AN ANXIOUS SERVANT met Will as he was emerging from the conference. The man wore the livery of the king. "Could you please come with me, My Lord?" he asked.

Shooting a glance at his wife, Will found that she had also been approached by another servant.

More curious than alarmed, Will followed the servants with Amyra at his side into a small reception room in another wing of the building.

"Please wait here," they were told. "King Krasmir will join you shortly."

KING KRASMIR WAS USHERED into a room to find the head of palace security waiting for him. The man appeared pale and drawn.

"There has been an incident, Your Majesty. The young son of Lord and Lady Torbury has been abducted."

"What?!" Waves of anger and distress washed over the king. "How is that possible? Our foreign guests were supposed to be well guarded at all times!"

The security chief hung his head.

"What have you learned?" demanded the king.

"The abduction was witnessed only by two of the other children. They looked out of an upstairs window and saw a man dressed in black. He appeared to be snooping outside a window of the room occupied by the Arvenian adults. The children ran outside. The man grabbed the five-year-old boy and ran off with him."

The king turned to his servants. "Round up my nobles. Immediately! I will speak with them shortly. And find the head of my agents. I will consult with him after the nobles."

The men hurried away to do his bidding.

He turned back to his security chief. "Go on," he said grimly.

"The children were followed outside by the monk who came with them from Arvenon. He told them to get their parents, then disappeared through the hedge near the building in pursuit of the abductor."

"Have you searched for the boy and the monk?"

"Yes, Your Majesty. We have found no sign of either of them, or of the abductor. The ground on the far side of the hedge was smeared with blood, and the imprints of several feet were visible. There were no bodies, and we have no way of knowing whose blood it might have been. It's possible that the monk was attacked when he reached the other side of the hedge. We also found hoof prints in the stand of trees beyond the hedge. Two or possibly three horses had been there. We have trackers trying to discover where they went."

"The chances of finding them are slim," growled the king. "Where are the other Arvenians now?"

"They have been moved to a more secure location. They are under heavy guard."

"Are Lord Torbury and his wife aware of this?"

"No, Your Majesty. They have been brought to a meeting room near here. They were told that you would meet with them soon."

A cold fury was building inside the king. "I want a full report within the hour," he barked. "I want to know how this happened and who is responsible. No effort is to be spared. Do you understand?"

The man hurried out of the room.

Another servant appeared in the doorway. "Your nobles have been assembled, Your Majesty. A few had already left, but most of them are waiting for you."

"Take me to them at once!" ordered the king.

He was led back to the room where the conference had been held. Most of the nobles were waiting for him. At the king's first glance, none of the faces revealed anything other than curiosity.

The king came immediately to the point. "The five-year-old son of Lord Torbury of Arvenon has been abducted!" he snarled.

Once more he took the opportunity to study their faces. He was not able to detect anything other than surprise and shock.

"That is indeed regrettable, Your Majesty," one of the nobles offered dryly. "It is surprising that he took the risk of bringing his children here in the first place."

"Especially given his past history," another noble added with a sage nod.

"All of you are fools!" hissed the king. "Don't you understand what this means? The boy was abducted from *my palace*. Under our very noses. Get your minds off the past and think about the future! We face the greatest threat our kingdom has ever seen. In our hour of need the king of Arvenon—the same man my predecessor tried to assassinate!—has sent us his best leader, with instructions to help us in any way he can. This incident threatens to tear our fragile alliance apart."

He stared them down. "There is no greater strategist alive than Lord Torbury. Maybe there never has been. Rogand has far more to lose than Torbury if his child is not found soon, and found unharmed!"

No one said a word.

His eyes flashed as he surveyed the nobility before him. "All of you have agents and informants. Forget whatever little schemes you have them working on. Get them onto this, and do it now!"

He glared at them coldly. "One more thing. If I should find that any of you have been involved in any way in this little conspiracy, then Malzakh have pity on you!"

Krasmir's nobles had known from the beginning that their monarch had teeth. He had chosen this moment to bare them.

They stared back at him wide-eyed.

"Get out of here!" roared the king. "Now!"

They scurried away like frightened rabbits.

Will and Amyra stood and bowed as King Krasmir entered the room.

He faced them grimly. "There is no easy way to convey this," he said. "I am very sorry to tell you that your son Ethen has been abducted."

A cry of anguish escaped from Amyra. Will went cold inside.

Somehow Will managed to hold down his growing agitation as the king outlined what was known of the circumstances.

When the king paused, he took a slow breath to calm himself. "Who has done this?" he demanded.

"I cannot say with any certainty, Lord Torbury. My best agents are already working on it. I have also recalled the nobles who attended our conference and insisted that they use their own networks to discover whatever they can."

"Do you think any of them might be responsible?" Will managed to push the words through clenched jaws.

"It is possible," acknowledged the king. "I don't think it's likely though."

"Who else?" Will managed.

"Ahran agents perhaps?" The king shrugged. "I am hoping that our inquiries will provide some answers soon."

King Krasmir passed a hand across his face. "I can well understand how distressed and angry you must be feeling. Let me assure you that no effort will be spared to find your son."

"Thank you, Your Majesty," said Amyra with a small bow. Then her composure crumbled, and she turned away, sobbing quietly.

The king inclined his head. "I will not intrude on you further. I will assign one of my most senior aides to you. You will have direct access to me whenever you request it."

Will dimly heard him speaking to one of the royal servants. "Leave them in peace for as long as they need it. Then take them to their daughter."

With that the king was gone.

Will moved to Amyra and put a comforting arm around her shoulder.

She stood stiffly, not returning his embrace. "Why did you bring us here?" she moaned.

VOLUME 2—THE YEARNING FOR VITALITY

18

Brother Ander woke to a pounding headache. Everything was black when he opened his eyes, and he wondered if he had lost his vision. He eventually decided that it was nighttime, or that he was in a dark room.

A small shuffling noise followed by a sob sounded beside him, and it all came back in a rush.

"Ethen? Is that you?" he asked.

The only reply was another sob, louder this time.

The monk pushed himself painfully up into a sitting position. His eyes were slowly adjusting to the dark, and he guessed that he was located in a cellar or something similar. A tiny amount of light was leaking through what appeared to be the cellar door.

His first concern was for the five-year-old beside him in the dark.

"Are you injured, Ethen?" After a pause, he added gently, "I need to hear your voice. If you're shaking your head I can't see it." He waited a moment longer before repeating, "Are you hurt in any way?"

The boy's breath hitched a couple of times, but he finally managed, "No."

"How long have we been here?" Brother Ander asked. Realizing that the question was probably too hard to answer, he decided on a different approach. "Have you been given any food or water?"

"Just a bit of water."

"More than once?"

"No."

So he probably hadn't been unconscious for long.

Before he could decide what to say next, the door opened abruptly.

Ethen scurried closer, and the monk responded by wrapping an arm around him protectively.

Brother Ander squinted in the sudden light.

Two men appeared in the doorway. Both of them wore hoods, and Brother Ander could see nothing of their faces. Having apparently decided that the monk was no threat, both men clambered down the few wooden steps that led into the room, each of them flourishing a naked sword in one hand.

One of the men held up a candle, and they stood silently for a moment, peering down at the monk and the boy. Brother Ander saw that the other man was grasping a small sack. The sack was tossed onto the floor, then both men backed out of the room cautiously, pulling the door shut behind them.

Brother Ander had stolen a brief glance at Ethen while the room was still lit. The boy's face was tear-stained and grubby, but he seemed uninjured. Their prison appeared to be a wine cellar, empty apart from a couple of old barrels lying on their sides. The cellar was large and the ceiling easily high enough for a tall man to stand upright without stooping.

As darkness descended, Brother Ander scurried across the floor and retrieved the sack. Groping inside as the light vanished, he removed what felt like a lump of bread and a water skin.

"They've left us some bread and something to drink, Ethen," he said softly, settling himself beside the boy. After quietly blessing the provisions, he pulled off a lump of bread and placed it into Ethen's hand. Hearing sounds of munching, he nodded with satisfaction.

The monk unstopped the skin and tasted its contents. It was

indeed filled with water, and he passed it to the boy the moment the sound of eating ceased. Then he handed over another chunk of bread.

When Ethen had eaten his fill, he leaned in to the monk, shivering slightly. Settling the little head gently onto his own broad shoulder, Brother Ander rested back against the cold wall and closed his eyes.

Ethen's breathing gradually became calm and regular. Concluding that he had fallen asleep, Brother Ander's mind turned to other things.

The monk smiled mirthlessly. The two men who entered the room had no idea of his past reputation, that much was obvious. He could easily have taken them out, with or without their swords. But he was no longer Ander the soldier. He had learned there were different ways to bring about change.

Bowing his head, he started to pray.

The hours passed slowly. When Ethen woke, he began shivering again. He leaned in close against the big monk, apparently needing the comfort of his protective presence.

At some point the door opened long enough for another water skin to be tossed into the room.

The monk had been waiting for just such an opportunity. "You can't keep a young boy in the dark for hours on end!" he called out in Rogandan as the door was closing.

No immediate response was offered, but Brother Ander felt hopeful anyway. These men were almost certainly not planning to kill Ethen. If that had been their intention they would have done so already. Expecting a child to remain placid while confined in a small space was one thing, but keeping that space permanently dark was another matter entirely. If the men had any sense they would quickly acknowledge that.

No more than an hour passed before a scraping noise could be heard outside. Daylight appeared suddenly in one section of the room near the ceiling. It quickly became obvious that the cellar was largely below ground, with a narrow strip of window looking onto the outside world above. Some object had been removed to admit the light. The window had little depth—certainly not enough to allow even a small child to escape through it—although it was quite broad.

The window must have faced west, because through it the setting sun was visible just above the horizon. After so many hours in unnatural darkness, the sunset was achingly beautiful. The monk and the boy sat together staring out the window, transfixed by the grandeur of the passing of another day. Brother Ander could not shake off the conviction that the extravagant display had been arranged just for the benefit of the two of them.

With the sun sinking low and the light beginning to fade, Ethen turned to Brother Ander. "I miss Mother and Father and Millie. Will I see them soon?" he asked, his lower lip trembling.

"I can't say when you will get to see them again," the monk answered truthfully. "But I know that your parents will not stop searching until they find you."

"ARE YOU READY, THOMAS?"

Thomas dragged open his eyes and peered blearily up at Will. "Of course. I was just having a quick nap, but I'm awake now."

Will grunted and headed for the door.

Thomas pulled himself into a sitting position and pulled on his boots. Clambering out of his bed, he hurried after the disappearing figure of his friend.

His mind was churning with the revelations of the stone when the princess and her spokesperson emerged from the meeting. He had said nothing to Will. The drama of the abduction and the search for Ethen had pushed everything else into the background. Thomas had concluded that Will did not need another distraction at that moment.

He had known Will for a long time, and he had never seen him so driven, so grim. The hunt for Ethen had become a consuming fire. Will barely ate, he rarely slept—the only thing he wanted to do was continue the search.

From the beginning Thomas had become a necessary accomplice. He was needed because of the Stone of Knowing. Normal living soon degenerated into an endless cycle of meeting people, sorting through the confusion of their thoughts and memories, and moving on.

It hadn't taken even a day before Thomas wearied of it. His mind was soon spinning, leaving him overwhelmed.

Thomas hadn't used the stone on Will, but he sensed that his friend was struggling as never before with the desire to take possession of it. He had resisted making any request to borrow the stone, but the pressure must have been building.

Thomas hadn't waited for the issue to come to a head. He instead turned to Elena. In the end, they established a workable arrangement. Thomas went out with Will. When they returned he gave the stone to Elena. Taking Rufe along for protection, Elena went with Amyra while Thomas and Will tried to get some sleep.

Rufe knew about the stone now. Thomas wasn't sure how it had happened, but everything felt like a blur anyway. The burly guardsman hadn't seemed surprised. He gave Thomas the impression he'd long since guessed that something very unusual was going on.

Thomas pushed it from his mind. There were other things he needed to think about.

Finally catching up with his friend, he hurried along at his side.

"What can we say with any certainty?" demanded Will, his jaw set firm in stubborn determination.

"That there's no end to the intrigue in this place," Thomas replied wearily. Then he sighed. "We know that King Krasmir has a lot of spies. That's no surprise. We also know that the High Priest has spies, and the Archprimus does as well. Somehow I wasn't expecting that."

Will's brows furrowed. "And none of them know anything about the abduction."

Thomas shook his head. "Not anyone we've seen so far. It's hard to imagine that a lot of people would know about it though. If it was common knowledge they'd never keep it quiet."

"There's a missing piece to this puzzle," Will growled. "Where are the Ahran agents?"

"So far we've had no more than that single fleeting glimpse," agreed Thomas. "In that tavern. We must have managed to spook him."

"That's where we're headed," Will told him grimly. "If we can't find him in the tavern, we'll start searching the vicinity."

Thomas suppressed a sigh. It promised to be a long night.

KING KRASMIR SAT opposite the High Priest. It was the first time he had entered the Temple of the Dark Gods at Rog on his own, and he was finding everything about the place extremely distasteful. He had no choice though. There was no other way to meet with the High Priest.

The wizened figure peered back at him for a moment before dipping his head. "You are welcome in this holy place, Sire," he said.

"Thank you for seeing me, Your Eminence," the king replied.

Had Krasmir ever seen anyone so ancient? If he had, he couldn't remember it. Life seemed to somehow cling to the old man in defiance of his age.

He pulled his mind back to the reason for his visit. "I need your help," he said frankly.

One of the High Priest's eyebrows quirked upward. He offered no other response.

"There has been an abduction—the son of a visiting nobleman from Arvenon. The matter is distressing to the family. And the timing could not be worse."

A long silence followed.

"What do you wish for me to do?" the Superior finally asked, his face unexpressive.

"You have your sources of information," said the king.

The eyebrow went up again.

Krasmir shrugged. "Of late my agents have been more active than usual. As a result, very little is hidden from me." After a pause he added, "Your Archprimus also seems to have a network. His reach might not be quite as extensive as your own, but his agents are unusually energetic."

The other eyebrow went up as well.

After a long silence the king sighed. "I'm sure I have no need to make you aware of the threat posed by the Ahrans. We don't need distractions right now, and we certainly cannot afford a quarrel with Arvenon and its allies."

Had the High Priest's eyes narrowed momentarily when the king mentioned the Ahran threat? Did the priests have reasons of their own for mistrusting the foreigners?

With still no response forthcoming, Krasmir decided to be direct. "Did your people take the boy?" he asked bluntly.

The reply was immediate and unambiguous. "They did not."

"And the Archprimus?" asked the king. "What about his people?"

The High Priest's eyes narrowed, but he did not immediately reply.

Did the lack of response mean he didn't know? Or did it mean he knew but didn't want to say? Krasmir sat patiently, determined to wait for as long as it took.

"I will look into it, Sire," the High Priest finally offered.

So he didn't know.

"Thank you, Your Eminence. I will await your report with great interest."

Getting to his feet, the king offered a shallow bow before following a junior priest out of the building and back to the gates.

It wasn't until the temple grounds lay far behind him that Krasmir was able to release the tension that had gripped him during his visit to the High Priest.

GOULTZAR SHUFFLED into the High Priest's familiar little room and settled himself onto the low stool opposite his master. The Superior sat silent and unmoving as always. Goultzar waited for him to speak. He didn't have long to wait.

"What do you know of the boy?" the old man asked, uncharacteristically coming straight to the point.

"What boy?" asked the Archprimus, raising his eyebrows inquiringly.

"Do not dissemble with me," growled his master.

"I have heard that a boy was abducted," Goultzar admitted. "I know nothing of it."

The Superior studied him silently through narrowed eyes for a very long time.

"You have built a network of agents that answer to you, and you alone. You have done so without my consent," the High Priest finally said. "Dismantle it. And do it immediately."

The Archprimus stared back at him open mouthed.

The old man's eyes bored into him. "You are dismissed," he said curtly.

Goultzar left the room in shock.

His mind raced, reviewing what his Superior had said and assessing the implications. Goultzar had originally built an informal network solely for practical reasons, intending only to streamline his administrative operations. Since it had no broader purpose, he had not bothered to inform the High Priest.

But over the years the network had changed as its scope gradually broadened. The changes had occurred so slowly they were almost imperceptible at first. Priests attending the shrines dotted throughout the countryside regularly fed back information. With much of it sensitive in nature, Goultzar had responded by branching off a special network. His intent had been pragmatic—he wanted to ensure that delicate information was handled appropriately and kept confidential.

Without conscious design, the network had slowly metamorphosed, developing an independent life of its own. Over time, the knowledge base grew to the point where Goultzar could have used it to manipulate people in high places if he chose to do so. Of course he never did.

By then he realized that in keeping the network secret from the

High Priest he had crossed a line. He didn't doubt that if his Superior learned of it, he would demand that Goultzar shut it down. But the network was surely essential, even if the High Priest was too set in his ways to see it. How could the Archprimus effectively promote devotion to the dark gods with no way to accurately assess the attitude of the people?

Rather than making his Superior aware of the network, he had instead become more careful and secretive than ever.

How had the High Priest become aware of his activities? Could one of his agents have betrayed him? He scowled in indignation. The agent would pay dearly if the Archprimus ever discovered who he was.

Clearly the time had come to clean house. He would dismiss his agents as instructed. Most of them. He would retain only his most trusted associates. And he would ensure that from now on they operated with extraordinary wariness.

WILL SAT with King Krasmir in a private reception room, restless and uncomfortable. He was trying his best to put a bold face on the situation.

"My wife and I were greatly heartened by the substantial reward you have offered for information about our son, Your Majesty," said Will.

"It was the least I could do under the circumstances," the king replied sympathetically.

"Have your nobles discovered anything useful?" Will asked hopefully.

"Nothing at all, I am afraid," the king told him. "I also heard from the High Priest just this morning. His contacts have led nowhere." He shook his head gloomily. "My own agents have been vigorously pursuing every possible lead as well. But I am sorry to say that in spite of our combined efforts, we have yet to learn anything definite about the whereabouts of your son."

Will worked hard at maintaining his composure. He wasn't surprised at the news, but he was still disappointed. He'd hoped irrationally that the king might have unearthed information of some kind.

The intelligence networks in Arvenon could not begin to compare with their Rogandan counterparts. The number and extent of the tendrils that crisscrossed Rogand was nothing short of astonishing. Apart from the huge web maintained by the Rogandan crown, the priests supported no fewer than two rival networks, and each of the nobles had access to extensive information sources of their own.

Thanks to Thomas and Elena and the stone, Will probably knew almost as much as King Krasmir about the various networks in the kingdom. Nevertheless, Will had no way of tapping into them. King Krasmir did, and his best efforts had yielded nothing.

"I am coming to the conclusion that the kidnapping was not carried out by any of the established groups," Will told him.

"You think the Ahrans are involved?" asked the king.

Will nodded. "How else could it have been kept so quiet?"

King Krasmir looked troubled. "If you are right—and I suspect you are—it will make our job that much more difficult. We know that Ahran agents are active in Rog, but they seem highly disciplined and probably few in number. We've been able to identify and bring in only two of them, and they've given away nothing of significance."

"All we can do is continue the search," Will concluded grimly.

"We have no intention of giving up," the king assured him. "We will continue the search until we find him."

19

Thomas and Elena sat waiting anxiously in a small room set aside for the use of the Arvenian delegation. Elena appeared calm and untroubled. It was more than Thomas could manage.

"Are you sure about the timing of this?" she asked.

"We need to take the chance while we can," he told her restlessly. "It's impossible to guess when we might get another opportunity."

After a further morning of intense activity, Will and Amyra had decided not to resume the search until the evening. Will needed time to map the sections of the city they had covered thus far. He was anxious not to inadvertently bypass areas, and he was equally determined not to cover the same ground unnecessarily.

The break left Thomas and Elena free for the first time in many days. Both of them were exhausted, and they knew they only had a few hours to themselves, but Thomas was determined to take action while he could.

The children had been left in the care of Rufe, Haldek, and Breysen. Elena in particular had felt very uncertain about both of them being absent at the same time. But the children weren't far away, and the other adults could call for Thomas and Elena if they were needed. And since the disappearance of Ethen and Brother Ander, the contingent of royal guards responsible for palace security had been strengthened significantly.

Elena was fully aware of what the stone had revealed to Thomas when he was watching for the princess and her advisor. He had not told anyone else. The frenetic search for Ethen was completely absorbing Will and Amyra, and Thomas had decided it was his responsibility to follow through on his discovery. Elena would provide all the support he might need.

The stone sat in its clasp beneath his clothing as usual, suspended on the chain around his neck. It was not in contact with his skin. It had already revealed the secrets of the person they were meeting with, and Thomas wanted this conversation to proceed as naturally as possible.

They had been waiting for about thirty minutes when a face appeared at the door. Thomas recognized him at once. It was the old man who had been acting as spokesperson for the princess.

Thomas leaped to his feet. "Thank you for agreeing to meet with us," he said eagerly. "My name is Thomas Stablehand, and this is my wife, Elena."

"My name is Kamash," the visitor returned. "I must congratulate you on your mastery of Rogandan. When I heard that you were Arvenian, I wasn't sure what to expect. And I do not speak your language."

"Neither of us speak your language well," Elena volunteered.

He turned to her. "I will say that your accent is more...pleasant to my ear than your husband's."

Thomas felt himself color slightly. Kamash apparently did not intend his comment to be taken too seriously though, because he winked at Thomas before grinning broadly at them both.

"I have been curious about your invitation," Kamash told them. "It wasn't clear from your message what had prompted it."

Thomas exchanged a glance with Elena. Then he took a deep breath.

"You seem to have been blessed with a long life, Kamash," he began tentatively.

Kamash stiffened immediately, a wary look on his face.

"We have no desire to expose your secret," Elena said gently.

The old man stared at her for a long moment. Then he slowly relaxed.

Thomas could only look on with awe. Was it Elena's words or the way she had said them?

He had wanted to communicate what they knew while reassuring their visitor about their intentions. Had it been left to him, they would have danced around the subject for some time. In Elena's gentle way she had come directly to the point, accomplishing the goal in one simple sentence.

"We heard that you left Rogand when King Ugar was on the throne," Elena told him.

"And we have heard tell of a small stone—dark gray in color and crescent shaped—that grants long life," Thomas added. "It has a name: the Stone of Vitality."

"So you put those two things together and decided that I had this stone?" he asked incredulously. "That's quite a leap."

"Perhaps it is," agreed Thomas. "But having convinced ourselves it was true, we couldn't carry on with life as if nothing remarkable had happened!"

He gazed frankly at the old man. "I cannot imagine what it's like to possess such a gift. In the wrong hands it could be terrifying. But it doesn't seem to have twisted you, Kamash."

Elena nodded. "We know that you took pity on the princess and risked your life to save her. Your compassion says a lot about you as a person."

"And it shows clearly that preserving your own life is not your overriding ambition," Thomas added.

An extended delay followed while the old man studied them both.

"I have had opportunity to observe people in many different circumstances over the years," Kamash finally told them. "I do not always read people perfectly, but I have learned to recognize ambition and greed well enough, even on brief acquaintance."

He fixed his gaze on Elena. "I see a rare goodness in you," he said. After continuing to stare at her for a few moments, he added, "The eyes do not lie." Then he turned to Thomas and studied him in turn. "You are more complicated, but I sense you are a person of integrity."

Kamash contemplated them both. "Surprising as it seems to me, I believe I can trust you."

He released a deep sigh. "I have been hiding for so long. It actually comes as something of a relief to have been discovered at last."

Neither Thomas nor Elena spoke, and after a while he continued.

"It all began many years ago. Ugar was king of Rogand, and his son Agon was a small child. I was a senior advisor to the king. It was a hazardous role. The king was both unpredictable and brutal—a dangerous combination."

The old man paused, remembering, gazing into nowhere. None of this was new to Thomas, but he sensed that Kamash needed to express it. And Thomas had been able to convey little more than a brief summary to Elena.

"We traveled south, near to the border with Lestanor. It wasn't the first such trip, and it wasn't the last. I didn't know it, but the king had somehow heard of the object you spoke about."

Kamash reached into his tunic and retrieved a small leather pouch hanging on a chain around his neck. He emptied its contents onto his hand.

Thomas and Elena both craned forward, an involuntary gasp escaping from Thomas. The Stone of Vitality lay exposed in Kamash's palm. Dull in color and trifling in size, it seemed unexceptional to the eye. Yet Thomas could still sense its power.

The old man's fist closed over the stone, and Thomas discovered that he had been holding his breath. He released the air slowly as Kamash returned the stone to its pouch and tucked it under his tunic again.

Sitting back once more, Thomas fixed his attention on Kamash's face.

"I learned later that Ugar had heard of strange reports from the border with Lestanor. Tales of men and women with remarkable lifespans. But never more than one person at a time. Rumor said that a unique talisman was responsible for their longevity. The possessor could expect to far outlast the tally of years allotted to other men and women. Ugar lusted after the talisman and was determined to acquire it. His agents haunted the region, searching out anyone who even appeared to be older than usual. As soon as they were ready to round them up, they called for Ugar to join them.

"I was included in the small company that traveled south with the king. When we arrived, every old man and woman was brought in to be examined. The soldiers were not gentle with them, and I was forced to intervene on more than one occasion. I made it my business to ensure that the captives were treated with respect. Many of the old folk were frail, and I also arranged for them to receive food and drink." He shook his head sadly.

"One night I was walking near the place where these unfortunate souls were imprisoned. One of them called softly to me. I went to him, and he gazed steadily into my eyes for a while before speaking. 'I have studied faces over many years, and I believe I can read them well. Your king is a cruel man who lusts after power,' he said bluntly. 'His ambitions will not be satisfied by attaining long life. He will only become more vicious.' He studied me again. 'You are a different kind of person.'

"He pressed something small into my hand. 'This stone will grant you good health and long life. Speak of it to no one! Your life will be short indeed if anyone else learns of it. Use its gift wisely.' Then he turned away to rejoin his companions, leaving me with the stone. He told me nothing of its origins or how he had come to be in possession of it."

"What became of him?" asked Thomas. He had seen the outline of the history clearly enough in Kamash's memory, but some details had escaped his attention.

"I don't know," Kamash replied regretfully. "I wanted to return the stone to him after the people had been questioned, but I wasn't confident I would recognize him again. I hadn't been able to see his features clearly in the dark. But it wouldn't have been possible anyway. None of the old people were ever seen again. I wasn't able to find out what became of them." He ran a hand over his face. "Knowing King Ugar as I did, it wasn't difficult to guess."

"Did the king find out that you had the stone?" asked Elena.

"No. Thankfully not. I heard that he had learned nothing useful from his captives. He eventually left the region, furious at having been thwarted. When we returned to Rog, I was fearful of being discovered. I kept the stone with me at all times. But after a while, when there was no reason to suspect my secret would be exposed, I didn't think about it as much. Until I fell off a cart and was severely injured. I recovered in an impossibly short time. No one who had witnessed the accident could stop talking about it. I knew that sooner or later the story would reach the ears of the king."

"What did you do?" asked Elena, clearly gripped by his account.

"I decided I needed to leave. Having served the king for many years, I was beyond weary—largely from the effort of trying to survive. Very few others had lasted as long. Anyone who displeased him was disposed of without a second thought. The man was unfit to rule, and his young son Agon was already showing signs of inheriting his father's sadistic nature.

"I wasted no time in making preparations. I acquired a boat and extensive supplies through the services of someone who didn't know me and never actually met me. I had become wealthy over the years, and I had many servants. I sent them away to my summer house at the coast, telling them to expect me there in the near future. I planned to set sail from that location.

"By then the only thing preventing me from leaving was fear. I knew that I would be missed, and that Ugar would not rest until I had been hunted down. I was on the brink of deciding I couldn't remain any longer when an old acquaintance from my village appeared on my doorstep. He sought me out because he had nowhere else to turn. We were acquainted because both of us lost our parents when we were young, and neither of us had other relatives to care for us. We survived

—barely—thanks to the goodwill of a couple of kind-hearted individuals in the village. They had long since passed away. This man grew up bitter and without friends, and as he aged his health failed. The other villagers wearied of him and his attitude—so much so that they eventually drove him out. So he came to me. He arrived late one night. I was alone in the house, and I took him in out of pity. He was much sicker than I realized, because I found him dead the next morning."

He smiled grimly. "I saw that I'd been granted an unusual opportunity. That night I set fire to my own house and watched from a distance as it burned to the ground. I waited long enough to be certain that a charred body had been discovered inside the ruins. From that moment, as far as anyone knew, I was dead. Then I fled to the coast. I boarded my boat secretly and left Rog behind, determined never to go back."

"Wouldn't your servants have missed you?" asked Elena.

"I'm sure they missed me," he replied, "but they didn't need me. I had made certain they were provided for. Since I had no other dependents, I made out a will in favor of those who had served me faithfully over the years."

"So that's how you came to be on your remote island," said Thomas.

Kamash nodded. "I discovered that I was well able to endure my own company," he said. "Especially with the help of a succession of animal friends. I imagine that a big risk for many hermits is getting sick or being injured, but I had no such problem. I did occasionally get sick, but I always recovered quickly. I had the stone to thank for that."

"Did you always carry it with you?" asked Elena.

"No," he replied. "I went for long periods without any direct contact with it." He shrugged. "Perhaps that will affect my longevity. I can't say with any certainty. I eventually buried it somewhere safe on the island so I wouldn't accidentally lose it."

"But you brought it to Rog with you," said Thomas.

The old man's mouth twisted up in a wry smile. "When I set out in my boat with the princess and her guard, I left it behind on the island. I'm still not sure why. I think a part of me wanted to give it up. But after we arrived in Rog I decided I'd made the wrong choice. King Krasmir wanted to send a ship to the island to see if the Ahrans had visited it on their return voyage. I volunteered to lead them there mostly because I wanted to retrieve the stone. The Ahrans had turned the place upside down, but they didn't find my hiding place," he said with satisfaction.

He gazed at Thomas and Elena thoughtfully. "This conversation is most unexpected. I certainly wasn't anticipating anything of the kind when I came here today," he said.

"Elena told you that we wouldn't share your secret without your consent," Thomas said. "You have my word on that as well."

Kamash nodded slowly. "Thank you," he said.

"And in case you're wondering, we have no desire to take the stone from you," added Thomas.

The old man's eyebrow quirked up. "You're an unusual pair," he told them.

"It's true," acknowledged Thomas. "We've been on an interesting journey ourselves."

As he exchanged a knowing glance with Elena, her lovely face lit up in a smile of affection. He beamed back a smile of his own.

Kamash grinned at them, plainly enjoying their interaction. "Perhaps I'll get to hear your story sometime," he said.

"Perhaps," Thomas returned noncommittally.

The old man's face gradually became serious. "Why did you want to meet with me today? Apart from being curious about my story, that is."

"It's true that we were curious," Thomas confirmed. "Extremely curious. And we're grateful that you trusted us enough to share your history, and especially to show us the stone. But our main reason for meeting you was because we felt constrained to let you know we were aware of your secret. It would have been inconceivable to behave as if the discovery wasn't significant."

"Are you thinking that others might guess too?" the old man asked, looking at them uncertainly.

Elena shook her head. "I don't think that's likely," she said. "As Thomas mentioned earlier, we were already aware of the existence of your stone. I can't imagine any way someone else could guess without that information."

"Where did you hear about the stone?" Kamash asked. "I've had it for decades, but in spite of that I know nothing about it apart from what the old man told me. And from my own experience of course."

"We learned of it from an old scroll in a library," Thomas replied. "The librarian thought it was nothing more than a fable."

"Is the library in Rog?" the old man asked.

Thomas shook his head. "It's a very long way from here, and not at all easy to find."

"Does anyone else know about the scroll?" Kamash asked.

"Just two other people," Thomas replied. "They're here with us in Rog, but they're rather distracted at the moment."

Kamash looked at them sharply. "Is it Lord Torbury and his wife?" They nodded.

"Do you know anything about the abduction?" Elena asked him.

"Nothing at all," he replied without hesitation.

"What about the princess?" asked Thomas. He berated himself once more for having failed to catch a glimpse of her.

Kamash took longer to answer this time. "Not as far as I know." He looked thoughtful. "I can't imagine that she's involved. The princess isn't a bad person at heart, although in her eyes the glory of her empire takes precedence over everything. That makes her unpredictable." He shrugged. "I agreed to act as her spokesperson because I saw her as young and vulnerable. But perhaps I was mistaken. I don't know her well, and I have no real understanding of the agendas and influences that might be driving her."

The princess almost certainly knew a great deal more than she was letting on, and Thomas had a simple way to settle the issue. "Would it be possible for us to meet the princess?" he asked.

"I can try to set up a meeting," Kamash told him. "But I doubt that she will agree to it anytime soon. The questions from King Krasmir's lords, especially since the abduction, have begun to irritate her. She doesn't believe she's been shown sufficient deference as a princess of the empire."

Kamash's reply dispirited Thomas. Will had entrusted the task of investigating the princess to him, and he could only acknowledge that he had allowed himself to be distracted by Kamash and his stone. It was not the fault of the old man. No one was to blame but himself.

"I am grateful to you both for listening to me patiently," said Kamash. "If there is anything I can do for you, and especially for Lord Torbury and his wife, please let me know without delay."

"Thank you," Elena replied graciously.

"Yes, thank you," Thomas echoed. "We will contact you if we believe you can help in some way."

The old man bowed once and left the room.

After he was gone, Elena turned to Thomas. "So he knows nothing about the other stones?"

"Nothing at all," Thomas confirmed.

"I envy him," Elena said softly.

20

———————

As the days dragged by, it became evident to the monk that he and his young charge were likely to be imprisoned in the cellar for some time. At first Brother Ander worked determinedly to discover a way to escape, but the cellar proved secure against any such attempt. Short of attacking their guards, there was no obvious way to break free of their prison.

The monk remembered the subject of his meditation on the morning he was taken. He had been studying a passage of scripture that said, *'In this world you will have trouble...'* The words had been said long ago, by a man intimately acquainted with trouble. And since becoming that man's disciple, Brother Ander had seen the truth of it demonstrated many times. It was a disturbing promise.

He sighed. He couldn't entirely shield the boy from trouble. But he would do whatever he could to guide him through it.

Having acknowledged that escape was not an option, at least for the moment, Brother Ander instead redirected his attention to occupying Ethen usefully. He knew that five-year-olds needed open air and exercise to thrive. Large as the cellar was, it must surely be claustrophobic for a child. With no possibility of altering their environment, he decided to do everything in his power to at least provide some exercise.

Finding a few old rags in the cellar, the monk fashioned them into a simple ball. Games involving throwing, catching, and kicking the ball quickly became a regular feature of every day. Ethen also became quite adept at walking one of the empty barrels around the space. At first Brother Ander steadied him with one hand, but after a while the boy could stay atop the barrel with ease as it rolled across the floor.

Occasionally their fun became sufficiently boisterous to earn them a sharp rebuke from one of their captors, but for the most part they were left to themselves.

The monk also instituted lessons on a range of subjects. Having never taught a five-year-old, he saw himself as a learner just as much as Ethen, but they soon settled into an afternoon routine of exploring a broad range of topics that included history, geography, science, theology, and medicine. Ethen had inherited his parents' facility with languages, and the two of them spoke Rogandan all morning, reverting to Arvenian for the rest of the day.

Brother Ander's life had changed so much in the previous few years. In his former life, before he met Will and Brother Vangellis, he could never have imagined being willing to spend time in this way. Yet he was content.

One afternoon as they sat together sharing the latest delivery of bread and water, Ethen asked once more about his parents.

"They'll still be looking for you, Ethen," the monk assured him. "And knowing your father as I do, I wouldn't want to be one of our captors when he finds you."

"How did you meet my father?" the boy asked.

"I knew about him before I actually met him," the monk replied. "He was commanding soldiers at Arnost, the capital of Arvenon. He was quite famous because he managed to prevent the Rogandans from destroying a large town called Danford. Later, when we were at war with the Rogandans, their army commander wanted to capture other towns, and your father set out to stop him. He took a few people with him, and I was one of them. So I traveled with him for some time."

"Tell me about it!"

Brother Ander had many stories to relate that centered around Will, and as time went by he shared them freely with Ethen. The boy listened intently, his eyes wide.

"I never knew about any of this!" he said after hearing about Will's efforts on behalf of Baron Rudungen's oppressed villagers.

The monk smiled. "Your father isn't one to sound his own praises."

The stories entertained Ethen, and they had a way of settling him too.

Difficult times were impossible to understand when you were living through them. The monk hoped these stories might show the boy that the most harrowing experiences also became the best adventures once they were behind you.

ELENA CROUCHED in the shadows beside Amyra and Rufe. They had positioned themselves behind a wagon, keeping out of sight as they watched people come and go from a tavern.

Abruptly Elena gripped Amyra's arm.

"What is it? Have you seen one of the Ahrans?" hissed Amyra.

Elena shook her head. She pointed to the woman who had just emerged from the tavern. "She's had contact with one of them."

The woman paused in the middle of the street as if undecided about which way to go.

"Do you want me to grab her?" whispered Rufe.

"There's no need," Elena replied softly. "I already know everything of value she could tell us."

She peered at the woman briefly before nodding to herself. "Wait here for a moment," she said to Rufe and Amyra. Then, ignoring their frowns, she stepped out from behind the wagon.

At first the woman looked at her warily as she approached,

although she apparently soon decided that Elena presented no threat.

Elena drew close to her. "May I tell you something?" she asked quietly. "I think it will benefit you."

The woman stared at Elena suspiciously, clearly torn between irritation and contempt, but she didn't move away.

Leaning forward a little, Elena whispered in her ear.

The woman stiffened, then her eyes opened wide in surprise. Tears trickled down her cheeks, and she began to gasp, convulsively sucking in gulps of air. She abandoned any attempt to master herself, and great sobs wracked her body. No doubt realizing she would soon draw unwanted attention to herself, she scurried away without a backward glance.

Elena hurried back to the others, and they headed immediately for the palace.

"What was that about?" demanded Amyra. "If you have information from the woman, we need to get it back to Will without delay. Why were you wasting time on her?"

"She hates herself," Elena replied gently. "It's damaged her unnecessarily. I wanted her to understand that other choices are available to her."

"Her happiness isn't our responsibility," growled Amyra.

"I know you want to rescue Ethen," replied Elena, "and that's what I want too. But that woman has no knowledge of the abduction, and it only took a couple of minutes to help her."

When Amyra glared at her, Elena shrugged helplessly. "People's lives are often a mess, but sometimes a small change can tidy things up a lot. It can make a big difference to the person, and to everyone who depends on them."

Amyra showed no interest in her explanation, concentrating only on hurrying along.

How could Elena begin to explain what it was like to suddenly enter the mind of another person and become immersed in their life? How could she hope to account for the overwhelming sense of responsibility that came over her—the pressing need to make a difference when she knew she could?

Pushing the woman's inner turmoil from her mind, she tried to refocus on what had been revealed about the Ahran agents.

———

AMYRA PRESSED FORWARD RELENTLESSLY, trying to overcome her feelings of anger. Elena was far too soft. Didn't she understand that every minute counted?

Their path took them down a back alley. Turning a corner, Amyra found her way completely blocked by a pile of garbage. She waved an arm irritably at the reeking mound, and the pile instantly disintegrated. Refuse flew through the air, landing on roofs and plastering itself on the sides of buildings. Ignoring the astonishment of Elena, who was immediately behind her, Amyra pressed on through the newly cleared path.

The power of the Stone of Authority had given expression to Amyra's agitation. But acting on her frustrations did little to ease them. If anything she was left feeling more unsettled than ever.

Before long her attempts to contain her distress failed miserably. Her exasperation burst out again, this time with a different target. With an open scowl, she faced Elena. "Why do you care about that woman? You don't even know her!"

"Her life matters, even if I don't know her," Elena replied calmly.

"It doesn't matter to me!" Amyra shot back indignantly. "My son has been abducted! Anyone even vaguely assisting the people who did it deserves no pity, from me or anyone else."

"I wonder if any one of us really deserves pity," Elena returned quietly.

Amyra frowned. What was that supposed to mean? Had Elena been directing her last comment at Amyra?

"Are you looking into my mind?" she demanded.

"Of course not!" Elena exclaimed. "We've told you we never use the stone on our friends, and it's true. I wouldn't violate you in that way."

A grunt was Amyra's only response. She tried to ignore the interaction, but Elena's comment still pressed in on her, whether it had been directed at her or not.

Did she deserve pity?

She had been tense and unhappy. Of course she had. Who could blame her under the circumstances? Her precious son had been snatched away.

Her thoughts swirled restlessly as she revisited her behavior and her attitude, intent on justifying herself. But a niggle of doubt would not let go. The truth was that her unhappiness had not begun with the abduction. She had been irritable and unhappy from the very moment they set out on this trip.

To begin with she was angry with Will for leaving Arvenon and going to Rog. That reaction wasn't entirely fair of course, as she well knew. Refusing the king would have been unthinkable.

It certainly was Will's fault that she was in Rog with the children though. With both parents heading to Rogand, they couldn't possibly leave the children behind.

She hadn't wanted to come; she was only there because of the Stone of Authority. Will saw her stone as an important weapon in his armory, just as he did with the Stone of Knowing. He wanted the stones available in case he needed them.

She tried to tell herself his attitude was selfish and unnecessary. But it wasn't that simple. Will didn't care about the stones for his own sake. And they were undeniably useful. Her stone had been the reason their ship made it safely through the storm. And Thomas and Elena's stone had been crucial as well; she herself had come to rely heavily on it since the abduction.

Everything had become so complicated and messy. Even so, she had a right to her anger and distress.

An image of Will's face came unbidden to her mind. He had woken that morning with a haunted look on his face. Normally so unruffled in a crisis, Will's composure had deserted him of late. Ethen was his son too. How could he be expected to retain his equanimity?

Her husband was clearly hurting as well, and it occurred to her to wonder what she'd done to support him in his grief. She'd certainly made it very clear she blamed him.

And what about Millie? Amyra had scarcely spared their daughter a thought in the past few days.

Elena's words came to her again. *I wonder if any one of us really deserves pity.* Amyra frowned uncomfortably. Could she lay claim to deserving pity?

A groan of misery escaped her lips. Abruptly abandoning the battle to justify herself, she accepted the truth. She had been behaving badly—there was no way to pretend otherwise. She'd felt so demoralized and defeated though. What else could she do?

The royal guards admitted them to the palace grounds, and they arrived at their accommodation with Amyra still unable to find peace. She tried to push her inner conflict to one side as Will joined them and Elena passed on what she had learned.

"We saw a woman leaving the tavern," Elena was saying. "She sells bread. Two men with foreign accents approached the woman and bought a few loaves. She saw where they were staying. I can show you where it is."

"Maybe we should ask the Rogandans for support before we go in," Rufe suggested.

"No," said Will emphatically. "A big group of men moving in might alert the Ahrans. We need to take them by surprise. And King Krasmir's men answer to him, not me—I'm not willing to risk losing control of the situation. We'll take Breysen with us. The three of us can handle it. Amyra and Elena should both be resting, but we're going to need Elena. Haldek can come as well to protect her."

As they were moving out Amyra approached Will. "Be careful!" she urged him, touching him lightly on the arm.

Flinching at her touch, he turned away with a frown of bemusement. Then without an acknowledgment of any kind he hurried off, his attention entirely focused on the operation ahead of him.

Amyra stood staring after them long after they had gone. She didn't show it, but his response had shaken her. Until that moment she hadn't fully allowed herself to grasp the extent to which she had become distanced from other people.

A dull ache in her head was beginning to throb uncomfortably, and she knew she needed to lie down before the headache blinded her. Holding her head, she stumbled to her bed. An insistent thought poked and prodded at her as she lay down—she had done more than just allow herself to become distanced from others. She had been actively pushing people away. Especially Will.

WILL PULLED at the reins of the horse, and the creaking of the wagon slowly ceased as it came to a halt.

"That's it over there!" Elena said softly, pointing to a building a short distance away.

As he peered forward in the dark, Will's mouth twisted in a grim smile of satisfaction. They must surely be drawing close at last. Handing the reins to Haldek, he climbed down from the wagon, Rufe and Breysen behind him.

Haldek moved into the driver's seat and took the reins, with Elena settling herself beside him.

"Don't leave Elena's side, whatever happens," Will whispered to Haldek.

Haldek nodded without speaking.

Gesturing to his companions, Will set off casually along the street. Rufe walked a couple of steps behind him. Breysen headed away in the other direction and soon disappeared.

When they reached the building, Will waved Rufe back out of sight. Approaching the door, he banged on it three times with his fist.

Nothing happened for several minutes. Then the door opened a crack, a face peering out suspiciously.

"Good evening, friend," said Will cheerfully. "May I come in?"

"No! Go away!" The speaker could not hide a heavy accent.

As the door was about to slam in Will's face, he pulled a short beam of timber from behind his back and jammed it into the crack. Then the massive frame of Rufe appeared beside him. Throwing themselves at the door, the two men forced their way into the building.

The foreigner came at them with a sword. Dodging past him, Will moved deeper into the building. Rufe could handle the swordsman. Another man appeared out of the shadows, swinging a sword wildly in the confined space. Barely managing to avoid it, Will stepped forward and smashed his fist into his attacker's face. The man went down hard and didn't get up.

Stepping over him, Will scaled a flight of stairs. Candlelight flickered ahead of him, and he moved cautiously into a long narrow room with three beds. The room was empty. Finding no one else in the upper level, he hurried back down the stairs.

Rufe's attacker was also lying prone on the floor, and the big guardsman did not appear to be hurt.

Pausing for a moment, Will heard a commotion at the back of the building. He raced forward, Rufe close behind him, and surprised a third man trying to escape through a rear door.

Redoubling his efforts, the man finally forced the door open to find Breysen blocking his path. He barely had time to raise his sword before both men were upon him from behind. Will had picked up a large earthenware jug, and he smashed it down hard on the man's head. The man crumpled.

Rufe bent down to examine him. "He's dead," he announced evenly.

Will grunted. He hadn't intended to kill the man, but he was in no mood to be gentle.

"Drive the wagon around the back," he instructed Breysen. The blacksmith nodded, and hurried away at once.

"Bring the other two here after you've tied them up," Will told Rufe. "I'll check the rest of the building."

He didn't say it, but he hadn't abandoned hope of finding Ethen and Brother Ander locked in a basement of the building.

It wasn't until he had conducted an exhaustive search that Will finally accepted he wasn't going to find his son in this place. The exercise hadn't been a complete waste of time. He would turn the surviving agents over to King Krasmir for questioning. But only after Elena had stripped anything of value from their minds.

Barely conscious, the two men trussed up by Rufe were bundled into the wagon. After wrapping the body of the third, they loaded him in as well and set off for the palace.

Will took the reins once more, and Elena sat beside him. He had seen her examining the men closely as they were being lifted into the wagon.

"What can you tell me?" he asked quietly, trying not to sound too eager.

"If other agents are holding a man and a boy, these men are not aware of it," Elena whispered back.

"Do they know where other agents are located?" asked Will.

"They seem to have at least a vague idea," she replied. "I'm not confident I could identify the exact place, but I think I can find the general area."

"Who is their leader?" Will asked.

"They meet regularly with a man who gives them instructions. They know he isn't the main leader though. They don't know who that is, but they have their suspicions."

Will was instantly alert. "Who?"

"They think it might be the Grand Vizier."

The idea that the Grand Vizier was directing the agents personally seemed preposterous to Will, but he didn't say so. "How many agents do the Ahrans have?" he asked.

"They know of quite a few," she said. "I'm worried about what will happen if you try to take all of them on yourselves, Will," she added with a worried frown. "I think there are too many for the three of you to handle."

Will nodded. "When we came here tonight I thought these men might be the ones holding Ethen," he said, jerking a head toward their captives. "I was even hoping we might be able to free him and take him home. But now we're no closer to finding him."

"I'm sorry, Will," she said.

He shrugged helplessly. "The Ahran network is clearly bigger than we imagined. And since they haven't drawn attention to themselves, at least some of them must speak Rogandan without noticeable accents. It's time we involved King Krasmir."

21

———————

Having once again sought out King Krasmir, Will sat with him in a small reception room.

"My own inquiries have led me to three Ahran agents, Your Majesty. Unfortunately one of them was killed when we attempted to subdue them. I have questioned the other two closely without learning anything that could lead me to my son. I will turn the men over to you whenever you are ready to take charge of them."

The king's eyebrows went up in surprise. "To achieve results like that you must have an extensive network of your own, Lord Torbury. Yet its existence has escaped my detection. I confess to being astonished."

Will smiled humorlessly. "I have no such network, Your Majesty. This connection came solely from my own very vigorous inquiries. I am sure my success is due to little more than dumb luck."

He flinched internally as he said it. Such dishonesty was uncharacteristic for him, but nothing had felt normal since his son was abducted. And he had no intention of revealing anything to King Krasmir about the Stone of Knowing.

"If we have succeeded in identifying five agents between us," said the king, "the Ahrans must have more people out there than we supposed."

"I agree, Your Majesty," said Will. "Our questioning has pointed us to the general vicinity of other Ahran agents. I am hoping you might agree to a joint operation to flush them out."

"The idea of allowing an Arvenian nobleman to participate in an operation in my own capital city is beyond unusual, Lord Torbury. But these are unusual times. I am willing to allow you to join us. On one condition."

Will raised his eyebrows. "What is that, Your Majesty?"

"That you cease your independent activities immediately." The king's face was grim. "I cannot have foreigners roaming my streets and killing people without my knowledge or consent."

Will winced. "I accept your condition of course, Your Majesty," he said, bowing low. "And I freely acknowledge that my own intensely personal interest in this matter has led me well beyond recognized diplomatic conventions and into some very murky waters. I am indebted to you for your gracious response. Please accept my sincere apologies for placing you in such a position. It will not happen again."

RESTLESS AND ON EDGE, Bolnyk waited on a low hill above a secluded beach north of Rog. As the senior agent responsible for the entire Ahran network in Rogand, he had many pressing matters competing for his attention. The arrival in Rogand of his master, the Grand Vizier, eclipsed them all.

The dim outline of a ship appeared, sailing in close to the shoreline. At almost the same moment, the first glimmers of daylight appeared in the sky, slowly transforming the dark smudges around him into a series of low hills on either side of a pale beach.

As Bolnyk waited expectantly, longboats were lowered from the ship, and dark figures clambered down into the boats. Pushing away from the ship, the sailors pulled vigorously toward the beach.

As the boats approached the shallows, Bolnyk hurried down onto the sand and called a greeting in the Ahran language.

"Get on with it!" a voice called imperiously to the sailors. Bending to their oars once more, they caught a wave that pushed the boat up onto the sand. The boat remained fast as the wave sucked back toward the sea. Two sailors leaped from the boat into the shallows, hauling the craft further onto the beach with the next wave.

Once the wave had retreated, the Grand Vizier stepped carefully out of the boat, grimacing as the sand squelched beneath him, soaking his shoes.

Bolnyk hurried forward to welcome him, bowing low. The agent led his master to a horse and helped him into the saddle. The chief minister left the beach without a backward glance.

"Update me on what has been happening since I left Rog," he commanded, pulling alongside Bolnyk's horse.

"Her Highness the Princess Neira arrived in Rog not long after you left, Your Eminence," the agent replied.

The chief minister sat rigid in the saddle, clearly stunned. Bolnyk pretended not to notice, peering resolutely forward in the dim light.

"Tell me everything you know about the princess," the chief minister growled.

The agent found himself answering many questions. They had barely finished before arriving at a large house.

"We arranged for the purchase of this farm after the previous owner recently died of natural causes," Bolnyk informed his master. "The property is situated in a sparsely settled location relatively close to Rog, and the house is well concealed in the middle of an extensive parcel of land. We have been using it as our main base. It includes a separate building that we have set aside for the exclusive use of Your Eminence."

"What of my instructions regarding the High Priest?" the chief minister asked.

"I put Kaifet, my best man, on the job. After the High Priest refused to meet with him, Kaifet went to the temple at night with a team of twenty of our best men to bring the High Priest in for questioning."

"And?" demanded the chief minister.

Bolnyk lowered his gaze. "We have heard nothing of them since."

The Grand Vizier turned away. "The priest's time will come," he pronounced. "Once we have subdued this puny kingdom we will quickly bring him to heel." He spared a glance for Bolnyk. "Leave me now. I will call for you later."

"Certainly, Your Eminence," the agent replied with a bow.

Bolnyk hurried away. The Grand Vizier would have a great deal to think about. Having served his master from the time when he was merely Bisri Rheibas, the agent knew him well enough to know how much he valued time alone and undisturbed.

LESS THAN AN HOUR passed before Bolnyk was again summoned to the side of Rheibas. A parchment, apparently a letter, lay open on a table before the chief minister. A quick glance at the fire showed singed fragments of other parchments—Bolnyk guessed that a number of drafts had been consigned to the fire on the way to the final version.

Bolnyk was aware that his master made a habit of disclosing more information to him than to anyone else, so it was no surprise when Rheibas waved a hand lazily toward the parchment, inviting the agent to read it.

Picking it up, he scrutinized it carefully.

To Her Imperial Highness the Princess Neira,

I rejoiced more than I can possibly say when I heard of your safe arrival in Rog! The news brought me comfort beyond words after the treachery of Captain Gharpin on our earlier voyage. He waited until I was confined to my cabin with illness, then he secretly arranged for his men to abandon you on the island. I was entirely unaware of his action. I wrongly believed that you were still on the ship until the moment we arrived in Rog.

For failing in my solemn duty to protect you I can only humbly apologize. I did, of course, insist that the ship return to the island as soon as possible to rescue you. I was dismayed to discover that no trace of you could be found there.

Revealing the truth to the Rogandans was out of the question. I could not have lived with the dishonor it would have brought to our beloved empire. I was left with the painful task of concocting a report that would somehow present an act of treachery in an advantageous light. I accordingly stated that you had been forcibly removed from our ship in an act of piracy, and demanded that the Rogandans find a way to return you at once. I take what comfort I can from the knowledge that I did my best to ensure that this shameful setback did not injure the empire.

Given Your Highness's unshakable loyalty, I know I can rely on you to labor mightily with me to advance the cause of your exalted father. I will look forward to working closely with you as soon as we are able to make direct contact.

I trust that this letter finds Your Highness well and in good heart, in spite of the trials you have been forced to endure.

Ever your humble servant,

Rheibas, Chief Minister of Ahr

P.S. Powerless as I was to prevent the perfidy of Captain Gharpin at the time, it gives me satisfaction to assure you that he has since been dealt with appropriately.

P.P.S. I have ordered my agent Bolnyk to retrieve and destroy this communication as soon as you have read it.

BOLNYK DID NOT EXPECT his master to invite comment, and Rheibas did not surprise him. The agent was well aware that this accounting of events could not be reconciled with what the chief minister had told the Rogandans, and no doubt the emperor as well. Bolnyk didn't care about the discrepancy—his loyalty was to the Grand Vizier—but it was obvious that his master was faced with a major problem.

Whether the princess would be satisfied with the chief minister's explanation remained to be seen.

"Take this letter to the princess," the chief minister commanded. "It must be delivered into her hand, and her hand alone. Do you understand?"

"Yes, Your Eminence," the agent replied.

"Make sure she returns it to you as soon as she has read it. Destroy it as soon as you leave her. You have never failed me, Bolnyk. Do not disappoint me this time."

The agent dipped his head respectfully.

The letter was at least written in the Ahran language, which offered some security from prying eyes, but he could see why Rheibas wanted it destroyed. Its very existence constituted a grave risk, and leaving it with someone as unreliable as Princess Neira would be unthinkable.

As he was about to leave, Rheibas held up a hand to forestall him. "I want a report that covers all of our agents. I'll give you two days, no longer. They know what they are supposed to be doing—I expect details on their progress."

Bolnyk bowed low. Then he headed for the door.

***

WILL STOOD beside the Rogandan commander as his soldiers moved silently into position in the darkness. Lord Kulferan was a man of few words, but Will had quickly seen that he was both effective and focused.

Leaning forward, Will whispered in the commander's ear. "Your men have been instructed to keep some of them alive, My Lord. For questioning." He pulled away, looking expectantly at the Rogandan. "Have I understood that correctly?"

Lord Kulferan stared back at him for a moment before nodding once.

Satisfied, Will returned his attention to the dwelling facing them. Situated not far from the bustling city of Rog, it stood alone in a field surrounded by farmland. The commander's soldiers had been quietly observing the building all day, and they had reported seeing men coming and going constantly. They expected to find at least ten men sheltering in it. Some of the men had been monitored surreptitiously, and there was no doubt that they were foreign.

Will was confident that this house was an important center for Ahran activity in the region. It could well be the place they were looking for.

Thomas hovered nearby, no doubt hanging back in an attempt to remain inconspicuous. That suited Will perfectly. The stone was the only reason Thomas was there; he needed to stay well away from any action.

The dwelling was now surrounded, with men covering every point of access. The Rogandan nobleman now raised a torch high. At the signal, four soldiers rushed to the front door supporting a small tree trunk. Swinging it back, they shattered the door in a single mighty blow before stepping aside to allow a dozen others to race into the house.

Would this be the place where Ethen was being held? Will could barely contain himself from joining the soldiers. He looked pleadingly at Lord Kulferan. After what felt like an eternity, the Rogandan nobleman turned to him and nodded. Will sprinted to the house and pushed his way inside.

A chaotic scene awaited him. Furniture lay strewn about the building, with maybe a dozen bodies sprawled on the floor. The occupants of the house had clearly put up a fight, and it had not gone well for them. Four of the fallen appeared to be Lord Kulferan's soldiers.

A staircase led upward, and Will took it two steps at a time. Reaching the top of the stairs, he emerged into a passageway that led to three rooms. Two of the rooms were empty. The door of the third had been pulled from its hinges. Inside the room a man lay unmoving on the floor. Another, seemingly uninjured, was being restrained by two of Lord Kulferan's men.

A quick glance around revealed no sign of Ethen or Brother Ander, and no place where they could have been hidden. Leaping down the stairs Will began searching for a basement.

A trapdoor lay in the floor. Soldiers must have found and opened it, and sounds of movement drifted up from below. Spotting a ladder in the opening, Will drew his sword before lowering himself into the hole and clambering down the ladder. Two soldiers with torches could be seen ahead of him, peering around cautiously.

As he moved forward to join them, he was attacked from both sides. Barely avoiding the thrusting swords, he sprang deeper into the cellar before pivoting around to face his attackers. Lunging out in a series of aggressive thrusts, he forced the men back against the ladder. Both of his opponents—one stocky and the other taller—knew how to fight, and he soon had little chance to consider anything except survival.

Cries behind him suggested that the soldiers who preceded him were also under attack. Will could only hope that they would prevent anyone from attacking him from behind.

Other soldiers were now trying to push down into the cellar. The taller of Will's attackers directed his attention to the floor above, his sword flicking upward as he tried to keep them out. Driving swiftly forward, Will avoided a hasty swipe from the stocky man and took the taller one in the side. His target went down with a cry of pain. Confusion reigned as the stocky man fought Will while simultaneously struggling to prevent reinforcements descending into the cellar.

Will could not allow all of these men to die. For Thomas to be able to discover everything they knew, Will needed to keep as many of them alive as possible. Choosing his moment carefully, he leaned swiftly forward and punched the stocky man hard in the face. Stunned, the man dropped his guard. It was only for a moment, but it was enough. Punching him hard a second time, Will leaped at him and threw him roughly to the floor just as two soldiers hurried down the ladder.

"Tie him up," Will ordered. "And keep him alive for questioning!"

Leaving the new arrivals to assist their comrades in ending resistance in the cellar, Will began methodically searching the cellar for hidden doors. Nothing obvious could be found in the area near the ladder. He could not examine the rest of the cellar until the fighting had ended there. More men arrived even as he was considering throwing himself into the fray, and he decided to let them do their work.

The fighting soon ended, but the cellar was now crowded with soldiers, and Will was forced to wait for an opportunity to explore the rest of it.

Eventually he got his chance. An initial examination showed nothing that looked like an entrance to a hidden room. But upon closer inspection he found a section of the cellar that had been filled with old furniture. An opening was barely visible, mostly obscured behind a large cupboard. Calling for help, he positioned himself to one side of the object and began to strain. Others quickly joined him, and the cupboard was moved aside. Behind it lay a door.

Will forced it open. With heart pounding, he grabbed a torch from one of the soldiers and groped his way inside. He found a large space filled with empty barrels—apparently nothing more than an unused extension to the cellar. Dust covered everything. It was clear that no one had visited this room in a very long time.

Struggling to master his disappointment, Will left the room and carefully examined the cellar from one end to another. Finding nothing further of interest, he clambered back up the ladder and subjected the rest of the house to a close examination. His efforts were fruitless.

The only remaining hope was for Thomas to learn something useful from the survivors. Pushing his way out of the house into the night, he saw that the Ahrans had been rounded up. They huddled together, surrounded by a large group of armed men.

Looking around impatiently, Will eventually spotted Thomas. He had positioned himself near enough to the survivors to get a good look at them without getting too close.

Will hurried over to him. "Ethen isn't here," he growled.

This information clearly was not news to Thomas. He shook his head. "No, this is not the place where Ethen and Brother Ander are being held. None of the Ahrans know anything about the abduction, either. They are only aware of their own immediate contacts. They don't even know for certain who is leading their mission."

Frustration gripped Will, causing him to cry out in exasperation. A few heads turned in their direction, but most of the soldiers ignored them.

"Do any of them know of other safe houses being used by the Ahrans?" asked Will.

"Yes," Thomas replied. "One of them knows the location of another house." He pointed to one of the Ahrans who was sitting on the ground. The man was carrying injuries from the fighting, and he looked dazed.

Will shook his head in irritation. They seemed no closer to finding his son. Already impatient to explore the next location, he would be reduced to waiting in the hope that Lord Kulferan would eventually find out through questioning what Thomas already knew.

Could he speed up the process by encouraging the commander to focus all of his attention on the one man with information worth extracting? It didn't take Will long to decide that the risks outweighed the benefits. He could think of no credible way to explain how he had acquired such knowledge. King Krasmir had already expressed surprise at the amount of information Will had unearthed with limited resources.

As far as Will was concerned, that night's operation could only be viewed as a failure. Shutting down an active cell of Ahran agents would undoubtedly be seen as a useful outcome by King Krasmir. But it made no difference to Will. His only goal was to find and release his son. Nothing else mattered to him.

Time was running short. With a serious push being made against the Ahran agents, all of them would soon be aware of it. The risk of spooking them would increase with every unsuccessful operation.

Sooner or later they would decide that holding on to Ethen was too risky.

There was no telling what might happen then.

22

———————

Weary of continually finding himself at a loose end, the young king of Castel wondered what had possessed him to come to Rog. The stakes had certainly been high when Rupert first made the decision; responding effectively to the Ahran threat was easily the most pressing issue for Castel as well as for every other kingdom in the region. But after arriving in Rog it hadn't taken long before progress stalled completely.

The initial meetings with the princess had failed to bring any real clarity about a way forward. That was no great surprise to him.

Then Lord Torbury's son had been abducted. It had only just happened, and all of Lord Torbury's friends, including Rupert, were still reeling from it.

If the Ahrans were responsible for the kidnapping as suspected, it had been an astute move on their part. All attention had been diverted away from the broader strategic threat in a determined attempt to address the immediate issue. Yet the best efforts of King Krasmir had so far yielded nothing.

Rupert felt keenly for Lord and Lady Torbury. But beyond expressing concern and support there was little he could do.

Stranded in a foreign capital with no role to play and no compelling reason even to be there, he had rarely felt so useless.

It didn't help his confidence that he'd begun so badly with the Ahran princess either. Before they left Varacellan she had done a masterful job of exposing his insecurities, standing by and witnessing his discomfort with evident relish. Supremely embarrassing as the interactions had been, he decided they revealed as much about her as they did about him. Even her spokesperson, Kamash, apparently saw her behavior as volatile and inappropriate.

The wing of the palace where the foreign contingent had been accommodated was surrounded by an extensive area of cultivated gardens. With nothing better to do, Rupert had taken to wandering both in these gardens and beyond in the extensive grounds that surrounded the palace. He had no concerns at all about his safety. Royal guards had been conspicuous even before the abduction. The palace almost seemed to be swarming with them since.

On that afternoon, Rupert had been rambling aimlessly once more in the gardens. Finding a bench beside a large hedge, he sat down and closed his eyes, soaking in the sunshine. Only a few minutes passed before his peaceful reverie was shattered by an enthusiastic yapping sound. Looking down he saw an Alaunt puppy at his feet, its eager face turned up to his. The wriggling ball of fur leaped up repeatedly, its little tail waving back and forth frantically.

Reaching down, he scooped it into his arms with a welcoming grin. The puppy was soon desperately trying to reach his face with its tongue, causing him to hold it at arms length while he laughed at its antics.

"Maxie, come back here you little truant!" called a voice.

Twisting around, Rupert saw a face framed by a hole in the hedge. A girl of perhaps eighteen or nineteen emerged from the hedge, her face flushed and her dark hair disheveled.

"I'm so sorry!" she exclaimed. "He's such a scamp!"

"It's no problem," Rupert replied. "Maxie and I have been getting acquainted." Acutely aware of his limited mastery of Rogandan, he tried to hide his awkwardness with a smile.

Apparently sensing his self-consciousness, the girl switched effortlessly to Arvenian. "You must be a member of the foreign delegation, My Lord," she offered, bowing low.

Clearly she had no idea he was a reigning monarch—how could she? He dipped his head in response, choosing not to enlighten her. Why spoil the moment by standing on ceremony?

"You speak excellent Arvenian," he said.

"Thank you, My Lord," she replied humbly. "It is a useful skill to have in a palace."

"It is indeed," he confirmed with a nod.

It hadn't escaped his notice that a high proportion of the servants assigned to the delegation spoke quite passable Arvenian. Rupert had no doubt that some of them did much more than just serve. King Krasmir's agents would be scattered among them, reporting everything they overheard.

"Foreign language skills are highly prized with palace servants in our capital city, too," he observed.

She dipped her head gravely, not managing to entirely conceal the delicate flush that tinged her cheeks.

It occurred to him to wonder if this young woman might herself be an agent. He promptly dismissed the idea. She had a delightfully artless air about her.

"What kind of service are you involved in?" he asked, glancing down at the puppy, who had nestled comfortably in his arms as he stroked it behind the ears.

"I attend to the princesses," she replied seriously. "And the crown prince."

His eyes widened in surprise. "Tell me about them," he suggested, recovering himself.

"There are three daughters and one son. Crown Prince Rimek is the oldest." She eyed him appraisingly. "You must be about his age."

He looked askance at her. "And how old might that be?"

She laughed. "I think you must be in your mid-twenties."

He brought his eyebrows back under control, granting her a modest smile. "Go on," he commanded.

She grinned at him. "Did you know that Crown Prince Rimek arrived in the world just minutes before his sister, Princess Ashloh? I think he's been running hard ever since to stay ahead of her." Her eyes twinkled merrily. "Then there's the neglected middle sister, Princess Kyla. She isn't really neglected, of course," she assured him. "Finally there's the youngest, Princess Teylee. She is my age."

This latest piece of information was accompanied by another delicate blush.

Rupert found it endearing. Nevertheless he nodded wisely. "And what is your role?"

"I try to keep them out of trouble, My Lord." A dimpled smile lit up her face.

He grinned back at her. He couldn't help it.

"But my most important task seems to be to lend a listening ear to them," she added seriously.

He quirked an eyebrow.

A merry laugh burst from her lips. "I don't wonder that you doubt me. I've done no listening at all—I've been talking your ear off!"

"No you haven't," he insisted. Then he frowned at her. "You've talked about everyone except yourself. You haven't even told me your name."

She paused, as if uncertain about sharing such a confidence. Then she seemed to come to a decision. "My name is Tasha. And what's your name?"

It was his turn to pause. "I'm Boyd," he replied.

"Lord Boyd," she corrected.

He executed a sweeping bow in response.

It never occurred to him to say he was King Rupert. And he hadn't told her a lie. 'Boyd' was the affectionate nickname his sister had used throughout his childhood. He still had no idea where it came from. Having now set a course, he decided to steer by it.

"Tell me about your home and what you do there, Lord Boyd," she said, trying vainly to bring her hair under control as she settled herself on the ground.

"Well," he replied. "There are just two of us in my family. I have an older sister, called Sandy. She's the talented and successful one in the family."

She eyed him skeptically.

"As for my home and what I do there, I live at Castel Citadel, the capital of Castel, and I'm learning to do administration. The capital is truly striking, Tasha. The citadel is crowned by a fortress built from gray stone with tall battlements. Behind it is a towering cliff face, and below it is the city, bounded by a wall that follows a broad sweep of river. The houses are built largely of stone. It is a beautiful city. The kingdom is much smaller and less populous than Rogand, but it is prosperous and peaceful, and for the most part its citizens are contented."

The afternoon slipped away as he told her about the fishing villages by the sea, and the fruit crops famous throughout the region.

She soaked in his descriptions and smiled at his enthusiasm for his country. She also asked many intelligent questions, listening intently to his answers. He could scarcely recall a more attentive and responsive audience.

"I could keep talking for hours," he told her. "But that would hardly be fair. Tell me about your home!"

In her turn she gave her perspective on the city of Rog. Having traveled a little with the royal family, she went on to describe the attractive coastline that fringed the city and the shipping that frequented its waters. Above all, she talked about the people and what shaped them. He felt as if he was beginning to see and appreciate Rogand for the first time.

He had no idea how long they had been there. He only knew it wasn't nearly long enough.

"I've talked far too much," she said apologetically.

"But you haven't told me anything about your family!" he protested. "You've only mentioned the royals."

Before she could respond, a voice broke across their conversation. "There you are, Tasha! Whatever have you been doing all this time?"

Twisting round once more, he saw another face poking through the hole in the hedge.

"I've been chasing Maxie," Tasha cried. "He's so naughty!"

Turning to Rupert, she bobbed her head quickly. "I'm so sorry to have troubled you, My Lord. Thank you for your help with our dog!"

The puppy had found its way back to him, and she held out her arms for it. Then before he could think of a word to say, she was pushing her way back through the hedge with Maxie grasped securely in her arms.

He shook his head in bewilderment, trying to understand what had just happened. He remained in the garden, striving to convince himself he was lingering there to enjoy the sunshine.

Eventually the dark and the cold drove him inside.

THE NEXT DAY Rupert hurried out into the garden as soon as he could manage it without attracting undue attention. Making his way directly to the bench he had occupied the previous day, he was dismayed to find that the hole in the hedge had been stopped up. Until that moment he hadn't honestly acknowledged to himself how much he wanted to see Tasha again.

What was wrong with him? Having allowed himself to be flustered and humbled by the vain princess of Ahr, he was now pining for a pretty Rogandan servant girl. He knew he ought to be ashamed of himself, but it didn't stop him wishing he could spend more time with her.

With no reason to remain where he was, he headed out into the palace grounds, hoping to catch a glimpse of what lay on the other side of the tall hedge that separated the adjoining gardens. He soon discovered that a high stone wall enclosed any sections of the garden not bordered by hedges. No access to Tasha's garden would be possible from anywhere except the palace buildings. The area was private and concealed, which came as no surprise since it was apparently used exclusively by the royal family.

No passageway joined the adjacent wings of the palace. He would connect with Tasha out of doors or not at all. It was immensely frustrating to be so close to someone but with no way of seeing them, much less meeting them.

After a long period of hesitation, Rupert tentatively approached a large gate in the outer wall. Several guards appeared from nowhere, eyeing him suspiciously. He changed direction immediately, hoping he had merely seemed curious.

Over the next couple of days he tried to put Tasha out of his mind. His attempts resulted in dismal failure. He could not forget the sparkle in her eyes and her guileless laugh. His final resort was to tell himself that sudden infatuations always withered over time. What else could he do?

Ridiculous as it seemed, the week that followed Rupert's meeting with Tasha began to feel like one of the most gloomy periods he had endured for years. He hadn't felt so disconsolate since Lord Eisgold's treachery.

Then everything changed abruptly, thanks to an unexpected encounter. Walking in the outer palace grounds, Rupert heard a sound he recognized. The excited yapping of a puppy grew suddenly louder as a familiar figure bounced into view.

"Maxie! What are you doing here alone?" he asked, reaching down for the eager little Alaunt.

Moments later, several horsemen rode up. A young man about his own age dismounted and approached him.

"Does Maxie belong to you?" Rupert asked.

"He does," the other replied, reaching out for the puppy. "Thank you."

As Rupert handed over the Alaunt, a memory came to him from a brief glimpse of the royal family at the palace. "You're Crown Prince Rimek, aren't you?"

"I am," he replied.

Rupert bowed respectfully.

The crown prince gazed at Rupert with considerable curiosity. "You wouldn't be Lord Boyd by any chance, would you?"

Rupert started, his heart skipping a beat. Tasha must have spoken of him to the crown prince. Not trusting himself to speak, he nodded.

The men who had accompanied the prince were still mounted. Gazing at one of them in particular, the prince pointed at the puppy before flicking his head meaningfully to one side. Taking his meaning, the guard approached the prince and took the wriggling Alaunt. Then he guided his horse out of earshot, calling to the other guards to join him.

The prince turned back to Rupert. "You want to see her again, don't you?"

A deep blush warmed Rupert's face. Pushing down his embarrassment, he nodded once more.

"Are you from Castel?" the prince asked pointedly.

Rupert nodded again, more uncomfortable than ever. His unplanned deception had seemed so innocent, but it was already becoming complicated. His supposed identity would not long survive careful scrutiny.

He soon discovered that the prince had guessed the truth. "Does she know who you really are, Your Majesty?" he asked, his eyes narrowing.

Rupert swallowed. There was no way to lather this situation with honey. He shook his head. "She has no idea that I'm King Rupert, Your Highness. I know how it must seem—a king wanting to spend time with a servant girl. But I have no improper designs on her." He shrugged helplessly. "I found myself drawn to her, and I would simply welcome the opportunity to get to know her better."

"To what end?" asked the prince.

"I can't pretend to have a definite goal in mind," he replied honestly.

"You introduced yourself as Lord Boyd," said the prince. "Did you invent the name?"

"Boyd is the nickname my sister used for me when we were growing up. As for the title, she assumed I was a nobleman, and I didn't correct her." He ran a shaky hand over his face. "I never set out to intentionally deceive Tasha. I just didn't want her to feel like she had to bow and scrape around me. I never imagined the situation would become so complicated."

The prince stared at him with an unreadable expression on his face. Then he said, "Well, Lord Boyd, this situation is undeniably complicated. Somewhat to my own surprise, I'm willing to help you. Within reason. Tasha will need a chaperone. But I will try to arrange an opportunity for you to speak with her again."

Rupert bowed again, blushing deeply. "Thank you, Your Highness. You are most gracious." It did not escape his notice that the prince had referred to him as Lord Boyd.

"Your Majesty," the prince replied, dipping his head.

The prince rejoined his guards, and they rode away.

23

_____

The chance meeting with the crown prince fully occupied Rupert's thoughts for the rest of that day. He had the clear impression that the crown prince had no immediate plans to expose him. Surprising as that seemed, it did not mean that Rupert could continue with his pretense. He owed it to Tasha to be honest with her. Assuming she was willing to meet with him again.

Being a monarch required a delicate dance. Since his disastrous miscalculations when first thrust into the kingship, he had enjoyed a relatively smooth period that spanned several years. Now his missteps seemed to be multiplying once more. Having recovered from the awkwardness with Princess Neira, he had managed to maneuver himself into a worse position. The crown prince of Rogand was directly involved this time, and he could only berate himself for his own immaturity and lack of wisdom.

He wasn't left stewing for long. Early the next morning he received an invitation to meet with Tasha that afternoon. At the appointed time Rupert was led to the location, arriving in a state of considerable agitation.

He found Tasha accompanied by a chaperone—a woman who looked like she would take nonsense from no one—and an armed guard. After briefly introducing themselves, both of the new arrivals withdrew to a respectful distance before settling down to monitor their charge.

Thankfully it took no more than a minute with Tasha to restore Rupert's equilibrium entirely.

"I hope the crown prince was not too harsh on you, Lord Boyd," she said anxiously.

"You needn't worry, Tasha. He was actually very kind."

She looked relieved. "He might seem fierce," she said with a warm smile, "but in reality he's sweet."

Her declaration felt like an arrow to Rupert's heart. There was no denying it—he'd suffered a pang of jealousy.

She was so beautiful. Her dark hair, admirably tamed on this occasion, accentuated her lovely features, and her simple blue dress emphasized her shapely figure while making her seem elegant.

He needed to speak before he became tongue tied. "I'm glad you were willing to spend more time with me," he offered, feeling himself reddening again.

She looked almost as discomposed, but she replied calmly enough. "I enjoyed being with you, and I was hoping we might meet again." She gazed at him shyly. "To be honest, I'm surprised that the prince was willing to help," she said frankly.

"I'm equally surprised," he told her. He glanced toward her protectors. "He seems to value you highly," he added, trying hard not to resent it.

Another endearing blush briefly flooded her face. "I am fortunate," she acknowledged. "More so than I deserve, I'm sure."

He frowned at her in mock anger, setting her eyes sparkling.

He opened his mouth to ask about her family before abruptly changing his mind. Their previous conversation had been veering toward such a discussion. That topic was much too hazardous, at least until he revealed who he was.

She needed to be told the truth of course, and he needed to do it soon. It didn't take long to reach a decision—he would leave it until their next meeting. A wave of relief washed over him. Delaying it would allow both of them one last opportunity to be relaxed and informal.

"How did you manage to convince the princesses and the crown prince to give you some time off?" he asked instead.

She shrugged. "It wasn't difficult. They're not as demanding as you might expect. And when the prince makes up his mind about something he can be quite determined."

Repenting of his ambivalence toward the prince, Rupert beamed at her. His smile broadened as she matched him with a radiant smile of her own.

Having sensed there was more to her than a lovely face and an attractive smile, he was not entirely taken by surprise when she asked him seriously, "What is important to you? What are you hoping to achieve with your life?"

To give himself time to think, he took a breath and released it slowly. "I have a great responsibility to those who depend on me. 'When someone has been given much, much will be required of them.' Or so I've been told."

She gazed at him thoughtfully. "I haven't heard that before. It's sobering. Where did it come from?"

"My priest says it. I think it's from our Holy Book." He gazed off into the distance. "I want to do the best I'm capable of. I know I need to be wise and compassionate in the decisions I make. I don't doubt my compassion, but I have a long way to go before I can make any claim to being wise." He rolled his eyes. "I do manage to get myself in a tangle at times. I can only comfort myself with the thought that I'm still young. I sincerely hope and expect that I will learn from my mistakes."

She didn't make light of his concerns. "Do you have wise counselors available to you?"

"I do," he acknowledged. "Some very good people have gone to considerable lengths to help me. I suppose I mostly get into trouble when no one's on hand to advise me," he added ruefully.

She gave out a merry laugh. "My father says he mostly relies on my mother to keep him out of trouble."

"It sounds like I need to get myself a wife," he replied, feeling instantly foolish for having said it.

Seeing the look on his face, she burst out laughing, a playful twinkle in her eye.

Had it been anyone other than Tasha, he would have responded with embarrassment or shame. But he felt sure she was mostly laughing at the absurdity of the situation.

Embarrassment was becoming far too much of a habit for him anyway. Casting pride to the winds, he began laughing as well, allowing himself to be caught up in the carefree attitude of the servant girl. And having relaxed, he discovered it wasn't even hard to laugh at himself.

Tasha's protectors stared at them curiously, but didn't intervene.

When they had recovered their poise, he posed a similar question to her. "What about you? What do you want to achieve with your life?"

"I want to do anything I can for the most disadvantaged and hurting," she replied firmly.

"There is no shortage of such people," he acknowledged.

She nodded. "Sometimes it happens due to natural causes. But more often injustice seems to be at the heart of it."

"Injustice or just plain cruelty," he agreed. "Like abducting Lord and Lady Torbury's son."

A fierce look came to her eye. "I would be willing to risk a lot if it meant I could return the boy to his parents," she said. "And bring whoever is responsible to justice."

He didn't doubt that she was in earnest. However much her eyes sparkled with merriment, she still radiated quiet determination.

"I hope I'll manage some adventure too," she said seriously.

He smiled at her. He could not imagine her ever leading a boring life.

Two hours passed in a moment. It was the protectors who finally ended the interaction. Rupert didn't part with Tasha before extracting a promise that she would meet with him again.

He left feeling like he was floating on air. They had covered a lot of ground, from deeply felt concerns to lighthearted banter. By the time it ended he could not remember ever feeling so relaxed with another person.

She was a servant, and a foreigner at that. Neither consideration bothered him in the slightest. He sensed they were slowly building something unique and precious.

At this early stage it remained fragile though. When they next met he would need to tell her who he was. He hoped and prayed the disclosure would not bring everything crashing down.

THE MORNING after Rupert's meeting with Tasha another invitation arrived, this time from King Krasmir. The invitation stated that His Majesty King Rupert of Castel was requested at his earliest convenience to attend King Krasmir.

A feeling of imminent doom hung over Rupert as he followed the messenger to one of the king's private reception rooms. He could only assume that his clandestine activities had been exposed. He decided grimly that he undoubtedly had the crown prince to thank for that. His mind churned as he tried to assess the implications. What protocols had he ignored? What conventions had he flouted? Was it possible that he had created an international incident?

The messenger left him alone in the room and set off to inform the king that he had arrived.

King Krasmir did not keep him waiting. He strode into the room, followed by Crown Prince Rimek and a woman who was undoubtedly the queen.

Rising hastily to his feet, Rupert offered a deep bow.

King Krasmir returned a stiff bow of his own. "This is my wife, Queen Deka," he said. "You have already met Crown Prince Rimek."

"Yes, Your Majesty." Rupert's heart sank. If the king knew he had met the crown prince, he must surely be aware of Rupert's meetings with Tasha.

"Will you understand me if I speak Rogandan?" Krasmir asked with a frown.

"Yes, Your Majesty," he replied evenly, working hard to at least project an outward appearance of calm.

"In my innocence I imagined we had more than enough to occupy our attention already," said King Krasmir sternly. "But it seems I am not to be spared a new distraction. I will come straight to the point, King Rupert. What are your intentions regarding my daughter?"

Rupert was too stunned to respond.

Krasmir frowned. "Have you or have you not been courting my daughter in the guise of a Castelan nobleman?" he demanded.

With his mouth hanging wide, Rupert glanced in the direction of the crown prince. Rimek shrugged helplessly.

Somehow mustering the composure to face his inquisitor, Rupert took a breath to steady himself. "There seems to be a misunderstanding, Your Majesty. I have met twice with one of your servants—a girl called Tasha," he replied. "It is true that I have not revealed my identity to her, but only because I did not want our interactions to be overshadowed by questions of status. I was planning to tell her everything at our next meeting."

Both the king and the queen had been studying him closely.

"He's telling the truth," Queen Deka told her husband. "Or at least he thinks he is."

"So he doesn't know," King Krasmir said to his son.

"I did tell you that, Father," Prince Rimek replied mildly.

The king grunted. Then he addressed Rupert once more. "It is my youngest daughter, Princess Teylee, that you have been meeting with. Tasha is an affectionate name used only by members of her family."

Realizing his mouth was hanging open again, Rupert hastily clamped it shut.

The king stared at him. "Now that all of us seem to be located in the same kingdom," he observed wryly, "I must repeat my question. What are your intentions regarding my daughter?"

King Krasmir's question was no less direct than before, but Rupert thought he had detected the tiniest softening in his tone.

Rupert made his best attempt at a formal bow. "King Krasmir, Queen Deka," he said, nodding to each of them in turn. "I would like to request permission to court your daughter, Princess Teylee."

The queen schooled her features into an unexpressive mask, but not before a triumphant smile made a fleeting appearance across her face.

King Krasmir appeared much less enthusiastic about the turn of events. "There are customs and protocols to be considered," he grumbled, "and there would need to be strict boundaries. Then there is the question of a dowry."

"Nonsense!" said the queen, waving a hand dismissively. "You'll frighten the poor boy away with all this palaver." She turned to Rupert with a genial smile. "You must pardon him, young man. He still thinks that Tasha is his baby. He probably also imagines that no one could ever be good enough for her." She glared at her husband.

King Krasmir glowered back at her, but he offered nothing more than a grunt in response.

"Of course we will allow you to court our Tasha," Queen Deka crooned.

With no immediate confirmation from her husband, she turned to confront him. "Well? Does this arrangement have the blessing of Your Majesty or not?"

She wasn't staring at him with hands on her hips, but from her tone she might have been.

"Very well," he finally conceded gruffly. "But I expect her to be treated properly! No more deceptions!"

"You have my word, Your Majesty," Rupert replied earnestly.

"Well, be off with you then," grumbled the king, flicking a hand toward the door.

Rupert hurried out of the room, relieved that the ordeal was over.

The crown prince followed him out. "You did well in there," he said with a grin. "Don't worry too much about Father—he isn't nearly as fierce as he seems."

"Thank you, Your Highness," Rupert replied.

"Please! Call me Rimek!" said the prince. "There's no need to stand on ceremony."

"Then you must call me Rupert," he said.

"Not Boyd?" the prince asked with a wink.

"Most definitely not Boyd!" he replied sheepishly. After a brief pause he asked, "Does Tasha—Princess Teylee I mean—know the truth about me?"

The prince smiled. "No, she doesn't. I think it's better for her to find out directly from you, and I imagine my parents will see it the same way. And a word of advice—I'd stick to Tasha if I were you."

"Thank you, Rimek."

"I'll organize an invitation for tomorrow," the prince assured him. "After that, the two of you can make your own arrangements."

Rimek clapped him on the back and headed off with a conspiratorial wink.

A servant arrived to lead the foreign visitor to his quarters. Rupert trailed behind the man with his thoughts whirling. The meeting with King Krasmir and Queen Deka had not gone as badly as he might have feared. At least he hoped he was reading that correctly.

But the whole situation had just escalated significantly. A puppy escaping through a hedge had led to an impulsive flirtation. It had seemed so harmless at the time, and it happened so quickly. Now it had assumed immense significance, for his future and also for Tasha's. He was struggling to get his head around it.

What would Tasha think about his meeting with the king and queen and crown prince? Nothing had been decided of course—no decisions could be made before she had her say. But, without her knowledge, her family had been deliberating with a foreign sovereign about her future. He didn't doubt she would have her own opinion about that.

After their last meeting, Rupert had been eager to see Tasha again. Given everything that had just happened, the prospect of facing her the next day felt unexpectedly daunting.

TRUE TO HIS WORD, Crown Prince Rimek set up another meeting in the same garden where Rupert and Tasha had met on the previous occasion. Having arrived first, the Castelan king paced up and down restlessly while he waited. He hadn't felt so anxious since his coronation.

His heart immediately began to pound the moment she appeared. Her two protectors afforded him a stiff bow before moving out of hearing range.

"Tasha, it's good to see you again," he said with a crooked smile. It was the best he could manage.

"Lord Boyd," she said with a quick nod of her head, gazing at him with an unreadable expression. She looked no less dazzling than before, but her manner seemed muted.

She'd called him Lord Boyd, which suggested she hadn't been told the truth. But she had clearly sensed that something was wrong. Perhaps her parents had been acting strangely since their meeting the previous day.

More likely the fault lay with him. He was desperately trying to behave normally, but he'd never been good at hiding his emotions.

There was no point in delaying the inevitable. His hopes and dreams were hanging by a thread, and he had no choice but to release them and hope for the best.

Taking a deep breath, he began. "There are some things I need to tell you, Tasha," he said. "I hope you will hear me out."

He could already see the light dimming from her eyes, but there was no turning back.

"My name is not Boyd, and I'm not a nobleman. Only my sister has ever called me Boyd—it was her nickname for me when we were young. My name is Rupert, and I'm the king of Castel." He paused to catch his breath. "I'm truly sorry I misled you."

She said nothing.

"I didn't intentionally set out to do it—somehow it just happened. I knew I needed to tell you the truth, but I wasn't sure how you would react. I decided to wait until we met a third time."

"Which is now," she said.

He nodded. She seemed almost relieved, and he wondered what she'd thought he might be going to say. But he wasn't finished.

"Yesterday I received a summons from King Krasmir," he continued.

A new wariness had come to her face, but she didn't speak.

"He demanded to know my intentions toward his daughter. I told him there must be some mistake. I said that I'd met with a servant girl twice, but that was all. He made it clear that Tasha and Princess Teylee are the same person. You're his daughter."

She stared at him through narrowed eyes. "And?" she asked.

"When I learned that, I requested permission from your parents to court you."

She didn't respond, so he pressed on. "Your father talked about customs and protocols and dowries. Your mother told him it was nonsense and that I was welcome to court you."

"Did it occur to you to include me in the conversation?" she asked. A dangerous tone had entered her voice.

"It did, but not until after I'd been dismissed," he admitted. "Your father took me completely by surprise! I was barely able to think straight for much of the conversation."

Her eyes were flashing now. "Do you imagine I want to be courted by someone who doesn't think to consult me when my future is being discussed?" She sent him a withering look. "You're supposed to be a king, yet apparently you don't have the nerve to stand up to my parents."

He hung his head miserably.

When he next glanced at her, her face had become expressionless again. It was almost more than he could bear.

"Goodbye, Lord Boyd," she said woodenly. "Or King Rupert, or whoever you are."

And with that she was gone.

24

———

Another long day was coming to an end at last for Brother Ander and Ethen. Two weeks had passed since their captivity began, and the monk had seen no sign that it was likely to end.

Something needed to change in their situation though, and change soon. Up to that point, the five-year-old had done remarkably well, but the strain was becoming increasingly evident. It had been especially difficult that afternoon to coax the five-year-old to spend time at his lessons. And in the morning he had refused uncharacteristically to speak Rogandan.

"Why hasn't my father found me?" Ethen asked irritably. "I miss him. And I want to see my mother!"

His lower lip trembled uncontrollably, and he began to cry.

Brother Ander comforted him as best he could.

Ethen had unusual energy and intelligence, which was no surprise given his parents. The daily routine of physical and intellectual exercise established by the monk had provided an important outlet for his restlessness. Nevertheless, steering the boy through the captivity had been no easy matter. Without contact of any kind with his parents, Ethen had become increasingly tempted to dissolve into despair.

The monk resisted the threatened downward spiral with thoughtful creativity and gentle compassion, supported by fervent prayer. Having carried his own childhood hurts well into adult life, he fully understood the bitter consequences of allowing unresolved disappointment and anger to grow and fester.

'In this world you will have trouble...' The words often came to his mind now. He shook his head sadly.

His efforts to redeem the captivity slowly assumed considerable significance for Brother Ander. He even wondered if he might one day come to see this undertaking as the main purpose behind his calling as a monk.

Ethen sat down beside Brother Ander as daylight faded from the sky. Resting wearily against the monk's shoulder, the boy confided, "I'm glad you're with me, Brother Ander. I don't like the dark."

The monk gazed down at him sympathetically. "God gave us darkness as well as light," he assured the boy.

"But why?"

"Do you ever think about light during the daytime?" asked Brother Ander.

Ethen shook his head.

The monk nodded. "That's the reason darkness exists. If it weren't for the darkness, we probably wouldn't think about light at all. We learn to value light because we have to live with darkness."

The boy went quiet for some time. Then his little brow puckered into a frown. "Is that the same as liking food better when you're hungry?" Looking at his burly friend, he screwed up his nose. "I'm sick of bread, but I wish I had some now."

"That's exactly right," Brother Ander told him with a smile. "I suspect you understand these things better than a lot of grownups."

FOR KAMASH, the familiar and comfortable patterns of his life had been upended almost from the moment he met Princess Neira. The turbulence that followed was unlike anything he had experienced before, even in his days as advisor to the unpredictable King Ugar.

Nevertheless, as he relaxed in unaccustomed luxury in the palace at Rog he found himself bored and lacking purpose. Meetings involving the princess had come to an abrupt end with the disappearance of Lord Torbury's son. The old man had no doubt that King Krasmir's attention would continue to be diverted until the matter was resolved one way or another.

Disturbingly, the rumors swirling around the palace suggested that the Ahrans were responsible for the abduction. Kamash had no way of establishing the truth. When he directly confronted the princess with the rumors, she responded evasively. He had the impression she knew no more than he did.

The princess must surely be feeling adrift herself. She had arrived in Rog as a sensation; now she was little more than a curiosity. Such a transformation must have been unusually difficult for someone who relished being the center of attention.

At first Neira had entertained herself by haunting Rog's markets, visiting them frequently, often daily. Since the abduction, King Krasmir had put a stop to that.

Kamash wasn't surprised. The Rogandans already had plenty to worry about with the Ahrans. It was asking too much to allow the princess to wander freely where her safety could not be guaranteed.

Conscious that the princess might not be coping well, Kamash decided to pay her a visit. He had been assigned a room in the same section of the palace, so he knew where to find her. And with her movements restricted, she couldn't be too far away.

The first person he encountered was Uman. The gloomy expression on the guard's face came as no surprise to Kamash. The Ahran hadn't seemed truly content since they left the island.

Kamash nodded to Uman. The guard nodded back once before turning away, ignoring him completely.

The princess spent a lot of time in a sunny room overlooking a stand of trees that lay within the grounds of the palace. Kamash headed for it, expecting to find her there. The room lay silent and empty.

Glancing out of the window, he noticed her walking swiftly away from the building in the direction of the trees. Concluding she had decided to take a walk, he headed outside to join her.

The park outside their building had become very familiar to Kamash. After so many years with the sea on his doorstep, he found it stifling to spend extended periods inside buildings. Accordingly he took every opportunity to wander outside in the open air. Guards were stationed all around the palace buildings, but they didn't interfere with their foreign guests provided they remained within the palace grounds.

Catching a glimpse of Princess Neira entering the trees, the old man set off after her. She didn't seem to have spotted him, so he needed to hurry to have any chance of catching her before she moved out of reach.

By the time he reached the trees he could see no sign of her. Guessing at the direction she had taken, he moved forward. He had been walking for only a few minutes when he heard voices ahead of him.

Without fully understanding why, he decided to remain hidden. Creeping forward cautiously, he concealed himself behind a tree, straining his ears to hear the conversation. Not a word of it made any sense to him—the conversation was clearly being conducted in the Ahran language.

Peering around the tree, he glimpsed a dark figure standing before the princess. The stranger held out something that looked like a parchment. Taking it, the princess opened it and read it slowly and carefully. The man held out a hand, and she returned the parchment. After concealing it within his clothing, the dark figure turned swiftly away and was lost to sight, leaving the princess alone.

Noticing her glancing around furtively, he pulled back quickly to avoid being seen. By the time he was willing to risk peering out again, she was gone as well. He waited for a considerable time before heading back to the building again, taking a roundabout path.

Princess Neira was emerging from her room when he reentered the building.

"Kamash!" she said vivaciously. "Where have you been? It's so long since I saw you last—have you been hiding from me?"

"I'm pleased to see you so buoyant, Princess," he replied. "Why the high spirits?"

"No reason," she assured him hastily. "I've just been for a short walk. Spending some time in the park has undoubtedly done me good." After giving him a cheery wave, she headed back to the privacy of her room.

The old man returned to his own quarters with a great deal to think about. Clearly she had been meeting with an Ahran agent, and the man appeared to have passed some kind of letter to her. Was this the first such meeting, or had it been a regular occurrence?

The change of mood in the princess raised many questions. Her contact with the agent—or perhaps the letter he had passed to her—had lifted her spirits enormously. Had the Ahrans somehow managed to heal the breach with their princess? He shook his head in bewilderment. They had abandoned her to die on the island. How could she overlook such a betrayal?

Should he inform King Krasmir of what he had seen? Uncertain and ill at ease, he decided to give himself time to think it through before deciding anything about what to do next.

THOMAS WATCHED ANXIOUSLY AS WILL PACED BACK and forth around the room. If Will's restlessness was anything to go by, he might have been dancing on hot coals.

"When I promised Krasmir not to work independently, I had no idea how it was going to turn out!" he growled. "We know exactly where to go next, but we're forced to wait while Kulferan tries to figure it out for himself."

"It isn't his fault," Thomas pointed out reasonably. "We have an unfair advantage."

"His people must be completely incompetent if they're still trying to squeeze details out of the Ahrans!" snapped Will.

"They don't know who to focus on," Thomas reminded him. "And even if they did, they can't force information out of him if he isn't willing to talk."

No further response was forthcoming, but it was nevertheless obvious that Will was not going to be placated.

Time passed in uncomfortable silence before Will seemed to reach a decision.

"We're not going to wait any longer," he said decisively.

"But we can't just ignore your promise to the king," protested Thomas.

"We won't go in with force," Will replied. "We'll head for the safe house and observe from a distance. You can watch people coming and going. All you need to do is find out if Ethen is there. If he isn't, find out the location of another Ahran safe house. We'll simply go there instead."

Thomas frowned. It all sounded very simple, but he had a feeling it was likely to prove anything but. He opened his mouth to argue but then closed it again without speaking. Will wasn't going to be convinced, no matter what he said.

How could he refuse his friend? Would he behave any differently if one of his children had been taken? Thomas sighed in resignation.

Thomas and Will stood hidden behind a building, opposite the house unwittingly identified by the Ahran agent. After watching vigilantly for almost two hours, they had caught a single glimpse of just one of the inhabitants of the house. It was enough to confirm to Thomas that Ethen and Brother Ander were not being held there, and that the Ahran knew of no other safe houses. But Thomas had seen that others lived there too, and one of them might have information worth knowing.

Will was becoming impatient. "Have they somehow spotted us?" he whispered, aiming a sideways glance at his companion.

Thomas could only shrug. "It seems unlikely. We've seen no sign of anyone."

"We've waited long enough," said Will. "I'm going in there."

"You can't be serious," hissed Thomas. "On your own, with no support?"

"I'm not planning to fight them," Will replied. "I'll pretend I'm selling something."

"Selling what?" demanded Thomas, frantically trying to dream up of a way of talking Will out of such a desperate plan.

"What does it matter?" Will replied dismissively. "Just make sure you're ready to get a good look at whoever comes to the door."

With that he was gone.

Thomas watched wide-eyed as he strode across the street. Reaching the door, he hammered on it hard with an open hand before stepping back to wait for an answer.

When no one appeared, he hammered on the door again.

It wasn't difficult for Thomas to guess what was happening. The occupants undoubtedly wanted to keep a low profile. If they weren't expecting visitors, they probably wouldn't bother to answer the door at all.

With no response forthcoming, Will hammered on the door a third time. Then, apparently concluding he was wasting his time, he turned abruptly aside and headed off down the road. Thomas watched on, bemused.

Many minutes passed before Will reappeared. When he did, he bore a flaming torch in one hand, while his other hand clutched something to his chest. Stopping once more outside the door, he opened his arm to release his oddly shaped burden. A pile of sticks fell to the ground. Reaching down, Will leaned the sticks against the door, then held the torch to them.

Before long the tinder began to smoke. A flicker appeared, growing steadily brighter. Will stepped back as flames licked at the door.

Torn between astonishment and alarm, Thomas gaped open mouthed at his friend's stunt. Apparently deciding that his work had been done, Will turned away from the door and hurried back across the road.

Thomas exhaled noisily in relief as the commander rejoined him, still scarcely able to believe what he had done.

"What are you doing?" Thomas asked in alarm.

"Since they refuse to answer the door, I'm going to smoke them out," Will replied grimly. He nudged Thomas in the ribs. "Make sure you keep a close eye on that door!" he commanded.

At first the fire did indeed seem to generate little more than smoke. After a while, though, the smoke gave way to an angry red glow. And with the door now ablaze, flames were spreading upward to threaten the eaves of the building. If the occupants of the house hadn't noticed the blaze yet, then surely they would do so before long.

By the time the fire reached the thatched roof, the roar of the flames could clearly be heard in the stillness. The door crashed suddenly outward, and smoke billowed from the opening—the interior of the house must also be burning. Men stumbled into the street, coughing and gagging from the smoke.

Three men had emerged before a fourth appeared dragging a man behind him. A glance at the prone form revealed no mental activity at all. Thomas knew that the man's life had ended.

Will's purpose had been achieved though. Thomas now knew of another location they could investigate.

Other people had appeared from nearby dwellings, and shouts filled the air as people hurried to fill buckets of water to fight the fire before it could spread to other houses.

Pulling at Thomas's elbow, Will dragged him away before anyone could spot them.

As soon as they were clear of the area, Will looked at Thomas sharply. "Did you learn about any other safe houses?"

"One of the men knows of another house—that was all," Thomas replied distractedly. "What if the neighbors can't put out the fire?" he demanded, his voice wavering in his agitation. "They'll lose their houses. Maybe more people will lose their lives."

Will waved an arm dismissively. "That won't be an issue. There's no wind to carry embers tonight, and there's plenty of water on hand and people to carry it."

Thomas covered his face with his hands, his mind filled with images of people frantic to protect their homes and loved ones.

Neither of them moved. Will's voice brought Thomas back to the present. "You're right, Thomas. Come with me."

Will immediately headed back toward the fire. After staring in amazement for a moment, Thomas hurried after him.

They arrived to find men and women in two ragged lines, passing buckets of water toward the fire. Up to that point it hadn't spread, but even a casual glance showed a major conflagration threatened every house in the street.

The bucket line was not stable. Thomas saw that people were coming and going constantly, running around in a panic to retrieve belongings from neighboring houses.

Will sized up the situation in a moment. Stepping forward, his voice rang out forcefully, issuing a series of clear commands. After staring at him in bewilderment for a moment, people everywhere sprang into action. Soon the two lines had stabilized, and two new lines had quickly formed as other buckets were brought to bear. Much more water was now being thrown on the fire. The houses on each side of the blaze were being preemptively soaked as well.

Having committed himself, Will threw all of his restless energy into the task. As well as directing the operation, he joined any bucket line that faltered, shouting encouragement as he passed buckets forward.

Even with Will's intervention, it was a near-run thing. By the time Will and his exhausted workers brought the fire under control, the original house had been entirely destroyed. The houses on either side were water damaged, but otherwise intact.

Thomas had not wasted a moment before joining one of the lines, and he labored tirelessly throughout the battle. He now collapsed in exhaustion.

Will came and slumped down beside him, utterly drained from his exertions. His face sagging with weariness, he faced Thomas. "Thank you for bringing me to my senses, Thomas," he said. "I...I'm not proud of what I did. It wasn't intentional. I never expected to start an inferno."

Thomas placed a hand on his shoulder. "No other lives were lost. And the surrounding houses were not seriously damaged."

"But someone owned the house I destroyed." Will turned away, closing his eyes and allowing his head to sink to his chest.

Thomas could think of nothing to say.

Glancing around, he could see no sign of the Ahrans. They must have taken advantage of the chaos to slip away, taking the body of their comrade with them.

Thomas did notice that the number of people milling around had increased significantly. A body of soldiers had arrived on the scene. Too late to help fight the flames, they were working to assist the locals.

To his alarm, Thomas saw that the soldiers were led by Lord Kulferan. Worse, the nobleman had recognized Will and was striding toward them.

"Lord Torbury! What brings you here?" he asked. The question was phrased respectfully, but it was clear he would not welcome a superficial answer.

"We were in the area when the fire started, My Lord, and we decided to help," Will replied.

One of Lord Kulferan's soldiers came and whispered in his ear. The Rogandan commander frowned for a moment before addressing Will again. "I am told that you took charge of the effort to extinguish the fire." He sounded mildly surprised.

Will dipped his head. "The locals were struggling, and they seemed to need guidance. It was the least I could do."

Lord Kulferan turned his focus on the cleanup effort, directing his soldiers to help the residents and make sure that no burning embers remained to spark another fire. He nevertheless continued to hover nearby.

After a few minutes, he addressed Will once more. "Could you please join me, Lord Torbury? The king will wish to express his appreciation for your assistance. Two of my men will accompany your companion to ensure he returns safely to the palace."

"Of course, Lord Kulferan," Will replied flatly. He appeared exhausted, but Thomas knew him well enough to recognize his discomfort.

Two soldiers approached Thomas, motioning for him to join them. Waving a farewell to Will, he followed them back to his quarters.

***

ARRIVING AT THE PALACE, Will was ushered into a small reception room and left there alone. Feeling gloomy and disheartened, he was grateful for an opportunity to recover himself.

In the end he was forced to wait for a considerable period. It was late at night when King Krasmir finally arrived, and Will wondered if His Majesty had been called from his bed.

Getting to his feet, Will bowed low.

The king nodded in response, one of his eyebrows raised quizzically. His expression couldn't be mistaken for a smile. "I understand we have you to thank for putting out a fire earlier tonight, Lord Torbury," he said.

Will dipped his head again. "I was pleased to be able to assist, Your Majesty."

"My soldiers were told that you didn't arrive until after the fire had started. How did you become aware of it?"

"I was wandering in the area with Thomas Stablehand. The glow in the sky and the smoke made it apparent, even from a distance."

The king peered at him shrewdly. "I am also told that the people in that particular dwelling were foreigners. Do you think it possible that they were Ahran agents?"

"I did not speak to them, Your Majesty. My entire focus was on extinguishing the fire."

The king studied him silently. Then he frowned. "I will be frank with you, Lord Torbury. There has been no suggestion that you were in any way involved with whoever or whatever started the fire, and I am told that the surrounding houses were saved only thanks to a prodigious effort on your part. Nevertheless, a house that could have been harboring Ahran agents caught fire, and somehow you were on the scene. That is a strange coincidence, is it not?"

Will did not reply.

The king sighed. "This is a delicate situation, Lord Torbury. I am responsible for your protection, and I can only imagine your king's reaction if anything should happen to you. Ensuring your safety is a key priority for me. I have ordered that senior soldiers will be assigned to you, and to your countryman Rufe Sarjant. From now on both of you will be accompanied whenever you leave the palace. I trust that you will not misunderstand this precaution."

Will had nothing to say in response, and it was abundantly clear from the king's tone that the conversation was at an end. Almost as an afterthought, King Krasmir added, "And may I once more express my thanks for your help tonight."

With that, Will was dismissed. After bowing low, he turned and left the reception room.

25

———————

Arriving at the Arvenian quarters in the palace, Thomas found himself subjected to a barrage of questions from Amyra and the others. After quickly describing all that had happened, from finding the Ahran safe house to fighting the fire, he answered their questions as best he could.

When he finished they settled in to wait for the return of Will.

The night was well advanced before Will reappeared after his meeting with the king. His face wore a grim expression.

"What happened?" asked Thomas anxiously.

"Krasmir has decided to clip my wings," Will replied with a shrug. "We should have left as soon as the fire was under control," he grumbled.

"What did the king say?" asked Amyra.

"From now on I won't be leaving the palace without one of Krasmir's men on my tail. The same with Rufe. The rest of you should still be able to do as you please."

"Does the king know what actually happened?" asked Thomas.

Will shook his head. "Thankfully not."

"Whatever were you thinking, setting fire to that house?" demanded Amyra in exasperation.

"I was doing what I could to find our son," he replied fiercely.

The others remained silent.

Amyra sighed. "The question is what the rest of us can do now that Will and Rufe are grounded," she said. "I certainly won't be giving in. I won't be attempting anything adventurous though." She raised an eyebrow in Will's direction. "Don't expect me to burn any houses to the ground."

Will winced, but didn't comment.

"Elena or Thomas can come with me if they're willing. Given what's just happened, maybe Elena is a better choice next time."

Elena and Thomas both nodded.

"Will you accompany us, Haldek?" Amyra asked.

"Of course you must count me in," Haldek replied.

Amyra's head dipped once. "Thank you all." Her face was set firm in determination. "Since Thomas has a location we can start with, we will leave early tomorrow morning—a little before dawn. We need to give ourselves the best possible chance of catching anyone leaving the house for the day."

"You should assume you'll be followed," Will warned them.

"I'll be able to tell if that's what's happening," Elena said calmly. "Provided I can catch sight of whoever is tailing us."

***

Dawn was near when Elena followed Amyra and Haldek out of the building.

"Are you sure you know where it is?" Amyra whispered to her.

"Yes," Elena assured her. "Thomas gave me the details."

"Let's be off!" called Amyra loudly, speaking in Arvenian. "I want to get to the markets early."

Dark as it was, Elena kept her eyes open. She had the stone at the ready to allow her to be certain about the intentions of anyone who appeared to be following them.

As the first light dimly brightened the sky, Haldek nudged Elena gently, jerking his head behind them and off to one side. Elena waited a few moments before casting a glance back in that direction. Two men were walking along some distance behind them. The men were talking quietly to each other, apparently taking no interest in them. But they could not hide their intentions from the stone. Elena was immediately aware that these men had been assigned the task of tailing them.

She leaned closer to Amyra. "Two of King Krasmir's men are following us."

Amyra nodded curtly. "We'll lose them in the markets. Stay close."

They arrived at the main market in Rog as the sun was clearing the horizon. Stalls were laden with produce and prospective buyers bustled about everywhere.

Elena and Haldek followed Amyra into a tent filled with carpets. They were greeted by a brightly clad woman who welcomed them with a smile and waved them to some seats, calling for tea to be served. Amyra ignored her completely, heading for the back of the tent and disappearing through a loose flap. Haldek was not far behind her. The carpet vendor watched them open mouthed. Elena shrugged helplessly before turning and following the other two out of the tent.

She found Amyra peering back the way they had come.

"Our admirers have taken the bait," said Amyra quietly. "By the time they realize we're not in the tent we'll be long gone."

With that she headed swiftly away from the tent, weaving her way through the market. Elena was hard pressed to keep up with her.

No more than thirty minutes after the sun rose, they were in position. The Ahran safe house was close by, with them located far enough away to avoid attracting attention.

They settled down to wait.

In the end they didn't need to wait long. Two men soon left the house, hurrying away without looking back. Then a third arrived, disappearing inside the house.

"Anything useful?" Amyra asked tensely.

Elena nodded. "The man who just arrived has come here from another house. And he's aware of a boy being held captive!"

Amyra gave a little cry, covering her face with her hands.

"Unfortunately he doesn't know exactly where, though," she added hastily. "It isn't at the house he came from."

A slow intake of breath greeted this news. Elena understood Amyra's reaction. This latest information might be a step in the right direction, but at that moment they were no closer to finding him.

BOLNYK HAD COMPLETED his report on the progress made by the agents. "There is one other matter, Your Eminence," he added tentatively.

"Well?" demanded the Grand Vizier, eyeing him suspiciously.

Berating himself for allowing even the tiniest trace of discomfort to show, Bolnyk hardened himself. "Some of our agents were foolish enough to be observed spying on the Arvenian delegation at the palace," he said. "As they escaped they were pursued by a boy and a monk. They took the opportunity to capture them both. The child is the son of the Arvenian army commander. He is being held along with the monk in an abandoned cellar in one of our safe houses in Rog."

The chief minister had gone red in the face. "What possessed the fools to allow themselves to be caught spying in the first place? And why compound their error by risking an abduction?" he hissed.

The agent didn't flinch. "I have asked them similar questions," he replied. "Nevertheless it occurred to me that the boy might provide us with useful leverage. Perhaps we can use him to drive a wedge between the Arvenians and the Rogandans." He bowed very low. "I did not raise the matter when you first arrived because there seemed to be many pressing matters that required your attention. I apologize if I have erred in these decisions."

Rheibas stared back at him, apparently assessing the possibilities.

"What do you know about the boy's father—this Arvenian army commander?" he asked.

"Very little of substance, Your Eminence," Bolnyk told him. "I will make inquiries."

"How secure are these prisoners?" Rheibas demanded.

"I believe they are very secure," Bolnyk replied. "They have been in our keeping for some days without escaping. And no one has discovered their whereabouts."

"Bring them here to me," ordered the chief minister. "I want them alive. The boy might have value as a hostage. We can use him to make sure the Arvenians do not interfere with our plans. He might also be useful to us dead, provided we make certain the Arvenian commander believes the Rogandans are responsible."

Bolnyk bowed.

"I am holding you accountable for them," Rheibas told him. "Your priority is to get them here alive. Whatever happens though, do not permit them to be rescued. As a last resort, kill them both," he added coldly.

KAMASH HAD BEEN unable to get the interaction with Thomas and Elena out of his mind. He had little concern about them exposing his talisman to unwanted attention. Something told him they would keep his secret as they had promised.

The interaction had been unsettling for a different reason. Recounting his history with the stone had highlighted the dramatic ways in which it had changed his life. The process had left him with a simple question. Would he be better off without it?

He had never sought the stone—it came as an unexpected gift. King Ugar had been the one who lusted after it, to no avail. Now Ugar and his son were dead.

Kamash had outlived them both. Did he want to outlast King Krasmir as well? Could he find the energy to adapt to a new king when Krasmir's life came to an end?

Living was a pursuit that required energy, especially when it took place around other people. And there was no escaping trouble. It came along for the ride. Trouble was inevitable, and the longer you lived, the more trouble came your way. A war with Arvenon might have passed him by on his remote island, but sooner or later another war would come—perhaps even an Ahran invasion. Would he be able to avoid that conflict too?

He faced the truth: well preserved he might be, but he was becoming weary of the ceaseless toil of daily existence.

Even on the island he had begun to tire of life. Since returning to Rog, his days had been consumed with wrestling—with Krasmir's nobles, with the princess, even with himself. The intensity of it was overwhelming. His energy for life was slowly being leached away.

The arrival of the princess brought his musing to an abrupt end. The merest glimpse of her had been more than enough to increase his weariness.

Princess Neira arrived with her nose in the air as usual. She eyed him haughtily before turning away with a disdainful toss of her head.

Kamash rolled his eyes. He had remained with her in the hope that he might be able to do her some good. Was he deluding himself?

Confronted by so many questions, he could only shake his head helplessly.

Uman belatedly arrived, positioning himself near the princess. His face, normally expressionless, suggested he wasn't entirely content.

The princess was almost strutting today, and Kamash eyed her curiously. She seemed much more buoyant than usual, and he wondered what might account for it.

"This city is unsafe for my countrymen," grumbled Neira suddenly, turning back to him with a scowl of displeasure.

"What do you mean, Princess?" Kamash asked with a puzzled frown.

"King Krasmir thinks they are wild animals, to be hunted down for sport. They are being hounded everywhere in Rog."

"How do you know that?" he asked.

"Everybody knows," she sniffed.

Her pronouncement confirmed his worst fears. "You have been in contact with Ahran agents."

Glancing at his expression, a snort of laughter escaped her. "Just look at you, Kamash! If only you could see your face!"

It was not lost on him that she had not denied his assertion. "Did your people have anything to do with the abduction of the boy?" he asked in growing alarm.

She waved an arm dismissively. "Why should I care if some grubby little brat has gotten himself into trouble? It means nothing to me."

Uman was following the interaction closely. He seemed more dispirited than ever.

Kamash faced the princess, his eyes narrowed. "It matters to me," he said. "If you're involved in the kidnapping—even if you're just aware of who has done it—you'll get no further help from me."

The princess stared at him. The irritability on her face was slowly replaced by a look of dismay. Her lower lip drooped miserably, and a tear came to her eye.

"Don't try to wheedle your way out of it, Neira," he said coldly. "I'm not interested in your manipulation. I mean what I said."

Ignoring her wide-eyed stare, he turned on his heel and strode away.

THOMAS BURST into the room in search of Will and Amyra, barely able to contain his excitement. They were exactly where he expected them to be, but the mood in the room quickly brought him back down to earth.

The children were playing energetically and noisily, to the point where he almost needed to cover his ears. Will and Amyra sat apart, haunted looks on their faces. They seemed entirely unaware of the commotion around them. Elena was shooting concerned looks at her two friends, interspersed with repeated requests to the children to tone it down. The other Arvenians had wisely fled the area.

Leaving the room, Thomas sought out Haldek. "Could you please look after the children for a while, Haldek? I need to speak with Will and Amyra and Elena."

Haldek grimaced. "These children have too much energy. They should be outdoors." Then he shrugged. "Of course. I am happy to help."

Haldek led the way back into the room. "Children!" he called. "It is time for a game with Uncle Haldek."

It took two more attempts before he managed to get their attention, but soon they were bouncing eagerly around him.

Catching Elena's eye, Thomas jerked his head significantly toward Amyra and Will and headed for the door. He led the way to a smaller room where he knew they were able to talk in peace. Elena arrived with an eager look on her face. Her companions appeared distracted and lacking energy. They looked at Thomas dully, like people who had lost hope.

"I'm beginning to think we've been approaching this the wrong way!" Thomas began breathlessly. "I just spotted Kamash—the spokesperson for Princess Neira—and the stone showed me what's on his mind. The princess has been in touch with Ahran agents—he witnessed one of them handing her a document. And he suspects she might know something about Ethen's captivity."

He seemed to have succeeded in capturing their attention. Will was frowning, and a hint of life had returned to Amyra's eyes.

"What are you suggesting?" asked Elena hopefully.

"I think we need to try to enlist Kamash's help," he replied.

"Why would we do that?" asked Will dismissively. "He's the princess's puppet."

"Perhaps not as much as it might appear," Elena replied thoughtfully. "He agreed to help her mainly out of compassion."

"I discovered that he feels very strongly about the situation with Ethen!" Thomas told them excitedly. "So much so he spoke to the princess about it. He told her he'll have nothing more to do with her if he discovers she's involved in any way in Ethen's captivity. Even if she just knows who's holding him captive!"

"That's all very well, but it sounds like he knows nothing more than we do," said Amyra. "How can he help us?"

"I haven't been able even to catch sight of the princess," Thomas replied. "Her suite is on the opposite side of the palace, and she barely seems to leave it now. If Kamash could arrange for us to meet her, we could find out everything she knows. I only need a glimpse of her, of course."

Will didn't share Thomas's enthusiasm. "Even if the princess has spoken to an agent who knows about Ethen, that doesn't suggest she's been told anything about where he's being held. She doesn't know her way around Rog, so locations would mean nothing to her. And the agents have no reason to give her details anyway."

Thomas left feeling deflated but determined not to give up.

KING STEFFAN STOOD with Queen Essanda on a battlement of their castle at Arnost, gazing distractedly into the distance. A courier accompanied by a contingent of guards had just ridden in from Rog, weary after the long journey on horseback.

"A king isn't supposed to be completely helpless. But that's the reality in this situation," said Steffan gloomily.

Essanda was holding her head. "I feel helpless, too. Will and Amyra are so far away!"

"The worst is that I feel responsible," said Steffan. "I was the one who sent him to Rog." His shoulders slumped. "Will seems to have led a charmed life, and I've taken that far too much for granted."

She shrugged helplessly. "You've never been able to protect Will when he's been off serving the interests of the kingdom. Or anyone else who's ever acted on your behalf."

Steffan threw his hands into the air. "Why did he have to take Amyra and the children? I don't understand it!"

"Would you want to be parted from your family if you were in

Will's position?" Essanda asked. "Don't forget that in our darkest time, after the attack in the barn, we had each other. I was heavily pregnant and unusually vulnerable, but when you look back on everything that happened, would you have wanted me to be somewhere else?"

"I suppose not," he admitted. "But all that aside, I can't make any sense of Thomas and Elena's decision to go, especially with their children. Apart from the risk to them, having a crowd of children running around—in Rog of all places—was almost inviting disaster!"

"I imagine Will and Amyra would have thought their children would cope better if they had friends their own age." She put a gentle hand on his shoulder. "All we can do is hope and pray that Ethen will be found alive and unharmed. At least Brother Ander is with him— we can take some comfort from that. It would be terrible if he was entirely alone."

He nodded. "I need to write to Krasmir. It's going to be delicate. I intend to convey in the strongest possible terms that I expect him to make extraordinary efforts to recover Ethen safely. But it can't come across as inflammatory." He passed a hand across his face. "I'll need you to read it before I send it."

She nodded. "Of course."

"And then I need to write to Will and Amyra. I have no idea even where to begin."

"Would you like me to draft that letter for you?" she asked.

"I would!" he told her with a sigh of relief. "However would I manage without you, Essanda?"

He put an arm around her, and she leaned in, resting her head on his shoulder.

26

———

For Rupert the two days that followed his calamitous interchange with Tasha were bleak beyond words. Unable to face people, he kept to himself, telling anyone who asked that he wasn't feeling well. Lord Mardone and the other Castelans who had accompanied him to Rog offered to call for a doctor, but he dismissed their concerns.

Based on the content of his conversation with King Krasmir, it seemed to Rupert that Tasha's response had been an overreaction. But even if he was right, what difference did it make?

He would have given a great deal to consult with his sister or Count Gordan, but they were far away. Elena had impressed him as both kind and unusually empathic, and he briefly considered confiding in her. But he quickly discarded the idea. She was entirely preoccupied with Lady Torbury.

Wandering alone in the garden, his melancholy was interrupted by the arrival of a servant with a visitor in tow. The visitor was Crown Prince Rimek.

The prince turned pleading eyes upon him the moment the servant had gone. "You have to see her, Rupert!" he exclaimed. "She's irritable and unhappy, and it's so unlike her! She refuses to speak to my parents."

"She won't want to see me," Rupert replied miserably. "She was very angry after I told her about the meeting with your parents. She had some harsh things to say."

Rimek nodded. "That accounts for it then," he said. "She never speaks harshly to anyone." He paused, musing. "Well, almost never. There was that time she came upon someone mistreating a horse..." He shook his head. "This is different. She's upset with herself."

"She isn't just upset with herself," Rupert assured him.

"Probably not," Rimek conceded. "Either way, you need to speak with her!"

When it became obvious that the prince wouldn't take no for an answer, Rupert reluctantly allowed himself to be dragged back to the royal wing of the palace. Leading him out into the garden, Rimek pointed him in the right direction and gave him a gentle push.

Rupert's feet carried him forward, presumably toward Tasha, although he had no idea what he was going to say to her.

Moving around a large bush, he found himself face to face with the princess. She looked at least as unhappy as he felt.

"What are you doing here?" she asked dispiritedly.

She had left her accusation hanging in the air when they parted. *You're supposed to be a king, yet apparently you don't have the nerve to stand up to my parents.* Those words had plagued him relentlessly since. Standing before her once more, he decided it was time he showed some spine.

"Look at you!" he exclaimed. "You're clearly every bit as miserable as I've been. Are you willing to do anything about it?"

She didn't rise to his challenge. "There's nothing I can do."

"There is something," he said. "You can hear me out."

She didn't respond.

"You owe me that much," he insisted. "I wasn't the only one who muddied the truth!"

A spark of defiance rose momentarily in her eyes, but it just as quickly died away.

Not waiting for permission, he began speaking. "I haven't been blessed with an easy life. My mother passed away when I was seven. I have a sister, Essanda, who is a wonderful person. But my father married her off to a foreign king the day after her fourteenth birthday! I was twelve years old. Once she was gone, it was just me and my father. I know he loved me, but expressing it directly wasn't something he ever learned to do.

"He was assassinated when I was seventeen. I was devastated. I became king long before I expected to, and well before I was ready for that kind of responsibility. I made some dreadful mistakes. I trusted people I shouldn't have trusted—people who were secretly working for your father's predecessor. They arranged for my food to be laced with poison, and I almost lost my life, not to mention the kingdom."

When he started she'd barely been able to look at him. Now he glimpsed compassion stirring in her eyes. She probably couldn't help herself.

"I was rescued by some wise and loyal people who risked their lives to expose the traitor and his accomplices. I gradually recovered, and the kingdom was saved. Since then I've slowly been growing into my role. I've been working hard at it, because I know how much power a king has to influence the well-being of every person in the kingdom.

"I have intelligent and capable advisors I can call upon, but it's a lonely job. Crushingly lonely at times! Plenty of young women have been lining up to ease my burden, as you might imagine. They're eager to wear the crown that sits on the head of the queen. But do any of them care about me for my own sake?" He shrugged helplessly. "I have no way of knowing."

He fixed his eyes on her face, his heart beginning to pound. "Then I met you," he said.

She was staring at him wide-eyed. He had her full attention now.

"You didn't know I was a king. You were willing to spend time with someone you thought was a nobody. You told me about yourself, and you asked me questions. And when I answered, you listened as if

I was saying something worth hearing. It was intoxicating to be with someone who took me seriously, just as I was. Your eyes seemed to light up because you enjoyed being with me." He gazed at her intently. "Do you have any idea how your eyes sparkle when you're happy?" he asked.

Was that the ghost of a smile on her face?

"I haven't known you for long," he continued, "but it was quickly obvious to me that we share similar values and passions. Everything changed for me after the time we spent together. I honestly can't remember feeling so contented."

He sighed. "I knew it could all come crashing down, because I needed to tell you the truth. I wasn't sure how a carefree servant girl would cope with knowing she was being pursued by a king."

He made sure he had caught her eyes. "I didn't care that you were a servant, Tasha. I didn't care that your skin was a different color. I didn't even care that you were better at languages than me!"

That earned him a grin.

"The reason I didn't care about any of that is because I care about *you*. You might be Tasha, you might be Princess Teylee, you might be the daughter of a king who's sometimes compared to a bear."

Taken by surprise at his own brazenness, he stole a quick glance about him. "Please don't tell him I said that!" he blurted awkwardly, sparking a brief burst of laughter from her.

His face grew serious again. "Whatever people might call you and however they might think of you, to me you'll always be the unpretentious girl with the sparkling eyes who spares a thought for the most disadvantaged—a girl who was willing to treat me as someone who mattered, not as someone to be used."

She stared back at him. "That's the most wonderful thing anyone has ever said to me," she breathed.

He abandoned any attempt to calm his racing heart.

"Of course it doesn't hurt at all that you're also very beautiful. Have I told you that?"

"No, you haven't," she replied forthrightly. Her eyes were definitely twinkling now.

"In that case let me rectify the omission. You stunned me from the moment you stepped through that hedge. You have the most bewitching eyes, in case I haven't mentioned it already. And when you smile it's like sunshine bursting through the clouds." He gazed at her dreamily. "As for your figure..." His eyebrows went up, and he slowly released a deep sigh.

A beaming smile lit her face, only to be replaced by a mock frown. "You haven't mentioned my hair!"

"Your hair..." He scrutinized her thoughtfully. "It's positively lustrous," he finally pronounced. "When seen at the right moment."

A merry laugh escaped her lips. Her smile truly was a ray of sunlight on a stormy day.

He gazed at her in frank admiration. It was impossible to imagine ever getting tired of looking at her.

She met his eyes. "I'm very sorry I said such mean things to you," she told him penitently. "I've been so ashamed of myself! What I said wasn't true at all. I *am* willing to be courted by you." She flushed delightfully.

"And I don't blame you for being taken by surprise by my father. He can be fierce at times, especially on behalf of his children. But he did agree to let you court me, and that says a lot about his opinion of you."

She sighed. "I owe you an explanation for the way I behaved. Unexpectedly becoming a princess hasn't been easy for me. I've never been able to get used to the idea that I could be married off to someone just to benefit the kingdom. Maybe it would have been different if I'd been born a princess. But I wasn't. When you told me about your conversation with my father, all of my worst fears just came rushing in. My reaction wasn't fair, and I'm truly sorry for the way I treated you. I can be impulsive at times, and it gets me into trouble."

There were no words for his relief. "Thank you for being honest with me," he said earnestly. "I can't begin to tell you how wretched my life has felt since our last interaction."

"It's been just as bad for me," she confessed. "I've been desperately unhappy, and I've treated my family abominably."

Taking her delicate hands in his own, he gazed down into her twinkling eyes. "I would like to spend whatever time it takes to get to know you properly, Tasha," he said. "Can we make a new beginning?"

"I would like that very much," she replied. Then with a cheeky grin she added, "Lord Boyd."

He laughed. "You're allowed to call me Boyd—that offer applies only to you, mind—but no more of this Lord business!"

"In private I think I'll call you Boyd. When I'm happy with you, that is," she said, her lips quirking into another smile.

"That suits me fine," he said happily.

She became suddenly sober. "We need to leave," she said. "We'll get into big trouble if we spend this much time together without a chaperone."

He nodded. Her face fell for a moment when he released her hands, which didn't displease him at all. Then they headed back toward the building, maintaining a respectable distance between them.

She led the way inside.

It soon became apparent that her entire family had been watching from one of the windows.

"Well thank goodness for that!" exclaimed the queen. She eyed Tasha critically. "You finally look like your normal self again."

Tasha cocked an eyebrow at her mother. Then she turned away to introduce Rupert to her two sisters. Some time passed before her family saw fit to release him.

As Rupert approached his wing of the palace, he released a quiet whoop, barely able to contain his elation.

So much had changed since the crown prince pressed him to meet with Tasha. If he'd ever felt happier in his entire life, he had no memory of it.

King Krasmir retreated to the royal apartments that evening overcome with weariness. It had been another long day with more than its share of challenges. On his way he was intercepted by an unusually buoyant Tasha. The affectionate kiss she bestowed on his cheek went a long way toward improving his mood.

He arrived to find Queen Deka in raptures.

"It's so gratifying to see our Tasha well placed," she gushed. "She'll make a wonderful queen! Insisting that the children learn Arvenian was a canny move, even if I do say so myself."

Krasmir frowned at her. "There's a very long way to go before anything of the kind is settled."

"Nonsense," she replied decidedly. "He's every bit as smitten as she is. What he said to win her back was positively moving!" She heaved a dramatic sigh, brushing a tear from her eye.

He frowned at her. "They were supposedly talking in private! How do you know what he said?"

"I have my sources," she sniffed.

He grunted. "That explains why she begged me to give them space. I told her I had no intention of agreeing to any such request. You've just changed my mind!"

She glowered at him for a moment then threw up her arms. "Do whatever you want. Nothing will prevent me from keeping a close eye on her. I'm her mother!"

When he failed to respond, she sighed once more. "If only there was an advantageous match for Rimek. Steffan and Essanda's daughter is much too young for him."

"There's always the princess of Ahr," he replied dryly.

"Don't make light of such an important matter," she protested, frowning at him fiercely.

Then she brightened. "Our Ashloh will do very nicely for Delmar of course."

"I wouldn't count on it," he replied. "Delmar is planning to return to Varacellan imminently. I expect an announcement from him at any moment."

A look of dismay came over her face. "How do you know that?" she demanded.

"You're not the only one with sources," he grunted.

KRASMIR DIDN'T KNOW IT, but at that very moment King Delmar was indeed planning his return to Varas.

Delmar had invited King Rupert and Count Ranauld to join him.

"I'll be leaving for Varacellan as soon as my ship is ready to sail," he told them. "Two of my senior noblemen will remain to represent me."

"What has prompted your desire to return?" asked Ranauld.

"I've been receiving persistent reports about Ahrans arriving in Varacellan. Posing as merchants, of course, but many of them are undoubtedly agents of the emperor. Right now I'm needed there more than I'm needed here. If the situation in Rog changes, I will return without hesitation. It isn't a particularly long journey."

He turned to Rupert. "You're welcome to travel with me if you like. Once we arrive in Varacellan a ship can easily take you on to Castel."

"I appreciate your consideration, Your Majesty," Rupert replied. "I'm in no hurry to leave, though. I left Count Gordan in charge, and he has been sending me regular reports. He is extremely capable, and I trust him implicitly." He paused to steady himself. "My other reason for staying is that I have requested and received King Krasmir's permission to court Princess Teylee, his youngest daughter. Unless a pressing reason arises to return to Castel, I plan to remain in Rog for some time."

Delmar was taken completely by surprise by this announcement, and it was obvious that Ranauld was as well. "You have my hearty congratulations!" he said with a smile. "Krasmir is a good man, and I have only heard favorable reports about his children. I can also see many benefits in stronger ties between Rogand and its western neighbors."

Ranauld expressed similar sentiments, and Rupert thanked them both sincerely.

"This news might also help to explain your distraction of late, Rupert," Delmar told him with a smile.

A sheepish grin came to Rupert's face. "I won't deny that the process thus far has been challenging," he said. "But I am hopeful that we're on firmer footing now. Beyond that, though, it is likely that I will see more of King Krasmir in the immediate future. I would be happy to act as a conduit in passing information back and forth if it is helpful."

"I have no doubt that it would be helpful," Delmar assured him. "Ready access to King Krasmir could prove to be invaluable. I plan to meet with him one more time before I leave. Our agents have uncovered some information about the Ahrans that he needs to know."

Both of them looked at him expectantly, and Ranauld in particular leaned forward intently.

"Unfortunately it doesn't help directly in the search for Ethen," he told them. Ranauld's face fell. "There are indications that the Grand Vizier has returned to Rogand, and that he has based himself in a large farmhouse not far from Rog."

"That should give Krasmir something to work with," Ranauld said hopefully.

Delmar nodded. "Please treat this information as highly confidential. I would appreciate it if you speak of it to no one."

"Not even Lord Torbury?" asked Ranauld.

Delmar hesitated before replying. The matter was extremely delicate.

"The agents have discovered no evidence to suggest that Ethen is being held in the Grand Vizier's headquarters," he said. "For that reason it might be a mistake for Lord Torbury to redirect his attention away from Rog. The king is the one with the resources to search multiple locations at once."

Ranauld nodded reluctantly. "I see your point. I will honor your request to keep this information completely confidential, at least for the time being."

The meeting broke up almost at once, allowing Delmar to resume his preparations for departure.

Regrettably, Delmar would not be leaving with any great sense of achievement. He felt confident that his presence in Rog had strengthened the goodwill between Rogand and Varas. Beyond that, he could not identify a single return on his investment of time in Rogand.

27

———————

Bisri Ahuzza watched as the Grand Vizier clambered up the rope ladder from the longboat accompanied by his senior agent, Bolnyk. The chief minister was clearly irritated that he could not meet the emperor's captains in a more civilized environment.

At that moment though, Rog harbor was not a place where Ahran warships could dock openly. Ahuzza had no choice but to keep his ships at sea. Whether Rheibas liked it or not, if he wanted to meet in secret with the captains in Ahuzza's squadron, the only option was for him to join them on one of the ships.

On this occasion, all three captains had joined Ahuzza, the chief minister, and Bolnyk on one of the ships.

The Grand Vizier eyed them haughtily. "As you are aware, the emperor sent me to Rog with instructions to inform the Rogandans that he was granting them one month to retrieve the princess. Events have now rendered the emperor's instructions obsolete."

The captains stirred uneasily, shooting glances at Bisri Ahuzza and at one another.

"After landing secretly, I learned through our agents that the king of Rogand has already produced the princess. Either he had her all along, or less likely, he came to an arrangement with the supposed pirates. However it came about, the Imperial Princess is now in Rog."

The news was greeted with general relief, but Rheibas did not leave them cheerful for long.

"The princess might be near at hand, but that does not mean she has attained her freedom. I have it on good authority that this King Krasmir has no intention of allowing her to return to her countrymen."

"What do you plan to do, Your Eminence?" asked Ahuzza.

"Nothing impulsive," he replied. "The situation is extremely delicate and needs to be handled with great care. I am informing you to keep you appraised of the circumstances." He turned to Ahuzza. "I must insist that you and your captains take no action of any kind without consulting with me first. I also need your assurance that my efforts will have your full support."

Bisri Ahuzza assessed the situation rapidly. Even if he had wanted to operate independently, he had no real choice. They were a long way from Kat Ahket, and while the emperor had placed him in command of the squadron, the practical reality was that the Grand Vizier outranked him. He might be independent in theory, but in practice he could not disregard instructions from the most senior official in the empire.

Embracing the only path available to him, he agreed not to act independently. He also confirmed that the chief minister had his full support.

Rheibas had maneuvered himself into position as the only person able to deal with the complexities of the situation. Ahuzza could only hope that the chief minister's legendary mastery over impossible situations would not desert him in this remote corner of the world.

AFTER RAPPING TWICE on the door before him, Bolnyk stood back to wait.

"Enter!" a voice growled.

Pushing through into a spacious study, the agent bowed to the Grand Vizier. "I understand you summoned me," he said.

Rheibas offered no immediate response, staring narrow eyed out of the window instead.

The look on the face of his master suggested he was not in a good mood. It wasn't hard to guess at the reason. The chief minister had given Bisri Ahuzza and his captains a report that accounted for the reappearance of the princess in Rog. He had laid the blame at the door of the Rogandan king, accusing him of first abducting the princess then producing her when it suited him. The Rogandans and their allies would deny it of course, but that need not concern him. No true Ahran would believe the Rogandans over their own Grand Vizier.

The problem was that the princess knew what had really happened, and she could refute this story in a moment if she chose to. Bolnyk had no idea how Rheibas planned to deal with this problem.

The Grand Vizier had told the princess that Captain Gharpin had been responsible for her abandonment. Perhaps he had managed to convince her, but even if he had, this alternative account could not be reconciled with the story he had told Bisri Ahuzza and the captains.

The central difficulty was that the princess had survived, against all expectations. Bolnyk had no idea how that had happened. With her now established in Rog under the protection of the Rogandan king, his master's options were limited.

Nevertheless, Bolnyk had personally witnessed the rise of Bisri Rheibas to his current position as Grand Vizier of the Empire of Ahr. The promotion had not come as a gift. Rheibas had earned it the hard way. He would never have scaled such heights were he not a master at retrieving impossible situations.

Turning his attention to Bolnyk at last, Rheibas demanded, "The boy. The one who was abducted. Why hasn't he been brought here?"

"As you are aware, Your Eminence, King Krasmir has been pursuing our agents with unusual vigor over the past few days,"

Bolnyk replied. "A number of our safe houses have been overrun. I have delayed the transfer in the hope of a lull in the king's activities. At the moment there would seem to be a significant risk of detection."

"Risk or no risk, I want it done within the next forty-eight hours," the chief minister demanded.

Bolnyk bowed.

"Is the monk still alive, and if so, why?"

"He is alive," Bolnyk confirmed. "I am told that the monk has managed to keep the boy calm and occupied. By doing so he has preserved his own life."

Rheibas grunted. "You're growing soft, Bolnyk."

The accusation was untrue, of course, but Bolnyk was well aware that the Grand Vizier was more interested in keeping his men ruthless and focused than in constraining himself with the truth.

The agent's only response was a stiff bow.

"Are you too weak to kill the boy should it come to that?" Rheibas demanded.

"Your orders are clear," Bolnyk replied coolly. "Bring them here alive. If that proves impossible, kill them both. I'll do it myself if the need arises."

The chief minister grunted.

Bolnyk knew he would never have risen to his current position if Rheibas had ever found him unable or unwilling to be ruthless. As for killing an innocent child, the chief minister knew he'd done worse than that. And he'd done it without hesitation.

"While you are here, you can give me a status report," the Grand Vizier said.

"There is one matter of immediate concern, Your Eminence," Bolnyk began. "It is possible that our location here may at some point become compromised. I have ordered one of the men to oversee the search for an alternative location."

"Why should our location be compromised?" Rheibas asked.

"Rog is seething with agents. The Rogandan king, the priests, even the Varasans have people snooping around. The father of the boy has been particularly determined. Every safe house that is compromised quickly leads to the detection of another."

The chief minister scowled. "Captured agents are spilling our secrets? I thought they were being told nothing beyond their own missions."

"Agents are told only what they absolutely need to know. Very few have any information about other locations in use by our people."

"How are the Rogandans learning about other locations then?"

Bolnyk shrugged. "They seem to have unusually effective interrogation techniques."

The chief minister shook his head. "It makes no sense. A few of the weaker agents might crumble under torture, but on this scale?"

His master was right of course. It didn't make sense.

"Do we have enough agents in place?" Rheibas asked with a frown.

"Your steady buildup over recent months has achieved what was needed, Your Eminence. I suspect our men are far more numerous than King Krasmir could imagine."

The chief minister had certainly not been idle. As head of the spy network of the empire, he had almost unlimited resources at his disposal. The emperor might have placed the squadron of ships under the command of Bisri Ahuzza, but that was little more than a symbolic act. The Grand Vizier's own ships were quietly coming and going from Rogand almost continuously, delivering agents, money, and anything else that could possibly be needed to further his purposes.

The Ahran web had already been well established by the time Rheibas arrived in Rog to accuse King Krasmir of piracy. It was now spreading out wider, both across Rogand and into Varacellan. Arvenon would be next.

"Our infiltration went undetected for months," said the chief minister. "Why the sudden interest in exposing our agents? Is it the arrival of the princess?"

Bolnyk shook his head. "It is more likely related to the boy," he replied. "We can expect pressure to be applied for as long as we continue to hold him."

Rheibas scowled. "We'll stay the course however many agents we lose. If the Rogandans are weeding out the careless ones, they're doing us a favor."

The agent offered no response apart from a tight bow.

"Have you investigated who is behind the raids on our safe houses?" the chief minister asked Bolnyk.

The agent's brows drew together. "I have made discreet inquiries, Your Eminence. Unlikely as it might seem, the only common factor seems to be Lord Torbury, the boy's father. My sources have revealed that bystanders frequently report sighting a man matching Torbury's description in the vicinity of raids."

Rheibas was clearly surprised. "The boy's father? How is he involved in this? And how did he conclude that his son was taken by Ahran agents? He couldn't possibly know that with any certainty. Why wouldn't he suspect the Rogandans? They were his enemies for long enough." He shook his head in puzzlement.

"I instructed you to learn more about him," the chief minister reminded Bolnyk. "What have you discovered?"

"As you already know, he is the Arvenian army commander," Bolnyk replied. "It is said he has never been defeated in battle. More than ten years ago he led the combined armies of Arvenon and Castel against a much larger Rogandan force that had invaded Arvenon and annexed Varas. His soldiers crushed the Rogandan army in a major battle at Torbury Scarp."

"This commander is beginning to interest me," said the chief minister, his lip curling in a sneer. "Holding his son might prove more valuable than I had imagined."

Bolnyk could readily guess what his master might be thinking. A man like Rheibas would find it especially satisfying to vanquish a celebrated strategist. The boy gave him a unique opportunity to demonstrate to the Arvenian commander that his run of victories had come to an end.

"He is a nobleman?" asked Rheibas.

Bolnyk nodded. "Yes, Your Eminence. He was formerly a commoner, but after his successes the Arvenian king gave him a title —Lord Torbury—in honor of his greatest victory. The Rogandan nobles despise him. Every use of his title is a constant reminder to them of their humiliation at his hands. Lord Torbury speaks Rogandan as if it were his native language, and that only deepens the insult."

"How does Krasmir view him?" asked the chief minister.

"The king is said to tolerate him. Krasmir needs an alliance with the Arvenians. He also has no strategist of his own to equal Torbury."

Rheibas nodded slowly. "Bring the boy to me alive if at all possible. If it becomes necessary to kill him though, don't hesitate. After Torbury's attacks on the agents of the empire, killing his son would be fitting retaliation."

His agent dipped his head in acknowledgment.

"There are perplexing riddles here," growled the chief minister. "What has made Torbury so certain his son was being held by Ahrans? And how has he become so effective at rooting out your agents?" He shook his head.

"Leave me now," the chief minister told his agent. "I need time to think. But before you go, I expect to be informed well ahead of time if the Rogandans are planning to move on this location. In the meantime, complete your search. As soon as you have secured a suitable base, ensure that we are ready to relocate to it at a moment's notice. If we move, we will leave this place occupied. Krasmir can raid it. Let him think he has taken out our headquarters."

Once more Bolnyk bowed.

"Another thing. You've been in contact with the princess?"

"I passed on your letter myself," Bolnyk confirmed. "And destroyed it afterward as you ordered."

Rheibas grunted. "Contact her again, and find out if she knows anything useful about Krasmir's intentions. You are dismissed."

Hidden in the darkness, Goultzar conversed in low tones with two dark-clad priests. Others hovered watchfully nearby, ready to warn the Archprimus of unwanted attention.

He had dismantled his spy network as instructed. For the most part. Only the closest of his associates remained now—including the men engaged at that moment in his clandestine meeting. He could no longer meet with his supporters openly, and it was increasingly difficult to meet with them at all.

"Two of our agents have disappeared," one of the men told him.

He scowled. "Disappeared? How can they just disappear?"

"We can't say with any certainty," he was told. "They last reported in yesterday. They'd been observing Ahran agents while also dodging some of our own people."

"The High Priest's agents," Goultzar concluded darkly.

The only response was a grunt, presumably in affirmation.

"So who was responsible for their disappearance?" he growled. He didn't wait for an answer. "You've done well," he told them. "Keep me informed, and make sure you stay out of sight."

The men nodded silently. Within moments they were gone, as unobtrusively as they had come.

He glanced toward the temple building, extremely uncomfortable about his own mixed feelings upon reentering it.

Of late the atmosphere in the temple of Rog had been thicker than usual. It had nothing to do with the habitual odor that filled Goultzar's lungs and clung to his nostrils even when he ventured outside. The change in climate had everything to do with the coolness that had opened up between the High Priest and his Archprimus.

Perhaps it was more accurate to say that a coolness appeared to have opened up. The High Priest had never referred to it. He remained as taciturn as ever, and what he did say was about as cryptic as it had always been. But the subtle signs were there. He rarely called for Goultzar now, and when he did, the Archprimus felt the Superior's eyes boring into him, weighing him up and finding him wanting.

Goultzar tried to maintain his focus on worshiping the dark gods as before, but his thoughts increasingly wandered, and he was much too distracted to concentrate as he should.

He continued to direct the other priests—it was an essential part of this role—but he did so with uncharacteristic hesitancy. He had his own loyalists, but what the rest of the priests thought and whether they were choosing sides he couldn't say with any certainty. But he was conscious of feeling watched wherever he went.

Pushing aside his doubts, he headed for the door, suppressing an audible sigh as he walked inside. A familiar sense of belonging had always accompanied his return. It seemed to have deserted him, and the extent of his new ambivalence alarmed him. He made his way to his own private office, eager for solitude.

A single question nagged him incessantly: what should he do about the fault lines opening up in the temple? In his darkest moments he had even imagined putting the High Priest's famed longevity to the test. He was, after all, the designated successor to the High Priest.

The question of longevity took his mind back to the twenty fools who had invaded the sanctity of the temple. They had hoped to drag the High Priest away bodily to explore that same question—Goultzar's own agents had exposed their plans well in advance of the abortive raid, and the Archprimus had been ready for them. Having led the operation that ended with the disposal of their bodies, he had derived considerable satisfaction from the outcome. Allowing them to succeed would never have occurred to him in his wildest imaginings. Yet in recent times he had found himself daydreaming about exactly such a conclusion.

He shook his head, trying to apply himself to more immediate questions. Who was responsible for the demise of his agents? Most likely it was the Ahrans, but he could not rule out the possibility that the High Priest's men were responsible. Finding replacements was out of the question. He would be forced to make do with the dwindling resources that remained to him.

A niggling pain in the small of his back intruded on his deliberations. Perhaps the High Priest had found a way to conquer mortality, but if he had, the Archprimus wasn't privy to it.

"What progress can you report, My Lord?" King Krasmir asked his commander. "I'm not in a patient mood. We need to find Lord Torbury's son, and we need to do it soon. I've just received a strongly worded communication from King Steffan. He stopped short of holding me accountable for the outcome, but he will not be at all pleased if the matter is not resolved satisfactorily. Meanwhile, the threat of an Ahran invasion hasn't gone away, and it's getting little or no attention. The abduction has distracted us for far too long."

Lord Kulferan dipped his head in acknowledgment. "We have been pursuing information provided by King Delmar before he returned to Varas, Your Majesty. The information is promising, and I'm cautiously optimistic."

The king frowned. "How have the Varasans managed to outdo us? This is supposed to be our backyard."

The commander winced. "They clearly have an unmatched network. It's small, but it seems remarkably effective."

"The Varasans are allies—use that fact to find out as much as you can about their methods."

The nobleman dipped his head.

"What information have you learned from them?" asked the king.

"They believe that the Grand Vizier has returned to Rogand and is directing his agents from a large farmhouse somewhere near Rog."

"If that's truly what he's done, it amounts to a declaration of war," growled the king.

"I agree, Your Majesty, although we have not yet confirmed this information," Lord Kulferan reminded him. "Nevertheless we believe we have almost finished identifying likely locations that involve land transfers. We will be moving the moment the investigation is complete."

The king eyed his commander soberly. "I don't need to tell you that the death of the child is not a result I'm willing to accept. I trust you are operating accordingly."

"Of course, Your Majesty."

28

The morning after Rupert's reconciliation with Tasha, he received an invitation to meet with her. Accepting eagerly, he was escorted to a section of the palace he had never visited.

"Good morning, Rupert!" Her vivacious welcome made him feel like king of the world.

"Good morning, Tasha. I'm delighted to see you again!"

After they had exchanged pleasantries, she asked casually, "Are you interested in books?" Her face wore a simple smile, but he couldn't shake off the suspicion that her question had a right and wrong answer.

"I enjoy reading very much," he replied honestly. "So I am definitely interested in books."

"I am, too!" she told him, her face beaming with delight.

He shook his head in relief at having provided the correct answer. Apparently misinterpreting the gesture, she stared at him in alarm. "You're surprised! Is it possible you imagined I was all sparkle and no substance?"

"Of course not!" he sputtered.

"I was only teasing!" she laughed. "Nevertheless, it is a reminder of how little we know each other," she added seriously.

He nodded his agreement. There was plenty to learn about Tasha. He was confident he would never find her boring.

"There was a reason for my question," she told him. "I'd like to show you something."

An ornate door stood nearby. Pushing it open, she disappeared through it. He followed at once, trailed by her chaperones. A large chamber lay inside. Wooden shelves covered every wall, the shelves lined with books, rolled up scrolls, and piles of parchments.

Gazing about in astonishment, he admitted to himself that he had not imagined Rogand as a center of learning.

"I love this place," said Tasha, speaking in little more than a whisper.

He understood her restraint. The accumulated knowledge surrounding them was breathtaking. Approaching one of the shelves, he removed a book and opened it. After peering at it for a few moments he replaced it on the shelf.

He grimaced. "I'm afraid that I'm no better at reading Rogandan than I am at speaking it. Much worse, in fact."

Tasha chuckled. "I read Arvenian poorly," she admitted.

She led the way to another section of the library. "There are books and parchments here written in Arvenian. I've made little headway with them."

Pulling a few volumes from the shelf, he examined them carefully, finding they dealt with medicine, theology, and astronomy. Many appeared old and extremely fragile. Picking an aging scroll at random, he unrolled it with great care.

"This appears to be a history," he said.

"Can you read it to me?" Tasha asked.

Rupert nodded. "If you lose interest, let me know."

He began reading.

This chronicle is recorded by Burnett of Earlsford, scribe to King Attalnar of Arvenon.

I set out on midsummer's day with the host of the king, marching east toward the disputed lands beyond the Blue Mountains.

From ancient times the border of Arvenon has run along the eastern skirts of these mountains, giving the king a rightful claim over territory on both sides of the mountain range.

Of old these lands were sparsely inhabited, the cities of the Aen-ur lying further to the east. With the fair cities of these peaceful folk torn down by the Rogandans, the Aen-ur were pushed west, establishing themselves at last in the great fortress of Ishitar Ataye in the foothills of the Blue Mountains. Rumor had it that even this final refuge had fallen.

Following the main trading route east, we cleared the Blue Mountains and swung north. After many days and frequent skirmishes with Rogandan patrols, we came at last to the ancient fortress. Nothing but desolate ruins remained. Since the bridge had also been broken down, we turned south and followed the great river until we reached a ford.

Once most of the host had crossed, a small group of men approached from the treeline on the same side of the river.

"Who are you that trespasses in the lands of the Aen-ur?" the chief among them asked.

"I am Attalnar, King of Arvenon," the king replied. "These are my lands, and we are no trespassers."

The other man bowed. "If you are indeed the king of Arvenon, you speak truly," he replied. "I am Jae-Nairan, ruler of what little remains of the Aen-ur. It is we who are the miscreants, and I beg your pardon."

With that he waved an arm, and many archers appeared from behind rocks and trees, lowering their weapons.

King Attalnar replied courteously, "I do not begrudge you and your people refuge on our lands, King Jae-Nairan."

A man approached the Aen-ur king and whispered in his ear.

"May I suggest that your men complete their crossing quickly and establish themselves on this side of the river?" King Jae-Nairan said. "We have experienced heavy rains in this region of late, and I have just received warning of an imminent flash flood."

King Attalnar gave the order, and the ford was cleared.

As the last of his men climbed the bank, the king was informed of the arrival of a new force from beyond the river.

A man stepped from their midst and stood at the edge of the ford. "These lands belong to Rogand," he called threateningly.

"I had not heard of it," King Attalnar replied. "These mountains have belonged to Arvenon for generations. As king of that country, I claim sovereign rights."

"Your claim is bold," sneered the other. "We shall see if you can support it." He waved an arm, and a large body of men began moving into the ford. They proceeded warily, the opposite bank being held against them.

King Attalnar was a man possessed of great learning. His subtlety was likewise rarely equaled. Raising his voice, he called out in the Rogandan tongue. "In destroying the great fortress of the Aen-ur you have awakened the wrath of an ancient sorcerer of unmatched power. He now spies out the land in the semblance of an eagle. In the guise of a bear his authority is revealed. Those who dare intrude in this region will taste his fierce anger," cried the king.

As he spoke, an eagle flew overhead, and a bear was seen eyeing the host. Although such creatures were common in these parts, many of the Rogandans hesitated.

The Rogandan commander scoffed at the words. "You will not frighten us with such tales." Calling a harsh command, he pushed forward into the ford at the head of many men.

"You have provoked the enchanter's fury," called King Attalnar. "You will face the consequences."

The words had barely left his mouth when a roaring sound was heard. Flood waters poured down the river with great force, sweeping away the Rogandan commander and every person in the ford. Even *men on the far bank were overwhelmed before they could scramble to safety.*

The survivors retreated in disorder, crying out in fear. The host of King Attalnar and the men of the Aen-ur watched on in awe.

When the last of their enemies were gone, King Attalnar turned to the Aen-ur ruler. "They will long hesitate before coming here again," he said.

King Jae-Nairan bowed deeply. "We are forever in your debt," he replied. "Those men were sent with the sole purpose of destroying the remnant of our people who survived the fall of Ishitar Ataye. There is little I can do to repay you, but before you return to your capital I will give you a token. It is an object of no apparent value—just a small glazed tile with a brightly colored surface—yet its worth is beyond price to us. It is a tiny reminder of the splendor of the throne room at Ishitar Ataye. There may come a time when it will be of use to you or your successors."

"I thank you," King Attalnar replied. "For my part, you are welcome to remain here, or indeed to settle elsewhere in Arvenon if that pleases you better."

"We will remain in the land that nurtured us," King Jae-Nairan told him.

The Aen-ur ruler uttered a final warning. "Be aware that your kindness to us will not endear you to the Rogandans. In turning them away from this region you have injured yourself. Their attention will turn next to Arvenon."

"Let them come," King Attalnar replied. "They will not find us unprepared."

After receiving the promised token from the Aen-ur, the king bid them farewell and led his host back the way we had come.

I, Burnett of Earlsford, myself witnessed these events.

"THE SCROLL ENDS THERE," said Rupert.

"The scribe does not portray my forebears in a favorable light," said Tasha frankly. "Do you believe it to be a true account?"

He shrugged. "I cannot say."

After reflecting silently for a time, she said, "I know a little of the Aen-ur. King Agon hated them and pursued them ruthlessly. In recent years my father has reached an understanding with them."

She soon abandoned her musing. Facing him eagerly, she told him, "My parents instructed me to issue you an invitation. You must join us tonight at our evening meal!"

His heart skipped a beat, and his breathing hitched. "I...I would be honored," he told her.

Honor it might be, but the prospect of being paraded in front of her family and their invited guests was daunting to say the least. But small and insignificant though his kingdom might be, he was a reigning monarch, and for Tasha's sake he would do his best to behave like one.

"I will look forward to it," he said.

"Wonderful!" she enthused.

Undoubtedly sensing his apprehension, she added, "And please don't worry. I have no doubt that it will go very smoothly."

WITH HIS FIRST meal with Tasha's family underway, Rupert stole a glance at Tasha. Buoyed by her encouraging smile, he was finally able to calm his racing heart and master his breathing.

When ushered into the dining room, Rupert had been taken by surprise. Servants were bustling about in preparation for serving food and drink, but the only people seated at table were the royal family. He had fully expected to find them dining with members of the nobility, as he did in his own royal castle. Before he could decide whether it was easier or harder to be the only guest, they rose together and welcomed him warmly.

Vigorous conversation was soon underway. Rupert followed the interactions with mixed success. While it was quickly apparent that his Rogandan language skills needed work, he was able to participate remarkably well. Whenever he felt especially bemused, one of the princesses—usually Tasha—noticed his confusion and helpfully provided a translation.

The experience had been a revelation in a multitude of ways. Table manners clearly differed from Castelan customs, most of the differences being minor, but thankfully the royal family didn't stand on ceremony. Some of the food was unfamiliar, but thus far he had thoroughly enjoyed everything he had been served. Recipes for a number of the dishes would certainly be finding their way to his chefs at Castel Citadel.

The biggest surprise was the energy level, and most especially the noise. It felt like everyone was talking at once, and to his amazement King Krasmir didn't seem to mind a bit. Both the king and the queen engaged almost as energetically as their children. Crown Prince Rimek had plenty to say, but he couldn't keep pace with his vivacious twin, Princess Ashloh. The dark-eyed Princess Kyla, a beauty by any standard, was the demure member of the family. She sometimes struggled to get a word in, but it didn't seem to bother her. Tasha—*his* Tasha as a euphoric inner voice kept reminding him—was by no means the most talkative of the family, but she had no difficulty holding her own in interactions that occasionally bordered on the chaotic.

Rupert watched on wide-eyed. He'd even caught himself open mouthed on a couple of occasions when he wasn't sufficiently guarded. After getting over his initial astonishment though, he increasingly found himself enjoying the experience.

For the most part the conversation lingered around everyday topics. On one occasion, Prince Rimek had asked quietly, "Has Lord Kulferan made any further progress?"

The king's only reply was a warning glance, and the prince immediately took the hint, switching to a more mundane topic.

Rupert understood perfectly. His presence at the table was not the issue. With so many servants in ready earshot, it was safest to avoid matters of state entirely.

Queen Deka took advantage of a rare lull in the conversation to address Rupert directly.

"It is such a pleasure to have you here with us, Rupert," she said with a beaming smile.

Tasha aimed a scandalized look at her mother, but Rupert wasn't at all bothered by the queen's familiarity in using his name rather than his title. Her body language suggested she had accepted him as part of the family already, and he felt only gratitude.

"Does it remind you of meals around your own table at Castel Citadel?" she asked.

"Not even slightly, Your Majesty," he replied without hesitation.

An uncharacteristic silence settled over the table, every eye turning to Rupert. Realizing he could still play it safe by saying very little, he shot a quick glance at Tasha. The look of encouragement on her face decided him.

"I have never attended a family meal like this in my life," he confessed, "and I must say I feel the poorer for it."

The rapid flow of conversation had dried up entirely. Deciding to ignore the unwavering attentiveness on their faces, he continued.

"I come from a small family, one that only grew smaller over the years. My mother died when I was quite young. I have a few memories of her—I can still hear her laugh—but between the ages of seven and twelve my family was just me, my father and my older sister, Essanda. After my sister became the queen of Arvenon I had five more years with my father. Then he was gone too."

"For my part, I am sincerely sorry for the role Rogand played in the trouble visited upon your family," said the king soberly.

"Thank you, Your Majesty." Seeing no reason to dwell on the past, Rupert satisfied himself with a brief dip of his head in acknowledgment.

He continued. "Even before my father's passing, I never experienced family in this kind of way. If I ever have children of my own," he added, feeling his face coloring as he said it, "I want them to grow up with this, not what I had."

"You poor boy!" crooned the queen. "We will just have to adopt you for as long as you're in Rog."

"My own experience was not dissimilar to yours," the king told him. "We have my wife, and her family before her, to thank for how we are today."

Queen Deka nodded wisely. "The best way to make sure your children experience our kind of family is, of course, to marry someone who grew up with it." As she said it, she beamed a smile in the direction of Tasha.

"Mother!" protested Tasha, her face turning beet red.

"I'm merely speaking the truth," her mother insisted.

The king raised his eyebrows imploringly, causing Rimek to snort with laughter. That set Ashloh off, and before long boisterous banter reigned supreme once more.

Occasionally one of them thought to include Rupert directly in the conversation, but for the most part he was happy to listen and observe.

When the meal came to an end and they had all risen from the table, he left satisfied. And not just from eating his fill of good food. He decided his contentment was mostly due to Tasha's family making it so obvious that they accepted him.

Odd as it might be, he felt completely at home with a family he barely knew, a family who spoke another language. Only a few years previously his kingdom had been at war with Rogand. Now his fondest hope was to marry a Rogandan.

Tasha accompanied him when he left. "They like you," she told him with an elated smile. "I'm not at all surprised, but I'm still very pleased."

"You have a wonderful family," he told her. "I'm more grateful than I can say that they're so welcoming of me."

"They are very special," she agreed. "Mother can be incredibly embarrassing though," she added, raising her hands helplessly.

He laughed. "She certainly isn't afraid to speak her mind."

Tasha went silent for a moment. "There's something I need to ask you," she said, casting an uncharacteristically tentative look toward him.

"Yes?" he asked, raising his eyebrows curiously.

"My sister Kyla. I know she's much more beautiful than I am." She lowered her eyes uncomfortably.

He stared at her in surprise. After an awkward silence, he asked, "Do you think I might be wondering if I'm pursuing the wrong princess?"

She didn't respond.

"You can't have much of an opinion of me if you think I'd pursue a girl just because she's beautiful."

She winced. "I didn't mean that," she said self-consciously.

He gazed into her eyes. "Kyla is beautiful—I would never deny it. But it wasn't your looks that first drew me to you. I was captivated by you as a person! It didn't take me long to notice how beautiful you were, but on its own your appearance—or anyone else's for that matter—would not have been enough to attract me."

She was looking up at him earnestly, her eyes wide.

"When I was with your family just now, yours was the smile I wanted to see," he confessed. "Your face is in my mind as I drift off to sleep, and you are the person I'm most eager to greet when my day begins."

Lowering her gaze, she released a sigh that might have been relief. "I'm glad we've sorted that out," she said.

He wasn't entirely satisfied. "You haven't told me what you're thinking about when you go to sleep," he noted.

"No, I haven't," she agreed, a twinkle in her eye.

Not long after his first meal with Tasha's family, Rupert discovered that the princess enjoyed riding. With the help of Rimek, who had promised to assist in any way he could, suitable mounts were soon secured for them both.

When they set off on their first ride, it felt to Rupert more like a procession than a private outing. Their mounted escort consisted of six armed soldiers along with a mature woman—an accomplished rider—as a chaperone. Tedious as it was, he decided to ignore it and enjoy the opportunity to spend time with Tasha. Their escort did at least allow them some breathing space.

Their conversation ranged over many topics, from the trivial to the weighty.

"Will you miss your family when you...when you leave them?" Rupert asked.

"Undoubtedly," she told him with a smile. "Especially if some foreigner wants to whisk me away to an unfamiliar place where they eat strange food and speak a different language."

"Would you be able to cope with that?" he asked seriously.

"I expect so," she replied. "You've told me that your sister managed it, and at the age of only fourteen!"

"That's true. But she didn't have a different language or religion to consider."

"I don't expect language to present too much of a problem," she said. "Assuming we're talking about one of the western kingdoms, that is."

He responded with a chuckle.

"I hadn't given any thought to religion," she told him candidly. "My father isn't a person you would describe as devout. He does what's required, of course—that's expected of the king. My mother is more attentive to the dark gods, but it's one of many areas where I'm more like my father."

"Would you be willing to consider adopting a different religion?"

She shrugged. "I imagine it would be expected if I marry outside Rogand. The religion comes with the kingdom. But if you're asking whether I would personally embrace another religion, I couldn't answer that without knowing more about it."

"Brother Ander would be the best person for you to talk to. His Rogandan is better than mine, and I'm told he has a gift for making complicated things easy to understand. No such conversation is possible of course, since he was abducted along with young Ethen. We'll need to wait until they're both freed."

"Do you think they will be freed?" she asked, her concern apparent on her face.

"I sincerely hope so," he replied. "I don't like to think about how Lord and Lady Torbury will take it if Ethen isn't found alive and well."

A fierce look came to her face. "I wish there was something—anything—I could do!" she said passionately. "I wouldn't care about the risk."

"I feel the same way," he agreed. "Unfortunately it's completely out of our hands."

After they had been riding silently for a while, he suggested, "I'll race you to those trees!"

Without bothering to reply, she urged her horse forward, charging past him with a laugh. He took off after her, leaving the guards and the chaperone scrambling to catch up.

Rupert and Tasha's time together came to an end all too soon. When they parted their farewells were surprisingly awkward.

He recalled Princess Neira's question: *Would you like to kiss me?* The question had been as disconcerting as Neira herself, but it wasn't difficult to answer. He had no interest in Neira.

Tasha was so different.

He understood the constraints of courtship, and he would have respected the boundaries even without her chaperones hovering nearby. But it didn't make her lips any less full and inviting.

29

After a day of frustration, Elena returned to the palace with Amyra. Will met them at the door, the strain plainly visible on his face. Fortunately Thomas was waiting for them as well. Elena's face must have told him all he needed to know, because he came and put his arm around her. She leaned her head onto his shoulder and tried to will herself to relax.

"Well?" demanded Will.

Amyra threw up her hands. "Nothing! Again!"

"I'll check on the children," said Elena.

"I'll come with you!" Thomas chimed in immediately.

The two of them slipped away together.

"I don't think they can take much more of this," Thomas whispered.

Elena shook her head miserably. "You're right. Amyra is barely holding it together."

"Will she want to go out again?" Thomas asked. "If she does, I'll go with her. You need a break!"

"We have no obvious leads to follow," Elena told him. "I'm hoping she'll decide to rest. She desperately needs it."

The children were squabbling when they reached them. Haldek, Breysen, and Rufe were all trying to calm them.

Elena sighed. The general tension was clearly affecting everyone.

Rufe looked especially relieved to see them. He sidled up to Elena. "Is this what happens when people get married?" he whispered. He looked terrified.

Seeing his reaction, Elena barely prevented herself from bursting into laughter. She smiled broadly at him. "You're imagining what might happen if you marry Peggy, aren't you?" He didn't answer, but it wasn't necessary. "I don't think you need worry," she said soothingly. "Peggy strikes me as the kind of person who wouldn't be overawed by a horde of children, even if they were all big and fierce like you."

The burly soldier looked back at her, wide-eyed and shaking his head. He headed for the door with a fatalistic look on his face. His expression seemed so pitiable that she was torn between sympathy and an almost uncontrollable desire to laugh out loud. "You're good for me, Rufe," she finally managed, holding open the door with a grin that split her face from ear to ear.

Out wandering in the sunshine, Kamash noticed a familiar figure hurrying purposefully toward the trees. Diving behind a bush, he managed to disappear from sight at the very moment Princess Neira cast a furtive glance around her. Peering out cautiously from behind the bush, he was in time to see her disappear through the large hedge bordering their section of the garden.

After witnessing her earlier interaction with the Ahran agent, the old man had no doubt what the princess intended on this occasion. Not yet ready to expose her to the Rogandan soldiers, he cast about in his mind, trying to decide what to do. Abruptly remembering his time with Thomas and Elena, he recalled his offer to help Lord Torbury and his wife in any way he could.

Racing back inside, he hurried as quickly as he could to the wing where they were staying. To his relief, the person he spotted first was Elena.

"Please! Can you and your husband come with me urgently?" he cried. "I believe the princess is meeting with an Ahran agent."

"Of course," she replied at once, calling urgently for Thomas.

Thomas soon appeared, trailed by two people Kamash recognized from King Krasmir's conference. It was Lord and Lady Torbury, the parents of the abducted boy.

A burly soldier had followed them out, and Elena addressed him in Arvenian.

The big man gave a tight nod and turned back immediately, a long-suffering look on his face. Lord and Lady Torbury remained, both of them looking agitated and overwrought.

"We must hurry," urged Kamash, restraining his impatience with difficulty.

Leading them outside, he headed quickly toward the location where Princess Neira had previously met the Ahran.

King Krasmir had ordered that one of his men should accompany Will any time he left the palace. Seeing Will hurry away with the others, the soldier immediately sprinted after him.

With no horses on hand and the stables too far away to be accessible, they were forced to follow on foot. The princess reached the treeline well ahead of them. By the time they were pushing among the trees there was no sign of Neira, and Kamash began to lose hope of finding her. He also realized that he had no settled plan about what to do if they did spot her with her contact. It didn't take much imagination to guess what Lord Torbury would want to do. At the very least, he would expect the Ahran to be taken in for questioning.

As for the princess, her life would also change very abruptly if she was caught meeting an Ahran agent. Having been mostly treated with sympathy and consideration, she would likely find herself an object of mistrust and suspicion. At best her freedom of movement would be drastically restricted. She might even find herself locked away in a prison.

Kamash found the thought confronting. Was he doing the right thing?

His doubts vanished when he reminded himself that the lives of an innocent child and a monk were at stake. If the princess was even vaguely involved, she deserved the censure that would come her way.

Then, through the trees ahead, he caught a glimpse of the princess. She was talking to a man in a hooded cloak. Looking back over his shoulder, Kamash held up two fingers and pointed emphatically in the direction of the conspirators. Then he tiptoed forward furtively.

Behind him a crack sounded loudly as a fallen branch snapped underfoot. Peering ahead in alarm, Kamash saw that the intruder had heard the sound. The hooded man melted immediately into the trees. The old man set off after him, followed closely by the others. The princess stood frozen to the spot, watching pale faced as they ran past.

With no idea where the man had gone or where he had hidden his horse, they searched fruitlessly among the trees for a while before pushing into the open. They could see no sign of him.

MEETING with the princess was proving to be an immensely frustrating experience for Bolnyk. He had been charged with extracting any information of value she might have. It quickly became apparent that the mission was a waste of time. She plainly did not enjoy the confidence of King Krasmir, so she had nothing useful to tell him.

He instead found himself assaulted with words—an insistent torrent that amounted to barely coherent rambling. It gradually dawned on him that the princess, accustomed to being the center of attention, craved reassurance about her place in the world.

If she wanted coddling, she'd come to the wrong person. He simply didn't care. And even if he had the inclination to humor her, he could not afford the time.

"Take me with you!" the princess insisted. "I command you to take me to the Grand Vizier!"

"I have no horse to offer you, Your Highness," he replied.

"We will ride double," she sniffed, her nose in the air.

He shook his head curtly. "I have no such orders from my master. Even if I did, I could not simply spirit you away from King Krasmir's palace."

"*My* command overrides any order *Rheibas* might have given you," she retorted, her eyes flashing. Her disparaging emphasis on the chief minister's common name was not lost on Bolnyk.

The princess might imagine that her command was Bolnyk's most compelling obligation, but she was wrong. He had no sympathy for her whims and no interest in pandering to a fragile and sensitive young princess.

Bolnyk's situation had been beyond desperate when the Grand Vizier had plucked him from the gutter. He would have expired on the street if it had been left to the emperor. Why should he feel loyalty to a family content to sit in luxury while their people suffered around them?

Neira continued to prattle on. Princess or not, the girl was a fool— her willingness to believe the Grand Vizier's explanation in his letter demonstrated that. To have abandoned skepticism so completely she must be desperate to avoid rejection.

The chief minister placed no value on her life. Having abandoned the princess on the island, it wasn't hard to guess what he might do if she fell into his hands right now. In leaving her here Bolnyk was doing her a favor, even if she didn't have the wit to understand it.

Weary of the girl and her impossible demands, he decided it was time to escape.

The situation changed in an instant when he heard the unmistakable sounds of someone approaching. The arrival of intruders felt both alarming and fortuitous at the same time. Turning away swiftly, he fled without a backward glance, weaving his way through the trees until he came to his horse. Vaulting into the saddle, he swung the horse about and kicked it in the flanks.

Fortunately for him, his pursuers had not found him. Galloping away, he headed for the broken section of wall that allowed him access to the palace grounds.

As soon as he was free of the palace, he slowed his horse briefly. He needed to clear his head before deciding on his next move. After this incident, the city would soon be swarming with King Krasmir's men, on the lookout for him and for any unusual activity. Most alarming of all, the transfer of the boy and the monk to the Grand Vizier was due to begin at any moment. Perhaps it was already underway.

The timing of the move had seemed sensible when he scheduled it. He had decided against a nighttime operation. While the darkness offered concealment, men with nothing to hide were not given to moving loaded wagons in the dead of night. Far too many people with watchful eyes were about, and the journey could not be completed quickly, especially in darkness. The same operation could be carried out more efficiently in the daytime without attracting undue attention.

However, everything had just changed. Bolnyk's clandestine meeting with the princess had been a disaster. After the supposed sanctuary of King Krasmir's palace grounds had been breached during the abduction of the boy, Bolnyk had penetrated deep inside it once more. When the king heard about it—and that would happen all too quickly—it would surely provoke an unprecedented response.

It was difficult to imagine a worse moment to carry out the transfer. Only one option made sense—he needed to get to the safe house in time to prevent it.

Putting his head down, he urged his horse to greater speed.

THOMAS PEERED AROUND IN FRUSTRATION. The Ahran had made a clean escape.

Will appeared, his face red with agitation. "Did you get a look at him?" he asked.

Thomas grimaced. "I barely caught a glimpse of him as he was disappearing, Will," he replied, keeping his voice low. "He heard us coming! I couldn't get all the details, but he's definitely the one we've been looking for. His head is crammed with information. I don't doubt that he knows everything we've been trying to find out."

A scowl of frustration twisted Will's face.

Thomas shook his head in exasperation. There'd never been a better chance to unravel the mysteries plaguing them for so long. They'd been so close.

"Look!" said Amyra suddenly, pointing back toward the palace. Other riders had come into view. Will began calling and waving his arms frantically, causing the riders to head immediately toward the little group.

Will turned urgently to Thomas. "Do you know where to go?"

"I'm confident I can lead you in the right general direction," Thomas replied with a nod.

Both of them directed their attention to the approaching riders. King Rupert and Princess Teylee soon arrived accompanied by six soldiers and a woman.

"We need horses urgently!" said Will. "We just surprised an important Ahran agent talking to Princess Neira, and he's escaping!"

"You can use our horses," the princess replied at once, dismounting and indicating to her chaperone and her soldiers that they should do the same. King Rupert dismounted as well.

Will, Amyra, Thomas, Elena, Kamash, and the guard assigned to Will all selected horses and mounted.

"You can't go without protection," exclaimed King Rupert. "There are three more horses—three of our guards can go with you."

The soldier in charge of the princess's guard detail shook his head stubbornly. "We were assigned to protect both Princess Teylee and you, Your Majesty. Other soldiers will need to be found to accompany Lord Torbury."

"There's only one solution," said the princess calmly. "If our guards must remain with us, then King Rupert and I will go as well."

"It wouldn't be safe, Your Highness!" protested the lead soldier.

"This is Rog, not the wilds of Lestanor," she reminded him. "Lord Kulferan's soldiers will never be far away. And we're following one man, not riding into battle."

The lead soldier didn't look at all convinced.

"Our kingdom is under threat!" she added firmly. "There's a great deal at stake, and there isn't time to argue. I'm going. Do whatever you please."

With that, she remounted her horse. "Would you like to share a horse?" she asked King Rupert. "It will allow another soldier to accompany us."

The king seemed far from certain about the wisdom of joining the hunt, but she'd left him little choice. Her unyielding look seemed to decide him. Taking her offered arm, he climbed up behind her.

No doubt inspired by their example, Kamash called to Amyra. "Please!" he said, pointing to his horse's back.

Accepting his invitation, she relinquished her horse and mounted behind him.

With only three horses remaining for the princess's six guards, Elena dismounted. Thomas patted the spot behind him, but she shook her head. "I don't need to go!" she said.

The six soldiers mounted, two of them forced to ride double.

"Ask the king to send reinforcements!" the princess commanded her chaperone. "As soon as we find where the Ahran has gone, we'll send someone back with directions!"

The chaperone hurried away with Elena.

Thomas did not linger for further conversation. Turning away with Will beside him, he set off after the Ahran.

The urgency of the situation had temporarily pushed everything else from his mind, including the fact that he'd finally succeeded in getting a good look at the princess. She had nothing worthwhile to contribute to this situation, and further follow up would need to wait.

EVEN BEFORE LEAVING the palace grounds they encountered two mounted soldiers riding patrol. The princess wasted no time in commandeering their horses.

All of her guards now had horses of their own.

Having lost his horse, one of the soldiers gave up his weapon as well. "Your sword! May I borrow it please?" asked the unarmed King Rupert. Bowing, the man unbuckled his belt and handed it over, along with the sword in its scabbard.

Even before the king had strapped on the sword, Will was urging Thomas forward. "We can't delay!" he growled. "The Ahran is long gone already!"

Locating the section of broken wall, Thomas guided his horse across it, the other riders following quickly. Loud muttering came from Princess Teylee's guards when they saw the breach. It wasn't Thomas's concern, so he thrust it from his mind and rode on.

He knew where the Ahran would be heading—even from the fleeting contact with the man's thoughts, the location had been fixed in his mind. The Ahran was heading for the place where Ethen and Brother Ander were held.

However there seemed little point in going there, because Thomas had the clear impression that the captives were imminently about to be relocated to the headquarters of the Grand Vizier. After what had just happened, the transfer would surely be accelerated. Unfortunately, he couldn't say where the Grand Vizier was based. The location was known to the Ahran, but Thomas had been unable to dig out specifics.

With no better alternative on offer, Thomas directed his horse toward the one other location accessible to him.

UPON REACHING the safe house where the boy and the monk had spent their captivity, it immediately became apparent that the house was empty. The transfer was already underway. Bolnyk gritted his teeth in annoyance. Their route to the Grand Vizier's headquarters had been decided in general terms, but he had no way of being certain exactly which roads they were planning to use.

There was, however, one segment of the journey that required them to pass through an extended section of open ground on a lightly trafficked road. Further, the road was in very poor condition, which meant that wagons were forced to travel at a slow walking pace. Because they would be exposed for a considerable period of time while passing through this area, it had received a disproportionate amount of attention during planning.

Unless his men had set out much earlier than agreed, he knew they would not yet have arrived at this location. Bolnyk accordingly hurried there, intending to join them as soon as they appeared.

He had no way of knowing it, but his own focus on this site had ensured it was the destination plucked from his mind through the agency of Thomas's stone.

BACK AT THE PALACE, a full hour had passed before King Krasmir learned about what had transpired. It alarmed him that Will was once more on the loose in pursuit of his son, even if accompanied by the soldier assigned to him by Lord Kulferan. He was even more alarmed that his daughter and King Rupert were off chasing Ahran agents, and with only six soldiers to defend them.

Calling urgently for his commander, he hastily prepared to join the search himself. Another crucial hour passed before a large and heavily armed group of soldiers set out, Lord Kulferan at their head. King Krasmir rode among them.

Heading in the general direction indicated by the princess's guards, they soon arrived at the broken section of wall. Krasmir eyed it indignantly. Such a lapse was utterly unacceptable, and he intended to have stern words with those responsible for maintaining security in the palace grounds.

Once beyond the palace grounds, they were confronted with the dilemma looming from the moment they set out—they had no idea where to go. The princess had promised to send someone back when they reached their destination, but the king refused to wait around for that to happen.

Pulling Lord Kulferan to one side, the king asked him, "Have your investigations given you any idea where the Grand Vizier might be hiding?"

"There are a number of possibilities, Your Majesty," the commander answered, as unruffled as ever. "One in particular stands out."

"Then why are we waiting, My Lord?" snapped the king. Lord Kulferan might be reliable and effective, but there were occasions when the king found his imperturbability little short of maddening.

The commander gave instructions to his men, and the column set out once more.

They were not moving quickly enough for the king. Positioning his horse alongside the nobleman, he insisted that the pace be increased. The commander calmly complied promptly with the request. Soon they were moving quickly enough even for the king.

Tracking down the Ahrans responsible for the abduction and releasing the child they held captive had always been Krasmir's most important priority. But the situation had just escalated significantly, and his gut was slowly twisting itself into knots.

What on earth had possessed Rupert and Tasha to become directly involved? If Rupert wanted to join the chase, he should have insisted that Tasha stay behind.

Krasmir shook his head. He couldn't reasonably blame everything on the young king. He knew his daughter, and he was well aware that Tasha would never have allowed Rupert to leave her behind. Nor would she have agreed to both of them abandoning the chase. The idea of pursuing the Ahran would have called out to her, whatever Rupert thought about it.

From the very beginning Krasmir had felt genuine concern for Lord and Lady Torbury following the disappearance of their son. Now, with his own daughter hunting a dangerous man with barely adequate protection, he began to catch the tiniest glimpse of what Torbury and his wife had been going through.

30

Thomas reined in his horse.

Will pulled up right beside him. "Why are we stopping?" he asked, frowning.

"This is the place," said Thomas. An open stretch of land intersected by a road lay before them, with no buildings of any kind in sight. A couple of men on horseback and several people on foot could be seen on the road, but none of them were of any interest.

Fleeting thoughts and memories had guided Thomas here—the legacy of his brief contact with the Ahran agent—but he had no idea what to expect.

Restless and on edge, Will was struggling to keep his emotions in check. "Do we need to find the nearest dwelling?"

Thomas shook his head. "I don't think so. I'm not entirely sure why this location was uppermost in his mind. I suspect he needs to pass this way. Or if not him, someone significant."

Will scowled. "I don't care about anyone except Ethen."

"I understand that," Thomas replied. "But finding the Ahran agent is the next best thing. If I can get a proper look at him, all of our other questions should be answered."

Will subsided with an effort. "You're right, Thomas. All we can do is watch and wait." He immediately began scanning the area.

The only feature in the landscape was a rise not far from their current position. Will pointed to it. "If we're going to wait, we should stay out of sight."

Thomas nodded. Both of them directed their horses over the rise and dismounted, the rest of the group not far behind them. Having positioned themselves to observe the road, Thomas and Will settled down to wait.

It seemed an ideal opportunity for Thomas to pass on what he'd learned from the princess. "I finally got a good look at the princess," he whispered to Will. "She's willing to do almost anything for the sake of her father's empire, and in that sense she's dangerous. But she isn't privy to the plans of the Grand Vizier, and she knows very little about his agents. She knows nothing that's useful to us in recovering Ethen."

Will responded with a grunt.

An hour passed without incident. Thomas could see that Will was becoming impatient, although thus far he had managed to restrain himself. Amyra had also spent time watching with them, but she was too fretful to remain in one place for long.

In the distance a wagon rolled into view. Two men sat on the driver's bench seat and two more followed slowly on horseback. The wagon had high sides, obscuring its cargo. Nevertheless, a glance at the men was all Thomas needed. In the bottom of the wagon, hidden beneath heavy covers, Ethen and Brother Ander lay bound and gagged.

As he opened his mouth to tell Will what he had discovered, several other riders come into view. To a casual observer, they had no connection with the wagon, but Thomas knew otherwise. Will, King Rupert, and five soldiers were now facing off against a dozen Ahrans.

He leaned toward Will. "It's time for one of your plans!" he said urgently, keeping his voice low.

Will tensed immediately. "Are you saying that Ethen's in that wagon?"

Thomas grabbed his arm, physically restraining him from leaping into action. "He is. But there are twelve men down there, Will! All fighters, and all well armed. Charging down there is likely to get you killed. That isn't going to rescue Ethen."

With Will straining away from him, he added tersely, "You need to know that they have orders to kill both Ethen and Brother Ander immediately rather than allowing them to be freed."

Will slowly relaxed. Peering around him, he assessed the possibilities. Behind them, the road forked, with one path continuing on and the other bending out of sight on its way to the center of Rog.

He addressed the others calmly. "We've finally found what we've been looking for," he told them.

Amyra's breath hitched, and she went suddenly pale.

"But we have a problem," Will continued. "These men have orders to kill Ethen and Brother Ander if anything goes wrong. So we need to catch them completely by surprise. And we're also outnumbered two to one."

He turned to Princess Teylee. "Could you please ride back and tell your father's men where we are?"

"If she goes, her guards go with her, My Lord," the lead soldier informed him.

"I think that answers your question, Lord Torbury," she replied tartly. "My men are needed here. And I am more than willing to do anything I can to help."

Will clearly wasn't happy about it, but there was little he could do. He turned instead to the soldier assigned to him by King Krasmir. "Someone needs to tell the king where we are. It will need to be you."

The man shook his head. "The king instructed me to stay with you, no matter what happens."

With a masterful effort, Will maintained his composure. "You are well aware of the importance placed by the king on freeing my son," he told the soldier bluntly. "Now that we've finally located him, we find ourselves unable to free him because we're outnumbered. We need Lord Kulferan here with reinforcements, and we need him now, before we lose contact with the Ahrans. If he doesn't arrive in time because you refused to notify him, the king will not thank you for sticking blindly to your orders."

Will had managed to dump a huge weight of responsibility onto the guard. Conflicted and uncomfortable, the hapless soldier could not come up with a response.

Princess Teylee resolved the matter. "You need to do this," she told him. "My men can take on the responsibility of staying with Lord Torbury."

That decided it. Mounting immediately, the soldier rode swiftly away.

Will turned to the remaining members of the party.

"I'm going to need your help," he told them. He faced Kamash. "Beginning with you," he said. "Are you willing to play a role?"

"Of course!" replied Kamash without hesitation.

"Here's what I need you to do then," Will replied.

Thomas heaved a sigh of relief. The old Will had reappeared at last.

KAMASH STRODE PURPOSEFULLY ALONG the road, careful to avoid the deep ruts that dotted his path. He soon came upon the wagon, bumping along at little better than a crawl.

"Good morning!" he called cheerfully to the driver. "It looks like slow going."

The men on the cart ignored him.

Coming to a stop, he shook his head, planting his hands on his hips. "No need to be rude," he told them. "I'm only trying to be neighborly."

The cart bumped past him without any kind of response from the driver.

"Suit yourself!" he said with a shrug. Resuming his journey, he called back over his shoulder, "Whether you're interested in hearing it or not, you're going to want to get off this road. I've heard from another traveler that a large company of the king's soldiers is heading this way, and I'm told they're riding fast. They'll be on top of you before you know it."

With that he continued his journey, not bothering to wait for a reply.

Even without looking back, he could tell that his words had caused consternation. He passed the two men riding behind the wagon. The alarm on their faces made it clear they had heard what he said. Smiling, he waved an idle hand as he passed.

Hearing hoofbeats approaching from behind, he turned his head in time to see two of the princess's soldiers approach the wagon.

"Are all of these men in your party?" one of the soldiers called roughly to the wagon driver, waving a hand to include the riders following some distance behind the wagon as well as the two immediately behind it.

The driver shook his head.

"Then you'd better pull over and let the men behind you pass," the soldier told him. "Lord Kulferan is right behind us, and he's looking for a wagon escorted by a large group of men." Then he shrugged. "I suppose it doesn't matter. He'll want to see what you've got in there anyway." He pointed into the wagon.

With that, the two soldiers rode on, one of them aiming a subtle wink at Kamash as they passed him. When they reached the second group of Ahrans, they rode beyond them without pausing.

As soon as the soldiers had gone, one of the two men riding with the wagon passed Kamash, heading rapidly back to the group trailing at a distance. Meanwhile, the driver wasted no time in pulling the wagon off the road.

The road was bumpy, but the ground beside it was much worse. The wagon slowly lurched and jolted in the direction of a stand of trees four or five furlongs away. The remaining rider followed it.

Kamash counted eight men in the second group of Ahrans. The rider from the wagon soon reached them, and after a hurried conference, all of them turned off the road, riding swiftly toward the same trees. The second group of riders soon passed the wagon. Clearly they did not want to be seen with it.

Kamash grunted in satisfaction. Lord Torbury's ruse was working perfectly.

The princess's two soldiers were under instruction to return as soon as all the Ahrans were out of the way, and he could already see them heading back. He began retracing his own steps.

As soon as a suitable gap opened up between the two groups of Ahrans, Lord Torbury, King Rupert, and the remaining soldiers would gallop over the rise and take control of the wagon.

Together they would free Lord Torbury's son and the monk, remove the horses from the wagon, and leave before the larger group of Ahrans could return.

With everything going precisely to plan, the entire situation changed abruptly. A lone rider appeared, riding hard along the path originally taken by the Ahrans. The remaining horseman beside the wagon spotted him first, calling out sharply. There could be no doubt that the newcomer had been recognized. The wagon came to an immediate stop.

It was soon apparent that the other group also knew who he was, because they were already racing back toward the wagon.

There was no longer time for Will's group of would-be rescuers to stop the wagon and free the prisoners. Once more the Ahrans had them outnumbered.

———

THOMAS WAS WATCHING the road as Will, King Rupert, and the soldiers prepared to ride for the wagon.

"Wait! That's Bolnyk!" Thomas exclaimed in alarm, pointing at a horseman who had recently appeared on the road. He was heading straight for the wagon.

Will hurried to his side. "Who's Bolnyk?"

"The Ahran we surprised with the princess," Thomas told him, pointing toward the new arrival and lowering his voice. "I'm finally getting a look at him. He leads the agents, and he's dangerous, Will! Don't underestimate him."

"What's he doing?"

"He's making sure his men stay together. He wants to get the prisoners to the Grand Vizier." Thomas paused before adding, "He intends to deliver them—dead or alive."

"That isn't going to happen," said Will flatly.

Thomas was squinting at Bolnyk, who had now reached the wagon. "His men have told him what Kamash and the princess's soldiers said, and he's very smart. He's guessed that it was just a ruse. He's also guessed we don't have enough people to risk fighting all of them."

"Where's Lord Kulferan?" asked Will, clenching and unclenching his fists in frustration.

"He'll be here soon," Thomas replied, hoping fervently it was true.

Will narrowed his eyes. "We can't wait—we'll attack them anyway. There mightn't be another chance."

"No! It isn't necessary to attack them now," Thomas replied urgently. "There's another option!"

"What option?" asked Will with a frown.

"I know where they're going," said Thomas. "There's a place where we can lie in wait for them. We'll have to hurry, but the wagon will slow them down."

"Lord Kulferan won't find us," Will replied.

"Not unless we send someone else," Thomas agreed.

"What makes you think this location is any good?" asked Will.

"It's the one place Bolnyk is wary about," Thomas told him.

"It'd better be worth it," Will growled.

"I sure hope so," mumbled Thomas under his breath.

They waited until the Ahrans were almost out of sight before moving. Then Thomas directed them on a roundabout ride through a forest, across a river, and over more rough ground.

By the time they arrived at their destination, Will was becoming testy. "Surely this can't be the place!" he exclaimed.

Thomas shrugged. "It's the location on Bolnyk's mind."

Will frowned as he rapidly scanned the terrain. "He might have reason to worry if an army patrol is waiting for him," he said. He pointed. "Over there."

They followed him to a rocky outcrop near a stream surrounded by trees on both banks. A rough path ran through the stream, with a steep bank on the far side.

"So they'll have to come this way?" asked Will.

Thomas nodded.

"I'd give a lot for two or three good Erestorian archers," said Will regretfully. "We'll have to make do. I need someone to watch the approaches and warn us when they're getting close."

Kamash volunteered without hesitation and soon rode away.

"Someone also needs to tell Lord Kulferan where we are," Will added, shooting a hopeful glance in Princess Teylee's direction.

She wasn't having it. "I'm not going anywhere," she told him. "You already know that my guards will leave if I go. And you need them."

Will had no choice but to accept it. "Decide among yourselves who to send. I'll be conferring with my wife and Thomas," he announced, ignoring them and heading toward the stream.

As soon as Amyra and Thomas joined him, he pointed to the path leading out of the water. "That's where we have to stop them," he said. "We need a hole so the wagon will get stuck. Or even better, so one of its wheels breaks."

With no response forthcoming, he spoke directly to Amyra. "There isn't time to dig."

She cocked an eyebrow at him. "You're the one always telling me not to use the Stone of Authority in front of other people."

"We don't have much time," he reminded her, ignoring her sally.

Turning toward the bank of the stream, she flicked a hand back and forth a few times. "That should do it," she said.

Thomas watched on in surprise. He'd barely seen the earth move, but both Amyra and Will seemed satisfied.

"I don't suppose you could arrange for the ground to open up and swallow some of the Ahrans?" Will suggested.

She snorted, not bothering to reply. She did, however, engage in quiet conversation with Will as they returned to the others.

"Who are we sending to Lord Kulferan?" Will asked.

"One of my guards," the princess replied.

Their leader looked mutinous, but eventually he pointed at one of the men. "Get back here promptly!" he ordered.

The soldier mounted and moved out at once.

Thomas shook his head. Bolnyk had boosted the Ahrans' numbers, while their own numbers had been further reduced.

"What now?" asked King Rupert.

"We keep out of sight, and we wait," replied Will.

"What will we do when they arrive?" the king persisted.

"We've examined the ground in the stream," Will replied, "and we're expecting the wagon to get stuck after it crosses. We'll attack while they're distracted trying to pull it out. That should even the odds."

He glanced at Princess Teylee. "That assumes your soldiers will be willing to help."

"The men are well aware that the king has placed a very high priority on recovering your son," she replied. "They will do their part."

"Your safety is our highest priority, Your Highness," asserted the lead guard.

"And I will be staying well away from any fighting," Princess Teylee replied.

Will nodded firmly. "That isn't open to discussion. Your father would never forgive any of us if something happened to you. Your senior guard will stay with you at all times for your protection. My wife will be at your side, and she knows how to use a weapon if the need arises. Thomas, Kamash, and King Rupert will also remain here. If anything goes wrong, none of you should hesitate—get out of here as fast as your horses will take you!"

"I will be fighting beside you," King Rupert insisted. Seeing that both Will and the lead guard were about to object, he added, "I have been training under the best fighters in my kingdom since I was a boy. You need me with you! And I'm not offering you a choice," he added grimly.

Whatever they might be thinking about it, neither Will nor the lead guard had anything further to say.

The Ahrans now had nine fighters to their seven. From the grim looks on the faces of the soldiers, they knew the odds were against them. And it wasn't just a matter of odds. It wouldn't be enough to overcome the larger force. They also needed to prevent the Ahrans from killing the captives.

Nevertheless, Thomas knew something the soldiers didn't. Amyra had access to a talisman of staggering power, and he had noticed her exchanging glances with Will. It gave him hope that there might be more to the plan than Will was letting on.

He thought it wisest not to ask.

THE HASTY RETURN of Kamash offered the first indication that the Ahrans were approaching. Thomas had an anxious moment as the old man splashed his horse across the stream, but somehow he managed to avoid the section of ground undermined by Amyra.

Pulling in behind the rocky outcrop, he told them, "They're coming. Not quickly—the wagon is slowing them down—but they'll be here before long."

31

———

Peering out around the outcrop, Thomas saw four horsemen ride into view, the wagon bumping along close behind them. Bolnyk and the other mounted Ahrans were bringing up the rear. All of them cast frequent glances over their shoulders. Thomas could see from the stone that they were expecting trouble, but only from behind.

As the first two riders crossed the stream, Thomas noted with surprise that the flow of water had greatly diminished. The wagon driver cracked a whip, urging his horses forward. The wagon bucked and swayed as the animals surged across the stream. No sooner had the carriage cleared the water than the ground beneath the rear wheels collapsed.

The water was barely ankle deep now. Bolnyk dismounted, shouting instructions, and the horsemen riding with him dismounted as well, approaching the wagon to examine it. A sudden noise caused them to look upstream. Before any of them could move, a wall of water smashed into the ford, sweeping the men away. Even the horses were overwhelmed, disappearing downstream. Water briefly flooded the wagon, but it was resting at a steep angle, and the water just as quickly drained away.

With a wild cry, Will rode to the ford. Recovering from their surprise, King Rupert and five soldiers raced after him.

The four mounted Ahrans barely managed to draw their weapons before they were set upon by all five of the princess's guards.

Pulling swords from beneath their seat, the two men on the wagon driver's bench jumped into the tray of the wagon and began frantically removing the covers that lay atop the load.

Will vaulted into the wagon, his sword in his hand. The wagon drivers abandoned their efforts and spun around to defend themselves. King Rupert quickly joined Will and side by side they fought the Ahrans. The space constraint made fighting unusually hazardous, but Will was in a dangerous mood.

The princess's guards brought down one of the Ahrans on horseback. When another tried to ride away, it cost him his life. The other two Ahrans now faced five attackers.

One of the princess's guards now jumped onto the wagon, attacking the Ahrans from behind. The fight in the wagon ended at the same moment the remaining Ahrans on horseback went down. Six Ahrans now sprawled lifeless on the ground.

Throwing off the remaining covers, Will finally reached his son. Pulling a knife, the nobleman cut Ethen's bonds before removing a gag from his face. Then he held the boy to him fiercely, his body trembling violently. Amyra had already left the princess, and she joined them in the wagon. Her husband pulled her into the embrace, and they stood there together, their joyous tears flowing freely.

One of the soldiers released the monk. The big man stood and stretched, his appearance disheveled and his once-white robe soiled and crumpled. Leaning toward the boy, he ruffled his hair, receiving a tearful smile in return.

All of them clambered down from the wagon, everyone talking at once, overflowing with the release of pent-up emotion and relieved distress.

As they celebrated together, a disheveled horseman emerged unnoticed from the trees. Seeing at once who it was, Thomas ran into the open, shouting a warning.

Bolnyk reached the little group at the same moment. Stepping forward protectively, Brother Ander took a vicious sword thrust to his stomach. He crumpled helplessly, his blood soiling the ground.

As Thomas looked on with horror, Bolnyk turned to Ethen, poised to strike again. Will stepped forward into his path, his sword extended. The Ahran swung downward, all of his force behind the stroke. The weapons clashed deafeningly, and Will stumbled back, desperately trying to keep his feet.

Ignoring him, Bolnyk drove his horse forward, shoving Amyra aside and knocking Ethen to the ground. The boy went down hard. The Ahran bent low, brutally plunging his sword into the boy as he lay defenseless on the ground.

Before anyone could respond, he spun his horse about and galloped away.

The princess's guards immediately took up defensive positions, but it was too late for Ethen and Brother Ander.

Through the agency of the stone, Thomas had seen the Ahran's intention. But everything had happened too quickly for him to prevent it.

Reaching their son, Amyra and Will bent over him in horror. Amyra began to wail, a piteous sound that shattered the stillness. Will had gone white with shock.

Kamash appeared at their side. Peering down at the boy, he shook his head sadly. Then he moved to Brother Ander.

Thomas brought the stone in contact with his skin, desperate for a sign that the monk's spirit still lingered. Brother Ander's life was flickering like a candle guttering in a breeze, but it hadn't yet gone out.

As he watched, Kamash bent low and placed his stone into the monk's unmoving hand. "I want you to have this," the old man whispered. Then he stood upright again, a satisfied smile on his face.

How much of what Thomas saw and heard came through his own senses, and how much through the stone, he couldn't say. But he looked on in amazement as life flowed back into the monk, filling him to the brim.

Brother Ander sat up, holding his side and wincing. Then he slowly got to his feet.

The old man leaned forward. "Don't lose that stone I gave you," he whispered. "Keep it safe and keep it hidden. It will grant you good health and long life." He nodded. "Vitality. Yes, that was the word." He studied the monk. "I think you will have more use for it than me."

Brother Ander looked baffled. Straightening his back and flexing his muscles, he peered at Kamash, at the stone in his hand, and finally down at his blood soaked robe. He shook his head in bewilderment.

Amyra's anguish reached him at last, and he shuffled to her side.

Looking down at the boy, the monk was overcome with distress. With the Stone of Knowing resting against his skin, Thomas glimpsed the toll of the ceaseless days and nights of captivity. He saw the way that Brother Ander had carefully sustained the child, laboring to shield him from the full intensity of the fear and suffering, guiding his spirit through the darkness. All of it had counted for nothing.

The soldier-turned-monk was no stranger to death. He had encountered it many times from his earliest years, eventually dealing out death himself more often than he could count. Now, as he stared at the small, limp form, indignation began to build within him. An act of casual malice had ended the boy's life, but it was not the cruelty of the deed that so provoked his affront. The monk had undergone a transformation, learning to heal, to rescue, to redeem, and in that moment, his spirit was overwhelmed with indignation at death itself.

The monk recalled the words of the man he now followed—words that had played so often in his mind. *'In this world you will have trouble…'* It came to him that the words hadn't ended there. They had continued, *'…but take courage; I have overcome the world.'*

Reaching down for the boy, he lifted him into his arms. The boy's blood stained his robe, mingling with the blood from his own wounds, but Brother Ander saw none of it. His attention was not on the grief-stricken figures huddled beside the stream, nor upon the child.

The monk began mouthing his prayers, speaking almost inaudibly, only his face revealing the intensity of his focus. Pouring out his entreaties to God, he assaulted the gates of heaven with an authority that filled Thomas with astonishment.

Thomas stood transfixed, scarcely aware of the passage of time. It was the stone that first alerted him to the faint glimmer of returning life in the child. Slowly the boy's eyes opened, and he gazed up into the face of his friend. "Brother Ander," he said softly.

Completely undone, the monk began to shudder, his entire body wracked with sobs as tears rolled heedlessly down his cheeks. The boy's parents had been looking on with mouths agape. Even before the monk had fully mastered himself, he came to them, placing their son in their arms and enfolding them in an embrace. Then all three of them lifted their voices and wailed together, tears of joy and relief flowing freely as their pain and anguish were washed away.

Ethen had lain silent in the arms of his parents throughout it all. When at last their voices grew still, he opened his mouth once more. "Mother, Father," he said. "I missed you!"

The sound of his voice set them off again.

Thomas had broken his contact with the stone as life was returning to Ethen. But he needed no assistance to feel the impact of the raw emotion emanating from his friends. He turned away, struggling to deal with his own responses.

Kamash sidled up to him, smiling and shaking his head at the same time.

Thomas took a deep breath to steady himself. "You gave him the stone," he said.

Kamash nodded. "I decided he needed it more than I did. I think I was right."

"So the stone healed him?"

"The monk? Yes, that was the stone."

"And Ethen—the boy?"

The old man frowned in puzzlement. "I can't claim to fully understand the stone, but I have always been able to sense what it is capable of. The monk was still alive when I gave it to him, and his recovery is no surprise to me. I have lived through similar experiences myself. But the boy was dead. I had no hope for him at all." He shook his head. "No, I do not think the stone can be credited with his return to life. It must surely have played a part, but your monk deserves most of the credit."

"He would say that God deserves the credit."

Kamash shrugged. "Perhaps he is right," he said. "I cannot say." With a brief nod to Thomas, he wandered away, musing thoughtfully.

Memories came to Thomas's mind of Brother Vangellis in a small hut in Arvenon, bending wearily over a stricken Ander. He recalled too the words of Ander at Hazelwood Ford after the battle of Torbury Scarp. Ander had aspired to become like Brother Vangellis. He had truly achieved his goal.

A large company of mounted soldiers appeared, and Thomas realized that Lord Kulferan's reinforcements had arrived at last. Four of the Ahrans remained unaccounted for, but it no longer mattered.

Glancing at the soldiers, he was surprised to see that King Krasmir himself had ridden with them.

"Where is the Princess Teylee?" asked the king.

"Sheltering behind that rocky outcrop, with one of her guards, Your Majesty," Thomas replied, pointing the way.

Guiding his horse around the outcrop, the king briefly disappeared. He emerged moments later, his face taut.

Spotting Will, the king rode to his side. "You have your son back!" he exclaimed. Seeing blood all over them, he asked more tentatively, "Is he injured?"

"To our astonishment, he is well, Your Majesty," Will replied with a strained smile. "Thank you for coming so quickly to our support."

"Where is my daughter, Lord Torbury?" the king asked, an edge to his voice.

Will looked at him in surprise. "I left her in safety with her senior guard, over there," he replied, pointing to the outcrop of rock.

"She is not there now," the king replied.

"Perhaps she is with King Rupert," said Amyra.

"He fought with us," added Will. "Where is he? I didn't notice him leaving."

All of them looked around, a couple of voices calling King Rupert's name loudly. There was no reply.

"Where are her guards?" asked Will.

Several men stepped forward.

Will's brows drew together. "Where is your leader—the one who stayed with the princess?"

"He was with the princess," one of them replied apprehensively. "He hasn't joined us."

Everyone fell silent.

"Is it possible they decided to follow the Ahran leader?" asked Thomas.

"Why would they do that?" asked Will, puzzled.

The king scowled. "It is just the kind of thing the princess might decide to do," he said. "Where else could they be?"

No one had an answer.

"Where did this Ahran go?" demanded the king.

"I can show you the direction, Your Majesty," Thomas replied.

"I will join you!" said Will.

"You will not!" replied the king. "Return with your son to the safety of the palace. Lord Kulferan will leave you enough men to ensure you are protected."

Lord Kulferan responded immediately, choosing a leader and telling him to retain fifty soldiers. The leader proved no less efficient than his commander, selecting the men swiftly.

Even before the process was finished, the king addressed Thomas. "Lead the way," he ordered. "One of my trackers will ride beside you."

The main body of soldiers moved swiftly away from the ford. Thomas rode at their head.

32

The moment Ethen and the monk had been freed, Rupert headed around the outcrop to satisfy himself that Tasha was safe. He arrived in time to witness a debate between Tasha and her senior guard.

"This is ridiculous!" Tasha was saying. "The fighting is over."

"We don't know if other Ahrans will arrive, Your Highness," the guard replied. "You're safest here."

Before the issue could be resolved, an Ahran reappeared, killing Ethen and Brother Ander and galloping away. They watched on help-lessly, paralyzed with horror and shock.

Tasha was the first to recover. "We have to go after him!" she said.

"It's much too dangerous, Your Highness!" exclaimed her guard in alarm.

"He's right," agreed Rupert. "What could we achieve by following him?"

"We could find out where he's going! He must be heading for their headquarters." She frowned at them. "Don't you see? It won't end here. This will just be the beginning."

Rupert shook his head stubbornly. He wasn't willing to put her at risk for any reason, and certainly not on the off chance of locating the main Ahran base.

A wild look came into her eyes. "That man just murdered a child! A helpless child! And the monk as well—the one you wanted me to talk to."

Her jaw set firm. "There isn't time to argue—he's getting away."

Before they could respond, she had mounted her horse and set off after the Ahran.

Leaping onto his own horse at once, Rupert turned momentarily toward the ford. Someone needed to let the others know what was happening. But he quickly turned away. Lord Torbury and the others were distracted with grief, but more importantly Tasha was alone and unprotected. He couldn't waste a minute. Even if she knew how to defend herself, she wasn't armed. Shaking his head in frustration, he set off after her.

The guard must have come to a similar conclusion. He had set off in hot pursuit of the princess even before Rupert did.

Tasha had a head start, and her horse was fast. After riding hard for some time, Rupert realized he wasn't gaining on her at all; he was barely keeping pace with her. The guard was doing a little better, but he hadn't reached her yet.

His mind was racing—what were they going to do when they caught up with her? They couldn't forcibly restrain her.

Frustrating as this situation was, Rupert realized he shouldn't be entirely surprised. Twice in their brief acquaintance she had told him she would do anything in her power in response to the abduction. She'd said the risk didn't trouble her. And Rimek's story about her angry response to someone mistreating a horse had reinforced his impression of her concern for the vulnerable.

Tasha's huge heart for the hurting was a wonderful quality. But she had also told Rupert she was capable of being impulsive. He shook his head with unease.

Throughout the ride Rupert had not caught so much as a glimpse of the Ahran. He presumed that Tasha still had him in sight though, because she hadn't slowed. She had been right about one thing—if they wanted to follow him, there hadn't been time to argue.

The path rose before him, and for a moment he caught a complete glimpse of the chase. The Ahran had just topped a rise. Strung out behind him were Tasha, her guard, and finally Rupert.

As he watched, he saw the Ahran glance back the way he had come. He must surely have seen that he was being followed, and that his pursuers were not traveling in a group. Then he was gone. A sense of foreboding began to niggle away at Rupert.

To Rupert's relief, as the princess neared the top of the ridge, she proved she had not entirely abandoned caution. Slowing her horse to a walk, she approached the crest cautiously. He guessed that with no way of knowing what she might encounter on the other side, she recognized the danger in proceeding alone.

The instant she topped the rise, she spun her horse around and raced back the way she had come. He watched in alarm as horsemen spilled over the ridge, riding hard in pursuit.

She quickly reached the guard, and he swung his mount around to race beside her. Rupert spun his horse around in turn.

"I saw their base!" Tasha cried as she drew level with him. He swung in behind her.

A glance back over his shoulder showed seven or eight men pursuing them. They were gaining.

Rupert had already been riding hard for too long. His horse was tiring. The guard was doing no better. Both of them would soon be overtaken.

Tasha had outpaced them. When she looked back, he called, "Don't stop! Find Lord Kulferan!" To his immense relief, she urged her horse forward without hesitating.

With the Ahrans almost upon them, the guard called to Rupert, "Ride on, Your Majesty! We need to protect Her Highness. I'll try to slow them!"

But it was too late. Their pursuers had already cut them off. One of them barked a command, and three of the Ahrans set off after the princess. The remaining men rode in close, forcing Rupert and the guard to bring their horses to a halt.

The two men drew their swords, but they were heavily outnumbered.

"Throw down your weapons, or accept the consequences," said a cold voice.

Turning to the speaker, Rupert recognized the man they had been chasing. The gloating tone of the Ahran almost prompted him to do something stupid. He barely mastered himself in time.

"There's no need for violence," the man asserted.

"And yet you just murdered an innocent boy and an unarmed monk," Rupert retorted disdainfully.

The Ahran shrugged. "It was regrettable, but I had my orders. Besides, the blame lies entirely with the father. If he hadn't interfered, both the boy and the monk would still be alive."

So the Ahran blamed his murderous rampage on the grieving victims. Rupert clenched his jaw in anger.

"Throw down your swords!" the man repeated in a growl.

After a moment's hesitation, Rupert complied. The guard did the same.

They were distracted by the return of the three Ahrans who had pursued the princess. They rode in leading a dejected Tasha.

Rupert looked on in dismay.

A self-satisfied smile covered the face of the Ahran. "I bid you welcome," he said to them all, executing a clumsy bow from his saddle. He turned to the princess. "I heard your guard refer to you as 'Your Highness,'" he said, his lip curling in an ironic grin. "So you must be one of Krasmir's daughters."

He considered her thoughtfully. "Princess Kyla?" He frowned, then shook his head. "No, I'm afraid not. Much too rash. And nowhere near beautiful enough. You must be Princess Teylee."

The princess flushed with anger, but she didn't speak.

The Ahran turned to Rupert. "And 'Your Majesty,'" he said, raising his eyebrows. "I am impressed! I can only assume that I have the honor of addressing King Rupert of Castel."

Rupert chose not to respond.

"The two of you will come with me. Do not be alarmed about your fate. You are more valuable alive than dead. Don't test me though," he added in a growl. "If one of you attempts to escape, I will order the other killed. You have seen for yourselves that I will not hesitate."

As if to reinforce his message, he cast a casual look at the guard. "I have no use for him."

Rupert watched in distress as one of the Ahrans pushed forward and thrust his sword into the side of the unarmed man.

Even before the guard hit the ground, the rest of the company began to move out.

Ringed in by Ahrans with drawn blades, and anxious about the safety of Tasha, Rupert had no option but to leave the guard to his fate and ride away with them.

A bitter anger began to well up inside him. If there was a way to destroy these men and everything they stood for, he would find it.

ALMOST AS SOON AS they were captured, Rupert and Tasha had been blindfolded. Their hands were tied in front of them and secured to their saddles. The party paused after their horses had been led for only a short time. A great deal of activity was going on around them, along with frequent chatter and shouting of instructions. Rupert could not understand a word of it, but he guessed that the Ahrans were abandoning their headquarters and moving to a different location.

For the most part, the two of them were left alone. They managed to snatch a brief whispered conversation before a harsh voice demanded silence. After that they sat restless and uncomfortable atop their horses.

Eventually, after a long delay, they set out again. From the sounds around him, Rupert concluded that a large party was on the move. During the ride he tried to pay attention to their surroundings, but he quickly lost count of every rise and fall in the terrain. He did feel confident that they had crossed four streams and one river.

They rode for at least three hours before Rupert's horse was finally brought to a complete halt. He and Tasha were allowed to dismount and sit on the ground. Further hours passed before they were led into a building. After descending some stairs, their blindfolds were removed and their hands released.

Rupert found himself in a large cellar. Crude but sturdy partitions had been erected, splitting the room into three sections. A narrow space at the bottom of the stairs held a table and chairs, presumably for the use of guards. The rest of the cellar had been divided in two, with a door providing access to each and a window in the middle of the partition. A narrow skylight set high in the outer wall dimly illuminated the two sections.

Rupert was led into one of the makeshift rooms, and Tasha into the other. He found a simple bed before him, with a small table beside the bed. No other furniture adorned the space.

One of the guards placed a pitcher of water on the table along with a small loaf of bread. Then he was left alone.

Moving to the partition window, he found it had been placed at head height. Wooden strips subdivided the window, preventing either of them from climbing through the opening. The window held no glass. They would at least be able to talk together as well as see each other.

Tasha appeared on the other side of the window. Tears glistened in her eyes.

"I imagine we'll have plenty of opportunity to talk," he said brightly, speaking in Rogandan. "And there will be plenty to talk about."

Lowering his voice, he switched to Arvenian. "They're allowing us to talk for a reason. They'll listen to everything we say. But they're probably not expecting that both of us can speak Arvenian. It might take them a while to find someone who understands it. This might be our only opportunity to speak in private. We need to make the most of it."

She immediately began speaking in Arvenian. "I'm so sorry!" she said tearfully. "All of this is my fault."

"Blaming yourself won't help," he said calmly. "We'll only make it through this if we stay positive. We need to remember that everyone will be working hard to find a way to free us. They'll be more cautious after what happened with Lord Torbury's son, but they won't give up."

"Is anyone even going to know we've been captured?" Tasha asked.

"I don't think there's much doubt about that," he replied. "If they don't figure it out for themselves, the Ahrans will soon let them know."

Tears were running freely down her cheeks now. "Aren't you angry with me?" she said miserably. "I've been feeling so wretched, and you being reasonable just makes it worse."

"I'm not angry with you," he told her gently. "From all I've seen, your father is a strong ruler, and a good one. His authority hasn't been seriously challenged before. So learning to be cautious and suspicious hasn't been necessary for you. Not like it has for me. You're learning the lesson the hard way."

"Learning the hard way hasn't just affected me. My guard is dead! And I'm responsible!"

He shook his head. "You didn't murder the guard. That wasn't necessary, and the Ahran is the one who bears the responsibility for it."

He sighed deeply. "What you did was foolish, Tasha. Very foolish. But you weren't entirely wrong either. Murdering Lord Torbury's son was only going to be the beginning. And the current situation isn't entirely bad. The murder of Ethen along with our capture will cement the alliance between our kingdoms as never before. Our people will oppose the Ahrans with all their might."

"But capturing us just weakens our kingdoms," she said despairingly. "They'll bargain with our lives. And I'm afraid that my father won't be able to be strong—not when he knows my life is at stake."

He shook his head. "There's a limit to how far they can go with that. Don't forget that your father has their imperial princess in his custody. He might be able to negotiate an exchange."

Her hand was resting on the window, and he placed his own hand on it. "You're a great deal more resilient than you give yourself credit for," he told her. "We're going to make it through this, and we're going to do it together. Agreed?"

Setting her jaw, she brushed the tears from her eyes.

"Agreed?" he repeated.

"Agreed," she finally replied.

"Now, who is your favorite storyteller?" he asked, speaking once more in Rogandan.

She hesitated, but she did reply. "My grandfather—my mother's father."

"Then I want to hear his stories. Every one of them. In full," he told her.

She nodded. He had the impression that her normal self was gradually reasserting itself.

"You've told me it wasn't easy to become a princess," he added. "I want to hear what it was like to wake up one morning and find your whole world had changed."

Without waiting for her to respond, he offered another promising topic. "This is also a perfect opportunity for me to find out more about your siblings. And your mother. She seems like a determined woman!"

She cocked an eyebrow at him. "Unless you pause for a breath once in a while," she said dryly, "I'll have no hope of telling you anything."

* * *

Thomas might have pointed the way at first, but before long the tracker was doing all the work. They were moving quickly—the king made no secret of his restlessness.

Thomas's heart skipped a beat when he spotted a body sprawled on the ground ahead of them. Others saw it as well, and the whole party raced forward.

Even before he reached the prone figure, Thomas twisted the clasp to bring the stone into contact with his skin. He saw at once that it was the princess's missing guard, and that the man was barely clinging to life. He was immediately able to learn everything he needed to know about what had happened.

The king was the first to reach the guard, kneeling at his side.

The man recognized his sovereign. "I...sorry, Majesty," he gasped. The effort of talking was clearly exhausting him. "They took...her...and the king...too many."

"Why did you come here?" the king asked, speaking as gently as he could.

"The...princess. I tried...king tried...to stop her..."

The king grimaced. It was the princess who had precipitated this situation.

Getting to his feet, the king remounted. "Do what you can for him," he told Lord Kulferan.

The nobleman in turn nodded to a man who had already positioned himself beside the guard.

"Move out!" called the king, prompting the whole company to set off once more.

This time Thomas hung back. He had nothing further to offer, not until they reached the Ahrans.

The trail led to a large farmhouse not far from the crest of the ridge. This was the place Bolnyk had been heading for. Aware that the Ahran had been planning an imminent move to another location, Thomas knew that the best hope of retrieving the captives was to find them here.

The king waited while his men investigated the farm building and its barns.

One of the king's scouts soon returned. "The farmhouse has been abandoned very recently, Your Majesty," said the scout.

Thomas's heart sank. Access to Bolnyk's thoughts had not shown him where the Ahrans were heading. Having delegated the search to one of his men, the chief agent did not know specifics of the location.

The scout was pointing. "The tracks lead in that direction."

With no sign of his daughter at the farmhouse, the king was impatient to resume the search. The company was soon on the move again.

They came to a broad stream, and beyond it the tracks disappeared entirely.

"They must have ridden along the stream, Your Majesty," said the tracker. "We'll see if we can find where they left it."

The trackers were gone for some time, but they did eventually locate the trail. The company set off again, only to discover an even larger stream before them. This time the trackers searched in vain.

"There are many places where they could have left the stream without leaving tracks," one of them reported to the king. "It will take a long time to explore every possibility, and we might not succeed."

The scout's prediction proved accurate. Nevertheless, the king didn't permit them to abandon the search until darkness had almost fallen. When he finally gave Lord Kulferan permission to lead the company home, they rode away with spirits as weary as their bodies.

33

———

Will and Amyra stood side by side, waiting for King Krasmir and Queen Deka to receive them.

"I have my life back again," Will told Amyra seriously. He had an arm wrapped tightly around her. He'd been doing it a lot lately; fortunately she didn't seem to mind.

He didn't understand his fierce hunger for closeness with Amyra since the incident by the stream. Perhaps it was because no one else fully understood the depths they had been through.

Seeing Ethen killed before his eyes had easily been the most devastating experience of his life. As for what happened afterward with Brother Ander, he was still unable to speak about it with composure.

He knew about the Stone of Vitality now. Thomas had told him everything. As to the role it might have played in bringing Ethen back, he didn't understand it at all.

Brother Ander seemed to have no clear idea either. All he had said was, "Recovery relies on the body's natural recuperative ability. A healer simply encourages and supports that process. Sometimes an unusual outcome might be prompted by prayer, but every healing is the gift of the Creator who designed us." Gazing curiously down at the Stone of Vitality in his hand, he had added, "I imagine this little object is simply another expression of that gift."

For Will, the important thing was that Ethen had been revived. Understanding the mechanism held little interest for him.

He was, however, determined to understand how Ethen's abduction had managed to shatter his closeness with Amyra. Thankfully their relationship had been fully restored. After all they had been through together he was confident it had emerged stronger than ever.

Would their oneness have been restored if their son had died? It was an uncomfortable question.

A servant finally appeared, and the two of them were ushered into the presence of the king and queen. It was immediately obvious that Queen Deka had been crying, and the look on King Krasmir's face was painfully familiar.

The king managed to push his own problems to one side. "We rejoice with you at the safe return of your son, Lord and Lady Torbury," he said. The queen's breath hitched at his reference to 'safe return', but she managed a nod in support of his congratulations.

"Thank you, Your Majesties," Will replied.

"Some remarkable stories have been circulating about your boy and the monk," the king observed. "I hardly know what to think of them."

"Storytellers love to embellish the truth," Will replied. "Nevertheless, it seems safe to say that without Brother Ander the outcome would have been very different."

"I would like to hear more about it at some point," said the king. "For now I wanted to say that I am beginning to understand what you must have been going through, and I am sorry for the insensitivity I sometimes showed."

The king's willingness to own his behavior surprised and impressed Will. In his experience kings were rarely given to such displays.

"You were not insensitive, Your Majesty," Will replied. "You provided the practical support I needed. And I freely acknowledge that my behavior was inappropriate at times. You were well within your rights to speak and act as you did."

He could only look back with shame on some of his actions. Especially burning down the house—he still winced when he remembered the reproach in Thomas's eyes.

"It is generous of you to say so, Lord Torbury."

"It is you who was generous, Your Majesty," Will insisted. "On reflection I can see that I completely lost my sense of perspective for a while."

"How so?" asked the king.

"I allowed my own pain to blind me to almost everything else."

Arguably Amyra had been the first casualty. Having fought in a battle line, Will knew from experience the importance of facing the enemy shoulder-to-shoulder with his comrades. Yet he had failed to apply the lesson within his own marriage. It was easy to see after the event that he would have been stronger if he'd faced the challenge with Amyra. But he had let her down, withholding the support she so desperately needed.

He had since vowed to Amyra that whatever came in the future, he would face it with her. Having done her own share of agonizing, she had made him a similar promise.

"Thank you for your forthrightness," the king replied. His face was grim. "I assume you will return to Arnost now that your family is intact again."

"Yes, Your Majesty. We will travel overland."

"And the rest of your party will return with you?"

"Yes, although Brother Ander wishes to remain if you will allow him to."

"He would be welcome to continue to stay with us in the palace," the king replied. "Perhaps his services might be of use at a future time," he added vaguely.

"I will convey that to him, Your Majesty. For my part, I am planning to return to Rog as soon as my family is safe in the capital."

"Why?" asked the king in surprise.

"Because your daughter is a captive of the Ahrans. You supported me in my hour of need, and I will do no less in return."

The king raised his eyebrows. "I suppose I should refuse your offer," he said. "But I am not sure I can bring myself to do it. Your wisdom and experience will be invaluable of course. But you are also unusually well equipped to grasp the delicacy of my situation."

Will responded with a bow.

"I must somehow find a way to preserve my own sense of perspective," the king concluded with a sigh. "Perhaps you can help me with that too."

KING STEFFAN WAVED the latest dispatch from Rog in his hand. "Will and Amyra are returning," he told Queen Essanda. "With both of their children!"

A cry of delight escaped Essanda's lips. "How did they manage to get Ethen back?"

"There are no details. We'll have to wait until we can hear the story from them in person."

"I am so relieved! I can only imagine how Will and Amyra must be feeling."

"Unfortunately the good news ends there," Steffan told her grimly.

"What else has happened?" she asked in alarm.

"The Ahrans have somehow captured both your brother, Rupert, and King Krasmir's youngest daughter, Princess Teylee."

Her earlier excitement vanished instantly, replaced by a look of horror.

"How could they have captured them both?" she asked in dismay.

"It seems they were pursuing an Ahran agent," he replied. "They were together because they are formally courting."

Her eyebrows went up in astonishment. She shook her head, struggling to take it all in.

He understood her confusion. He could barely make sense of it either.

"What of Castel?" she asked. "This news will be devastating for them!"

He raised his hands helplessly.

"Perhaps I should go to Castel Citadel," she said. "As a gesture of support."

"It might be a good idea," he agreed. "Provided we send a large enough escort to guarantee your safety."

"What do you mean?" she asked, frowning.

"These abductions make it clear how bold the Ahrans have become," he said. "You are aware that their agents have been infiltrating Rog and Varacellan in large numbers. I've received word from Lord Burtelen that we're beginning to see similar incursions in Erestor."

She stared back at him in surprise.

"Supposedly I am in authority over the docks at Maranelle. As you know, the reality is that the Peerless Mariner is in control. Fortunately, one of Burtelen's retainers, Jaxin, has an understanding with the Peerless Mariner's people. They monitor every ship that comes and goes, and they've been passing information freely to Burtelen through Jaxin. I've told Burtelen to be ruthless with any Ahran agents. But it would not be wise to assume that Arvenon is free of them. The same applies to Castel."

She shook her head in dismay. "So we will have further need of our army. It never ends. It will be good to have Will with us again."

Steffan shook his head. "He is planning to return to Rog as soon as his family are safe in Arnost."

"Do you know his reasons?" she asked.

"Krasmir lost his daughter almost at the moment Will got his son back. I imagine that's behind it. Krasmir did everything he could to retrieve Ethen. Perhaps Will feels obligated."

"Will is doing the right thing," Essanda asserted. "We'll just have to manage without him. It isn't only about the princess. There's

Rupert to consider as well. We need to do whatever we can toward recovering him safely."

"I agree," Steffan replied.

He sat down with a grunt, reaching for a parchment and his quill. "I sent Krasmir a strongly worded note after Ethen was abducted, letting him know that I expected his full support. It's time I thanked him for his efforts." He shook his head, still trying to grapple with the implications of this latest incident. "Given what's just happened, I will also express our deepest concern and offer our full support in his efforts to recover his daughter and Rupert."

As far as Bolnyk was concerned, the location chosen by the priest for the meeting would have seemed desolate in the daytime. On a dark night it was positively eerie. He waited restlessly, the chief minister at his side.

"Where is he?" demanded the Grand Vizier. "He should have arrived by now."

"I am told that priests do not reckon time in the same way as normal people," Bolnyk replied evenly.

At that moment a dark cloaked figure appeared abruptly before them, barely distinguishable from the darkness. His sudden arrival, without warning from the guards, almost startled Bolnyk out of his wits.

A voice came from within the priest's cowl. "I bring you greetings," he said coldly.

"I greet you in return," said Rheibas. "I trust all is well with you and your...your people."

"How can anything be well when a monk has established himself in the royal palace?" growled the voice. "The pretender styles himself as a healer."

The Grand Vizier offered no response.

"Do you intend to honor your agreement?" asked the priest.

"I do," Rheibas asserted.

"What guarantees do you offer?" the priest persisted.

"The same guarantees you offer me," replied the chief minister coldly. "None at all."

The priest fell silent.

"I will do my part," Rheibas told him. "I suggest you focus on doing yours."

Then suddenly the dark figure was gone. Bolnyk peered into the darkness in confusion. It almost seemed that he had vanished.

"It is time we were gone," the chief minister told Bolnyk.

Mounting up, they rode away, their guards trailing behind them.

Bolnyk cast a last glance back over his shoulders. The priests could only be described as unnerving. He would be wise to keep a very wary eye on them.

RUPERT WOKE from a deep sleep to find rough hands shaking him. Three men were standing beside his bed.

"Get up!" one of them ordered curtly.

As soon as he complied, his hands were tied in front of him. Shoved toward the door, he headed up the stairs. Tasha was ahead of him, her hands tied as well. Once they reached the top of the stairs they were led out of the building into the darkness.

After being taken to waiting horses, they were instructed to mount. Once more their hands were secured to their saddles. Tasha was silent, but she seemed reasonably calm, and he gradually allowed himself to relax.

Looking around curiously, he saw that they had been imprisoned in a large farm building that stood alone in a broad open space. Their stay had been surprisingly brief.

Intense activity was going on all around them. It didn't appear to Rupert that the building was being abandoned entirely, but a number of the occupants were clearly preparing to leave.

Eventually a group perhaps twenty strong rode away into the night, the two prisoners positioned in the middle of the column.

They had been riding for little more than an hour when Rupert began to smell sea air. Before long he could hear the crashing of waves onto a beach.

Clearing the clouds, the moon granted him a glimpse of two longboats drawn up onto the sand. A ship was anchored further out to sea. The implications were alarming, and his unease grew as the column made its way onto the beach.

Rupert and Tasha were ordered down from their horses and led to one of the longboats. When they tried to get Rupert into the boat he began to struggle until a voice growled, "If you value the life of your friend, you'd better cooperate." All the fight went out of him.

Others clambered aboard, and the longboats put out to sea. When they reached the ship they were expected to climb a rope net hanging over the side of the boat. The task would have been difficult even without his hands being tied, but there was little risk of him falling. One man climbed on each side of him, grabbing him if ever he lost his grip. They were probably willing to manhandle him all the way to the deck if necessary. Tasha was similarly shadowed.

The minute they reached the deck, men with lanterns hurried them to the hatchway, leading them down into the bowels of the ship. Finally they reached a modestly sized storage room. Once inside, their hands were freed. In the lantern light Rupert saw that the space boasted two hammocks and little else.

After setting down a single lantern with a candle, the Ahrans filed out, shutting and bolting the door behind them. The sound of footsteps slowly faded as the men departed, leaving their prisoners alone in the confined space.

When quiet sobbing filled the room, Rupert made his way to Tasha. She had slumped to the floor.

Sitting down beside her, he drew her close, guiding her head onto his shoulder. "At least they left us together," he whispered.

They sat uncomfortably on the hard wooden floor, lurching back and forward with the motion of the ship and clinging miserably to each other.

After a few minutes her sobbing stopped. Her breathing slowed, and she sat up straight.

"Where do you think they're taking us?" she asked. Her voice was quavering, but she seemed calm again.

"I don't know," he replied. "Beyond the reach of anyone who might want to rescue us, I imagine."

"No one will have any idea where to find us," she said dejectedly.

"No," he agreed. "If we're going to escape, it will be up to us."

They fell silent.

After musing darkly for longer than was healthy, Rupert frowned.

"We'll make it through this, and we'll do it together," he said defiantly. "Agreed?"

"Agreed," she replied, her voice clear and unwavering.

34

An endless succession of waves rose and fell, moving with the tide and a gentle breeze. Pitching about on the swell was a cluster of driftwood, the upturned remnants of a longboat. Two men lay sprawled across the wreckage, lost in the vastness of the open ocean.

How long they had been adrift in the water, Gharpin couldn't say. Nor could he clearly recall the reason why he was so determined to stay alive. All he knew was he needed to cling desperately to life for as long as possible. It surely couldn't be too much longer.

He wondered when last he had eaten, or drunk fresh water. Vague recollections of a rain squall came to mind, of lying face up with his mouth wide to capture the life-giving drops.

A smudge on the horizon had steadily been growing in size, and it dawned on him that they were drifting close to an island. Slowly, painfully, he began to move his dangling legs, hoping his feeble efforts might direct the makeshift craft in the right direction. He continued kicking until, spent by the effort, he lost consciousness entirely.

He woke to find himself floating near a sandy beach, tantalizingly close to the shore. With each wave the tide drew the wreckage in toward the sand before sucking it back out again. A bigger than usual breaker rolled in, and Gharpin called upon a final reserve of strength as dry land beckoned. Clutching hold of his prostrate companion and waiting until the wave reached its furthest extent, he tumbled off the wreckage and dug into the sand. The wave sucked and pulled at him as it retreated, but somehow he clung on.

When it had gone, he crawled forward a full body length before slumping in exhaustion. He knew he had no strength to haul his companion further up the beach. He could only allow the tide to do whatever it pleased.

Several hours must have passed before his eyes opened once more. He was lying above the waterline, the waves lapping gently below him. His companion had not moved.

Dragging himself the short distance to the other sailor, he saw that life had departed from him. After coming so far, his shipmate had stumbled as safety beckoned at last.

If Gharpin could have managed it, he would have scooped out a shallow grave in the sand. But any such gesture was beyond his capacity. Spotting a stream trickling down onto the beach, he crawled to it instead, struggling as far upstream as he could manage. The water tasted surprisingly fresh, and he took his fill before lying down beside the stream. He drifted off to its merry tinkling.

It was late morning when he awoke. After once more slaking his thirst, he managed to struggle to his feet. No sign of his companion's body remained on the beach. The sea had apparently claimed him.

It was just Gharpin now. He didn't doubt that he alone had cheated the elements—the sole survivor of his entire crew.

This latest reminder of the treachery of Rheibas infused him with fresh determination. He would do more than just cling to life in this place—he would thrive. The island appeared to have a ready supply of fresh water, so his highest priority would be to find food and shelter. Since he knew how to catch fish using available materials, seafood would provide the foundation of his diet.

Somehow he found the strength to climb a low hill. No other land was visible nearby. Perhaps if he climbed to the highest point of the island, he might glimpse another tiny splotch on the horizon.

Glancing about in every direction, he saw that the island on which he stood was extensive. That encouraged him. Nesting birds might make their home here. If they did, their eggs would supply a welcome addition to his menu.

The island also boasted an accessible beach—the one he had washed up on. That encouraged him too. If fishermen ever came there to replenish their water supply, they might provide him with an opportunity to escape.

On his way back to the beach he stumbled upon a hut. Could it be possible? Had he washed ashore on an inhabited island? Heart pounding painfully, he approached the structure, calling out a greeting before pushing inside. Quickly realizing that the hut lay abandoned, he slumped to the floor, struggling to overcome a crippling sense of desolation. He remained there until sleep claimed him once more.

A new day had dawned when he discovered the cultivated strips of land. Left untended, they were overgrown and marginal, but he was confident that at least some of the crops could be coaxed back to life. His prospects were surely improving.

It wasn't until he found the strength to climb the highest point of the island that a growing suspicion was confirmed. Unlikely as it seemed, he had arrived at his intended destination. Drifting in the boundless expanse of the ocean, a helpless subject to the wind and tides, he had somehow reached the island where the princess had been abandoned.

The Grand Vizier had been lying, of course—there was no sign of her, just as Gharpin expected.

He was alone, but he was alive. He would endure, and he would never stop searching for a way to exact revenge on the slithering creature who had destroyed his ship, doomed his crew, and condemned him to this forsaken bolthole.

EPILOGUE

Kamash sat at the tiller, relishing the salt air that filled his lungs. The wind might be whipping his hair about wildly, but for the most part the elements seemed intent only on reinforcing his smile.

He watched with delight as his little craft rode the swell and capered in the wind. It was a beautiful vessel. It wouldn't be easy to abandon it when the moment came.

He had Lord Torbury to thank for the boat. The grateful nobleman would probably have given him almost anything he wanted. After laying bare Kamash's longing to renew his solitary life, Lord Torbury had enlisted the aid of his friend Breysen to locate an ideal little craft. In spite of the nobleman's eagerness, Kamash had wrestled with himself long and hard before accepting it. He had admitted freely that he disliked being obligated to anyone. Lord Torbury had pointed out that he was heavily in Kamash's debt. By refusing the gift, he would be dooming Lord Torbury forever to just such an obligation.

In the end Kamash had yielded and taken possession of the boat. Now, with Rogand disappearing in his wake, he was willing to admit that any other decision would have been foolish pride.

King Krasmir himself had sought out Kamash before he left. "When you arrived in Rog, you promised never to do anything to the detriment of Rogand. You have kept that promise, and I thank you for it."

Kamash had offered a bow in return.

"I understand you were responsible for exposing the meeting between Princess Neira and the Ahran agent that led to the recovery of Lord Torbury's son. I thank you for that too." He paused before adding, "That meeting also led to the series of events that ended in the capture of my daughter. But I am not so unreasonable as to lay the blame for that at your feet."

The old man winced. "I sincerely hope that your daughter will be returned to you very soon." He could find nothing else to say.

The king had changed the subject. "I understand that you no longer wish to act as Princess Neira's spokesperson," he continued.

"That is correct, Your Majesty. I told her that if I discovered she had any awareness of the abduction, I would no longer act on her behalf. I cannot represent a person who places the glory of their empire above every other consideration."

King Krasmir nodded in satisfaction. "Lord Torbury has informed me that you are leaving the mainland. I wish you safe travels."

"Thank you, Your Majesty," he had said with a final bow.

They parted without further comment.

He had sought out Princess Neira before he left. She no longer had her freedom. Heavily guarded, every moment of her life was closely monitored. Their time together had been strained, which was hardly surprising since he had been the one who exposed her meeting with the Ahran agent. But he had meant it when he wished her well.

It was a great relief to him that she was no longer his problem. Uman at least remained with her, although he seemed more despondent than ever.

Perhaps the advance and retreat of Kamash's relationship with the princess best symbolized his reengagement with humankind in general. At first, after so many years alone, a part of him had welcomed human contact. He had quickly wearied of it. He wouldn't miss the political machinations, nor the frustrations that came from dealing with difficult and capricious people.

The absence of a few individuals might cause him regret. He was glad to have met Thomas and Elena, the Arvenian couple who uncovered his secret. The three of them shared a very pleasant evening over dinner before he took possession of the boat. For the most part, though, he felt only eager anticipation at the prospect of being alone once again.

Loneliness would not greatly trouble him, but the absence of the stone would prove more consequential.

He thought about the times it had healed his hurts and even saved his life. On one occasion, while wading in shallow water, he had come upon a strikingly colored sea snake. When he approached too closely, the creature had bitten him. By the time he reached the stone he was panting for breath and barely capable of crawling. Upon clutching it, the venom quickly lost its potency.

He winced as he remembered the time he broke his leg. The injury itself was not life threatening, but he could not have lived long if he'd remained disabled. Once more he had dragged himself to the hiding place of the stone. The effort cost him dearly—he had barely managed to grasp the object in his hand before swooning. When he regained consciousness, his leg was completely healed.

The other impact would be on his life span. Nevertheless, he had no regrets about letting the stone go. When he was young he could never have imagined tiring of life, but of late he had felt increasingly worn down. Everything had its season, and the time had come to pass the talisman to another.

There would be a time to die too. He would face that when it came.

For now it was enough that he was going home.

He was returning to his island. Its location was no longer his secret alone, and he had no way to be certain that others would leave him in peace. But he intended to abandon his previous dwelling and establish a new one in a hidden location. He knew just the place. He would keep it well stocked with water and fresh provisions. Anyone who cared to could land and search the island. They might find his cultivated strips, but as long as he spotted them in time, they would never find him.

None of that would matter until he arrived at his destination. In the meantime, with sturdy timbers beneath his feet and the wind whistling about his sails, he was more than content.

The End

The saga will continue and conclude in the final book in the series
The Hope of Vitality (The Stone Cycle Book 6)

LIST OF CHARACTERS

- *Agon* - previous king of Rogand
- *Ahreitas* - imperial crown prince of Ahr
- *Ahuzza* - Ahran bisri (nobleman), special envoy of the emperor of Ahr
- *Aiden* - crown prince of Arvenon, son of Steffan and Essanda
- *Ander* - a monk; former Arvenian soldier who traveled with Will and later commanded soldiers at the Battle of Torbury Scarp
- *Andy* - son of Thomas and Elena
- *Ashloh* - princess of Rogand, daughter of King Krasmir and Queen Deka; younger twin of Crown Prince Rimek
- *Attalnar* - early king of Arvenon
- *Amyra* - wife of Will Prentis; holder of the Stone of Authority; formerly Ahnya, daughter of Sheylha
- *Anneka* - former noblewoman who leads a community hidden away in the forest near Erestor
- *Beldisel* - Erestorian nobleman with holdings adjacent to those of Lord Torbury
- *Bolnyk* - Ahran agent

- *Boedwyk* - Rogandan nobleman
- *Breysen* - retainer to Lord Torbury (Will Prentis); former sailor, soldier, and mercenary
- *Burnett* - scribe to King Attalnar of Arvenon, from Earlsford
- *Burtelen* - high-ranking Arvenian nobleman from Erestor who is a close confidante of King Steffan; played a crucial role in bringing an army from Erestor to the battle at Torbury Scarp
- *Charlotte* - princess of Arvenon, daughter of Steffan and Essanda
- *Dahra* - mother of Amyra; formerly Sheylha, the Seer
- *Deka* - wife of Krasmir and queen of Rogand
- *Delia* - daughter of Thomas and Elena
- *Delmar* - king of Varas, a neighboring kingdom to Arvenon, and ally of King Steffan of Arvenon
- *Drettroth* - high-ranking Rogandan nobleman who commanded the Rogandan army during the invasion of Arvenon; known as Vilkami during his childhood
- *Duke of Erestor* - King Steffan's uncle, and the regent during the king's absence during the Rogandan invasion; the senior member of the nobility in Erestor
- *Eisgold* - Castelan nobleman formerly commanding the Castelan army; exiled after the Battle of Torbury Scarp for ignoring orders at a crucial moment in the battle
- *Elena* - wife of Thomas Stablehand
- *Essanda* - Queen of Arvenon, formerly a princess of Castel
- *Ethen* - son of Will and Amyra
- *Gharpin* - captain of an Ahran ship
- *Goultzar* - Archprimus, second in command to the High Priest of the Dark Gods of Rogand
- *Haldek* - former Rogandan soldier who unwittingly helped Will on more than one significant occasion; living in a tiny forest community with Elena, Rubin, and Thomas
- *Hourahn* - emperor of Ahr

- *Istel* - king of Castel, a neighboring kingdom to Arvenon, father of Rupert and Essanda, and father-in-law and ally of King Steffan of Arvenon
- *Jaxin* - retainer to the Duke of Erestor and later Lord Burtelen and their key representative at the docks in Maranelle
- *Jonas* - senior army leader and close confidante of Will Prentis; fought at the Battle of Torbury Scarp
- *Hender* - bowman living in Anneka and Rellan's forest community
- *Kaifet* - Ahran agent tasked with meeting the Rogandan High Priest
- *Karevis* - Varasan nobleman and commander of the Varasan army; played a key role at the Battle of Torbury Scarp
- *Kamash* - Rogandan who chose to exile himself to a remote island
- *Krasmir* - king of Rogand, formerly a wealthy and powerful Rogandan baron
- *Kulferan* - Rogandan nobleman and army commander
- *Kyla* - princess of Rogand, daughter of King Krasmir and Queen Deka
- *Leonid* - prince of Arvenon, son of Steffan and Essanda
- *Millie* - daughter of Will and Amyra
- *Neira* - imperial princess of the Empire of Ahr
- *Ranauld* - Arvenian count and a senior leader in the army at Torbury Scarp; a close confidante of King Steffan and a friend of Will Prentis
- *Rellan* - Arvenian soldier from Erestor who led a cavalry force to the battlefield at Torbury Scarp with his twin brother Kuper; connected with Anneka's forest community
- *Rheibas* - Grand Vizier of the Empire of Ahr
- *Rimek* - crown prince of Rogand, son of King Krasmir and Queen Deka

- *Rubin* - father of Elena
- *Rufe Sarjant* - respected and physically imposing Arvenian soldier; a close friend of Will Prentis and a key leader in the army
- *Rupert* - king of Castel, brother to Essanda, son of King Istel
- *Steffan the Second* - king of Arvenon
- *Tamara* - daughter of Thomas and Elena
- *Teylee* - Rogandan princess, daughter of King Krasmir and Queen Deka
- *Thomas Stablehand* - possessor of the Stone of Knowing
- *Torbury* - title granted to Will Prentis by King Steffan; Will Prentis was elevated to the Arvenian peerage as Lord Torbury in honor of his efforts in defeating the Rogandans
- *Uman* - guard and servant to Princess Neira
- *Vangellis* - Arvenian monk who became a key mentor to Thomas; role model to Brother Ander; killed at Lord Drettroth's stronghold
- *Will Prentis* - commander of the Arvenian army, greatly respected by his soldiers as well as King Steffan due to his remarkable qualities; fluent in Rogandan and widely traveled

NOTE FROM THE AUTHOR

Thank you for reading *The Stone of Vitality*—I hope you enjoyed it. Please consider leaving a review on Amazon for the benefit of others. Reader feedback makes a big difference to me as well!

The Stone Cycle saga will continue in *The Hope of Vitality (The Stone Cycle book 6).*

To be kept up to date on new releases, sign up to my mailing list at *www.allanpacker.com.* New subscribers will receive an exclusive bonus novelette—a prequel to *The Cost of Knowing.* The novelette, *The Rending: A Prequel to The Cost of Knowing,* is a complete story four chapters (13,000 words) in length. It provides background information on Anneka and her community. The novelette is described below.

Endings may be beginnings in disguise

Anneka is comfortable and confident, a noblewoman of consequence living a life of privilege. Until the day her world is torn apart.

After losing everything she most cares about, she must abandon

her home and her way of life in an attempt to secure the future of those who depend on her.

No one, least of all Anneka, could anticipate a deeper significance to her struggle. Yet her journey will one day influence the fate of kingdoms.

How did the stone come to be where Thomas found it? The answer can be found in *The Seer: A Prequel to The Stone of Knowing,* a novelette 5 chapters (13,500 words) in length. It is a standalone story, and as such can be read independently of other books in *The Stone Cycle* series. The novelette is described below.

Eyes see no more than a glimpse

Sheylha is a seer—a woman with unique and extraordinary abilities. Powerful men want to control her, to use her to dominate others.

Kalvor is a warrior of unusual tenacity, a hunter who never gives up. Driven by his past, he has become a dangerous enemy.

When Kalvor is sent to find and capture the seer, each of them will be tested in ways they could never have imagined.

In time the outcome will determine the fate of kingdoms.

The Seer: A Prequel to The Stone of Knowing is available at Amazon's Kindle store.

ACKNOWLEDGMENTS

Huge thanks to my wife and alpha reader, Merilyn. She patiently reads the early drafts, offering useful feedback, and then follows up with feedback after I've made changes. Neither the process nor the story would be the same without her involvement.

Grateful thanks once more to my beta readers, Andrew Menzies, Stephen, Ray, Deborah, and Cherilyn White. I'm grateful for their feedback and encouragement.

My developmental editor, Mary Novak, always makes a positive difference to the final story. Her feedback is invaluable, and I very much appreciate it.

Thanks once more to Deborah, who has found time in her busy schedule to do another thorough proofread.

Karri did her usual great job on the cover. She's brilliant at taking a simple idea and turning into something evocative and moody.

I'm grateful to Brian Plush for his map, which continues to add depth to the story.

Finally, thanks to God, the foundation on which my life is built and the source of creativity, joy, and so much else besides.

ABOUT THE AUTHOR

Allan Packer writes epic fantasy. *The Stone of Vitality* is his fifth novel.

Allan grew up surrounded by books and became an avid reader during his childhood. In his university years fantasy displaced science fiction as his favorite genre, thanks primarily to J. R. R. Tolkien. He later shared this love with his four children by reading *The Lord of the Rings* to them aloud—a three-month marathon he completed twice during their formative years.

Born in Australia, Allan has lived and worked on three continents, and spent one quarter of his working years abroad. Having worked as an IT professional throughout his career, he was first published as a technical author.

Today he lives with his wife in Adelaide, South Australia, near their children and a small but growing band of grandchildren.

Allan is currently working on the sixth and final installment in his series *The Stone Cycle*.